FIRE WITCH

BOOK ONE OF THE FRONTIER WITCHES

ANNETTE GRANTHAM

This book is dedicated to Dale, my true love, for his continuing love and support.

CHAPTER ONE

MARY MAGUIRE WAITED FOR her older sister, Stella, to leave for work and entered her bedroom. She wasn't going to leave without their mother's necklace and grimoire, that Stella told her had unspeakable dark magick. *Now, where would she hide them?*

Mary stood still, dropped her hands in front of her, fingers interwoven, waiting for the necklace to whisper. It always did when she was near, even as a young child. The trunk. She pulled up the lid and grabbed a blue velvet bag, holding it to her chest. The power that radiated titillated her, sending shivers along her back. Passed to the strongest witch in each generation, it called to her, not Stella. She believed the silver necklace, dating back several centuries, possessed a curse that would imbue any witch wearing it with wicked abilities. Mary didn't believe it. She dropped the lid of the trunk. Their mother was not an evil person; the church had burned her at the stake from fear of her healing abilities.

Now she needed her mother's grimoire, because what good is the necklace without the knowledge? She had seen the book only once since her sister kept it hidden away from her. She looked in the dresser, the trunk, and even under the bed. Exasperated, Mary leaned over Stella's wooden carved altar with its triple moons. The worn, leather bound thick book appeared beside the altar under Stella's own thin grimoire. *She loved that invisibility spell their mother had taught her before they left her in that jail cell in Ireland.*

Boots, Stella's black familiar cat, unwound himself from Stella's bed, stretched and yawned. Mary sighed. She couldn't do anything without that cat snitching on her, including her sneaking in this morning. *I hope Stella gets a good chuckle.*

"Goodbye, Boots." *More like, good riddance, hope I never see you again.*

Mary left and returned to her own cramped room. She sat on her bed beside the bounty from her sister's room. What should she pack? She would not have any help once she left the train station in Independence, so her bag shouldn't be too heavy. *Ugh!* That meant she had to leave much behind, including the red silk ball gown her suitor, Henry, had bought her to wear last night at the Marshall Field party. She ran her hand down the skirt, remembering what they had done after she gave Henry a potion. If only they had not fallen asleep.

Mary dug through her clothes, pulling drawers out, rummaging through her wardrobe. Undergarments, practical dresses, and shoes. Just the basics, not too many. Necklace, grimoire, indigo blue silk hand-painted altar rolled up, and some important herbs. Last, she packed her special potion, for which she only had one more use in her reticle.

She hefted the bag to check its weight. Pretty heavy, but not unmanageable. Almost in a panic stage, she paced the floor, shaking her hands to release nervous energy, and ran through her list. "Pack. Write letters. Get a carriage. Train station. Buy a ticket. Get on the train. Arrive in Independence. Find George. Go on a wagon train. Live a life of adventure." *One down.*

She sat to write letters. One for Stella and one for Henry. Stella's was easy. It was what she had said over and over for many years. *Sorry for all your tears.*

Done.

Henry's letter would be the most difficult to put in words. No matter how she wrote it, it would crush him. There was no way to avoid it. No letter would be cruel.

Dearest Henry,

You are the most important person in my life. But I have caused countless problems for you, though you do not complain. I am convinced you are better off finding someone more appropriate for your life and your family's wishes for you. You will have no problem finding a better beloved.

Love always, Mary

Done.

Mary left the letters on her dresser. *Two down.*

Now it was time for an escape from a mundane life to head out for adventure. Her heart beat fast, so she grabbed her bag and headed for the door before she changed her mind. Her carriage would be there soon.

Carrying the heavy bag down the narrow steps of the tenement building turned out harder than she expected. *Not giving up.*

No more yelling from Stella like the shameful dressing-down this morning for coming home in the early morning disheveled and using a magick potion on Henry. Mary tried living up to her sister's standards, but she failed all the time. If Stella thought she had ruined her chances with Henry and he wouldn't propose now, then she wouldn't be a problem for anyone anymore. A few more steps banging her bag along the wall. Not Stella. Not Henry. Nor his parents with their down-their-nose glares. Mary got to the next floor. *Whew!*

Even if Henry proposed, she couldn't imagine trying to maintain a false front in his social circle with charity events, opera, and the seasonal balls. How boring. Then he would expect children. After she dragged the bag half a floor, she paused, blowing a stray black hair out of her face. Children are dirty, loud, and needy creatures. Her a mother. *No way.* A life without magick? She couldn't imagine it.

Should she remove something from her bag to make it lighter? There wasn't anything she would sacrifice.

At dinner the other night, Henry's brother, George, had discussed his aspirations to escape the constraints of modern society and find freedom in the untamed west, selling mining supplies. That's what she wanted—adventure and freedom. But he had left yesterday for Independence, Missouri. She had to catch him before he left on the Oregon Trail.

One more floor to go, but she was running out of steam. She set the bag on the step, kicked it hard, and watched it plop over and over a few steps. Nothing was breakable, so she kicked the bag all the way down the last flight, saving her energy.

When Mary pushed her way through the front door, she heard horses' hooves clip-clopping on the cobbled street. No one else in the tenement would hire a carriage. She had saved every penny she earned at the tea shop, and now she had good reason to use her savings.

Once the driver helped her in and secured her bag, she sat on the padded bench, releasing the tension in her neck and shoulders. *Three down.*

The carriage lurched forward. Mary pulled the curtains closed to shut the world out. Henry's letter exhausted her. Though short and sweet, it defied the effort to get her thoughts to paper. She didn't know what to say.

Mary stood amid the bustling train station, her bag resting at her feet. The air smelled of steam and the sound of chatter filled her ears. Her eyes scanned the crowd, taking in the sea of faces rushing to catch their trains. This was it—the start of her new life. Her heart raced, a mixture of excitement and nervous anticipation.

Spotting the sign pointing towards the ticket counter, Mary hoisted her bag and made her way through the throng of people. The brick two-story building loomed before her, its windows reflecting the sunlight. With each step, her resolve strengthened.

Inside the building, Mary located the ticket counter, a hub of activity. Her gaze met the clerk's, a short, fat man with furrowed brows and a perpetual frown etched onto his face. She felt small in his presence, like a mouse before a cat. But she refused to let her nerves get the best of her.

The clerk barked, "Next!" startling a young man who had just purchased his ticket. Mary waited until he gathered his composure and moved aside.

Approaching the counter, Mary felt her heart quicken its pace. She steadied herself, determined to face whatever challenges lay ahead. Dizziness swept over her, but she gripped the edge of the counter, refusing to let it consume her. This was her chance for a fresh start.

"Where ya going?" the clerk grumbled.

"Independence," Mary blurted out, her voice trembling. She slid her money under the metal cage, her hands shaking.

The clerk handed her the ticket, his gaze lingering on her for a moment before he pointed toward the boarding area. *Five down.* Mary thanked him, her voice barely a whisper, and turned away, clutching the ticket in her hand.

Mary lowered herself onto a nearby bench, her bag resting beside her. She wished she had brought a book to pass the time. To her side, she noticed a copy of Harper's Weekly abandoned on the bench. Curiosity piqued, she picked it up and thumbed through its pages. The news of President Lincoln's funeral and the trials of Confederate traitors dominated the headlines. With the war now over, she longed for more uplifting stories.

As she studied the sketch of the latest Paris fashions, Mary observed the other travelers around her. She wondered if they, too, were embarking on their own grand adventures. The queasiness in her stomach persisted, but she found solace in the thought of finding George. Together, they would navigate whatever challenges awaited them.

Minutes turned into hours as Mary waited for her train to board. Finally, the moment arrived, and she joined the bustling crowd, finding her seat. *Six down.* The reality hit her—this might be the last time she would ever see Stella or Henry. A pang of sadness tugged at her heart, threatening to bring forth tears. She pulled out a handkerchief from her reticule, pressing it to her eyes to hold back the emotions. With her head against the train window, she whispered a silent farewell to the life she was leaving, her mind a swirl of uncertainty and determination.

Chapter Two

Mary stepped off the train, her legs aching from the long journey. She found herself in the public square of Independence, a bustling town. The courthouse stood tall in the center, a symbol of order amidst the chaos. *Seven down.* As she looked around, her eyes caught sight of a bar on Main Street. She peered inside, hoping to glimpse George, but he was nowhere to be seen. Determined, she continued her search, walking from one bar to another around the square until she spotted him, sitting alone at a bar on Lexington Street. *Eight down.* Her feet throbbed with pain, and her bag felt like she was dragging a dead body.

Mary entered the bar, standing beside George for a few minutes, waiting for him to notice her. Impatience washed over her, and she narrowed her eyes, pursing her lips. She couldn't contain herself any longer. She jabbed him in the side with her elbow, prompting him to turn, a frown on his face.

"Hi, George! Fancy finding you here," Mary said, bouncing on her toes.

George's mouth dropped open, his eyes bulging. "What are you doing here?" He glanced around, his gaze searching. "Is Henry here? Did my father send you two to bring me home?" His bottom lip jutted out as he turned back to the bar. "Won't work. Never going back." He took a big gulp of his drink.

Mary's smile widened, as she was certain her next words would thrill him. "I'm not going back either. I'm here by myself." She placed a hand on his forearm, leaning over the bar to meet his gaze. "I came to find you. Let's go west together. Won't it be fun?" She hopped on her toes again, lifting her shoulders. She had endured George's advances right in front of Henry, threatening to steal her away.

"No. I'm going alone. Why would I want to bring you?" George replied, his voice carrying the bite of a lone wolf.

Mary fell silent, eyes widened, fighting the urge to step back and run. She searched for a way to save face. No man had ever rejected her. "I can cook. Can you? How are you going to keep yourself fed for several months? You've been taken care of all your life. You need to think about it."

Feeling a minor victory, Mary took a seat, and the bartender approached her, asking for her order. She contemplated ordering a whiskey to make a point. Before she could respond, George shook his head, interjecting, "Get her a whiskey on my tab. If she chugs it in one go, she can go with me."

Mary raised an eyebrow, a mischievous spark in her eyes. "A challenge it is." She took the glass to her lips, winking at George. In one swift motion, she tipped the glass, downing its contents in a single gulp, and slammed it back on the bar. The other patrons who had overheard the challenge cheered for Mary. She overheard a gentleman behind her remark, "She's a keeper!"

George patted her on the back. "Welcome to the wagon train. I won't buy your personal needs, but I'll cover the food supplies for both of us since you'll be cooking."

Mary extended her hand, and George took it, shaking on their agreement. "It's a deal, George. Happy travels to us."

"Now, tell me why you're really here? Last I heard, Henry was ready to propose, and here you are," George leaned in a little too close, causing Mary to arch her back away from him.

Mary sighed, her thoughts drifting to the jewelry box containing a gorgeous engagement ring that fell out of Henry's jacket pocket. "Think of the things your mother does. I don't want to do any of that. Dinner parties, social affairs, and children. Being proper all the time. I want a more interesting life." She also considered how hard it would be to hide her true abilities, which she didn't want to. She was a witch, and she wanted to live like one.

George folded his arms across his chest, rolling his eyes. "My mother has the perfect life. She has servants to do everything for her." He shook his head. "I wish I could have her life. Low expectations. My father expects Henry and I to be successful businessmen." He threw his hands up, sneering. "Women have it made."

Mary narrowed her eyes, tapping her foot in annoyance. George's gestures and attitude grated on her. She had never seen him behave that way at his house. It was clear he presented a different side to his parents. He was proper around them, though they still criticized him, as far as she saw. Henry insinuated George did nothing but party instead of showing up to work at his father's textile business, which led to the business being willed to Henry.

"Your mother has to manage the household, including that staff that waits on her hand and foot, as you say," Mary retorted, shaking her index finger at him. "And let's not forget the gardens she's responsible for, along with the staff that maintains them. How many servants is that so far? You should give her more credit." She added, tipping her head, "But it still seems like a boring life to me."

George shrugged. "Do you want another drink, or do I have to worry about you falling off your stool?"

Mary threw her head back and laughed. "Are you afraid you can't handle someone as small as me? Of course, I want another drink...to celebrate our trip."

George raised a hand to get the bartender's attention. He waved his hand around their empty glasses. Two more whiskeys appeared in front of them and the empty glasses cleared away.

They raised their glasses in a toast, bidding farewell to their old lives and embracing the unknown. Mary couldn't believe she was going West, where she had only read fascinating stories of frontier life in the newspapers.

Mary's achievement brought a blissful serenity to the evening. She engaged in conversations with other people who were also preparing to travel west. Some planned to mine for gold, others to establish ranches, and many more aspired to become farmers in the fertile valleys of Oregon. Each person had their own big dreams, and Mary felt a kinship with them. Her own big dream was coming true.

As George led her outside, and towards the river, Mary asked, "Where are we going?"

George smirked, his eyes glimmering. "To bed?"

Suppressing her repetitive question, Mary followed him to a small community of tents, observing as he dropped to his knees and crawled inside one. She looked around, shaking her head in disbelief.

On the ground? She hesitated for a moment until George stuck his head out.

"Are you coming?"

Surprised and at a loss for words to protest, Mary swallowed her reservations and entered the tent, stepping into the unknown alongside George.

George awoke to the biting chill of the frosty morning, his breath forming mist in the air. He rolled over, his gaze falling upon Mary, curled in a fetal position, fast asleep. He felt a twinge of exasperation toward her foolishness. How did she neglect to bring warm clothes or a bedroll for their trail adventure? Did she expect it to be a luxurious journey, with fancy hotels at every turn? His worry grew as he contemplated whether her high-maintenance nature would become a burden on their expedition. After all, he had left Chicago to escape such airs and sensibilities.

As George laid back, he found his thoughts consumed by the dilemma of convincing Mary to return to Henry in Chicago. Let him propose to her, provide for her, and deal with the inevitable brood of children. It would no longer be George's problem. That was the stark contrast between him and his brother. Henry sought comfort and structure, conforming to societal norms. George suspected Mary didn't quite fit into that world either, which explained why their parents disapproved of her.

George had never been one to engage in long-lasting relationships. It suited him better if the women he encountered lacked moral constraints, sparing him the need to pay for their services. But to entertain the notion of a more permanent connection and the expectations it entailed—George wanted none of that. Expectations had no place in his life, be it in relationships, family, friends, or work. It was always about what others would do for him, with no expectations placed on him in return. Was he a narcissist? Perhaps, but what harm was there in looking out for oneself? If you didn't take care of yourself, nobody else would. His family hadn't.

His nanny raised him; his parents were too preoccupied doting on his flawless older brother, Henry. Henry did no wrong, while George was perpetually in the wrong. No matter how hard he tried in his youth, he never measured up to Henry's achievements. Henry was superior in everything he pursued. Frustrated and defeated, George had given up, realizing that life was easier when he bottled his emotions and let them explode.

As George returned to the matter at hand—how to send Mary packing—he rose and slipped out of the tent. The sky veiled in a thick fog, cast an eerie ambiance over the campsite. A brisk walk would help clear his mind and perhaps spark some ideas. He entertained the thought of tossing her into the nearby river, but dismissed it. She might swim, and there were far too many witnesses who might rescue her. What if he found her a job and convince her that Independence held countless adventures? Doubtful that would work. The idea of stabbing her in her sleep crossed his mind, but how would he dispose of her body?

Ascending the hill toward the first street that ran alongside the river, George cast a glance towards the wagon shop. He had placed the order upon his arrival, but the increasing number of people arriving each day and setting up camp by the river left him concerned. With everyone heading west, the demand for wagons was substantial, and the supply limited.

The smell of freshly cut wood wafted through the air even before he reached the shop. A small hut stood beside a large, covered work area where sawdust covered every surface and floated through the air. The sounds of hammers striking nails and the rhythm of saws slicing through timber resonating while several men toiled away on four wagons. He hoped one of them was his. The two facing the street had buckboards, so they weren't. He hadn't opted for extravagant features, choosing instead a basic wagon with reinforced axles. He knew he could easily repair the rest along the way. Besides, the mining equipment he had ordered was heavy.

The question that plagued him was whether to have a team of four oxen or six. Nobody seemed to have a definitive answer. Four oxen might struggle on steep hills, while six would be a burden to feed on the limited grass found along parts of the trail. He embraced spontaneity and postponed his decision until tomorrow—it wasn't his style to overthink.

A man in front of him appeared to be his age, so George inquired, "Which wagon train are you joining?"

The man turned around, a piece of hay dangling from his mouth, and replied, "Grantham. And you?"

"Hmm, same here." George nodded. "Do you have anyone accompanying you?"

As the line inched forward, the man took a few steps, prompting George to follow suit. "My wife and my brother," he answered.

George mirrored the man's steps again, moving closer to the supervisor of the shop. "I planned to go alone, but someone from

Chicago suddenly showed up, insisting she wanted to join. Not sure I want that," George confessed, following with an enormous sigh.

The man twisted around. "Oh, having some help is always beneficial, but if she's not related to you, it goes against the rules for the Grantham train," he added.

A glimmer of hope flickered within George as he absorbed the man's words. A rule. This rule could be his salvation, a means to send Mary back home to Chicago. In that moment, a surge of relief filled him. Finally, something of benefit to him. Besides, he knew he could handle the trail by himself—what did this man know? George was sure he would conquer anything that came his way.

CHAPTER THREE

MARY AWOKE TO THE chill that seeped through the thin fabric of the tent, her body stiff from the unforgiving ground beneath her. It reminded her of the last time she'd slept like this, back when Stella and she had traveled to Chicago for Stella to be a nanny. But the child had died during their travels, leaving them stranded. They sought refuge in alleyways until Stella found work at the herbal shop, a job she still held. Mary hadn't considered her accommodations for this journey.

Was this yet another impulsive decision that would leave her rueful, akin to that ill-fated potion she'd slipped to the headmaster, compelling him to alter her grades? The shame he'd carried after succumbing to her concoction was palpable, leading to his resignation. Stella never let her forget it. Of course, there was also Henry, on whom she'd used the elixir to break through his prudent exterior. And now, here she was.

Mary located George's cooking supplies and yanked them from the tent. She arranged rocks she gathered into a makeshift ring, securing branches and a bonus log from an abandoned fire pit. A cautious survey of her surroundings revealed no prying eyes. With a sharp exhale, she ignited the stack of branches, flames voraciously devouring the offered fuel. Setting the log, she positioned a rock beside it to serve as a base for the pan.

A glance upward revealed George's approach to the tent. Perfect timing. She laid bacon slices in the sizzling pan, hoping he hadn't eaten yet. He needed a taste of her culinary prowess to realize her value on this journey.

As the aroma of bacon filled the air, George settled onto the ground. When Mary cracked a pair of eggs into the pan, he said, "Why don't we find the wagon master after we eat? Get you added to my wagon?"

The look on George's face didn't align with his words, leaving Mary puzzled. Was there an ulterior motive? Perhaps she was over-thinking. "Yes, let's do that. I'm eager to hit the trail." Was that a smirk? George was a far cry from his brother. She handed him a plate.

George devoured the eggs and bacon, discarding the plate. He reclined on the grass.

Mary finished her meal and tidied up, extinguishing the fire with a swift kick of dirt. "Ready."

George sprang to his feet, a surge of enthusiasm that heartened Mary after those cryptic smirks. She followed him along the river-bank, approaching a sprawling cluster of tents.

"Stay put," he barked at her, heading towards the heart of the encampment where a group of men congregated.

Too distant to eavesdrop, she found herself drawn to the fire near the men, captivated by the flickering flames, their warmth and hues enveloping her, oblivious to all else. A child careened around a tent corner, colliding into her, snapping the spell. "Ugh!" She swiped her hand down her dress, as if dislodging an imaginary speck.

Emerging between two tents, George retraced his steps towards their own. Mary caught up, inquiring, "Are we going to see the wagon master?"

George pivoted, brows knitted in a scowl. "I had to track him down first. Stop with the questions. It's irritating." He quickened his pace.

It was a struggle to keep up, but her resolve propelled her. Why was George so obstinate today? After all, he'd consented to let her accompany him.

Opposite a vast workshop with men toiling on wagons, George halted. Mary noted a few men pausing in their labor to cast curious glances her way. She offered a coy smile.

George stood beside a tall man talking with several men. As their discussion concluded, George approached the broad-shouldered figure—presumably the wagon master. "Good morning, Will. I enlisted a few days back, but someone's joining me. I need to include them on my wagon."

Will nodded. "Morning. Have you secured your wagon yet? They're getting backed up, it seems."

Chest out, George nodded. "Oh, yes. Ordered and ready today."

Will produced folded papers and a pencil from his dungarees. "Good on the preparations. So, who's the addition?"

George thrust Mary forward. "Mary Maguire."

Will's arm sagged. "Is she a relative?"

"No."

Will exhaled. "The families who hired me have a rule: all couples must be wed."

George shook his head. "No, no, we're not a couple. I'm just giving her a ride west. There's no romantic entanglement."

Mary murmured, "Oh, no! This is a problem."

Will folded the papers and stowed them away, along with the pencil. "Yes, it is. The hiring families are devout, and they have their principles. I'm bound to abide by them. So, she won't be joining us."

Mary stepped forward, intercepting Will's retreat. "But I must go. I want to go. What am I to do? I came all the way from Chicago, and I don't want to return."

"Then get married. It's a simple solution. She cooks, you drive." Will continued down the street, leaving George and Mary locked in a silent standoff.

Mary clutched George's arm. "Fine. Let's go get married."

George shook his head, edging away. "Absolutely not. I have no desire to marry you. I don't even like you. And I won't be anyone's second choice. You'll either go home or stay here. Take your pick."

A sense of despair washed over her, events unfurling too fast for her to grasp. She shouted at George, "You won't marry me? What am I to do now? This isn't fair." Mary hastened after Will. "Sir, what if I secure my own wagon?"

Will halted, leveling a steady gaze at Mary. "Do you comprehend the magnitude of that decision? This is a grueling expedition, not fit for a delicate lady to undertake alone. I won't permit it."

Mary wept, her voice a plea. "I want this so much. I'm certain I can manage it better than George. He's nothing more than a pampered rich boy."

Will chuckled. "If George falters, we will leave him behind. I can't have one party holding everyone up. Like I said, it's a hard trip." Will continued on his way.

She stood there frozen, unable to grasp how her dream was falling apart. This was not the way she thought it would go, and now her mind was a complete blank. The tears came hard. People stopped and stared at a woman nearly collapsed, sobbing.

George yelled as he stomped his foot for emphasis, "Stop making a fool of yourself! I'll buy your train ticket home, alright?"

How could her plans be defeated so easily? What was she thinking? Shaking her head, she straightened up. She would not be dispatched. Tears wiped, she pushed her shoulders back, thrusting her chin forward. George had taken off down the street and she knew what to do now.

Fuming, George stormed off, heedless of his direction. He needed distance from Henry's insufferable girlfriend, a relentless thorn in his side. He had his plans all laid out, and then she waltzed in, throwing a wrench into his carefully constructed life. As usual, his brother interfered, even from afar.

His steps brought him into the path of an unsuspecting couple, and he plowed through them without a second thought.

The man yelled, "Hey, watch where you're going!"

George didn't care. Was there no sanctuary in this town, no respite from the ceaseless clamor? How would he clear his mind with so much chaos swirling around him? If he didn't find solitude soon, he'd explode, and that never ended well. His father had bailed him out of trouble one too many times.

He slipped behind a row of buildings, a secluded alcove where no one intruded. On a tree stump, he unleashed his frustration, kicking it with fervor before collapsing onto it. He pounded his fists, shaking his head and body in a frenzy. To an outsider, it might have resembled a fit or a seizure, but it was the only way he could regain control, preventing himself from inflicting harm on others or property.

Then, in the stillness that followed, he rocked back and forth, plotting how to rid himself of Mary for good. He never wanted to lay eyes on her again. A bit of payback was due for the trouble she'd caused him. Perhaps he'd purchase a train ticket, but instead of Chicago, send her eastward. Would she even notice? He needed assurance before parting with his money. Time to test the waters.

He spun around as he rose and delivered one last kick to the stump, envisioning Mary's face. Pain shot up from his toe to his knee, and he hopped on one foot, cursing her name.

Surveying his surroundings for clues, he oriented himself and tuned in to the distant wail of a train whistle. The sound would lead him towards the station. He set off, limping and cursing.

The streets seemed less congested on the side roads, but as he neared the station, the throngs grew denser. He navigated through them more composed, no longer resorting to shoving. When a break in the crowd appeared, he found the ticket office line devoid of patrons.

Approaching the window, he cleared his throat. "Excuse me. I have a few questions."

The clerk, an older gentleman with snowy tufts of hair protruding from under his hat, a white mustache, and impressive mutton chop sideburns, peered out at George. "I've got answers, sir. Shoot."

George sighed. "If I were to buy a ticket for someone, would they have any inkling of their destination?"

The station clerk's lips twisted in contemplation. "That's an unusual inquiry. Sounds like you're hatching quite the scheme. But it won't work. We print the destination on the ticket to ensure the traveler boards the right train."

George's face fell, shoulders sagging. "Well then, how frequently do trains depart for Chicago?"

A broad smile spread across the mutton-chopped man's face. "Every single day!"

As George turned to leave, he offered a nod. "Thank you."

The clerk replied, "Pleasure's mine, sir."

George kicked at the air, hands buried in his pockets, and head bowed. He retraced his steps toward the river, thoughts churning. Mary, Henry, and his parents all doubted him, believed he couldn't handle this wagon train alone. To hell with them. He was tired of their skepticism and was determined to prove them wrong once he rid himself of Mary.

Chapter Four

Mary trailed behind George, keeping a discreet distance to ensure he remained oblivious to her scrutiny. Negotiating the teeming streets and bustling boardwalks challenged him as he shoved his way through the throngs of people. Disappointment washed over her, struggling to fathom why he felt the need to be so aggressive. Navigating the crowded streets was manageable without resorting to such tactics.

The mere thought of returning to Chicago was unthinkable. The only conceivable path ahead involved marrying George, but the notion settled in her stomach like the sour tang of a freshly bitten lemon. Yet, sometimes, acquiring what one desired was a battle. Why did she shy away from Henry in Chicago? He embodied perfection, perhaps to a fault. He was at the pinnacle of society. She couldn't measure up to such impeccable standards, which led her to this juncture. It might not be the right path, but it was the one she craved for the moment. She refused to abandon this venture with George.

Nestled within her bag rested the remnants of the potion she'd employed on Henry, where he loosened up and they ended in a bed in the Marshall Field mansion. If she slipped it into George's drink, she could exploit his newfound lack of inhibition to lead him to the town hall for a marriage certificate.

However, she needed to persuade him to join her for a drink or dinner first. George was a challenge, an understatement if ever there was one. She harbored doubts about the man's capacity for forming lasting relationships or friendships. How on earth did his mother tolerate him? She chuckled to herself. He was far from a commendable person, yet here she was, plotting to marry him. It didn't seem wise, but who was she to adhere to wisdom? How many times had Stella expressed her ire at Mary's choices? Stella was probably seething now. *Oh well.*

As George darted behind a row of buildings, she observed him with furrowed brows, kicking at a tree stump and flailing his limbs in frustration. What was he doing? Perhaps this was his peculiar way of indicating his willingness to marry her. So she pressed her back against the corner of the building, sneaking glances now and then to monitor George's antics. If only she possessed the power to read minds. Although, deciphering his thoughts might prove rather disturbing.

When George rose, she melded into the building's facade, hoping to evade detection as she resumed her pursuit. This street was sparsely populated, allowing her to maintain a reasonable distance, yet still keep him in her sights. From her vantage point across the street, it seemed he was purchasing a ticket. Afraid to stop him, she ran to the other side of the building and positioned herself around the other corner from him at the ticket counter. To her delight, she heard every word. To her despair, she overheard his plan to send her astray on the train. The stars aligned and the protocols of the train company thwarted his plan.

Continuing to follow him back to the tent, she knew what to do. No need to feel guilty about tricking him now, since she learned of his plan of deception. At least her idea would work.

"George," Mary called out, her voice carrying across the bustling street. "I've been scouring the town for you."

"Don't," George responded curtly. "You're heading back tomorrow."

"Indeed," she agreed with an exaggerated gesture, palms open. "So why not give me a proper farewell over dinner?"

The surprise that flashed across his face was a prize. "Fine. So you're leaving. Good. I want you gone. Let's go."

Mary kept pace with him, though her feet ached from all the walking. Still, her plan was proceeding as intended. She could endure a bit more discomfort.

George led her to a quaint café, courteously holding the door for her. Her reticle harbored the remaining potion, a secret ace up her sleeve. She needed to divert his attention and slip it into his drink. How difficult could it be? George was a predictably pampered buffoon.

Seated at a table, with George nursing a beer, Mary scanned the room, searching for something, anything, of interest to draw his attention. Patience, she reminded herself. When their food arrived, a woman entered, her corset straining to contain her ample curves. Mary chuckled, retrieving her vial from her bag.

"What's amusing you?" George inquired.

"Oh, what does it matter?" She glanced down at her own modest chest and laughed again, imagining the challenge of seeing her toes with such an ample bosom. "My word, those are the largest I've ever seen!"

George swiveled in his chair, his gaze locked on the woman. It was just the opportunity Mary needed. Swiftly, she added the potion to his beer and stashed the vial away. "I've seen bigger," George declared upon returning to his meal and beer.

"I suppose so," Mary mused, a pause punctuating her words as she waited for the potion to take effect. "Even without an ample bosom, I'd be perfect for marriage."

"Hmph. Maybe for Henry. He has questionable taste." George rubbed his chin, tilting his head to one side while pursing his lips. "Perfect for marriage?" He looked up as if deep in thought. His face lit up in a daze. "You're right. I'm sure of it. Henry thought so, and he's the clever one."

Mary seized her moment. "Don't you want to be the clever one? If we wed, *you*'ll be the clever one, not Henry."

"You're right. My father never acknowledges my brilliance. Let's marry and prove them wrong. We'll make a fortune together." George's excitement was palpable as he tilted his head back. "I come up with the best ideas, don't I?"

"Yes, you do. Let's get married right after we eat. No reason to wait! Then we can find Will and prepare for our adventure together. Cheers!" Mary raised her glass, and George clinked his against hers.

"Cheers!" George turned to the other patrons, announcing, "We're getting married!"

Amid the polite applause, Mary felt a surge of satisfaction at surmounting yet another hurdle. She was eager to accomplish this before the effects of the potion wore off. She knew George would likely be irate later, but that was a problem for tomorrow.

"Where in town can we get married this afternoon?" Mary inquired of the waitress.

"Check at the town hall. I heard you can tie the knot pretty quickly there. Good luck, you two." The waitress cleared their dishes.

Mary seized George. "Let's go! Time is of the essence. We need to get this done today so I can secure my place on the list. I refuse to be left behind."

George made no protest and followed her to the town hall.

"I'm looking to arrange a swift marriage. Can you assist us?" George's demeanor was endearing, though Mary knew it was temporary.

The elderly woman beamed and tilted her head. "How sweet! So you two are ready to tie the knot. Fill out this form and sign it - both of you. I'll have Mr. Harris with you shortly. There's a two dollar fee."

George completed the form with his information and passed it to Mary.

She hesitated. Who would want to marry George with his smug, entitled demeanor and nasty disposition? She craved the West, so she didn't have a choice. She sighed as she completed the form and returned it to the petite woman behind the counter.

Mr. Harris entered. "So, who's the lucky couple? Follow me. Miss Emmy will be your witness, since it appears you didn't bring anyone."

They trailed the middle-aged man into his office. "I'm the mayor, but I wear many hats in this town. We're growing fast. Stand right here."

Before Mary knew it, Mr. Harris had concluded the ceremony. "I now pronounce you husband and wife. You may kiss your wife." George leaned in for a passionate kiss. Mary pulled away, wiping her lips while gagging. The things you have to do to get what you want and need as a woman. If she was a man, she would have bought the wagon and left George on his own.

"Thank you, Mr. Harris." She led George out of the town hall. "We have to find Will."

"He'll be at the large group of tents around this time of day."

Two hours later, Mary half-dragged a tipsy husband back to their tent, a far cry from the vision she'd harbored of securing her passage on the wagon train. She was a woman driven, unapologetically determined to get what she wanted, a trait her sister often labeled as selfishness.

An uneasy pit gnawed at her stomach in anticipation of the morning when the effects of the potion wore off, and reality would bite George's head off. Then he would bite hers.

CHAPTER FIVE

THE NIGHT AIR CLUNG to Mary's skin as she stirred, a shiver coursing through her frame. The sound of George's frantic movements jolted her fully awake. There in the dim light, George struggled free from the blanket, sitting upright.

"What are you doing under my blanket?" His voice was sharp, slicing through the chill air.

Mary yawned, her breath misting in the cold. She rubbed her eyes, then her arms, still feeling the lingering bite of the night's frost. "Well, where else should your wife sleep?" she retorted, trying to inject a note of levity into the tense atmosphere. "I'll need to get my own blanket today. It's freezing out here at night and your blanket is too small for the two of us."

George loomed closer, his breath, a harsh gust, washed over her face. "What do you mean, 'wife'?" She noticed the hint of stale alcohol on his breath.

Mary laughed, a tinge of nervousness threading through the sound. She knew his hangover would amplify his irritability. "We got hitched yesterday, ran into Will last night, and he sorted out all the paperwork. So, it's all official now. Don't you remember? Though we did celebrate quite a bit."

"All I recall is a meal at the cafe," George muttered. He lowered his head to the ground, and his hands at his temples. A pained moan escaped him.

Mary resisted the urge to sigh.

"I never wanted this. Now, I'm stuck with you. I had my sights set on a lifetime of a confirmed bachelor." His hands dropped, revealing a look of disbelief as he turned toward her. "Oh no, no, no." He shook his head. "You must've tricked me. Where did we even get married?"

"Town hall," Mary replied, as George crawled out of the tent. The notion that he could simply stroll into the town hall and undo their marriage was laughable. It wasn't a pair of shoes that didn't fit, after all. Good thing she'd taken pains to stow the certificate away after showing it to Will the previous night.

As he dusted off his clothes, George muttered, "You stay here and don't cause any more trouble." He added under his breath, "Women are always trouble."

Mary chuckled to herself. If only he knew the half of it. But he should have remembered last night. When she used the potion on the headmaster and Henry, they did. What was different with George? Did it get more potent with age, or had she not mixed it up each time? She had to record this in her grimoire, though she never planned on utilizing that recipe again.

The morning light was seeping through the canvas of the tent, casting a soft golden glow over the campsite. As the reality of their situation settled in, a mix of apprehension and determination welled up within Mary. She committed to this path now, ready to embrace whatever challenges lay ahead.

Three days passed before Henry mustered the courage to face Mary after his disgrace at the Marshall's party. He dispatched a messenger, but no reply came. Desperation gnawed at him, drowning any concerns for etiquette. Arriving in his carriage, he emerged, his heart pounding, and ascended several flights of stairs to Mary's tenement. Clutched in his arms were offerings of flowers and chocolates, a silent plea for forgiveness. After deep breath, he rapped on the door.

Stella answered, her expression a tableau of surprise and disdain. Her lips curled, her eyes freezing over. 'Why are you here? Mary's gone.'

"No! She can't be. Why?" The air grew thin, Henry's chest constricting. It was like a sucker punch to his gut. Thoughts swirled, fragments of Mary's voice, her laughter, as he tried to grasp onto something, anything, that might explain her sudden departure.

Stella motioned him inside, her voice tight. "She left in the middle of the night. Left a note for you, which I intended to send, but... but I'm very disappointed in you."

Henry stepped into the parlor, the weight of his actions bearing down on him. He contemplated dropping to his knees, begging for forgiveness, but his words stumbled out instead. "I'm terribly sorry. I don't even know what happened. We had only kissed, just a peck on the cheek, before that. I came to apologize to her. But..."

The door slammed shut, and Stella pointed a trembling finger at him. "And it's your fault she's left."

"Please. I'm sorry." Henry fumbled with the bouquet, the gift, and the chocolates, extracting a small ring box from his jacket pocket. He held it out, trembling. "I've been carrying this around for weeks, waiting for the right moment to ask Mary to marry me. I want her to be my wife."

Stella's face crumbled, her shock palpable. She sobbed into her hands. "I had no idea that's how you felt. I told her you wouldn't want her anymore, that she was soiled because you come from a higher social standing. It's all my fault!"

"No, I would never do that. I love Mary!" Henry's composure shattered, tears streamed shamelessly. His body trembled, and he sank to his knees in the middle of the room, everything slipping from his grasp.

Stella's hand rested on his shoulder. "Let's sit. I'll get the note Mary left for you."

Henry regained his wobbling feet, gratitude mingling with heartbreak. "I would appreciate it so much. If it could give me a clue why she left, I need to know."

As they settled, Stella handed him the note, her eyes downcast. Handkerchief in hand, she dabbed her eyes.

Henry unfolded the note, his heartache intensifying as he read each word. His throat tightened, his vision blurred. He read it again, as if expecting a different outcome. Each sentence was a blow, a cruel twist of fate.

Stella sat beside him, her presence a balm to his wounded soul. "Henry," she began, her voice gentle, "Mary and I have always been each other's protectors. When we came to America with our uncle, I promised to keep her safe, to shield her from harm. She's a lot like our mother—impulsive, passionate, a handful, but so full of love."

Henry's eyes met Stella's, gratitude and sorrow swirling in their depths. "I love those things about Mary. I don't know how I'll go on without her. It must be so difficult for you. You two share a bond I wish I had with my brother."

Stella handed him a handkerchief, her gaze still averted. "Her note speaks of her pain, Henry, but also of her love for you. She believes she's doing this, for both your sakes."

Henry wiped away his tears, his breath hitching as he absorbed Stella's words. He longed to hold Mary, to reassure her they could face whatever trials lay ahead together. But now, the distance between them seemed insurmountable.

As the minutes stretched on, the weight of the world pressed down on Henry. He could sense Stella's concern, her own heartache for her sister palpable. They sat for a time in shared sorrow, bound by their love for the same woman.

Finally, Henry mustered the strength to speak. "Stella, I can't thank you enough for being here, for caring for Mary. Please, if there's any way you can help me reach her, to make her understand... I'll do whatever it takes."

Stella turned to him, her face softened, eyebrows furrowed. "Henry, I believe in your love for Mary. I'll do whatever I can to support you, to help bridge the gap between you. But you must promise me one thing."

"Anything," Henry vowed.

"You must prove to Mary that you're willing to fight for her, to stand by her side, no matter the challenges. Show her that your love is unwavering, that together, you can overcome anything."

Henry's heart sank as he realized the weight of his responsibilities back in Chicago. "My father is too ill to oversee the company anymore. The responsibility has fallen to me. I can't leave." The weight of duty settled heavily on his shoulders, conflicting with the ache in his heart for Mary.

Stella placed a comforting hand on his arm. "Henry, I understand the dilemma you face. Your duty to your family is paramount."

Torn between love and obligation, Henry nodded. "Thank you, Stella. I must stay in Chicago for now, but I promise you, as soon as circumstances allow, I will find Mary and bring her back to us."

"I'll be here, Henry. Waiting for both of you."

As he left the tenement, Henry's steps were heavy with the weight of his decision. He glanced back one last time, hoping to catch a glimpse of the woman who held his heart. He stepped into his carriage, determined to fulfill his responsibilities, though his thoughts remained with Mary, far away on the Oregon Trail.

CHAPTER SIX

THE MORNING AIR WAS crisp as Mary finished her breakfast and cleaned the dishes in a bucket of water from the nearby river. George rose from the campsite and walked away.

"Where are you going, George?" Mary called after him.

He increased his pace, barely audible as he replied, "I'm getting the wagon, oxen, and supplies."

Mary wasn't about to let him dictate her actions. She scrambled to her feet, determined to catch up. "Wait! I want to come."

Racing after him, Mary drew near, breathless. "You can't... slow down... for your wife?"

George rolled his eyes, maintaining his swift pace without a word.

As they approached the livestock yard, a pungent scent assaulted Mary's senses on the wind. The sight of dozens of horses, mules, and oxen penned in small corrals greeted her. Mary wrinkled her nose and voiced her concern. "Will the smell of the oxen be unbearable during our travels?"

George retorted, "If it bothers you too much, go back to Chicago. But since we know you won't, you might as well enjoy the aroma."

Determined to make the best of the situation, Mary wandered over to the nearest pen. A horse approached, and Mary tried her luck. "Can I have a kiss?" To her surprise, the horse nuzzled her shoulder. The man talking to George suggested, "She has a knack with horses. Do you want horses instead?"

"Nope. Four oxen. And I'm not paying over fifty a pair."

Mary turned to ask the man, "Where are the oxen?"

"Let me show you." The man took her to a pen where several oxen laid along the back rails on hay.

Mary leaned over the top bar of the metal fencing to survey the largest beasts she had ever seen. If the horse came, maybe the ox will, too. "Come here." Two of the closest oxen rose and walked over to Mary. The larger one nudged the other away, bringing his head in front of her. Mary rubbed him like she would a dog. It didn't offend her nose as bad as she feared, as most of it was the excrement in the pen. What a relief.

"If I didn't see it myself, I wouldn't believe it," the man exclaimed. He turned to George. "You're a lucky man. I guess she'll help you take them to your new wagon. Good luck on the trail!"

The man took four out of the pen and put a yoke harness on each set of oxen. Mary watched to know how to do it. With the harness ropes handed to her, Mary learned the commands: Gee for right, haw for left, and whoa to stop. Leading her two oxen out of the livestock building, she marveled at the unexpected ease.

George sought to dominate over his two oxen, who weren't having any of his harsh treatment using a stick. Every time he hit the closest oxen, it would back up. "Go, dammit. You stupid animal." He smacked it on its hindquarter and it lurched forward, spooking the other oxen who tried to get away in the other direction.

Mary glanced over her shoulder. George toiled to keep his oxen moving in the right direction and had a scowl on his face. Mary laughed. He must have been born scowling. To save his poor oxen any more abuse, she called out, "Come on." The oxen fell in line behind the oxen she led.

Mary didn't require the commands, as she just spoke to the oxen when they needed to turn the corner. "What shall I call you?" She looked at the bigger oxen. "I'll name you Aengus, which means strength in Irish." Then turned to the other. "You'll be Niall, meaning champion. I hope you like your names. I'll take proper care of you." Aengus and Niall beat Stella's cat, Boots, on all accounts. What if they were her familiar?

When she arrived at the wagon maker's shop, she waited for George while he straggled behind, his chin to his chest. When he arrived, she said, "This is Aengus and Niall. Please bow to George." Both oxen lowered their heads. Mary clapped her hands, smiling. "Good job!"

George rolled his eyes. "They're not pets. They work for us." Shaking his head, he disappeared into the shop.

As they brought out their Prairie Schooner wagon sporting an off-white canvas cover, Mary watched as several men motioned for them to bring their oxen. George struggled, tugging and pulling at his oxen, while Mary's obedient pair followed her without resistance. The man overseeing the wagon raised an eyebrow at Mary's ease and frowned at George's struggle.

Mary smiled. "I have the finest oxen, don't you think? I want to learn how to secure them to the wagon, although that will be George's job, right?" She fluttered her eyelashes. "You never know if something might happen to him and I'll be all alone."

George fumed. "You don't need to learn any of this. Why don't you start on our list of supplies?" He pushed her away.

"Hey!" A larger man approached, causing George to step back. "That's no way to treat a lady. If something happens to you and she can't fend for herself, they'll leave her behind."

"Fine." George's eyes blazed like fireballs as he uttered a firm "Stay," leaving her with no doubt that she had pushed him too far. At least for today, because tomorrow would be another day.

Mary smiled and followed what the man did to hook the oxen to the wagon. He explained why she should use the stronger oxen as her wheel oxen because they can stop the wagon on steep inclines. Mary felt a lightness in her chest and a sense of calm that she could take care of herself. She tilted her head and shoulders back, her hands hung behind her. The prospect of the impending journey filled her with eager anticipation.

In the bustling supply store, Mary surveyed towering stacks of provisions—cooking utensils, farming tools, mining gear—all marked for the journey west. A quick glance at the list sparked a realization. "Wait. There's not a bigger tent?"

"I already have a tent. For myself." George seized the list, dismissing her with a curt command. "Be quiet and stand there."

Mary's eyes widened, and her hands found her hips. "Where am I sleeping?"

"I don't know, and I don't care. If you want a tent, get one yourself." George strutted toward the counter.

Unyielding, Mary snagged his arm. "Can't I sleep in the wagon?"

George sighed, his shoulders sagging. "No! The wagon will be full of supplies." He emphasized each word, jaw clenched. "That's what the wagon is for—to take mining supplies to California to sell."

While George handled the transaction, Mary paced beside a stack of flour sacks, contemplating her uncertain sleeping arrangements. A woman in a blue dress approached. "Sorry, I overheard your conversation and I want to suggest something, if you don't mind."

Not surprised this woman overheard since George was loud, she hoped it wasn't a lecture about his behavior. "Oh, please. I have never done this and I feel so ill-equipped for this journey."

"This is my second trip. The first one, I traveled as a missionary. This time, we are moving to Oregon. A woman showed me how she had arranged their supplies until there was a flat area. Then she put a mattress on top. She said it was comfortable. On this trip, I'm doing the same for me and my youngest children. Let's look at the mattresses." The woman took Mary's hand and leaned towards her. "Are you sure you want to make this trip? It is difficult, and an ill-tempered man will make it even harder."

Mary flitted her other hand. "Don't worry about him. Do show me the mattresses. I love this idea. Thank you! We're leaving on the 14th. When are you leaving?"

"Same. Our church organized the group and opened it to others to lessen the cost for each wagon. My name is Katherine."

"I'm Mary and I'm glad to meet you." *That's why there's a marriage requirement. Better check what other rules there are.* Rules weren't what she bargained for.

Grateful for the insight, Mary made her purchase and loaded it with other supplies, curious about George's reaction. The mattress was only large enough for one person.

Mary walked along with George, their wagon loaded.

George yelled, "Hee!" The oxen didn't move.

Mary said, "I think it's haw, not hee."

"No. I heard him say hee. They gave us the stupidest oxen."

Mary thought to speak to the oxen, but she remembered George's foul mood, embarrassing her in the supply store.

"HEE!" George whacked the oxen with his stick several times. He snorted through his nose and clenched his jaw.

Mary pinched her lips together, crossing her arms in front of her chest. Witnessing the man's stubborn refusal to change his approach, she took charge and instructed the oxen on where to go until they reached their campsite. A sense of dread filled her. Would this be the way it is for the entire trip? She felt the icy glare from George, sure it injured his pride that she handled the oxen when he failed.

At the campsite, George inspected the supplies. He yelled, "What is this, Mary?"

Mary walked around to join George. She raised a brow, wondering why he only checked the supplies now, but it saved her from having him yell in front of other people. "You said I had to get my own bedding, and I did." She cocked her head, pointing in the wagon. "I need some things moved to lay the mattress out flat."

George smirked. "Well, if you need help, that's not happening. You're on your own!" He lifted his arms and walked towards the river, laughing.

Mary went around to the back of the wagon, looking for a way in, but it was too high for her. She found a lever on the side, played with it until she figured out it lowered the back end and allowed her to enter. Proud of herself for doing that, she felt confident to arrange her bed without George's help.

Grabbing a sack of flour, Mary couldn't move it, no matter how much she tugged. Not the container of tar, either. Her confidence flagged, but she was determined. The arrangement had to be smart, so she didn't sleep on items she needed every day. She pulled the strings that tightened the canvas on the end of the schooner for privacy. Hands out over the heaviest objects, she whispered a spell.

With gentle touch and whispered word,
Let this burden be like a bird.
Lighten the load that we see here,
Ease the weight, make it clear.
So mote it be!

Mary lifted, shoved, and dragged the lightened boxes, barrels, and bags, wishing she was an air witch like her sister whose magick would move it without a touch.

But wouldn't life be easier if she could use any magick all the time? It's not like she would change someone into a pig, though some deserved it. She didn't understand the fear of magick. She might even help others like Katherine. Her mother's prosecution in Ireland reminded her every day to keep it to herself for her own safety. The religious aligned it with their devil. Her beliefs had no devil, only karma.

Mary surveyed her work, pleased, before stepping out of the wagon and closing the back. George was nowhere to be found to show him. Not that he would appreciate it, anyway. Humming, she strode towards town to have a victory meal at a cafe she had discovered when taking Aengus and Niall to the wagon shop. She paused and turned to see the oxen feeding on the grass. Today was a good day indeed. She even made a new friend.

When she returned, she found George had prepared his tent and had warmed up the leftovers. So he could do things for himself. Unfortunately, he left a mess of dirty dishes and seemed to expect her to clean them. Better to do it now than wake up to it. At least she would sleep in more comfort than a blanket on the ground. Which worked perfect since they were to leave in the morning for the Oregon Trail.

As the golden hues of the setting sun bathed the campsite, Mary took a moment to appreciate the serenity before tackling the pile of dirty dishes George had left behind. She sighed, rolling up her sleeves, reminding herself that the promise of adventure lay beyond the Oregon horizon.

The rhythmic clinking of cutlery against plates echoed in the still evening air as Mary scrubbed away the remnants of his meal. The sun's last rays painted the landscape in warm tones, casting long shadows across the uneven ground. Mary stole glances at the oxen grazing nearby, oblivious to the human drama unfolding in their midst.

George lounged in his tent's entrance, his eyes narrowing as he watched Mary work. The unspoken tension between them hung heavy in the air, like the impending storm clouds on the distant horizon.

Mary finished the last dish, her hands dripping with soapy water. She shot George a defiant glance, unwilling to let his disapproval dampen her spirits. Rising from her crouched position, she dusted off her hands on her apron.

With a confident stride, Mary approached George. "You know, we're in this together. It won't hurt you to lend a hand once in a while."

George scoffed, dismissive. "I'm not here to play house. We're on the Oregon Trail for a reason."

"And I'm not asking you to play house. Just to be a decent human being," Mary retorted, her voice firm but not confrontational. She turned away, leaving George to stew in his own frustration.

As the evening settled in, Mary strolled to the wagon, eager to witness the sunset's last spectacle of the day. The hues of orange and pink painted the sky, a stark contrast to the brewing storm clouds on the distant horizon.

A soft breeze rustled through the grass, carrying with it the scent of adventure and the promise of a new life. Mary's thoughts drifted to the newfound friend she had made, Katherine, and the camaraderie she hoped to find on this journey.

The makeshift mattress in the wagon beckoned, and Mary climbed in, feeling the cool evening air on her face. She gazed up at the stars beginning to emerge, a celestial display that seemed to whisper tales of the unknown.

The campfire crackled nearby, casting flickering shadows on the canvas of the wagon. Mary lay there, contemplating the challenges that lay ahead. She was not just a passenger on this journey; she was a participant, ready to face whatever the Oregon Trail had in store.

As the night settled in, Mary drifted into a restless sleep, dreams of distant mountains and unexplored territories dancing in her mind. Tomorrow marked the beginning of their adventure, and despite the uncertainties, Mary couldn't deny the thrill of the unknown that awaited them on the Oregon Trail.

Chapter Seven

As the first light of dawn kissed the edges of the horizon, Mary stirred within the confines of her wagon. The murmur of activity outside seeped through the canvas walls, coaxing her into the new day. With a languid stretch, she embraced the remnants of a restful sleep—the best she'd had since departing Chicago.

However, a reluctant consciousness tugged at her, urging her to face the day. Mary left the haven of slumber rolling off her makeshift camp bed and set about the mundane task of dressing in the dim light.

As she emerged into the vibrant hues of sunrise, Mary's eyes sought Katherine, already immersed in the routine of camp life at the adjacent wagon site. The flickering flames of her fire hinted at the promise of breakfast soon to come. Mary waved in acknowledgment, a silent recognition of the bond forming between them. If this journey held any chance of success, emulating Katherine's kindness and efficiency seemed the prudent path.

With purpose, Mary busied herself choreographing the morning ritual. A sense of responsibility nudged her to prepare a pot of coffee, setting the tone for the day ahead. Her gaze flitted toward George's tent, harboring a quiet hope that the aroma of breakfast might coax him into a better mood.

As the bacon sizzled in the pan, Mary's mind danced between the rhythmic flip of the spatula and thoughts of Henry, the man she'd left behind. Unbidden, the tendrils of uncertainty wound around her, questions of regret lingering.

Today, she resolved, she would discuss her role in this partnership with George. If taking on more responsibilities would foster civility, then so be it.

When the meal was ready, Mary approached George's tent, her intent clear. A gentle prod at his foot and a call to breakfast, her attempt at a harmonious beginning.

However, George's response reverberated with irritation. "Stop poking me! That's no way to wake me!"

His early-morning grumpiness cast a shadow over Mary's optimism. "We have to get ready to leave for the trail today. I'll get the oxen ready while you eat," she declared, a veil of determination masking the unease beneath.

"Good. Go away," George dismissed her.

Mary redirected her steps toward the oxen, her mind occupied by the impending departure. In town, grazing space was scarce, so the oxen fed on a bale of hay tethered to the wagon. "Aengus, Niall. You will be in the wheel position today and Fionn and Conall in the lead." She led Aengus in place and drugged the yoke close. She silently beseeched a clandestine plea for strength in the mundane under her breath while focusing on summoning her magick.

Great goddess Brigit, goddess of fire and light.
I summon you to lift this yoke upon my ox without fright.
So mote it be!

The yoke raised and slid over the ox's broad head while Mary kept her hands upon it and made motions as if it was a struggle. Of course, the spell took a little energy, but there was no way to get it done without magick; it was the cost of getting it done. Mary reveled in the illusion of strength, a facade she wielded with purpose. Who's going to bother a woman who can lift an oxen yoke by herself?

While she placed the bowed part under his neck, she stroked the enormous beast. She repeated it for the other three oxen. There was immense satisfaction working with the animals. It made her feel connected, but now she needed to speak to the other beast, George.

After she readied the oxen, a string of swear words lured Mary to the other side of the wagon. George grappled with his unruly tent, putting on a spectacle for all to witness. She approached, shaking her head and, in a calm voice, said, "I will do that for you."

"Fine." George huffed off towards the river.

Mary unraveled the tangled tent, a quiet resolve in her demeanor. Folding the canvas shelter with ease, Mary aimed to dull the spectacle George had created.

As the morning unfurled, Mary walked the wagon closer to the ferry dock to observe Katherine and her husband, Marcus, get loaded on the ferry. Their oxen were being released from their wagon and tied to a rope system suspended over the river so they could swim across.

George came running up. "You thought you'd steal my wagon and leave without me? I knew I shouldn't trust you."

The accusation hung in the air, a testament to their fractured partnership. Mary threw her head back and smirked. "If I waited for you, we would miss the train. I told you we were getting ready." Heat rose along her back. "If you don't mind, I'll lead the oxen. You are free to do whatever, since you aren't used to working."

"I worked. I slaved at a boring job at my father's company. Don't say I'm lazy, woman." George hurried over to Marcus and Katherine's wagon and took the ferry with them, leaving Mary to manage the loading on her own.

Her humming Irish folk tunes served as a shield against the rising heat of frustration. No need for a fire at the moment. All she yearned for was to embark on the adventure that lay ahead. California beckoned, and Mary, with her magick and oxen in tow, felt ready to face the challenges that awaited on the Oregon Trail.

Once her oxen were released and tied to the crossing ropes, Mary said, "Goddess Aine, keep my oxen safe." As the ferry embarked on its river crossing, Mary's eyes remained fixed on her oxen—her companions on this arduous journey. They were strong swimmers and ended safely on the other bank, waiting.

As the ferry reached the opposite bank, Mary released a breath she hadn't realized she'd been holding. How many more rivers would she face before she reached the golden coast? She would rather walk on hot coals or step through a fire than end up in water, especially when she couldn't see the bottom. She hadn't even gotten out of Independence, Missouri, to face her greatest fear. Water. What was next?

Once they crossed the Missouri River, the daily drive west became a routine for Mary. Since she slept lightly, she arose when Katherine started her fire before sunrise. How Katherine woke when she did was beyond Mary. If Mary hoped to get everything done in time to line up for the day's journey, she had to follow Katerine's lead.

One morning, Katherine said, "You have a knack for starting your fire. I don't know how you do it." Mary smiled. Her fire magick would remain a secret.

The most annoying part of every morning was waking George. *Why was he so grumpy all the time?* She wished she had brought more chamomile with her, but she needed what she had to keep her temper under control for safety's sake. Since she hadn't found a decent way to wake the grump, she banged on his tent near his head and carried on with her chores. Most of the time, she would tend to the oxen and get them yoked to miss his morning tirade.

A week after they left Independence, he leaped out of his tent before she made her get-away. George whined, "Why do we have to leave so damn early? I need more sleep to walk all day."

Mary replied, "Retire earlier, like I do."

"You're boring as hell. I enjoy talking with the other men."

"Ride in the wagon." Mary shoved his breakfast at him with one hand and his coffee with the other.

"That's for the elderly and snot-nosed children. I should have bought a horse, dammit."

Mary was sure he got that idea from the men he hung around. She walked off towards the oxen who were better company.

The next morning, she was quicker at getting away before he crawled out of his tent and listened to him complain from a distance. After the oxen were prepared, she saw George dump his dishes on the ground and walk away. Sighing, she walked over to clean the breakfast dishes, took down his tent, and stow it all in the wagon.

Mary dropped to the ground and yanked off her shoes and stockings. Out of her apron pocket, she pulled out a salve she made. In the past, she had used it on her hands when she gardened, but now applied it to her feet before the daily ten to twelve-mile walk. It helped heal blisters fast. She scrambled to get stockings and shoes back on when she saw Katherine's wagon moving.

When she rode in the wagon, there was too much jostling and jolting around. Mary's feet felt better, but the rest of her body suffered.

While walking, the rhythm kept her calm, allowing her time to think without being yelled at. The feel of nature, the tall grasses with small birds swishing through, chasing insects and eating seeds. Creatures taking long drinks in small creeks startled by the wagons. Mary felt the unseen larger animals, the predators, watching the train go by. Some following, some lurking in the shadows at night. Nature barely disturbed by her presence, letting her be. She let them be except to collect herbs along the way. A quiet interlude in her life.

When the wagon master signaled for lunch, Mary warmed leftovers of rice and beans. Butter, made in a churn tied to the side of the wagon, spread on the crusty biscuits, made them more palatable.

"Nothing is more frustrating than a woman who's an awful cook. Can't believe you expect a living being to eat this." George crossed his arms across his chest while sitting on the ground. He looked like one of Katherine's youngest children pouting after she corrected them.

Mary turned away to stifle a laugh. It was unfortunate that there were not better options for eating, but there was no way to avoid it. Beans and rice kept on long journeys. How many ways can you prepare a meal with those ingredients? The only time to bake was on Sunday when the wagon train rested, and what you baked had to last all week.

As she walked over to check the oxen, she said, "Sorry. If you're planning to eat, you'll have to do it quick. We'll be leaving soon." Once she was out of anyone else's sight, she took a long blade of prairie grass and tied a loose knot in it. As she spoke her spell, she pulled the knot tight.

Great Goddess Morrigan, this man wants to battle his food.

Let him choke on a biscuit chewed.

So mote it be!

When she returned, she found an empty plate except for a biscuit with one bite taken, which she cleaned up and put away. Mary hoped he enjoyed his biscuit. Too bad she missed him choking. He should learn to be thankful, but she doubted he had it in him.

Time for a long walk made more challenging by the heat of the day. Katherine and her older children could walk in the shadow behind the wagon since Marcus walked their oxen. It wasn't an option for Mary.

When the train stopped for the day, Mary leaned against the closest oxen with a deep sigh. Head back, she would only stay as long as she could bear the heat coming off the large animal. She wished she could cool them and herself off at the same time. But it would tire her too much and she had work to do.

Mary unloaded her cooking supplies. She had to hurry. George would show up and yell for his dinner. She dreaded the spectacle. There were many others who overheard, since the train made a tight circle every night to keep predators out and the horses in. Plus, the sooner she fed him, the sooner he would disappear. She cleaned right after dinner to avoid any critters. Then it was time to prepare his tent to avoid another tirade.

After their work, the women would talk until it was time to tuck children in for the night. Mary didn't speak, as she had nothing to offer, but it gave her the opportunity to relax and listen to how the other women coped on the trip.

Mary heard her name repeated a few times and jerked her head up.

A woman she didn't know asked, "Please ask your husband not to use profanities around my children. I bring them up in the way of the Lord."

Mary sighed, head bowed. "I can try, but he doesn't listen to me. I'm sorry." *Why didn't she ask her husband to talk to George?* Mary rose, spun around to walk to her wagon.

The woman protested, "You don't need to leave. I don't have any hard feelings towards you."

Mary said without turning back, "I'm tired. I'm ready to retire. Good night." Walking away from the circle of women may give them the message to raise problems with George differently. She had no power there, but she flared the fire they sat around to add to the message. The verbal reactions she heard made her smile, head held high.

After a while, Mary noticed George return. She peeked out of the wagon. "Don't be mad at me, since I'm only a messenger. They don't like you using profanities around their children."

"I'll speak how I want. There is no way I'm about to travel in such an unspeakable way that causes my entire body to hurt just to have someone tell me what to do. How's that even possible? I'm traveling west to get away from everyone telling me how to be. It's not fair. I deserve better. Tell me how their way is more significant than mine. Well?"

Wanting to end the discussion, Mary said, "They asked me to say something, and I did. I'm tired and going to sleep." She popped her head back into the wagon and tried hard to tune out his cursing. It hit her just right that evening and the heat of her reaction rose. The woman's complaint and his response were too much.

Mary climbed out of the wagon and walked away. But the prairie was tender with waist high grass and she was a spark. She found the rutted trail and stood there until the heat dissipated. Angry, frustrated tears flowed. George was a catalyst, and she didn't know how to prevent a disaster. She better figure it out before she started a wildfire where there was nothing to put it out.

Chapter Eight

Nearly six weeks had passed since Mary's departure from Independence, each day an arduous traverse, but the river crossings gnawed at the core of her fears—the Blue, Wakarusa, Kansas, Vermilion, Big Blue, and Little Blue. The oxen strained against the rushing waters, and Mary battled her own apprehensions, wondering if the incessant encounters with rivers would ever dull the sharp edge of her fear.

Fort Kearny, a pivotal trading post, loomed on the horizon, promising respite and a chance to replenish supplies. The prospect of sending a letter home ought to have ignited a spark of excitement, yet Mary found herself mired in a weariness that resisted enthusiasm. The women around her busied themselves with missives to family, their pens dancing across parchment. Mary, however, remained tethered to an overwhelming desire for more sleep.

In a moment of half-hearted distraction, Mary observed ants diligently cleaning plates, contemplating how long it might take before such chores became obsolete. Her mind meandered to avoid the other pressing tasks that awaited her attention, a list left unattended.

Katherine's approach interrupted Mary's contemplation, and a flush of embarrassment painted her cheeks. What would Katherine say about the chaotic state of the camp? George's abandoned dish, now a feast for ants, mirrored the surrounding disorder—the untidy tent, the oxen unprepared. The simplest tasks had become Herculean struggles, a silent testament to Mary's perceived failure.

"Are you okay, Mary? You don't look well."

"Ugh! I'm sick every morning, and all I want is to sleep. It's wretched." Mary's attempt to retrieve the dish from the ants ended in a bout of dry heaves, leaving her gasping for breath once the episode subsided.

"Have you considered you might be pregnant, dear? You have all the signs." Katherine took charge, accepting the dish and fork, submerging them in a basin of water.

Mary's face drooped, a silent gasp escaping her lips. "No. I can't be pregnant! Oh my goodness, no. Can you just imagine me with a child?" Laughter turned to tears, emotions tumbling out unbidden.

Katherine walked over and hugged her until Mary controlled her sobs. "How will I know for sure? How long will I suffer like this?"

As they restored order to the wagon, Katherine, a beacon of calm assurance, shared her own past. Mary, thoughts racing, wondered how she would navigate this new reality. The specter of telling George loomed large, a storm gathering on the horizon.

While walking alongside the oxen, Mary felt the cool breeze against her sunburned skin. Her thoughts drifted to the night she'd given Henry the magick potion, a night that now echoed with unintended consequences. The child she carried would be a constant reminder of impulsive decisions and a looming confrontation with George. How would she face him?

Lunch approached, and Mary avoided George's gaze. When Katherine's oldest daughter came over to assist Mary, he asked,

"Why are you helping her? You should help your mother."
George used his hand to shoo her away.

The girl stood her ground, her arms clasped at her waist. "My
mother sent me over here to help her since she's pregnant." She
went to grab the Dutch oven handle using a towel.

"What!" George turned towards Mary, taking the steps needed
to be in her face. "You're pregnant! When were you planning
to tell me? Is it Henry's? It's sure not mine!" Accusations and
questions hung in the air, the fragile threads of Mary's composure unraveling.

Tears streamed down her flushed face as George stormed off,
leaving Mary to pick up the shattered pieces of her secret. She
stammered, "Thanks for your help, but I have it now. You can
go back." She dropped her head, shaking, wanting to hide. *This
can't be happening!*

Katherine's daughter fumbled pulling the Dutch oven off the
hook on the tripod, almost spilling it all. "Uh, um. I'm sorry.
So sorry." Her frown pulled the corners of her mouth, her eyes
watered between furrowed brows. She wiped her hands on her
apron. Taking off, she sprinted towards her mother's camp.

Mary retrieved the cast-iron pot from its cockeyed position
to place it in the wagon. She dreaded George's words reaching
Katherine's ears. She only hoped her neighbor was not a gossip.
The last thing she needed was the entire camp, knowing she
carried another man's child. She didn't need all that judgment
to surround her every day.

Later in the afternoon, Katherine came alongside Mary. "I
understand my child spoke out of turn this morning. She's an-
guished for causing any problems. I hope you can forgive her."

Mary bowed her head, embarrassment clinging as she struggled to articulate her gratitude, her emotions still raw. She wasn't sure if Katherine heard what George said or what her daughter repeated to her. Tears welled up again. "Tell her I have no quarrel with her. She was very kind and tried to help."

Katherine tipped her head. "Do you want to talk about it? It's better to get your troubles off your chest."

"I don't think I can right now, but I appreciate the company. I'm homesick and I didn't think I would ever acknowledge that." She sought to laugh through her crying. "Never want my sister to find out that." Or that she was pregnant. Judgment from her was the last thing she needed. How could she raise a child when she can't even manage her own life?

Mary lifted her head to let the breeze dry her tears. A chuckle masked in tears escaped her lips, a feeble attempt at humor. In Katherine's company, the ache of loneliness momentarily lifted, replaced by the warmth of simple, meaningful conversation. As the afternoon unfolded, Mary, still grappling with her troubles, found solace in Katherine's presence, a respite from the harsh judgment that awaited her on the trail.

Alfred, Stella's fiancé, persuaded her to expedite their wedding, culminating in a swift and quiet ceremony before the justice. Stella, now married, left the tenement behind to embark on a new life in Alfred's elegant brownstone. She started her new life alongside a man who was not afraid of who she was or what she did.

Optimistic and hopeful, she arranged a bedroom for her wayward sister, Mary, yearning to reunite their fractured family.

Despite the joy of her union with Alfred, Stella couldn't shake the gnawing despair lingering over Mary's unexplained disappearance. Why did she leave? Nights slipped away in sleepless torment, relief elusive as she tossed and turned. Eventually succumbing to slumber, vivid images of Mary, lost and vulnerable in the wilderness, consumed Stella's dreams.

Upon waking, Stella, unable to return to sleep, brewed a calming chamomile and lavender tea in the kitchen. She retreated to her sitting room adjoining their bedroom, draped in a blanket. Days unfolded in pacing and worry, Alfred voicing his concerns over her restless behavior. Gardening and herbal remedies languished, and Stella found herself unable to focus on any magical endeavors without spoiling the results.

Guilt shadowed Stella, the weight of failing to protect Mary pressed tears from her eyes. Despite their mere four-year age difference, Stella had taken on a maternal role to her impulsive sister. Reading tales of women in the west trapped in brothels and succumbing to laudanum, Stella fretted over Mary's potential fate.

Sleep reclaimed Stella, cradling her in a slumber that birthed a troubling vision. In the dream, a child lay nestled on Mary's chest—a girl. Stella observed as Mary, wielding magick, cooked over an open flame, a surly man nearby who bore a resemblance to Henry but with a rougher edge.

Mary effortlessly handled heavy yokes, performing chores and tending to the baby slung on her chest. Stella's concern deepened, contemplating the repercussions of Mary's carefree use of magick. Fearful of history repeating itself, Stella pondered the absence of laws in the west, haunted by the specter of their mother's persecution in Ireland.

As Stella awoke, tears flowed anew. The sight had revealed a child born into unfortunate circumstances, yet the vision offered no clues to the father's identity. Stella grappled with the idea that Mary's departure might be linked to the pregnancy, questioning whether Mary had left to give birth elsewhere. The want of her sister and niece left Stella feeling cursed, aching to be an aunt but unable to revel in the joy of their presence. The sight, a cryptic revelation, left the mystery of the child's paternity unsolved—was it Henry or the enigmatic stranger in the vision?

CHAPTER NINE

THE NEBRASKA SKY BROODED under a canopy of dark storm clouds, threatening to unleash its fury. The north wind, relentless, pushed the impending tempest across the Platte River, a harbinger of treacherous water and soft sandbars that devoured wagons.

Mary sensed the crackling electricity in the air, the very oxen seeming to share her unease. Her calming voice and soothing strokes on their necks aimed to pacify the agitated beasts. The first large raindrops splattered, and the wind intensified. Struggling to stay by her oxen in the slippery mud, she feared being trampled and retreated to the wagon, knowing they would follow the one ahead.

Mary pulled the canvas drawstrings tight as the storm intensified. The wind howled against the wagon's side, threatening to lift it off its wheels. As thunder roared, lightning cracked, and wind-driven debris struck the wagon, Mary and her mattress flung across the flat supply area. Magick surged through her, shifting heavier items to the northern side. She gripped a barrel of beans and huddled on the floor as the canvas stretched taut, pulsating with the onslaught.

The canvas stretched across the hickory bows on each gust. *Thank the Goddesses, the wagon makers made the canvas watertight.* Mary's pulse pounded in her chest and temples. *Breathe.* A silent plea echoed in her mind—someone, anyone, assure her that everything would be alright. Tears escaped, vulnerability piercing her facade. She wasn't as strong as she believed. *I will be strong,* she vowed, envisioning the wagon toppling and careening across the prairie. The storm seemed endless, her muscles aching from the fierce battle.

Sounds of rain and wind abated. Mary's hold on the beans relaxed, arms stiff and trembling. As the storm passed, she had no energy left. Shaking uncontrollably, she collapsed on the rough floor, as she knocked wood to acknowledge the benevolent spirits that spared her.

It was time to check on the oxen. After she climbed out of the wagon, Mary found Aengus had a long gash on his side. When the trail master called for the last stop of the day, she unfastened the soaked oxen, allowing them to graze, holding Aengus back to tend to his wound. She grabbed some comfrey and yarrow from her bag in the wagon. Ground into a powder, she poured the herbs into the oxen's wound and covered it with axle grease. She released him to join the others grazing.

Mary marveled at how still and quiet everything was after the storm. The air, now fresh, offered a moment of respite.

Mary pulled some wood out of the wagon, using the same spell she used for the yoke, and summoned the fire for the evening with a breath. Extra tired and stressed, she moved slower than usual.

George jumped out of Jasper's wagon, which was behind theirs, and entered their camp. "Hurry up. I'm hungry and I want to eat. You're so slow. Do you see everyone else? They're working and you lolly-gag. I don't want to hear any whining about your damned condition." He threw his hat to the ground. "When we get to Fort Kearny in a few days, I'm leaving you there."

Mary stepped back, pinching her mouth in a tight line. Tears welled and ran down her cheeks. She turned away, not wanting George to see. Even though she was determined not to go home, her voice trembled as she spoke. "I'm trying to make this work. Don't you want someone to cook, clean, and take care of the oxen?" The fire sputtered and died, her tears dampening her magick. She centered herself to focus on the fire, taking a deep breath and letting it out slowly. It took. She got the rice and beans heated.

"No, you are getting out of my sight as soon as possible." George mumbled to himself, "Story of my life. My brother continues to ruin my life. Now I'm supposed to take care of his damned child."

My child is not damned! Fury raged through Mary, igniting every nerve in her body. The fire, a virtual extension of her, exploded, sending burning embers raining on George. He jumped up, brushing off his head, neck, and shoulders. "You're trying to kill me. Get it off!"

If I was trying to kill you, I would engulf you in flames.

Mary overheard Marcus and Katherine's laughter from their campsite. She scowled and put her index finger to her lips. If George discovered them laughing, it would escalate the situation, and she didn't know what she would do then. This man was like a small child because of all his temper tantrums. How were he and Henry so different? She never observed Henry getting angry at all.

George needed to regain his composure. She shoved his bowl at him and sought solace on the other side of the wagon, away from his venomous words. With distance between them, she allowed him to stew in his own temper. Plopping on the ground, she leaned against the wagon, guarding against explosive anger. Fire was dangerous around the wagons.

Mary's mind wandered to her fire gift, chuckling at the thought of her sister being a windbag while pondering her own status as a firebug. She chuckled when she remembered her sister screaming and breaking a glass. Her sister could blow her over using the tiniest breath or a slight movement of her hand. However, Mary never seemed to have a knack at much except starting fires spontaneously when she didn't want to.

George kicked his metal bowl on the other side of the wagon. "Mary! You haven't set up my tent! This place is a mess. Do something!"

She twisted around to peer under the wagon to see him storming off. *Good.* Mary found a fleeting sense of peace in his absence. She rose, cleaned the dinner dishes and pitched his tent. With more privacy, she'd use magick to complete the tasks, her energy waning from the storm's aftermath.

Feeling sympathy for the Perkins' servants, who endured George's daily abuse, Mary pondered if she deserved her current situation. As she reflected on her use of magick to manipulate others, she questioned if life's retribution had manifested in George. A resolution emerged—no more using magick to hurt or impose her will on others. A fresh start awaited a pledge to reshape her destiny.

Stella's heart fluttered with a mix of hope and apprehension as she awaited Henry's arrival. She needed to uncover more about the party night, a secret guarded behind the veil of her disturbing dream. If that was when Mary conceived, then she would have the baby in late

December, early January, in the dead of winter. She had too many concerns to count.

As Henry's knock punctuated the evening stillness, Stella exhaled a weary sigh. He was the epitome of punctuality, a trait that would have served Mary well. "He's too good for her," she muttered, shaking off the thought as she opened the door.

Henry, impeccably dressed, stood on her threshold, his hat in hand. "Good evening, Stella. May I come in?"

"Of course, Henry." Stella's voice wavered as she stepped aside. "I'll take your hat."

"No, thank you. I know where it goes." His gentle refusal was accompanied by a warm smile. "How have you been today?"

"Better," Stella replied, her voice barely above a whisper, as she led him into the parlor. "Sleep has been a stranger to me, though. And you, Henry? Are you feeling any better?"

She led him into the parlor. "Alfred, can you fix some drinks, please?"

Alfred said, "Henry, do you want yours neat?"

"Yes, that would be great." Henry's gaze lingered on Stella, his eyes reflecting a familiar sorrow. "Somewhat. Your tea was comforting, but my heart... it's still in pieces. How do we move on without Mary?"

Noting the 'we', it was another aspect of Henry she appreciated. The world did not revolve around him, though he was rich enough to consider it did. No, he had empathy and concern for others. A catch that Mary let slip through her fingers and now that she was pregnant, it was a grave mistake.

Stella felt a pang in her chest. "I don't know. But my biggest worry is how Mary will manage without us. Her path is fraught with hardship."

Henry frowned, and his brows furrowed. "If she is accompanying my brother, as I suspect she is, then she is in for a hard time. He is an irresponsible hothead."

A shiver traveled down Stella's spine. "Your brother?"

Henry shook his head. "The other day, I was so overwhelmed that I wasn't thinking straight. I neglected to tell you he went to join a wagon train taking the Oregon Trail following grand dreams of starting a mining supply business. He mentioned it to Mary at my house." He outstretched his arms. "And now it seems she followed him."

Then Henry's brother is the loud-mouthed complainer in her dream. That's why he looked familiar. "She'll be safe, though, right?" Stella feared the brother being cruel and hurtful to Mary and Mary's reaction being over the top, burning everything to the ground.

"I hope so."

The look on Henry's face told her he didn't believe it. Her fears were genuine. There it was, right in front of her. A brother knows. Like a sister knows. Two irresponsible adults caring for a child didn't bode well for the child. It was unimaginable seeing her sister as a mother.

Alfred entered, handing Henry and Stella their drinks. He sat to join them. "I overheard your brother is starting a mining supply company. That takes some capital."

Henry swirled his drink, watching it. "My father is not in good health, subsequently he redid his will. He gave George part of his inheritance early. The rest is in a trust to be distributed monthly after my father passes. George has no interest in the family business, therefore my father hoped he would start his own and finally find his footing." He paused, looking pained. "Sorry. I cannot think about my Mary at his side. My father expects me to hand him money after what he has done."

Stella rose. "I'm off to check on the roast. It should be done by now." Not only was she wrestling with her own emotions, but it also killed her to see Henry hurting. Her sister did this. It wasn't George. She entered the kitchen, grabbed a towel, and yanked the oven open. As she pulled out the roast, she wondered how much money George received. If it was enough, Mary wouldn't have to suffer too much. She could have the baby in a hotel. Still, not better than her own damn room. *Silly girl. Silly girl in the company of a mean boy. Damn them.*

Stella called out, "Alfred, can you help lift the roast for me?"

Henry entered, startling Stella. "I offered to help. There are too many servants in my house. That is the way my mother likes it. It is not to my liking. May I?"

Stella backed away. "Please do. Alfred has offered to hire some help, but I am not used to that. I prefer to do it myself." And if she wasn't able, she employed some magick. There were many practical uses for air magick.

As Henry lifted the roast from the roasting pan to transfer it to the broad china platter, he said, "How is that? And I did not splatter."

Stella chuckled at the sight of Henry being proud of himself for doing something ordinary. But then sadness took over when she thought of Henry and Mary being in their own kitchen. Mary ruined her life and Henry's. "Thank you, Henry. You did well. If you would take it to the table, I'll dish the rest."

Henry lifted the platter from the kitchen counter. "It looks delicious!" He headed to the dining room.

Stella entered the dining room to find Alfred teaching Henry the correct way to cut a roast. She set the serving bowls of roasted potatoes and green beans on the table. When she sat, she said, "I hope you're hungry."

Alfred and Henry chatted while they ate. Stella was silent. Alfred asked, "Are you alright, dear?"

Stella nodded as she continued to eat. Stella couldn't get the image of Mary and Henry in their own kitchen out of her mind. They were made for one another. Why did Mary run off? A sob. And another. *Not in front of Henry!* She could not stop.

Alfred rushed to her side, his embrace a slight comfort in the ocean of her grief. "It's alright, Stella. You're not alone in this."

Henry said, "Is there something I can do? Should I leave?"

Alfred shook his head and raised his hand. As he stroked Stella's shoulders and smoothed her hair, her sobs subsided.

Stella said between gasps for air, "No. Please. Stay." As soon as she was able to speak, she said, "I'm sorry you had to see that, Henry. I never know when the sorrow of Mary's absence will hit me hard. When you helped me in the kitchen, I imagined you and Mary in your kitchen. Oh, Mary!"

Henry let out a long sigh and closed his eyes for a moment. "I did not mean to cause you any grief when I offered to help. Grief is a wicked emotion. Attacking victims when they are trying to put their life together. I have had to excuse myself at work and retreat to the facilities to pull myself together."

Alfred returned to his seat and his meal. "You're welcome here anytime. We'll work through it together."

"Alfred is right. It's like I have part of Mary here when you visit." There was comfort that Stella would not be alone in her grief and despair. But how would she endure all the worrying about her sister and niece's safety? And she still needed to get Henry alone to ask about the party. She needed to piece things together in her head to have any peace.

Chapter Ten

Mary stepped alongside one of the creaking wagons wheels, as the wagon train lumbered along on the rolling plains with their tall and short green grasses. Her gaze fell upon the wheels, the wooden spokes groaning under the strain of the journey. She knew the secret to their preservation lay not in the blacksmith's forge, but in the latent power of her own hands.

With a focused breath, Mary extended her fingers towards the wheel. A soft, ember-like glow emanated from her palms, casting a warm, flickering light on the weathered wood and iron. The air around her hands shimmered with heat, an invisible dance of fiery energy that only she commanded.

As she ran her hands along the wheel's circumference, the metal rim heated and expanded subtly, melding more snugly to the wooden frame. Her touch was gentle, a caressing trail of warmth that tightened the rim without scorching the wood. Sparks of her magick flickered and died as they met the air, a silent testament to her control and precision.

The wagon wheel, once loose and precarious, now hummed with a newfound stability. Mary's fire magick, a gift often misunderstood and feared, in that moment became a silent guardian of their journey. With each wheel she tended to, the wagon grew stronger, each repair a whisper of her mysterious, yet indispensable, art.

At the sight of the tops of buildings and a flag on a flagpole as she crested a hill, she stopped. Her heart raced. As if it was possible to sweat more, she did. Fort Kearny. George had threatened to leave her once they reached the fort. Now she dragged her feet more. The closer they got, the more disappointed she became. It didn't look like a place she would want to be dumped off at.

After dinner last night at the women's circle, many talked of the letters they were sending home to family and friends. A few talked about replenishing supplies and eating at diners to spare them another meal of dried bacon and beans.

Fort Kearny featured an extensive field, flagpole and cannon in the center. Large cottonwoods circled the field, small sod one-story buildings on two sides and larger two-story buildings on one end. There were stables and other elongated sod buildings opposite the two-story buildings. Why would anyone want to live in a house made of dried mud? How would you make it comfortable or desirable? Everything was brown. Sad.

The other women made this fort sound like it would be more like Independence but on a smaller scale. The fort was nothing like anything she had ever seen. Soldiers must go crazy sitting out here in these hovels.

The plan was to stay two days to buy provisions and do maintenance on the wagons. She had already given George a list of items he needed to buy. But that was before his threat, and she had barely seen him all day. The axles had to be greased, and it looked like messy work. George would have to do it if she stayed there.

If George left her there, she would have to arrange travel arrangements for home since it was a fort for soldiers, not deserted women. Where would she sleep while she waited for her way home? As they passed to camp on the other side of the fort, she wondered if there was a hotel. More sweat trickled along her back.

After she guided the oxen around tight for the wagon circle, she let them loose to graze. She retreated inside the wagon, since it was too early for dinner. If George didn't see her, maybe he would forget his threat.

Mary pulled out her bag to retrieve her grimoire to record a few unfamiliar herbs she found on the hills. The book was not there. She dragged everything out and laid it on the mattress. Her mother's book was right in front of her, but not hers. How did she forget her very own grimoire? In a crazy focus for her mother's book, she forgot her own. She hunched over and slumped on the bed, her fists pounding the mattress. *What kind of witch am I?* Her mother would be disappointed if she were still alive. But then Mary would be a better witch, having her mother to teach her. Until she made another book for herself, the herbs went into her mother's grimoire. She stuffed everything back into her bag and curled up for a nap, hoping to sleep away her dreadful life.

When she woke, she peered out of the wagon, surprised to find George had purchased the food items on her list and left them by the back wheel. Since it was late afternoon, Mary figured she had time for a card reading before she headed to the post office. Mary had two letters ready for her sister. One told Stella about the pregnancy, the other didn't. How was she going to decide? She would let her tarot cards choose for her. She pulled them out from under her mattress.

Mary shuffled the deck while thinking about her question. The first card she pulled was her motivation. *Do I want Stella to know or not?* She turned over the Son of Wands and sighed. A card she pulled often and meant just for her: I do what I want. She chuckled. *The cards don't lie.* The second card, the ideal outcome, was The Sun. Which meant goodness, truth, and beauty. *Who doesn't want that?* She wondered what the cards would show for her principles and values. It wasn't ever positive and always troubled her. The High Priestess was reversed. She scrunched her face. It was conceit and selfishness. *Thanks. Now do I tell Stella?* She pulled a card and turned it over. The Justice card. She nodded. The card of honesty. *And if I don't?* The next card pulled revealed The Ten of Swords. It would seem like she was stabbing her sister in the back. Somehow, it didn't feel right, and the cards told her the same. She pressed the cards to her chest and took a moment to take in the occasion where she was being honest.

Mary climbed out of the back of the wagon, truthful letter in hand, and walked towards the larger buildings of the fort to find the post office. She had to work her way along the boardwalk since everyone from her wagon train and another was fulfilling their errands.

She wondered why there were men standing around the front of one building. As she got closer, it appeared to be a saloon from the smell of beer and whiskey emanating from the breath of a few drunken men approaching her. Forts would have that, she guessed. What else would they do in the middle of nowhere? They parted to let her through, and she peered into the window. *George!* She rushed past, hoping not to be seen, her heart racing. Of course, he would be there, but it would be better to avoid being seen than to remind him of his threat. Let him spend his whole time in the saloon then. She stepped off the boardwalk before passing the door and the second window. She wove around groups of people, hoping to traverse by the saloon like a ghost.

Once past the saloon, she returned to the boardwalk to continue to the post office. Still, her heart pounded. She quickened her pace, wanting nothing more than to get this errand done and get back to start dinner. If he returned to eat, it would be there since she would cover his food and place it near the fire to keep warm.

Once inside the simple, small building, Mary handed the postmaster her letter, relieved her errand was complete, and she told Stella the truth. She had asked Stella to reply by letter to Fort Laramie, the next fort. For the first time, she sensed a warmness inside that brought tears to her eyes. She longed for her sister to be understanding and show unconditional love and acceptance. That's what she needed, and she left it all in Chicago with Henry and Stella. *I'm so stupid.* She doubted she would ever find love again. Not that she deserved it.

The landscape turned browner, scrubby plants grew in sandy soil as they follow along the south side of the Platte River. While George walked with Jason after leaving Fort Kearny in the afternoon, he panicked about the decision to let Mary stay with him. He had said nothing to Mary and continue about their usual routine. She stayed by default.

Father always said he didn't make good ones. He had the knack of making George feel small and inconsequential.

George didn't want to look at Mary every day, or ever. But, and it was a big but, he didn't want to cook or deal with those damned beasts that never listened to him. It wasn't that he needed her. It was just easier for him. He convinced himself he could do everything but why should he if she'd do it. He grimaced as he dealt with his indecision and threw his hands up. "I should've left her."

"Na." Jason knitted his brows together. "Better to have someone take care of the cooking. Hell, she even starts her own fire. I wished I had someone cooking for me."

"You're not stuck in a marriage you don't want." George stuck his hands in his pockets and kicked loose dirt.

Jason laughed. "Who would marry such a sourpuss? Cheer up. Let's talk about something else. Some men were talking about the good hunting in Wyoming. Might get an antelope."

"Hmm. I only shot turkey before." George had no fond memories of hunting with his father and brother. They would always get one and then make fun of him because he couldn't shoot fish in a barrel. His father would compare him to Henry and then say he should have stopped with one child. Not allowed to cry, he did what he did best—throw a tantrum. That got him sent off to his nanny for the rest of the day, which was better for him. "Don't think I'm going to do any hunting, but I hope you get an antelope, though."

Relieved when the wagon master called it for the day, he walked over to his camp. They had stopped at an older camp since there were logs alongside fire sites. George sat down to take off his boots and socks. Blisters on top of hardened blisters. The dried blood on his socks had formed a crust, making them stiff and uncomfortable.

When would his feet become tough enough to take the daily beating? He replaced his socks and boots.

Mary had the fire started before anyone else. George wondered what the trick was. Too bad he had found nothing he was good at. At least he'd be eating soon. He was starving.

Mary handed him a plate of rice and meat. He took a bite. It was tasty and way better than beans. After he ate several more bites, he asked, "What is this?"

"Chicken."

"But there are no chickens here and none at Fort Kearny."

George swore she smirked. She had lied to him. His mother did that all the time, making up reasons he couldn't play outside with other children. He knew the real reason was the other parents didn't want him around. It wasn't always his fault that a fight broke out. But his mother's lies cut him every time. "What the hell is it?"

Mary cocked her head and smiled. "Frog legs. They're delicious, aren't they?"

George flung his plate at her, but she ducked so it narrowly missed her. *Damn.* He wanted to see the frogs hit her in the face and give her warts. Frogs do that, don't they?

"What the damned tarnation! I'm not a redneck. You strumpet. Cussed scalawag!" George wanted to destroy everything around him. He should have left her. His father was right. He didn't make decent decisions. "I have to use the necessary." George stormed away from camp to calm and relieve himself.

While focusing on the sunset over the surrounding hills, footsteps behind him interrupted his search for tranquility. George clenched his jaw and tensed. *No peace to even take a piss.* After he fastened his pants, he swung around with balled fists and his chest thrust out.

Jim, the wagon master, stood there, hands on hips and not looking too happy. "George, we're gonna talk man to man."

George crossed his arms across his chest and leaned his head back. Speaking through his teeth, he said, "Alright."

"I witnessed you throwing a plate at your wife and cursing. There's been many complaints about the cursing and your attitude. That has to change. No one wants to hear it. Personally, I don't want to see you assault your wife again. I do have the option of leaving you at any time." Jim turned to go back to the wagons.

George shouted while throwing up his hands, "Wait! Don't I get a say?"

"No."

George felt the bile in his throat. He always got treated like a child. Where was the freedom he was walking miles for every single day? Now he can't cuss. Might as well be at home listening to Mother. A growl escaped as he pulled his hair, looking to the sky as if the answer to all his problems was there.

He took his time walking back. George hated his life. His feet hurt, the food sucked, sleeping on the ground was uncomfortable, and now he couldn't cuss. And then there was Mary.

George twitched his whole body and scrunched his face when he didn't see his tent. He hesitated and thought about how to say what he wanted without cussing. In a careful, controlled tone, he said, "Mary, where's my tent?"

He swore she smirked at him and pointed at his tent on the ground, still folded. Then she walked over to the center of the train to sit among the women.

George yelled, "You're in cahoots with him, aren't you?"

There were so many other things he wanted to insinuate, but he didn't know how to say it without cursing. It took too long to figure out how to say it 'properly'.

Mary could have shown him how the tent went up, but she was determined to make his life miserable in every way possible. He would show her. George would do it himself. After he figured out how. In Independence, a friendly passer-by had helped him, and George left it that way until Mary dismantled it. He was never proficient at assembling things. But he wouldn't sleep on the ground without his tent, as the fear of wild animals kept him on edge.

On his knees, George unrolled the tent. Mary's meticulous folding technique made assembling it seem straightforward. He pushed the front poles up. With the rope resting on his shoulder, he exerted force to pull it taut and used a rock to drive one stake into the ground. Then the other stake.

George stepped back, mentally patting himself on the back. If his father saw this, it would impress him. Well, maybe not. Doesn't matter. George moved to the other end of the tent to pull up the back poles. As he did in front, he secured the ropes with stakes as well. Now his tent was upright, ready for him to sleep in. He hooked his thumbs in his dungaree belt loops and rocked on his heels.

One pole leaned inward, threatening to collapse his tent. George rushed over to pull the rope and banged the stake into the ground harder. Now his tent was tighter. He grinned from ear to ear. He'd show her he didn't need her. Then he would leave her at Fort Laramie.

CHAPTER ELEVEN

MARY SQUEEZED HER FINGER and contemplated the small mound of blood on her fingertip. She had poked it hard, trying to push a needle through the leather of her boot to repair it. Frustrated by the difficulty, but knowing she may not get to replace them for a long time, she kept pushing the needle through. *If there's already a hole for the stitch, then why is it difficult to stitch it again?*

"Mary!"

She lifted her head as Katherine raced towards her. "Good morning. I didn't see you earlier."

"I've been at a prayer vigil for Mr. Frasier. He has cholera."

"Oh, no! Do you want me to fix some herbs for that? I've been collecting blackberry, raspberry, and strawberry leaves along the way." Stella taught her the remedy a long time ago when they lived with their uncle in Pennslyvania.

Katherine kneeled beside Mary. "He's probably going to die. They think prayer is enough to heal him. The Owens might have a need for herbs though. Their five-year-old has taken ill. It's their only child."

George asked, "Is it contagious?"

"No."

"Good." George slid his hat down over his face.

Mary got to her feet, dumping her boot and needle. She climbed into her wagon, grabbed bundles of dried vines hanging from the inside of the canvas, and then clambered down.

Katherine picked up Mary's boot and began stitching. "Do you need my help?"

"You are helping by mending my stupid boot. I have spilled blood all morning." Mary pulled leaves off and pulverized them in her fingers into her pot. She flinched every time she hit the spots that were stuck by the needle. "Do you have any water at your camp?"

Katherine didn't look up from the boot in her hand. "Yes. Take what you need."

Mary ran over to Katherine's water bucket and ladled the water into her pot. She took care to not spill any on the way back. Using a small amount of magick with breath and hand, she worked the fire, placing her back to Katherine so she couldn't observe. In a race against time, every second mattered, especially for a child. Once she set her pot on the tripod, the only thing she had to do was wait until it boiled and simmered for an hour.

She turned to Katherine.

Katherine held out Mary's boot. Where a gaping hole in the side had been, now lay a row of neat blue stitches, the end tied off to resemble a flower poof.

Mary placed her hands on her cheeks. "Thank you! I have struggled all morning."

Katherine rose and shook her skirt, sending dust flying. "I've practiced six times as much with four children. How long before this is ready?"

"An hour."

"I'll come back and we can walk together." Katherine rushed off toward the Frasier wagon. Mary wondered if it was to pray more, or if it was to prepare old man Frasier's body for burial. Cholera could be a quick, if not agonizing, death. Fine in the morning, dead by evening.

Mary sent a puff of air from her cheeks to stoke the fire, wanting her tonic to boil quicker. She was glad Katherine had left, since she needed privacy to add a healing spell boost.

The child would need every help possible to survive. The young and the old were ready victims of cholera. Mary was sure there would be more victims before long.

Kneeled over the pot, she waved her arms around, centering her energy and focus on the tonic, chanting low.

From the fields where you have grown, to this potion, your power loan.

Heal the sick, soothe the weak,

Grant the wellness that we seek, so mote it be!

A glow emanated from the center and spread throughout the tonic and dissipated.

Now her tonic was ready. When Katherine had returned, they poured the liquid into an old tincture bottle she found at another wagon. They raced to the Owens' wagon to stand at the back.

The poor young boy was bent over in cramping pain, his blond hair plastered to his contorted face. The mother waved them into the wagon and returned to soothing her child.

Mary gave her a bottle. "Give him all you can a spoonful at a time." When the young woman nodded, Mary noticed the pain in her eyes. *Will I know this anguish in the future with my child?* She remembered the pain in her own mother's eyes when they said their last goodbyes in her jail cell.

The child tried sipping from the spoon and turned away, his face scrunched. "It tastes bad."

Mary asked, "Do you have any honey?"

When the mother shook her head, Katherine said, "I know where to get some." She jumped out of the wagon.

"I'm Sophie. How did you learn about this tonic?"

Mary smiled. "I'm Mary. I learned from my sister, who has worked in an herbal shop for several years."

The wagon shook when Katherine ran up the ramp into the wagon. "Here."

Mary poured some honey into the tonic and shook it. Then she handed it back to Sophie. "Now try."

Sophie's hands shook when she poured the tonic onto the spoon. In a lull after his last spasm, she gave it to her son. He took it and nodded.

Sophie turned to Mary and then to Katherine. "Thank you. I pray this works."

Mary placed her hand on Sophie's shoulder. "Have faith. I'm leaving now to make more tonic. I'm sure there will be more who need it."

Mary and Katherine left the Owens' wagon and walked back to their own.

"How much more tonic can you make?"

Mary shrugged her shoulders and let out a sigh. "Not enough. While the next batch simmers, I'll venture out to look for some brambles."

"I can help."

"Thanks. If we pin them to the outside of the wagons, they will dry faster while we travel. Hopefully, it won't rain."

Mary stoked her fire once she reached her campsite. Crushing more dried leaves, she started her next batch. The sounds of men repairing wagons and splitting wood echoed in the background.

She ruminated on the idea that if she saved a life, would it satisfy a debt for the wrong she had done? How many would she have to save to settle her account? Can doing good cancel previous evil? It didn't matter since she would continue making the tonic to help her fellow travelers, even George. It would be unconscionable for her to stand by and do nothing.

The week sped by while Mary tended the sick once cholera took hold of the wagon train. She had lost no one to the dreadful illness. No matter how much they prayed, even the most devout took her tonic. Some gave prayer credit for their healing, but it didn't offend Mary. When the cases dwindled, she collapsed on her mattress from exhaustion, arms stretched wide. *How did I manage this?*

Tuesday night, Jim called for a meeting after the evening meal. Mary made her way to the growing circle, slipping through to see. Once they had all gathered, he explained how they would descend Windlass Hill the next day into Ash Hollow, where they would camp through Sunday.

Mary looked forward to a well-deserved rest. But the longer she listened to Jim, the more the hairs stood on the back of her neck and sweat beaded on her forehead. The three-hundred foot Windlass

Hill sounded dangerous where any small thing could spell disaster. It required coordination beyond the men handling the ropes, but also the work animals to traverse the twenty-five degree slope. If you arrived at Ash Hollow in one piece, the pure water, trees, and grass sounded wonderful.

On Wednesday, they climbed California Hill under a hot cloudless sky. The oxen handled the slow drive well, but the wagons drawn by horses struggled, making Mary grateful for her steady beasts. But it meant no afternoon nap for her.

The next morning when the wagons came to a halt, she knew they had reached the treacherous steep hill. The scenarios in her mind came fast and furious when the line didn't move for a while. She paced alongside her wagon. What if an overturned wagon or an injury happened? It took some time for the line to move again, and she continued to fixate on why there was a delay.

Instead of their usual noon break, they continued descending the hill one by one. The sun was high in the sky, casting its warm rays on the landscape, when Marcus and Katherine's wagon, leading the line, made it to the top of the hill. Mary watched as they locked their wheels, tied ropes and used a large exposed root from an old oak tree as a pulley to control the speed of the wagon.

Katherine and her children found the dirt hill hard to walk to the bottom, their footing slipped many times. Marcus shouted commands to the oxen. Mary could sense the trepidation radiating from their oxen and the strain in their muscles as they fought to keep from running out of control. The wagon crept the length of the hill until it reached the bottom. She realized she had held her breath and let it out hard and fast.

Mary froze at the top of the hill, next for her own descent. She scanned the area for George, but didn't see him anywhere. *I can't do this.* Where is he? Hands over her face, she peered between her fingers at the slightly less than vertical hill, deep ruts a testament to those who had passed before her. Her breath caught. Her shoulders tensed and lifted.

Marcus and Jim approached. It still didn't quiet her pounding heart, but the sight of them loosened some of the tension in her muscles to get her moving.

The men retrieved two lynch pins each from the toolbox on the side of the wagon. Marcus handed her one. "You should know what to do, since George isn't here. Take this and watch what I do. Do the same on the back wheel."

The smooth pin weighed more than she expected. Mary watched Marcus at the front wheel slide the pin into the wheel hub opening to lock that wheel, and she did the same at the back wheel. She walked around the wagon to see if Jim had locked the wheels to keep the wagon from rolling out of control. There was no room for error.

Mary told Niall to move forward. The oxen took a few steps, the other three following his lead. Now the men tied a rope from the metal hook on the back of her wagon and wrapped it around the worn tree root, grooved from previous settlers descending.

Marcus said, "We're ready. Work them downward, Mary."

She urged the oxen forward, her voice soothing and steady. She understood their resistance and didn't want to upset them with her own trepidation.

About halfway, Niall slipped, catching her by surprise. She lost her balance on the uneven ground, her arms windmilling. Unable to regain her balance, she fell, twisting her ankle. She heard a pop. *Oh, no!* Niall scrambled, trying not to step on her. *Please don't step on me!* All she saw were hooves. Mary curled into a ball, hoping to become a smaller target. Niall's movements scared the other oxen, causing them to shift away. The wagon twisted precariously sideways. Mary yelled at the top of her voice, "Stop!" Marcus and Jim wrestled the ropes to regain tension.

Mary stood and felt a sharp twinge in her ankle, unable to put weight on it without pain. No time to worry about it now. Mouth open, eyes wide, her whole body covered in sweat, she whispered, "Breathe." Determined not to lose her wagon, she closed her eyes to focus on the problem. "Hold on."

She found a large rock and carried it to the front wheel, half-crawling and limping as she went. She wedged it under the wheel since it was the furthest down the hill. "Niall, forward. Aengus, stay." The reluctant oxen cooperated. Men and beasts worked the wagon straight.

"Stop!" She tossed the rock. Then they proceeded as slowly as possible. She hobbled the rest of the way, hanging onto the wagon, letting out a huge breath when she and her wagon made it to the bottom. Her palms slid to her heart and she let her head fall back.

Once Marcus and Jim untied her wagon and left the rope for the next wagon, Marcus walked over to her, Jim following him. "Smart thinking about the rock. I thought we were going to lose it."

"Thank you. I've never been that scared."

"You did fine." He glanced at her feet. "Are you alright? You're lucky the oxen didn't step on you."

Mary tried putting weight on her foot and winced at the pain. It hurt worse than anything she had ever felt before, but she figured it would heal quickly. "I have an ointment for it and a few days of rest will help."

Jim said, "One family didn't fare well. They thought their youngest was asleep in the wagon, but he had woken and climbed on the buckboard. Before they could do anything, he fell off the buckboard and a wagon wheel ran over him." He dropped his head and shook it. "Poor thing didn't make it. That's why I said no one in the wagons."

Mary's hand covered her mouth, and an icy chill ran through her. She feared for herself as well. For her, the hill meant she faced her fear, but for another family, it meant loss and grief. Now they will bury their son in the vast prairie and leave without him. Was there something she could do to ease their pain? A tea, maybe? She understood loss, first her mother and then her uncle.

She glanced up the hill, Jason's wagon sitting at the top, and then George walking around from the back. *Of course. Nowhere to be found to help me.* She fumed. If he had helped, she might not have gotten injured. But then, he was usually worthless.

Marcus left to return to his own wagon. Jim shook his head. Did he not want to help them? The two men had caused a lot of trouble for him almost daily.

Mary put her hands on each side of her mouth and shouted, "Get the pins from the toolbox. Slide them into the hubs to lock the wheels."

Jason made his way closer to understand her. Mary repeated the instructions. One person from each wagon was to help the wagon behind them. But Mary couldn't make it up the hill since she injured her ankle. She had no faith in either of them; this would not fare well.

"Tie one end of the rope to the hook on the back of the wagon box. Then pull the rope up the hill from that root it's wrapped around."

George shook his head. "That makes no sense. How would that work?" His voice carried loud enough for Jim to hear him. Jim shook his head and headed towards George, mumbling to himself.

Jason yanked around to George. "Shut up! You can complain if it doesn't work." Jason guided the oxen and George worked the rope. Mary's heart raced at the thought of George running the rope, fearing it would end in disaster. It took two strong men to handle her wagon.

The oxen worked their way along, doing well. As George braced himself against a small tree, the rope slipped from his grasp, causing it to lose tension. A string of expletives exploded from his mouth. The oxen struggled to keep their footing, and the wagon lurched forward.

Jim increased his speed. "I told you, no cussing!" When he reached the top, he took the ropes, pulling hard, slipping. "I need a real man to help me."

Jason turned back to the next wagon and yelled, "Wilson, I need help!" A stout young man ran over to the ropes to assist Jim while the oxen strained to stay in place. George scrambled out of the way, scowling, crossing his arms across his chest. The wagon tracked its way along the hill.

Glad that the experience was over, Mary hobbled her way near Marcus and Katherine's camp to prepare her own camp surrounded by ash and dwarf cedar trees. She tended to her ankle with a comfrey salve and wrapped it snug with strips of fabric.

The hill had filled her with fear, yet there was an ominous feeling of impending trouble in the distance. It's what she gets for wanting an adventure. Right now, she would love a night out at the theater with Henry by her side. She carried the memories of their time together like a weight on her shoulders, a constant reminder that thoughtless decisions yielded disastrous outcomes.

Chapter Twelve

Two weeks after Fort Kearny, the wagon train reached Chimney Rock, a towering four-thousand-foot formation. Its peak, visible from their last night's stop, had stirred a buzz of excitement among the emigrants. For Mary, the sight of rugged cliffs and Ponderosa pine forests breaking the monotony of the endless prairie was a welcome change.

The train set camp early, near the iconic landmark. Children chased each other around the base of Chimney Rock, while Mary yearned for a breeze, even longing for the motion of the wagon that at least stirred the air. The stillness was stifling.

Mary sought respite from the oppressive heat by bringing her mattress under the wagon.

"Why are you sleeping under there?" George's voice, gruff and unexpected, broke the silence.

Startled, Mary looked over. George's presence seemed intrusive after days of his silent treatment. "It's cooler here," she replied, avoiding his gaze. "Why do you care?"

George shrugged, his form stark against the dimming sky. "Don't want any critters sneaking up on you."

George's reply confused her. He had never shown concern before and it was a welcomed respite from his constant insults. She tucked a lavender sachet under her pillow. Laying down, she took a deep whiff of its sweet aroma and sighed. Another good night's sleep welcomed her after a long day of walking, cooking, and cleaning.

As the night deepened, an unsettling feeling crept over Mary. Her heart skipped a beat as she locked eyes with two mysterious, glowing orbs while peering through the wagon's wheels. A cougar, massive and majestic, paced outside of their circle. "Leave me be, beast with beautiful eyes. I need to sleep."

Mary watched the eyes of an enormous cat and the shadow of its silhouette cast by the moon as it paced back and forth along the wagon. It stopped in front of her wagon and stared past her to the inside of the train's circle. Her breath burst in and out, her body trembled. What if it attacked someone sleeping on the ground?

The enormous cat trotted back to sit by the wheels in front of her. Mary sweated, and her heart raced. She had no weapon to defend herself but a sachet of lavender. The sachet landed in front of the cat when she threw it. It sniffed the sachet and pulled back. Then it batted the offending bundle, flicking its black-tipped tail.

Beads of sweat formed on her lip as she pressed herself against the wheel closest to George's tent. "George!" she hissed, tossing the rocks she had cleared from under the wagon towards his tent to rouse him. The cat's presence, dangerously close, sent her heart racing.

George emerged, disheveled and irritable. "God dammit! What's going on?"

"There's a cougar," Mary whispered urgently. "Get the rifle!"

As the night grew darker, the moon and stars became more prominent, casting an ethereal glow on the camp, which had become a stage for the unfolding drama of impending danger. Mary's heart pounded in her chest as George scrambled below the wagon, his voice conveying his panic. "Hot damned! The rifle is in the wagon!" He crawled for the back of the wagon.

The cougar moved with a predatory grace towards George. "Stop!" Mary's voice pierced the air like a sharp hiss, carrying with it a sense of fear and urgency in every syllable. "You can't get the rifle. Find the night guard." She watched him walk off. "Hurry!" Still, he didn't move fast enough.

Mary's eyes never left the cougar, its glowing eyes fixed on her. Every instinct screamed that it was a race against time. Trembling with fear and the weight of responsibility, she crawled to the outside edge of the wagon, struggling to center herself.

To summon her inner fire, Mary focused, her breath steady as she released a stream of flames towards the cougar. The animal recoiled, its eyes reflecting surprise and a hint of fury. "I asked you to leave me in peace. I have no choice but to defend myself," she whispered, half-pleading, half-defiant.

The cougar, undeterred, continued to pace. Mary glanced around, ensuring they were alone. She gathered her magick, her hands rolling together, conjuring a flame that grew from a spark to a blazing orb. Positioned on her knees, she launched the fireball. It struck the cougar, sending it fleeing into the night. Mary's heart raced, adrenaline surging through her veins. A few deep breaths calmed her as she sensed the cougar's presence leaving.

Breathe. George was not back yet. Mary crawled back to her bed but realized her lavender sachet was beyond the wagon wheels. Exhausted, she crawled back, reaching for her lavender sachet. Its familiar, calming scent was a balm to her frayed nerves.

Mary lay back, contemplating the significance of the night. Her powers had protected her, not George. His absence had been a blessing, freeing her to use her magick without restraint.

"Mary, wake up!" George kicked the wagon wheel in front of her.

"Oh. George, I must have fallen asleep waiting for you. The cat left finally. I have never been so scared before. If I wasn't under the wagon, I would surely be dead." Mary rested on her elbow.

The guard shook his head. "George, you need to have your rifle with you. It's dangerous out here. Well, glad it's out of here, but I'll keep an eye out. It might circle around for all I know. This area is prone to cougar attacks." He walked off, heading for the next wagon.

George waited until the guard was out of earshot. "You made me look like an idiot. Do you realize that?" He flung his arms out. "No cat," he spat, frustration clear in his voice.

"Ugh." Mary dropped her head to her mattress. "I know you hoped the cougar would eat me, but it didn't. Sorry, you're disappointed."

George kneeled to enter his tent. "How am I gonna get to sleep now? Delirious woman. All I can think about is that damn cat."

Mary resigned herself to a mix of disdain and pity for George. His disbelief, his failure to understand the danger they had faced, only solidified her realization that she was better off without him. She nestled the sachet under her neck, its scent calming her.

In the night's silence, Mary pondered her solitude witchcraft, never having a familiar. Perhaps she didn't have a familiar because her strength lay within, not in a companion. Her powers were her own, a secret she guarded among the wagons. As sleep overtook her, she embraced the solitude, finding strength in her independence. But curiosity about the cougar nagged her. Why didn't it attack her?

During the morning drive west in Wyoming, the wind whipped. The train slowed as they approached the North Platte River, which was always treacherous and unpredictable to cross. Mary blew her breath out while pacing. After a while, she saw they were to cross a bridge, not ford the river.

Mary handed a young man three dollars, an exorbitant price, and led her wagon across the bridge, a real bridge. No fording through a cold, rapid river for her, wading through swirling water where the bottom would drop off or a sudden current pull you away. No precarious ferry she always feared would tip. She hated water. Her face beamed so much, she touched both sides of her cheeks. The sound of her shoes and the oxen's hoofs on the wooden structure instead of in the roaring water made her worries and concerns evaporate. Shoulders relaxed.

Off the bridge, she took only a few steps into the thick, sinking sand, like on the beaches of Lake Michigan. In front of her, all she saw was more of the same. When her foot sank, it took effort to drag it back up while the sand rasped against her boots. Small, hot granules slipped inside with each step, creating an uncomfortable rub.

The constant irritation inside her boots through her threadbare socks stole her attention. Step by step, the pain increased like an endurance test. Clenched jaw, fists clasped, she struggled, determined to cross this piece of infernal land. She cursed cheap George for not paying to have a bench installed to drive the wagon instead of walking.

The oxen strained to pull the wagon. There was nothing she could do to help them but let them determine their own pace and hope they would find solid ground before they wore out.

The wind whipped the sand everywhere. Mary yanked her scarf from around her shoulders to cover her mouth and nose. At least the soft ruts created by the wagons before her held her on the right path.

After two of the longest miles she'd ever walked, she received and passed along word that the front of the train reached the Laramie River. Now water. Could she not have time to catch her breath? Trying not to think about the next river crossing, she leaned against the side of the wagon, holding her belly, eyes closed for a moment to rest them. As she pulled off each boot, she poured out the sand and stepped back into the worn leather.

The hairs on the back of her neck rose. She scanned the surrounding prairie. The enormous cat's presence returned. But where? She sensed it in her core, but since that night near Chimney Rock, she hadn't seen it. She no longer feared it; curiosity replaced fear. Why was it still near?

The wait for her turn to ford the Laramie was torture. While she picked her cuticles, she kept sighing long and heavy. It didn't matter how hard she tried to avoid the thought of crossing, the same fear remained. She was more afraid of water than the cougar.

As she came closer, she saw neither livestock nor wagons entering the water, but another bridge. She hopped, clapping her hands. Whatever the toll, she would pay it. There was nothing better than avoiding the cold, racing water that threatened to sweep her away to her death.

Mary skipped her way across this wooden structure. She counted her blessings one by one. The water was high and rapid. There was no way they would ford that. At least, not her. She kept close to the oxen to avoid the edge of the bridge.

The first step off the bridge was solid. Another relief. She had no more strength for any surprises.

By mid-afternoon, the wagon train had circled for the day, having arrived at Fort Laramie. Mary was quick to release the oxen, eager to check for a letter at the post office. Not wanting to get her hopes up too much and be disappointed, she thought of all the chores she should do before heading out. She glanced up to find Katherine glaring at her. Her and Marcus complained to the wagon master about George and Jasper arguing all the time and about Mary giving tarot readings to others in the train. Katherine had pulled any form of friendship leaving Mary alone on the journey.

But she wanted to hear from Stella. She followed the other emigrants to the only building that would warrant a visit - the post trader's store.

The long building, stone on one end and adobe on the other, an obvious addition, contained a store, a post office, and a small bar for enlisted and travelers. She headed inside and found the end of the line. From the grumbling people pushing their way out of the store, she heard outrageous prices. Sugar was $1.50 and flour $1 a pint. She needed nothing but a word from her sister. That was free, at least.

After reaching the ill-made counter, she didn't touch it to avoid splinters. "Is there a letter for Mary Maguire?" She bit her lip and rubbed sweaty palms on her apron.

"Hmph." The wild-haired man turned to stacks of letters in bundles, grabbed one, and ruffled through it. When he returned to the counter, he held two letters in his worn, calloused hands. He placed them on the counter. "That's all? Tobacco? Sugar?"

Mary shook her head. Her mind swirled, unable to make words. She retrieved the letters with trembling hands and checked for her name. No mistake on his part. In a daze, she made her way out of the building. The writing on the second envelope was familiar. Once outside, she leaned against the rough adobe surface of the wall. One from Stella. One from Henry! Her legs weakened. Her vision narrowed.

Someone had her under her arm, holding her. Blinking, she saw the silhouette of a soldier.

He held her envelopes. "Ma'am, are you alright? You fainted. I think I should take you to our post doc."

Mary shook her head, straightening enough that he had lessened his grip. "Thank you, but I'm fine now. I appreciate you catching me. So kind of you."

"If you are sure, you dropped these. Be careful now, Miss." He handed her the letters and returned to his station outside the post trader's store.

She stood staring at the letters, eager to know what they said, but she didn't want to do it here. Too many people milling around. She headed back to the wagon, her shoulders curled, clutching her arms. The letter from Henry was a shock. Why had he written? Was he going to lash out at her for what she did to him? He would be justified. Stella might have told him she was expecting, which caused her fear of what Stella had written. She didn't want another lecture.

At the wagon, the only sanctuary she had, she climbed in to sit on her mattress. Though the afternoon sun blazed on the prairie, she shivered. She grabbed her blanket and wrapped herself in it. Two letters had so much power over her. Her heart pounded against her chest and she tingled all over. She slid Henry's out and placed it on her bed, afraid of what he could have written. She would read Stella's first, since she had awaited a reply since Fort Kearney.

Mary broke the seal on the back of the envelope and the letter slipped out on its own, unfolding in front of her. Her sister enjoyed creating drama out of the mundane. She imagined her embarrassment had she opened it outside the post trader's store.

Mary shook her head and stared at the blank pages. *Stella, I want to read it.* In her native tongue, she said, "Nocht," for the words to appear. She watched, following the words as they spilled across the page. She sighed, her eyes tearing up. As she read, more tears flowed. A plea to come home. No lecture, only love like a warm hug. There was no better relief from the long days on the trail arguing with George, or the regret of leaving home. Aunt Stella. Her sister would be a capable aunt if she had the chance.

She plopped back on her bed, the letter on her stomach. What would it take to return and how? To suffer through all that twice and have nothing to show for it, like a whipped dog. Why keep moving forward? *What is out there for me and my child?* She wanted adventure, and she got it, more than she bargained for. Did she have something to prove? Here she was in the middle of the trail and she didn't have a convincing reason to continue. But she didn't want to go back yet. She couldn't put her finger on why, though. A gut feeling, nothing more.

She pulled herself upright on her bed, set Stella's letter aside, and picked up Henry's. There would be no antics in order to read his words. She placed her index finger along the side of the seal. A quick motion released it. The envelope and its contents rattled in her shaking hands. She hoped he would be kind. She held the letter taut to overcome her trembling. There were only a few sheets of paper, but it weighed plenty in her mind.

Dearest Mary. He, too, pleaded for her to return. If not to marry him, then for her safety. No mention of the child, so Stella didn't tell him. He poured his love onto the page and explained how lost he was without her. He asked if she would keep his brother alive if she didn't return. That was a tall ask, but one she would take to heart. She wanted to be *Henry's* wife, but her current condition would be embarrassing and cause ridicule in his social circle. Not to mention intense parental conflict.

Yelling outside stole her attention. George and Jasper engaged in another argument based on who was better at something or other. Neither yielded. She rose, tucked the letters under her mattress for later, and grabbed the bag of buffalo chips as she left the wagon. The two men stood as if ready for a duel.

"Are you two done? You have gotten everyone's attention. Again." She let the bag drop to the ground. Maybe she should leave and let the man-child die in the wilderness. George sat on the ground against a wagon wheel. While Mary tended the fire, he ranted about Jasper and how no one considered him good at anything. She nodded to his spiel, hoping her child would be more like Henry than George or even herself.

She sat against the other wagon wheel, deep in thought. The letters provided love, unconditional love. She placed a hand on her chest. Warmth tingled in her arms and legs. It overwhelmed her, but pleasantly. This was what she wished her child to have. It was the happiest feeling in the world. And she wanted to share it. Just not with George, who was still ranting about something being unfair. And as much as she wanted to drink in the moment, to savor it forever, she had to make dinner.

CHAPTER THIRTEEN

MARY HEARD CHEERS FROM nearby wagons, having traversed the unremarkable open saddle, South Pass, between the Wind River Range to the north and the Antelope Hills to the south. It was all anyone talked about the last few days. They had entered the Oregon Territory, a major milestone, though they had so much further to go.

Mary walked through the waist high sea of grass and sagebrush speckled with wildflowers of paintbrush, fireweed, lupin, and wild blue flax, adding color to the otherwise monotonous landscape.

Mary struggled with dread emanating from the pit in her stomach that had gotten worse the past few days. She knew it was a matter of time before something went wrong. Her cards told her something terrible lurked in the future, disturbing her sleep and her thoughts during the day. She kept a smoky quartz crystal in her pocket for good luck.

They stopped to camp at Pacific Springs, the first water source they had encountered that would end in the Pacific Ocean. She watched Katherine's oldest boy place a foot on the marsh to shake the ground for several feet. His siblings roared with laughter.

Mary steered her oxen away from grazing close by the bog when she saw someone else's oxen standing deep in the mire, struggling to move. She replenished all their water containers closer to one of many springs, a bucket full at a time.

Jim announced an extra day off to make repairs. Mary smiled as she considered the naps she would get. She had kept the rims on the wheels smooth, applying heat or cold from her hands to adjust them while traveling. No one was aware of her wielding her magick.

George grumbled, "At last, I get relief from this torture. Father was right. I should have waited a year and then taken a train." He sat, awaiting Mary's evening meal.

Jasper, next to them, overhead George while Jasper worked his fire. "Use the time to work on your wagon. It's a lot - wheel rim adjustments and axle tightening, not to mention the grease that needs to be applied. Do you need help?"

George rose and scoffed, pointing at the back wheel. "Ha! The rims on my wheels are in great shape and my axles already have enough grease. See for yourself." He gestured for Jasper to come closer and check.

Jasper examined each wheel, running his hands over the top. "Who built your wagon? You couldn't have driven it all the way here with these wheels."

George's face contorted into a scowl. "I've done nothing to them. Leavenworth Wagon Works."

Jasper placed his hands on his hips, skepticism radiating from him. "You're lying. I used the same builder."

George thrust out his chest, indignation written on his face as he stepped closer to Jasper.

Mary rushed over, desperate to defuse the situation. "George, dinner is almost ready. It doesn't matter," she pleaded, placing a hand on his arm.

George spat, pushing her away. "Nobody calls me a liar! You can't drive a wagon right. That's obvious." George took a step forward, squaring off to Jasper.

Jasper stomped his foot and thrust his chest out to meet George's challenge. "I ain't having no one tell me I can't drive a wagon. I've done more than you have." He pointed a finger at George in accusation. "Mary does everything for you."

Mary put both hands to her face. If they fought one more time, it would mean expulsion from the train, leaving them behind. Would someone allow her to join their wagon? She wasn't sure.

George scoffed. "Well, there's the tragedy right there. You can't get a woman with that face." He spun around, an arrogant smirk on his face, and walked over to Mary.

Mary's shoulders relaxed in relief while George retreated, thankful he hadn't gotten himself into another brawl. But then she noticed Jasper in the corner of her eye reach for his rifle. Her eyes widened in panic. "George, down!"

The sound of gunfire echoed through the air. An invisible force held everyone in place.

A piercing scream.

"No! Bethany! Oh God! Please, someone help!"

Mary whirled around in response to Katherine's desperate pleas and saw her three-year-old daughter, Bethany, clasped in Katherine's arms. Mary broke into a run.

"Go away! I don't want you here," Katherine begged through her tears. "You non-believers are the reason for this. You brought this upon us with those Tarot cards and constant fights."

Mary kneeled beside Katherine and her daughter, her heart sinking at the sight of the bullet wound in the little girl's left arm. "I can help. Let me help." How could Katherine put her beliefs before her daughter's health? "I want to help you. Please."

Mary knew healing Bethany would be risky to the unborn child she carried. She had to risk it.

"Please," Katherine implored Mary, "go. Never come near me or mine again."

Marcus approached with a glare, so Mary rose from her crouch and backed away from the scene of grief before her, making her retreat as discreet as possible. She wandered back to her wagon, dread filling her at the sight of men gathered around Jasper and George. A sigh escaped when she heard Jim, the wagon master, call for a trial first thing in the morning. Right now, she had a more pressing task at hand.

Mary wouldn't do nothing because of a difference in spiritual beliefs. A child suffered, and she had to do something. She made a wide circle around Katherine's wagon and crawled beneath it, scarcely daring to breathe as she centered herself deep within to begin the healing ritual. To pull heat took more from her than creating heat. Destruction was always simpler.

Mary suddenly sensed the cougar nearby, adding strength to her core, strength she needed. Still, fear coursed through her veins and the uncertainty of what this would mean for her unborn child, she persevered. With hands outstretched towards the child while Katherine cleaned the wound, she pulled the damaging heat away from the child's wounded arm into herself until no trace remained.

When all was done, she laid spent and gave thanks to the cougar. Mary crept out and made her way back on wobbly legs, dizzy to her own refuge, where she collapsed into a deep sleep until morning arrived.

As dawn broke over the wagon train, a bustling energy filled the air, the chatter of the settlers punctuated by the clanging of pots and the occasional neigh of a horse. Mary watched from the half-open flap of her wagon, the morning light casting long shadows across the circle of wagons. The tension was palpable, a stark contrast to the usual morning routine. Katherine's glare from a distance, aimed squarely at her, was heavy with blame for the incident with her daughter. Mary felt a twinge of injustice - she was no saint, but this trouble wasn't of her making.

The wagon master, Jim, stood at the center of the gathering, his weathered face as unreadable as the vast Wyoming sky above. "We're here to address the incident with Jason," he announced, his voice gravelly with authority. "Jason, how do you plead?"

"Not guilty," Jasper retorted defiantly. "It was George's provocation! He said I was too ugly to get a woman."

Marcus interjected, his voice thick with emotion, "My child is hurt because of your recklessness! He should face the law!"

Jim raised a hand to silence the growing murmurs. "Our priority is the safety of this train." His gaze swept over the crowd, settling on Jason. "You need to convince us why you should stay."

Jasper shouted, "You've already convicted me!"

"No. Why didn't you change your position in the train if you and George were having trouble."

"We're friends... were friends." Jasper lowered his gaze. "George approached me threateningly last night."

The wagon master said, "Did George pull a weapon on you?"

"No. But when he walked away, he might've been going to get his rifle."

"George walked away? He ended it, then?"

"Sure, but like I said, he could have been going for his rifle."

"And you responded with gunfire?" Jim's tone was incredulous. The settlers exchanged uneasy glances, the weight of the decision pressing down on them. "I'm going to end this right here. I recommend expulsion."

Marcus said, "I want a proper trial with prison time."

"That will not happen. Taking care of this train's safety and welfare is my responsibility. That's what you are paying me for."

Marcus grimaced.

"Can I get a yes for expulsion?"

Marcus shook his head while most of the men in attendance said 'yes.'

Jim turned to Jason. "One hour to break camp and leave."

"This isn't right. George started it." Jasper stormed off to his wagon, where he began yoking his oxen.

George yelled, "Good!"

Suddenly, the focus shifted to George. Mary clutched her throat as she felt a lump form. She sensed the cougar nearby once more, finding solace in its presence creating a blanket of security.

As Jim scanned the crowd, he said, "We are prosecuting George for regularly violating the rules and starting fights."

"Wait!" George, throwing his hands up as he spun around, exclaimed, "It wasn't my gun. I was the one shot at! I'm the victim!"

Marcus raised his voice, pointing at George. "My little girl has a bullet wound because of you. You start more arguments than anyone else. Of course, someone tried to shoot you."

A voice rang out. "You're a scalawag and a reprobate."

Jim rolled his head back. Around the circle, there were murmurs of agreement.

George turned around in the middle of the men, trying to storm off. However, the circle of men around him tightened as he stomped around, looking for an opening to escape his trial. There was no father to bail him out this time. He would have to account for his conduct.

Mary watched, a knot of anxiety in her stomach, as George, now the center of the trial, blustered and fumbled for words. His usual bravado was gone, replaced by a palpable fear of the consequences. The wagon master listed George's transgressions on his fingers, his voice steady and resolute. "Cursing when told not to, kicking other people's possessions, spooking horses with unruly actions, instigating arguments, and not doing your share of the work. I'm sure I forgot something."

Mary, stretching to see over the heads of the men, only looked on in frustration. She was the victim of an immature, spoiled rich kid's actions.

Her mind raced, trying to figure out a way out. She wished she knew a spell to change men's thinking. Her potion was gone and wouldn't have worked in this situation, anyway. There must be a way if she only had the knowledge. She was not like her sister, who was fearful of making a fold in the fabric of life, so as not to cause harm to some unknown person. As if it would.

Finally, Jim asked, "Is everyone in agreement that George will leave the train?"

Mary strained to see over the crowd, her heart racing. The agreements seemed loud to Mary as she pulled the canvas into place. George's expulsion felt both a relief and a new worry. How would she fulfill her promise to Henry now?

She glanced over at Katherine's wagon and noticed the young girl sitting up, her arm bandaged, hugging a doll. Relief flowed over her, though she still feared her own future.

As the crowd dispersed, Mary emerged from her wagon. She needed to prepare for the journey ahead, alone now with George. His anger was palpable as he cursed and stomped around their wagon.

As she set about her tasks, the letters from Stella and Henry weighed heavily on her mind. Their words offered a sanctuary of love and understanding, a stark contrast to her current predicament. She wrapped herself in the comfort they provided, a brief respite from the harsh reality of the trail.

With George's fate sealed and the journey to Fort Bridger looming, Mary steeled herself for what was to come. The path ahead was fraught with uncertainty, but she knew she must find a way to navigate it, for her sake and for the child she carried.

It was time to honor Henry's request that she try to keep his brother alive. She could only hope George would avoid his usual self-sabotage to get them to the next town, Fort Bridger. At least the tracks were obvious. They only had to follow them. Hopefully, George wouldn't have some wild idea of a shortcut.

Chapter Fourteen

Mary's yearning for the wagon train's camaraderie increased as George continued to complain nonstop. The echo of Katherine's icy stare haunted her, a reminder of the unjust blame she bore for the child's injury. Now, her only companions were the oxen and George's grating voice, a relentless drone against the backdrop of the ever-rising hills, their windswept grasses whispering secrets in the breeze.

Mid-afternoon, they approached a fork in the trail. Mary steered the oxen toward the well-trodden path, only to be interrupted by George's urgent call. "Stop!" He was pointing to the less traveled route, a wild look in his eyes.

Mary halted, her patience wearing thin. "What now, George?"

George was adamant, pointed to the other trail. "We take that route."

"That is not the right one. This one has wider ruts. More wagons go this way," Mary shook her head. This would lead to a major disagreement if she pushed it.

Leaning towards her, George displayed his misplaced confidence by puffing out his chest. "You don't know. Someone gave me advice to take this way to cut off forty-six miles to Fort Hall. That's three days of walking instead of six. He said to travel at night to avoid the heat, though."

Mary thought the plan had a myriad of problems. "Travel at night when wild animals prowl. How will we see where we are going?"

George chuckled. "I have my rifle and I'll use a lantern. I walk ahead and you follow. The way it should be." He puffed his chest out.

Mary rolled her eyes. "How do you know the advice is sound and not something to lead you astray?"

George spread his legs out and crossed his arms. "I trust him."

Mary smirked. How could he trust anyone since they voted him out? *Silly man.* "Fine. I hope you don't get us killed." How was she going to keep George alive for Henry if George gets her killed? She knew arguing with George was futile. Resigned, she guided the oxen onto the unmarked trail, her heart heavy with foreboding. "Shouldn't we break now to get some sleep before traveling at night?"

"Yeah. Take a break. Get some sleep." George walked over to the back of the wagon to retrieve his tent, and the sound of the rocks being disturbed resonated through the afternoon air as he cleared a spot.

Mary removed the oxen's yoke, and the animals wandered off in search of scarce grass, their hooves thudding on the dry earth. She gazed in the direction they were heading to the mountains ahead. She hoped for a decent pass through them.

Mary lay in her wagon, trying to calm her racing thoughts. Every instinct screamed that this decision would lead to misfortune. Her intuition, sharpened by years of reading tarot cards and interpreting omens, told her they were headed for trouble. He was being tricked.

Mary roused after dark. Dread weighed on her like a wet blanket, but she made her way out of the wagon. She called for the oxen to yoke them. Waking George was an arduous task that she loathed. She approached his tent. "George! Time to get going. It's dark now."

"Give me more time. You're always in a hurry."

Mary gave the side of the tent a swift kick. "You said after dark. It's going to take some time to cross forty-three miles. We have to get started."

"You won't quit, will you?"

"No."

"Fine. I'll get up. Then leave me alone."

Mary walked over to the oxen to stroke them to calm herself. George finally walked past her, the lantern lit. She coaxed the oxen along.

The night journey began under a canopy of stars. George led the way, lantern in hand. The dry, cracked earth stretched into the darkness, a desolate landscape devoid of life. The skittering of lizards and the rustle of unseen creatures kept Mary on edge, her skirt catching on thorny plants, adding to her discomfort. Mary hated to think about what this place looked like during the day. The night grew chilly. She crawled back into the wagon and dug out her wool coat to stop shivering. How could a desert be so cold at night and so hot during the day?

As dawn broke, revealing a stark, unforgiving terrain, Mary's worries deepened. The oxen, already exhausted, found nothing to graze on. Mary rationed their water supply, concern etched on her face. The harshness of the landscape was a stark contrast to the green fields she longed for.

As she fixed a hearty meal of bacon and beans while scanning the harsh gray and brown landscape and hoped this was not what her future held. Mary preferred green landscapes.

While half-listening to the long trail of complaints by George, she cleaned camp and made sure that the smells of their dinner would entice no animals. Mary retired to her mattress in the wagon. Even though all the walking and worrying drained her, it felt strange to sleep during the day, and it took her a while to drift off.

Mary woke, covered in sweat from sleeping in the intense heat of the day.

"Get up, lazy woman. We need to eat and get going. It will be dark soon."

George's eagerness to continue surprised her, but she complied, her stomach rumbling from hunger. They ate only two meals a day, not stopping at night. Two more days of this.

They ate a hasty meal, cleared away the dishes, and soon Mary had the oxen attached to their yokes, ready to go. As they set off again, Mary's anxiety mounted. They were far from any water source, and both the oxen and they needed more than they had.

The moonlit journey resumed, a surreal procession through the desolate night. Suddenly, a blood-curdling bellow shattered the silence. The oxen swerved towards her; the wagon tilted back and forth. Mary told them to stop and George ran over. Aengus, Mary's favorite oxen, had been attacked. Her heart sank at the sight of the gash on its hindquarters.

George swung the lantern around, its light casting eerie shadows on the surrounding landscape. In the flickering light, Mary glimpsed glowing eyes—a wolf lurking in the darkness. Fear and resolve battled within her. She knew she had to protect her oxen, her lifeline in this unforgiving wilderness.

As the wolf edged closer, Mary felt an overwhelming sense of responsibility. She had to keep both the animals and George safe, a daunting task on this perilous night. The weight of her decision to follow this path pressed upon her, a reminder of the consequences of each choice on this treacherous journey.

The moon cast a ghostly pallor over the scene as the wolf paced, its eyes locked on the injured ox. Mary's heart raced and pounded in her chest. She scrambled to the back of the wagon, her hands fumbling in the herbal satchel for dried yarrow and comfrey. Crushing them into a powder, she dashed back, her breaths coming in quick gasps.

George, wielding the lantern like a makeshift weapon, charged towards the wolf, his face a mask of fear and determination. It was an act of bravery Mary had never seen in him before.

A low, guttural growl rippled through the air, sending a chill down Mary's spine.

George jumped at the sound, causing him to drop the lantern and extinguish the candle.

The cougar emerged into the moonlight. Muscles rippling, ears pinned back, it fixed its gaze on the wolf.

The wolf snarled in response, ready to defend its future meal against this new threat. The tension in the air was palpable as the two predators circled each other, a dance of deadly intent.

With a powerful leap, the cougar pounced, its claws meeting the wolf's bared teeth. They crashed to the ground in a whirlwind of fur and fury.

Mary gasped, her hands flying to her mouth. "Oh, no!"

George rummaged through his pockets. "Now we've got two beasts to worry about!"

The battle raged on, a chaotic tangle of claws and teeth. Mary watched, transfixed, as the cougar and wolf traded blows. The cougar, larger but visibly injured, fought with a ferocity that belied its wounds. Each swipe of its paws was met by the wolf's agile dodges and sharp bites.

"Please, Morrigan, help the cougar," Mary whispered, her voice barely audible over the commotion.

George, lighting the candle again, shot her a puzzled look. "Who's Morrigan? I just want them to kill each other so we can leave!" The lantern gave an eerie glow to the fight.

Mary winced, realizing she had spoken her prayer aloud. The cougar, now bleeding from multiple wounds, seemed to falter. In desperation, Mary focused her energy on the animal for healing and strength to prevail.

As if responding to Mary's unspoken plea, the cougar unleashed a surge of energy, reclaiming its advantage. It locked its jaws around the wolf's neck with a sickening crunch that made Mary's stomach churn. The wolf's body went limp.

The cougar circled its fallen foe, panting. It gazed up at Mary, bloodied but victorious, and disappeared into the night.

Mary experienced a deep, inexplicable connection to the wild creature as she bowed her head in thanks to the cougar. She turned her attention back to Aengus, applying more salve to its wound, hands trembling, and used her remaining energy to add more healing.

"George, we need to stop here to let the oxen rest." She was the one who needed the rest, but she couldn't tell him that.

George's face flickered from the lantern he held in her direction, deep lines etched in his face. "Alright, but we're not safe yet. That cougar, or more wolves, could come back."

Mary nodded, her mind and body weary. "The cougar is not a problem. But you're right about the wolves. Don't they travel in packs?"

"I'm taking first watch. Then I'll wake you for your watch while I sleep. If you see any, wake me. I'll have the rifle beside me."

Mary headed to the back of the wagon. "It would be better to show me how to use the rifle since we are traveling alone."

"Go to sleep. Your mind is leaving you. Women don't use weapons." George headed to the front of the wagon, leaving Mary in the moonlight.

As Mary settled into the wagon for a few hours of rest, her thoughts lingered on the cougar. Its presence had been a constant shadow, an enigmatic guardian of sorts. She contemplated giving it a name, a symbol of the strange bond she developed with the wild creature. Exhaustion soon overtook her, and she drifted into a fitful sleep, the events of the night replaying in her dreams.

CHAPTER FIFTEEN

MARY OVERLOOKED THE BANK of the Green River, listening to the water roar, and jumped back as a large tree limb tumbled and tossed past her. It had been a couple of horrible days on the trail, a wolf attack, the extra night in the desert causing them to run out of water for a day. Her parched throat longed for a drink of water. But not this. Why not a little stream of water? Not a river of fury. She swatted mosquitoes from her face.

While the oxen ate lush grass, Mary and George surveyed the river, searching for a better place to cross. Here, past travelers had cut in the steep bank and the trail continued on the other side of the river.

George unhooked the tongue from the oxen, and Mary removed the yokes from the two smaller oxen, stowing them in the wagon.

"How did you get strong enough to lift those?"

Now he notices? Mary couldn't give George an answer, too focused on her dread about the task at hand, getting across this horrible river. The thundering torrent of frothy water swept everything in its path, an unyielding force. She knew they were the river's next victims.

George tied heavy ropes to the tongue and the other ends to the yokes of their largest and strongest oxen. Mary led the oxen to the river and touched each one.

Cross the river and pull us across.

I will meet you on the other side.

So mote it be!

The oxen stepped in, continuing across until the middle, when Mary saw they had to swim. She sucked her breath in as she saw them struggle against the currents. Her stomach crawled into her throat. As each oxen reached the other shore, she released some tension in her shoulders. She expelled the air from her lungs until she realized they still had to get themselves over.

George stepped into the river, a rope on either side of him. He tested each step before planting his foot and transferring his weight. River beds had sudden drop offs he could step into if he didn't pay attention. Mary could see he was fighting the current to stay upright. The wagon rolled in.

Mary gazed across the river to the oxen tethered to the wagon. *Keep pulling.* She went in, holding on to the back of the wagon. The tears came as she tested her greatest fear yet again. She had lost count of the river crossings. The wagon lifted, bounced, and headed downstream, towing her along. She refused to let go, not being able to swim. She swallowed icy water, increasing her panic. *Please oxen, pull!*

Mary tried to get a better hold, using all her strength. *Focus!* Her fear prevented her from focusing enough to reach her magick for extra strength. The relentless rush of water tugged at her skirt, wanting to take her to her watery death. She hung on, eyes closed. *I don't want to die!*

The wagon creaked and groaned as it swung closer to the other shore, its wheels banging on the rocky river bed. *What if the ropes don't hold?* Another large cottonwood branch bounced against the wagon, almost striking her on its fast-paced trip down the river.

The wagon bucked against the current, and Mary worked to get her footing on the slippery and uneven riverbed. She thought she heard George groan, but maybe it was the river tricking her ears.

Mary tried again to focus enough to access her magick, pushing with all her strength. The river rocks shifted beneath her feet until the reaffirming solidness of the shoreline consoled her soles. She collapsed on the dry ground, sobbing. Her jaw hurt from clenching. Her fists pounded the ground. Why couldn't she focus when it mattered the most to use her magick?

George laid on his back, chest rising and falling, loud and forceful, and they stayed there for an hour to recover.

Mary sobbed as she did after every river crossing. *I want to go home.*

As she filled the water containers, her tears fell onto her sleeve, and she wiped them away before yoking the oxen. This is what she got for wanting adventure. She trudged west, chin held high, and wished the worst was over.

A high pitch whistle made her shoulders rise and tighten. *What was that?* Mary thought of the whistles of the steamboats on the Missouri River. Civilization. She couldn't be that lucky. It got louder as they followed the trail.

Mary sniffed as she got a whiff of something. She wrinkled her nose as the odor of rotten eggs increased. A sheet of water, bubbling, its shore yellow. She asked the oxen to move faster, wanting a greater distance from such a foul spring.

Strange looking cones, blackened slopes and jagged peaks, were on both sides of the path. Steam rose from cuts on the ground and cones. She approached a cone, reaching out to touch it. Her finger came back black. She rubbed it using her other hand, but it didn't come off.

George approached a spring surrounded by white clay. He stuck his finger into the bubbling water and brought it to his lips. "This is good. Bubbly."

He reached a cupped hand into the water, and the droplets trickled down his fingers, dripping to his mouth, and drank. "Mmm. Quenches your thirst."

Mary tried it for herself. "Reminds me of seltzer."

Mary heard the next spring before she saw it, a hissing sound emitting the whistle they had heard at intervals of fifteen seconds. A white column of spray shot in the air five feet. Mary ran over. The water gushed out of a one foot hole. She reached her hand out until some warm water foamed over it. She touched her finger to her tongue and recoiled. It had a nasty metallic taste that left a burning effect on her tongue. She ran her tongue against her teeth and wipe it with a corner of her apron to no avail.

They passed a three-foot gray-orange geyser that emitted water and gas. Mary gave no thought to trying it. She focused on gathering small branches fallen from the cottonwoods along the Bear River.

When they came to the end of the mountain pass, a small wagon train camped, circled around cattle, near the remnants of something she wasn't sure. It had a rectangular mound surrounding foundations of several buildings, reminding her of the Fort Laramie, only smaller. Was it Fort Hall?

Mary asked, "Are we camping here?" It was late afternoon, and the oxen were exhausted.

George nodded while scanning the wagon train. He headed toward the camped wagons.

Mary watched George until he disappeared into the center of the wagons. She crossed her fingers that he would not find himself in another disagreement.

She returned her focus to lifting the yokes off the oxen using her magick, leaving them to graze. The grass in the lower valley was abundant. The oxen needed it after the ordeal through the desert. Aengus had healed well.

Mary's stomach growled. She grabbed her bag of fire supplies from the back of the wagon. The bag weighed more than it had been in the desert since she collected tinder and sagebrush branches as they came through the pass. She kneeled and reached into the bag for something that would catch.

A spider crawled on her arm. Mary plucked it off and set it free in the grass. On the bag's bottom were fluffs of oxen hair that she kept when she wiped their sides. She placed the fur in a pile, blew a slow long breath on it, and watched it take. A few broken cottonwood branches and some oxen dung. Today, she made a batch of beans that she added bacon to, a hearty meal to feed them for several days.

When the food was ready, Mary ate in peace, listening to the song sparrows.

George came back and sat to eat. Mary waited for him to tell her about his visit, but he said nothing. She twisted her mouth, lowering her brows. "Well?"

"Well, what?"

"Are you going to tell me about your visit?" She leaned forward.

George let a breath out before he spoke. "We are joining them in the morning."

Relief rushed over Mary until she remembered why they were traveling alone. How long before they kicked them out of this one? "What's the wagon master like?"

George tilted his head and nodded. "Nice. Not like the unfair bastard from the last train. There's a couple taking cattle to start a ranch. Another group of farmers is going to mine in Bannock, where they say you can pull up a sagebrush, shake its roots, and get a pan of gold. That's where I'm going to sell mining supplies."

"How many women?" Mary desired companionship. She missed it.

George laughed. "One. The cattle couple...she's..." He rounded his hands in front of his stomach. "So...yes. You two can whine together."

Mary pulled her face down, looked at George through her lashes. She wanted to punch him. She did more work than he did. At least she would have someone to talk to.

The next morning, after they ate and broke camp, they lined up at the end of the new train. As they pulled out, they headed north, which confused Mary. "George, why are we going this way and not following the trail over there?"

George gave her an evil smile and laughed. "We're going to Montana." He sped off.

Mary stopped in her tracks. *What has he done? I want to go to California.* "No! That's not what we agreed to, George. Come back here." She raced after him, but he ran faster.

The heat in her body rose to a danger point. Every fiber of her wanted to send flames everywhere, to burn everything. Mary slowed until the oxen caught up. She took long deep breaths, not wanting to start a fire. That would not be a pleasant introduction to the new train. *Flaming witch burned everything.* What in the world is in Montana? George mentioned gold. *That must be it. A gold rush.* But what does that do for her? It was closer. She wanted something good from this major change in plans.

Mary had to remember she, not George, got herself in this situation by leaving Chicago and the unconditional love of her sister and Henry. Especially Henry. Mary realized too late that his kindness, level-headedness and gentle nature were what she needed to balance her passion and fiery personality. She had to figure out how to survive his bull-headed, nasty brother in some godforsaken part of Montana. That's what she got for an impulsive decision.

Flaming witch under control.

The prairie grass brushed against Mary's skirt as she strode left of her wagon. Her eyes landed on only twelve wagons in the train, fewer people for George to argue with. The mountains in the distance spelled trouble for them if he got them kicked out again. Mary hoped the cattle woman was amiable to talk to.

The bugle blared for the noon break. Mary scrambled to warm up the bacon and beans and wolfed her food. She then hurried to the wagon, where she had spotted a tall man on horseback driving cattle into the center of the wagons. A woman, blond hair braided down her back, was struggling to get her fire going. Mary raced over.

"Hello. I'm Mary." She extended her hand, grinning.

The woman beamed, her eyes crinkling at the edges, and opened her arms. "Oh, I heard there was a new couple. One wearing her bustle wrong. I'm Anna." She hugged Mary.

Mary hugged her back, taken aback by the warmth. Anna's voice was light and cheerful, full of affection, hitting Mary to her core. A tug. A need.

"I'm four months. And you?" Mary asked.

"Same. Are you hungry?"

"No. I ate. But thank you. But if you don't mind, I'll sit a bit."

Anna knitted her eyebrows. "Of course, sit and get comfortable. Did you eat something cold? I'm still getting my fire going."

Mary laughed as she sat near the sputtering fire, letting out an inconspicuous breath on it, flames catching. "I'm a firebug." Shrugging, she continued. "Somehow, I just get it going."

The fire grew, reflecting in Anna's eyes wide open. "Ah, look at that. Maybe you can rub that off on me. When Peter has time, he starts it, but the cattle come first."

Mary giggled at the thought of George getting a fire ready for her. The inquisitive expression on Anna's face made her explain. "George would never start a fire for me. I won't say anything bad about him. You'll see for yourself soon enough."

"Hmm. It's never good to bad-mouth your husband. I'm sure he helps you in other ways."

George had been better in the desert and the last river crossing, so there might be hope. She saw Anna's wagon had a buckboard. "Do you ride in the wagon or walk?"

"Both, depending on how I feel that day. The buckboard bouncing makes it a little hard on the back. The walking is hard on my feet."

Mary took a deep breath. "We don't have a buckboard, more room for mining supplies. My feet are hard as rocks now. No blisters."

"I have a salve. I can get it for you."

Mary put her hand up. "Thank you, but I make my own."

Anna's mouth formed an 'o'. "You do? I do, too. What herbs do you use?"

A wave of warmth spread from her chest to her fingers and toes. A kindred spirit. "I use chaparral leaf, comfrey leaf, and echinacea flower. What's your recipe?" Mary left out the magickal spell that did the heavy lifting.

Anna dropped her hands in her lap, head tilted. "It's nice to find someone who shares the same interest in healing. I use plantain, mullein, and red clover. Sometimes I add self-heal. Depends on what I have on hand."

The tall man approached. "I see you have company, Anna."

Anna held out a wooden bowl to her husband. "Come rest. This is Mary," she introduced, turning towards the woman beside her. "And this is my husband, Peter."

Mary shielded her eyes from the sun's rays. "Hello, Peter."

"Good to meet you, Mary. My wife has had no one to talk to since we left the Oregon Trail," Peter replied, chomping on his food while standing.

Anna extinguished the flames of their cooking fire. "You really need to rest."

But Peter waved off her concerns. "Too much to do. This tasted good, Anna. I was starving."

Mary observed the couple, warmth emanating from their relationship. She was happy for them, though a pang of envy tugged at her heart. She longed for a connection like that.

After finishing his meal, Peter handed the bowl to his wife. "Glad you've joined the train, Mary," he said, nodding in her direction before making his way over to the cattle grazing nearby.

Anna rose to clean the dishes, a damp cloth in her hand while she spoke. "I swear he treats them like children. He loves ranching. We worked for a rancher in Iowa and saved to buy some cattle to start our own ranch. Then we learned about a valley in Montana where we could get some land. Where are you headed?"

Mary paused for a moment, careful not to sound negative or whiny. "George found out about gold in Montana yesterday while talking to some miners here. He figured there weren't many mining suppliers yet. I guess we're headed to a place called Bandock."

"Bannock." Anna swooped her arm in a grand gesture towards the line of wagons. "That's where everyone's going for the gold rush. But we'll continue on to the Bitterroot Valley."

When Mary saw others packing to continue the day's travel, she stood. "I better get ready to go. How about we get together this evening?"

Anna enveloped her in a warm embrace, and Mary leaned into it, feeling a sense of familiarity. "We can. I've set my heart on it."

As Mary made her way back to her wagon, each step seemed lighter, almost buoyant. The encounter with Anna had stirred something within her, a sense of kinship she hadn't realized she very much missed. The brief interaction had felt like a balm to her weary soul, providing a much-needed respite from the constant tension and loneliness of the journey.

In Anna's company, Mary had experienced a rare moment of genuine connection, a reminder of the warmth and camaraderie she had left behind. The encounter echoed memories of past friendships and the comfort of being understood and accepted. It was as if Anna's presence had lifted the heavy cloak of isolation that Mary had wrapped around herself since leaving Chicago.

The encounter also sparked an introspective reflection in Mary. Was it mere coincidence that brought them together, or was it a twist of fate? The thought that perhaps the universe had conspired to bring a semblance of joy into her tumultuous journey filled her with a quiet sense of hope. For the first time in what felt like an eternity, Mary allowed herself the flicker of optimism about the days ahead.

The prospect of having someone to converse with, to share experiences and stories, was something to cherish and look forward to. In Anna, Mary saw a potential friend, someone who could understand the struggles of the trail, and perhaps someone who shared her interests and passions.

As the wagon train moved, Mary glanced towards Anna's wagon, anticipating their next meeting. It was a small but significant light in the monotony of the trail, a reminder that amidst the hardship and endless travel, there were still moments of human connection to be found.

This unexpected encounter didn't no more offer Mary a new acquaintance; it offered a glimpse of a unique journey, one where friendship and solidarity could exist alongside the challenges of the trail. It was a subtle but profound shift in Mary's outlook, a gentle reminder that even in the harshest of circumstances, there can be moments of grace and companionship.

CHAPTER SIXTEEN

MARY HANDED GEORGE A biscuit she made when they had camped at the remains of Fort Hall. "Wayne, a miner in our new group, told me that a massive flood destroyed Fort Hall when the banks of the Snake River crested. They didn't bother rebuilding it, since the Fort Bridger treaty brought peace to this area, so we have one less worry about an attack from hostile natives."

George inspected the biscuit before taking a bite and setting it down in his bowl, grunting. "Who cares? This group has as many rules as the last one." He furrowed his brows. "Why can't people let people live without putting their thumb on someone? I can't do rules. Never have."

Mary took a deep breath, suppressing the urge to roll her eyes at George's constant rebellion. Although they had only been traveling among this new group for a few days, she had already grown fond of them. Wayne told stories in the evening, giving Mary another thing to look forward to each day. The Irish twins, Sionn and Seamas, were always on the lookout for their elusive pot of gold. The wagon master, Tony, had been cordial when she was first introduced. But her favorites were Anna and Peter.

Mary declared, her voice echoing through the night, "The wagon master's rules are there for our safety. We can't afford to be reckless. Why don't you become a hermit?"

George snorted. "You'd like that, wouldn't you?"

Mary chuckled, shaking her head. "Can you at least try this time? It's easier to travel in a group than alone."

George's grumblings were a pleasant distraction this morning. Today they were crossing the Snake River, which she hoped wouldn't be like the Green River. She didn't want to think about it.

Mary hustled to pack everything, yoke the oxen, and talk to Anna; anything to keep her mind from wandering to thoughts of water or rivers.

As the sun neared its apex, they arrived at the Snake River. The trail, worn flat from many past trains, made the ideal crossing obvious. Since the river wasn't wide here, they would keep the oxen hitched to the wagons. George yanked on the oxen's yokes to lead the wagon off the trail to the right.

"Why are you going this way?" Mary feared George would again defy a wagon master. She did not want to be kicked out of another train since Tony was more adamant that they follow his rules as the trail north through the Rocky Mountains was dangerous.

George flashed an angry glare and pointed. "Look! It's easier crossing over there."

Mary's gaze followed where George pointed. "The bank is steeper on the other side, and don't you see the swirl of water in the middle? I think we should join the others and cross here."

"No! We are crossing there!" George tried to get the oxen to go faster, but bellowed. The Irish twins yelled, "What are you doing, George? You're being thick going that way."

Mary muttered, "Oh great. Here we go again." She had no choice but to stay alongside or behind the wagon. She worried about the oxen and, most of all, water. Ever since they crossed the Green River, nightmares of water engulfing her had plagued her sleep.

Mary tied her skirt around her ankles, made easy by the slits she had cut earlier. The oxen entered the water, and Mary stepped into the icy water. A shiver ran up her spine. When she was in calf high, she felt the current's powerful pull. She struggled step by step to her thighs, waist, and chest. Where the water didn't swirl and foam as much, she could still see the river bottom, rocks of blue, red, and cream. The current pushed her against the wagon box as she tried to keep her head above water, holding on using all her might. She tried to stay calm but struggled, keeping the panic at bay.

The wagon pitched over to one side when the river bed dropped, right where Mary had observed the water swirling. As she struggled to keep hold, her grasp broke under the strength of the current and the river pulled her under the bed of the wagon.

To keep her head above the water, Mary kept grabbing for anything, but the current was stronger than she was. It pulled her back under, twisting and turning her. She did not know which way was up. The bubbles and swirling water made every direction appear the same. The surface should appear brighter on a sunny day like today, but it didn't.

This is not how I want to die.

A rock hitting her hip, though it hurt, gave her a clue of where the bottom was. Mary kicked, searching for something solid to push herself from. Her foot found a large rock, and she launched herself. When she reached the surface, she saw a branch ahead hanging over the water and lunged for it. Using what little strength she had, she held on, gasping for air, freezing.

The branch bent further into the water. Mary placed one hand over the other to get closer to shore, where she hoped the branch was stronger. Her feet hunted for the river bed. She closed her eyes, searching for the focus to use her magick to add strength to the branch and herself, but she was too wet and weak. A wet fire witch was a defeated witch.

Don't break, please.

"Quick! Take my hand, Mrs. Perkins! I'll pull you out!"

Mary heard the man's voice, but wasn't sure it was real. "I'm afraid to let go." She opened her eyes to see Tony reaching for her.

Tony moved into the water on the other side of the branch, bracing himself against the current. "I'm going to pull you over. Don't panic, or both of us will go downstream. I'm not sure how long this branch will hold. Do you understand?"

"Yes, yes, I understand.." Mary looked into his eyes and found kindness and concern.

Tony grabbed Mary under her arms and pulled her over the branch. They stood in waist high water facing a steep bank. Tony climbed and dragged her up the embankment. Mary, on hands and knees, could not move. Her wet skirts entangled her legs.

Tony ran to his horse and took a blanket out of his saddlebag, and brought it back to Mary.

Mary shivered as she rolled over to sit. She welcomed the blanket, wrapping herself in it. "Thank you, thank you. How will I ever repay you? I owe you my life." Mary gazed at him. This man who she only met a day ago was risked his life for hers. Her foolish, hasty decision to go on an adventure had led her to this place and put her life at risk. Regrets stacked on more regrets.

Tony shook his head, frowning, brows furrowed. "Ma'am, if you want to repay me, get away from that man. I watched when your wagon tipped and you disappeared. Everyone on the shore screamed. He didn't show any concern. There is something wrong with him. Walter, Sionn, and Seamas rushed to the shore, then ran alongside the river, and he continued on, not stopping at all on the other side. Not even paying attention to everyone yelling at him."

Mary cringed. George embarrassed her again, but she tricked him into marrying her. *Stupid girl*. "I can't leave him, as I owe it to his brother to make sure he doesn't get himself killed. He is my responsibility. Anyway, it's my fault I'm in this position. But I appreciate your concern."

"I guess I don't understand women. You're not the first I've seen in the company of horrible men. Especially a beautiful woman like you." He shook his head and offered his hand to Mary. "Are you okay to walk over to my horse?"

She took his hand. "Yes. I don't think I hurt anything."

"Well, I'll have you on a more experienced wagon team on the next crossing. Gotta keep you safe." Tony led her to his horse and helped her into the saddle. Then he directed the horse back the half mile to the wagon train to applause from all who gathered.

"Can someone start a fire for her to dry herself? We'll do our nooner here. I'll ride ahead to let the rest know we are stopping now. And have a word with George." The wagon master helped Mary to the ground. Mary handed him his blanket, but he raised his hand. "You keep it until you are dry. I'll be back to check on you."

Anna rushed over to give Mary a hug. Peter gathered wood and started a fire. Anna said, "I'm glad you're safe. The wagon master acted fast."

Mary sobbed. "I could have drowned. I owe him my life."

Anna sat next to Mary and held her until she stopped crying. "Are my oxen alright?"

"I'll ask Peter to check on the oxen. Don't worry about anything right now." When Mary continued to shiver, Anna sprang to her feet. "I'm going to get you another blanket." When Anna returned, she dried Mary's hair while Mary recounted what happened when she swept away. She perked up as she talked to Anna. It didn't surprise her that George did not check on her. He didn't realize he needed her more than she needed him.

Mary craned her neck to peer at the towering evergreen trees that surrounded their camp for the night. She had never seen such a sight. She breathed in the fresh scent of the forest while gathering boughs on the ground. This evening, she wouldn't need to resort to using oxen dung for fuel.

The clear night, accompanied by a half-moon, held thousands of twinkling stars. Mary relished the grandeur of the sight even more than usual after her near-death experience in the river.

George had been away for a while, leaving her to savor the peace and quiet, aside from the crackling of her fire and the rustling of her fellow travelers in the camp.

Mary tried to dry out her wet belongings, which had gotten soaked. She then busied herself preparing dinner and cleaning up after it. Hopefully, the warmth of the fire would dry everything out enough allowing her to stow it back on the wagon.

George stomped over, his pacing soon escalating into shouting. "Who does he think he is, telling me how to cross the river? It's not like I've never done it before. It's not my fault you let go!" He stopped his pacing to glare at Mary. "You should have held on." He resumed pacing. "But that's my fault. And now he wants to abandon me here and have you join Peter's wagon. What good would that do?"

Mary pursed her lips and regarded him through lowered lashes. She had grown weary of his self-centeredness. "What would you do if I died? Who would cook and clean for you?"

George flailed his arms about, raising his voice. "If you died? It doesn't matter because you didn't die. You just got your hair wet."

Mary was certain that everyone in the camp had heard his outburst. There was no placating him. Any attempt would only exacerbate the situation.

"Poor thing, taking a swim in the river, and it's all my fault," George continued to grumble.

The wagon master approached, but Mary shook her head, and he walked away. It would be a lonely night for her.

Perhaps it was self-pity, but her fury built as George went on and on about his complaints, revealing a complete lack of consideration for her. It was one thing to be spoiled, but there was something more to George's behavior. She couldn't bear to look at him or speak to him. The campfire flared, getting her attention. Mary stood and moved to a clearing, out of danger of starting a forest fire. The farther she walked, the smaller the flames became.

Mary held back her fiery temper to help others, while George's selfishness was palpable. Had his father given him money for this trip and business venture to get him out from under their roof? She wouldn't fault him if that were the case. But Henry had said their mother was upset, so at least she loved George a little.

Regardless, without her, George would starve, and the oxen would flee, leaving him stranded. No one else would help him, as they ostracized him for his behavior. Mary wanted to run away, but guilt would consume her. Perhaps the journey had worsened George's attitude, and a more stable situation when they reach Bannack in a couple of weeks could improve it. She would give him another chance there.

Mary scanned the dense forest surrounding her, her senses on high alert. She had wandered too far, unable to see her camp. Her nerves tingled as she returned to her wagon, but something caught her eye—a pair of glowing eyes staring back at her. Every fiber of her being fired when she realized they belonged to her savior, the cougar who had rescued her from the wolf.

The majestic animal paced before her, its tail waving in greeting. Mary's heart raced as she stepped back, her eyes locked on the cougar's as it approached her. She bowed, sensing the weight of the animal's power and grace, and without hesitation, she kneeled before it, humbled by its presence.

The rough tongue of the enormous cat raked across her head. She hugged it, feeling both the warmth of its affection and the danger of its strength. She whispered, "Thank you," grateful for its protection and friendship.

As she rose and ran her hand along the cat's back, Mary understood this was her familiar, a bond between witch and animal that would last a lifetime. The cougar rubbed against her, and though Mary longed to stay there forever, she knew she had to return to her fellow campers.

Giving a final rub on the cougar's head, she whispered its name, "Danu," before turning to leave. As she walked back to camp, her mind raced with thoughts of her new familiar and the power it might bring her. Mary smiled, knowing that her destiny lay ahead in the west, and that Danu, who she named after the mysterious queen of the Celtic Gods, would always be by her side.

CHAPTER SEVENTEEN

THE SUN BEGAN ITS descent beyond the rugged horizon, casting an amber glow across the vast expanse of the wilderness. A gentle breeze rustled the tall grasses, carrying on it the earthy scent of pine and wildflowers. At the heart of this untamed landscape, the small wagon train came to a halt, forming a makeshift campsite on the Idaho-Montana border.

Mary had her fire established and dinner warming in no time. She walked over to Anna's camp to help her build a ring and get her fire going. The past few nights, everyone gathered around Anna's crackling fire. They ate, talked, laughed, and sang to the serenade of crickets, drawn together by the shared warmth of companionship.

Except George. He sat by the fire Mary kept going for him. A pile of gathered dried oxen chips to keep him company. One day, the deep lines of his scowl would become permanent.

The campfire flickered, casting shadows across the faces of the travelers gathered around it. Mary asked Anna, "How did you and Peter meet?"

Peter, calloused hands and a weathered face, adjusted his worn Stetson hat, casting a curious glance towards Anna, a spirited young woman, eyes as bright as the stars that would soon adorn the darkening sky. A subtle smile tugged at the corners of his lips.

Anna, her face flushed, eyes with a faraway look, settled herself on a rough-hewn log. Her voice carried a gentle lilt as she spoke, the words wrapped in a delicate tapestry of memory. "It was back in '63, just outside Cedar Rapids, Iowa, where I lived," she said. "My dad was harvesting hay and me and my siblings helped."

Peter nodded, his eyes fixed on her, every nuance of her story captivating him like a well-woven tale.

"This tall boy on horseback rode up," Anna continued, chuckling. "He caught sight of me and stared for the longest time. Until my father told him to state his business." She laughed. "The concern in his voice for his lost mama cow and her calf, and his handsome face did me in. We haven't been apart since."

Mary recalled a time when her heart was full of hope, only to be replaced by a hollow ache that seemed to grow each passing day. Her eyes welled with tears.

Peter reached out a weathered hand, offering comfort.

Mary shook her head. "I'm sorry. It's me, not your story."

Anna's voice faltered for a moment as she said, "You poor thing. You have *us* now." In that flickering light of the campfire, they discovered solace, the warmth of friendship that could heal even the deepest of wounds.

Wayne cleared his throat and said, "We introduced ourselves when we first got going, but we haven't heard yours, Mary. You said you were born in Ireland. Can you tell us your story of coming to America?"

Mary leaned forward, thankful for the distraction. "Well, I came when I was a small child." Not wanting to tell them they burned her mother at the stake for witchcraft, she told an elaborate fib. "I'll tell it quick, as there's no good in it. Crops failed. There was no work for my father. My parents died of the fever on the ship. My uncle took me and my older sister in. He became a miner in Pennsylvania. But there was an accident, and he perished. My sister answered an ad for a nanny in Chicago, so we moved. But by the time we got there, the baby died. Now my sister had no job. But we're Irish. We persevered like we always do." She shrugged and splayed her hands out.

Sionn said, "Now that's a sad story. I think we need a song to lift the spirits. What would you like to hear, Mary?"

Mary lifted her head, her smile reappearing. "I remember all the Irish coming across the ocean would gather to sing and share stories in the bowels of the ship. How about Molly Malone?"

Seamus clapped the beat as he and his twin brother sang. Mary joined in.

In Dublin City, where the girls they are so pretty,
'Twas there I first met with sweet Molly Malone;
She drove a wheel-barrow, through streets broad and narrow.
Crying, "Cockles and mussels, alive, alive-o.
Alive, alive o! Alive, alive-o!"
Crying, "Cockles and mussels, alive, alive-o!"

She was a fishmonger, and that was the wonder,
Her father and mother were fishmongers too;
They drove wheel-barrows through streets broad and narrow,
Crying, "Cockles and Mussels, alive, alive-o."

She died of the fever, and nothing could save her.
And that was the end of sweet Molly Malone;
But her ghost drives a barrow, through streets broad and narrow,

Crying, "Cockles and mussels, alive, alive-o."

As the night wore on and the fire burned low, Mary's thoughts turned to happier memories of her sister. She sang an Irish lullaby that Stella had sung to her when she was young. Mary's voice, soft and lilting, carried across the clearing and into the trees beyond.

As the last notes faded away, Mary bid her companions goodnight and made her way to her wagon, glimpsing the glowing eyes of Danu in the dense brush. She whispered, "Good night, Danu." Now that the air was cooler in the higher elevations of the Rocky Mountains, she slept in the wagon. She settled in, wrapping herself in blankets against the chill, her thoughts still full of the memories she had shared around the campfire.

The stars shone overhead, casting a soft light across the clearing. The others talked and laughed, their voices carried on the night air. But for Mary, the lullaby she had sung was enough to soothe her troubled heart, transporting her off to a peaceful sleep.

As the wagon train rumbled into the burgeoning town of Bannack, a surge of excitement filled Mary. The main street, dotted with burgeoning buildings under the brilliant Montana sky, seemed to pulse with life. The sun cast playful shadows, making the windows of the saloon, the general store, and other establishments glint like scattered jewels. Bannack's vibrant energy, so different from the weary trail, was almost tangible, stirring a longing within her to explore every nook and cranny.

Unyoking her oxen, Mary sensed Peter's sudden presence beside her wagon. She always tensed when someone witnessed her handling the yokes—George's recent comments about her strength made her wary of prying eyes. "Sorry, I didn't mean to startle you," Peter said. "Anna mentioned you wanted to check out the town."

Mary ran her hand along her largest oxen, Aengus' coat, feeling the warmth of his body against her palm as she spoke in her mind for him and the other oxen to stay close. "Yes, that'd be great," she replied. "George is mulling over the idea of setting roots here."

Peter glanced at the oxen, then back at Mary. "We'll be heading west from here. Lots of grazing land in a protected valley. You can always join us later." Peter said. "I thought you might wanna go for a ride on Anna's horse."

"Ah," Mary considered for a moment, since she'd only been on a horse once when Tony plucked her out of the Snake River. "I guess. I have never really ridden, but I might as well if you'll help me."

"Don't worry!" Peter smiled. "No wild rides where you're holding on for your life. We'll walk and I'll help you on Anna's horse, Jill. She's a real sweetheart."

"Let's go." Mary made a beeline to Jill, a black and white paint. Peter hoisted Mary up. "You need to swing your leg over."

"Ugh, need some stairs." Mary wrestled her leg over far enough to pull herself upright. "Whew. Thank you, Peter. I didn't realize how hard it is to get on."

Peter headed to his horse, chuckling. "It gets easier. Paints are smaller horses. Perfect for small women." He mounted and led them into town, the sound of the horse's hooves clattering against the ground.

Mary held on tight, afraid she would fall off. Jill followed Peter and his horse, leaving Mary relieved for that. Peter stayed quiet, and Mary noticed a slight tension in the air.

Peter broke the silence at last, his voice solemn. "Anna and I have discussed George's behavior and our worries for you many times. You are welcome to join us."

Mary glanced at Peter out of the corner of her eye, letting go of a heavy sigh. "You know I love you and Anna, but I need to stay with George. He would get himself killed, and I don't want to bring that pain to his brother. I owe it to Henry. I've told you this before." She shrugged. "It is what it is. It will not change."

"Give it some thought, please. We worry about you." Peter said nothing else until they arrived at a supply store, where he hitched both horses and helped Mary off.

"Go explore and meet me here at noon. I promised Anna I wouldn't stay too long." Peter tipped his hat to Mary and entered the store.

Mary scanned the street, the smell of baked bread wafting through the air as she headed towards its source. As she walked along, she heard a faint clatter from the balcony of the brick two-story hotel. Next door was the small bakery that enticed her through the door. As she strolled out, she took a bite out of her pastry, savoring it as the best tasting thing since Independence, Missouri, which seemed long ago. She would love to eat anything other than beans, rice, and bacon.

The odor of cigars and whiskey wafted out of the saloon as she walked past, and she heard the men inside hooting and hollering. Mary licked her fingers when she took another bite. She looked up, mid-lick, to see a table of drunk men grinning back at her. She quickened her pace. A small bank and assayer office got nary a glance from her.

A green dress caught her eye in the window of the next shop. Mary had no power to resist; she walked in. It startled her, as it wasn't like any dress shop in Chicago. The dresses here were calico and utilitarian. She wasn't ready for drabber styles and colors. Her dresses from Chicago were of more vibrant rich colors, like the dress in the window. But she had to admit, she was self-conscious on the trail wearing more expensive dresses. That's what she packed. *Silly girl.*

A woman came over. "Can I help you find something?" She smiled and winked. "Maybe the green dress in the window?" The woman's demeanor was pleasant and warm.

Mary pulled her head back and stuttered, "Oh, I don't need anything right now. We are on the Montana Trail, but considering staying here to sell mining supplies." *But that dress would be more my style.*

"My name is Suzette. If you're staying, welcome to town. If you're not, good luck on the trail. But I hope you're staying all the same. This town needs more women." Suzette had her hair braided into an intricate crown around her head. Mary couldn't imagine having hair that long.

"My name is Mary. Thanks for the welcome." Mary scanned the shop and still her eyes landed on that same dress.

Suzette followed her look and retrieved the garment from its hook in the window. "There is one man selling mining supplies. I bet miners would rather buy from a pretty woman than a bloke. I would bet my bottom dollar on it."

Mary twisted her mouth. "My husband would disagree." Suzette was right, but how would she convince George? And she knew whatever she did, she would use magick. Why not? "If you're right, I'll come back for the dress."

"I'll hold it for you." Suzette placed it on her work area where there laid bobbins of thread, a pair of scissors, and pieces of blue-gray fabric.

Mary said, "How long is your hair? That is a lot of braid!"

Suzette laughed as she placed her hands on her head and then moved one to mid-thigh. "To here. I can't bring myself to cut it. I have to braid it again every few days. It's silly, I know."

Mary wondered how long it would take to grow her hair that long when she saw the sun overhead out the window. She realized she spent all her time in the dress shop. "I have to go meet my friend to head back to camp. It was lovely to meet you. I'll see you soon to get the dress."

"See you soon, Mary." Suzette smiled and waved.

Mary stepped out to a bright sun and put her hand over her eyes. As she retraced her steps to meet Peter, she plotted her strategy on how to convince George to allow her to sell the mining supplies for a few days, demonstrating her sales superiority. There was no way George would win against her.

Peter was loading the horses with provisions when Mary arrived. "Did you get everything you needed, Peter?"

"I did. But prices are high here." Peter pulled the last strap tight and turned to Mary. "Did you get enough exploring done?"

Mary nodded, a determined glint in her eye. "I did. And I think we might stay awhile." Her voice was steady, but inside, the turmoil of her decision churned. She wondered if Bannack could be the fresh start she craved or another chapter in her saga of regret and compromise.

Peter frowned.

Mary said, "Oh, I would love to join you, but we need to make some money and this is a good a place as any to do it. That much I learned while exploring the town."

"We worry, that's all. But you're a strong woman." Peter's face relaxed some but still showed lines of worry.

"I'm lucky to have such great friends. This journey has taught me that is worth so much. Ready to hoist the biggest load on the poor beast." Mary faced the horse, getting ready for Peter's boost. As her waist expanded over the last month, she became self-conscious of her weight.

Peter approached Mary from behind, putting his hands around her waist. "Ready, go." He hoisted her up, and she leaned across the saddle. *There has to be an easier way to get on.* She swung her leg over and arranged herself upright. She blew out a raspberry.

Peter mounted his horse and steered them toward camp.

"Sorry, Jill," Mary said while patting the horse's neck.

As they rode back to the wagon train, Mary's thoughts wandered to George. Could she reshape their future in this new town? Or was she bound to the cycle of his whims and follies? Bannack represented a crossroads, not just geographically, but in her life's journey—a place where the promise of gold and the allure of new beginnings met the harsh realities of her choices.

Chapter Eighteen

Mary approached George, eating his breakfast atop a rickety wooden box. Sunbeams caressed his features, casting a warm glow over his strong jawline and chiseled cheekbones. *Are you mad? He's not Henry!* She dismissed such thoughts and focused on the pressing matter at hand.

"What would you say to a challenge? You and I," she said, her voice steady and pitched low, lips pulled to the side.

One of George's eyebrows arched, and a smirk tugged at his lips. "Ha. You believe you can outdo me?" An arrogant sneer deformed his face.

Fire surged within Mary, but she quelled it, refusing to set anything aflame. "The challenge is who can sell the most supplies. You sell for a few days, and then I take my turn."

As she awaited his response, Mary cleaned the breakfast dishes. George's mind was as speedy as a snail. She wondered if his bravado masked a dearth of intellect.

George stretched when he left his perch atop the box. "Before you challenge me to sell mining supplies, consider your lack of knowledge in mining. Know your product, as my father always said. This will be effortless for me. I'll start today, and you in two days' time. But I don't want you anywhere near while I'm selling. Get lost."

Mary stifled a laugh. George knew nothing of mining beyond purchasing the wares.

She planned to profit while the challenge forced George to toil for a day. She had secured Suzette's permission to offer tarot readings outside her shop. Mary departed without a word, her reticule swinging from her wrist.

Throughout the day, as Mary mulled over the challenge, she worried whether agreeing to it had been a mistake. She endeavored to focus on her tarot readings; the cards making a soft whisper as she shuffled them, their placement on a three-legged stool done with steady hands.

When she returned to the wagon in the early evening to prepare George's dinner, Mary was giddy finding all the supplies intact. She bit her tongue to keep from provoking George's ire. As she cooked, apprehension gnawed at her, fearing he might end the challenge.

George finished his meal in silence, not noticing she didn't eat. His departing footsteps echoed down the dusty street. She crossed her arms and shook her head as she watched him go. He was ever a vexation, and she relished the solitude.

While she strolled toward the diner, Mary's gaze fell upon the sun's descent behind the mountains, casting an orange glow on the town. For a fleeting moment, her troubles dissipated as she admired the breathtaking sight.

The bustling restaurant teemed with miners and townsfolk. Mary settled at a small table in a corner, ordering a satisfying meal of fried chicken, potatoes, and green beans. She savored each bite, gratitude swelling for the tasty food.

The food brought on homesickness, thoughts drifting to Henry and Stella. She yearned for their presence and pondered whether they still missed her as well. Henry had been her unwavering supporter, even in her darkest hours. Stella possessed a compassionate heart, ever ready to lend an ear or a comforting shoulder.

Her mother's tragic fate wormed its way into her consciousness. Mary's heart throbbed as she contemplated what had befallen her family. The townspeople had accused her mother of witchcraft. As a child, Mary hadn't understood the enormity of the events, but the memory of her mother in an Irish jail cell sobbing for her children brought a chill to her spine.

Mary shook her head, determined to cast aside the haunting memories. Dwelling on the past offered no solace. Her focus must be on the present in Bannack, a town teeming with opportunities.

The following day, Mary found herself immersed in a reading, her cards laid out before her, when a group of women intruded upon her session. Their voices pierced the air, brimming with judgment, and their intense gazes bore into her. She tried to ignore them, but their cries kept growing louder, their shrillness ringing through the air.

Suzette, the shop's owner, appeared uneasy. "Mary, perhaps you should move. Try the blacksmith's shop. His dark skin unnerves them. It will stop their interference."

Mary shrugged, her eyes scanning the surroundings. "But no one else would venture there either."

"They are merely the church ladies," Suzette said, rolling her eyes. "The others hold no such judgment."

"They *are* driving customers away. We'll talk later," Mary said, collecting her cards and departing down the boardwalk. The women refrained from following her, yet their resentment and disapproval lingered in the air, weighing upon her from a distance.

As the rest of the day unfolded, Mary endeavored to disregard the hateful glares from across the street. She recognized some individuals would forever resist accepting her for who she was. Yet, their approval held no sway over her happiness. She needed only herself, her newfound companions, and the magick coursing through her veins.

The jingling of coins within her purse sent George spiraling into a fit of rage when she returned to the wagon. He cursed and kicked up dust, resembling a wild animal. Mary sighed, rolling her eyes at his petulant display, pondering when he would learn to rein in his temper. She prepared dinner, clanging the metal spoon against the pot to drown out George's continuing diatribes.

Once George had eaten, he departed without a word, leaving Mary to clean and take stock of their supplies. She knew he would never offer an honest account of what he had sold. Thus, she recorded every item, lamenting that she had not done so from the very beginning. She had little hope that George would come to recognize the truth of their financial predicament, as his muddled mind made such clarity seem out of reach.

The next morning, George flexed his knuckles, his eyes cold and flinty as he offered a mere "Good luck" before sauntering down the street to indulge in his vices. Their fate hinged on her ability to generate enough sales. Failure would leave them burdened with a bar tab they could ill afford.

Mary had altered her finest dress to conceal her burgeoning belly while accentuating her blossoming bosom. She arranged picks, shovels, and gold pans around the wagon, weaving an illusion of prosperity. Perched atop the box, a glimpse of her boot peeking from beneath her dress hem, she awaited potential customers.

Soon enough, a man approached, followed by another, captivated by the enchanting aura she exuded. Mary employed her magical allure to coax them into purchases.

Mary grimaced and shook her head as a man attempted to use a nugget to pay for his purchase. "Hmm." It lacked the familiar resonance she had sensed from other pieces. Something felt off about it—perhaps it was gold-plated lead or fool's gold or she was tired from all the enchanting. She knew better than to accept it without conviction. "This isn't real. I won't take it," she said, her voice firm.

The man leaned in, his expression hardened. "It's real."

Mary pressed her lips together, her eyes narrowed. She stood her ground, crossing her arms. "It's not, and that's final. Go to the assayer and get cash."

Fury etched across his face as he stormed off. How had she discerned the falseness of the nugget?

As dusk settled, George remained absent. Mary safeguarded some of the money she had earned, shielding their future from the grip of his drinking. They required a safety net to endure, and she would not allow George's vices to unravel their chances.

George returned to the wagon, his gaze sweeping over its contents, resulting in a frown. He stomped over to the box by the fire and slumped, emitting a heavy sigh. Mary served him dinner, but the only sounds that punctuated the silence were the clinking of utensils against his plate. When he finished, he extended his hand, palm upturned, as though expecting something. Mary reached into her pocket, retrieving the money she held aside for him, and watched as the bills vanished into his grasp. He departed without a word.

"Remember, we need some of that to buy supplies," Mary called after him, but he continued walking, disregarding her plea. She exhaled an enormous sigh, her gaze fixated on the small pile of coins within her palm.

The next morning, the sun bathed the landscape in radiant light, though a crispness in the air hinted at the encroaching change of season. Stepping out of the wagon, Mary discovered George dozing on the box leaned against the wagon, a fresh shiner marring his face. She giggled, pondering who he had riled this time. *Must be his charming personality and fine manner of speaking.*

After tending to George's needs and sending him on his way, Mary set about arranging her wares for another day of sales. Men, she realized, were susceptible to manipulation—her successes from the previous days attested to that. Why had she not used her charms without a potion on everyone before? Yes, it tired her, but the results would alter her life's trajectory.

The day unfolded without incident, yet proved fruitful when almost all the remaining supplies found eager buyers. Now, she needed to persuade George to invest time and money into restocking. She harbored little doubt that the proceeds from the earlier days had vanished, squandered on his drinking.

An idea took shape in her mind. Maybe she should use her enchantments on George, as she had the past two days. She tucked away the money from her upsells, ensuring it remained within reach. At least they could buy some supplies.

When George wandered back in time for dinner, Mary unleashed her charm. Her words oozed like honey, her tone disarming. "You only need half, right? That way, we can go to Butte to buy more supplies. You are going to be a rich mining supplier."

George tilted his head to one side while pursing his lips. "What?"

Mary maintained her poised stance, her head tilted, radiating an air of confidence. "Save half for supplies, and the rest you can indulge yourself. We shall rise as prosperous mining suppliers," she said, her smile stretching wider, her fists on her hips.

A flicker of understanding dawned in George's eyes. "Sure. Give me half."

Mary relinquished half of the day's proceeds she had prepared for him. She took deep, satisfying breaths, knowing she had secured the lion's share to safeguard their business.

As George departed, Mary settled into another tranquil evening, feeling the cool breeze on her skin and the warmth of the setting sun.

Mary strained her ears, listening for any sign of George's approach. She had prepared the wagon and oxen, its wheels creaking in anticipation. Exhaustion weighed upon her, draining her of the strength to perform the simplest tasks. But they couldn't delay any longer; they had to leave for Butte before the sun rose. Supplies were a lifeline, their means of survival.

"Mary!" George's words slurred, his unsteady footsteps drawing closer. He attempted to climb into the wagon but tumbled backward onto his backside. "Damn it!"

Mary stuck her head out the back of the wagon, glanced around, hoping his commotion wouldn't attract unwanted attention. She leaned over the back of the wagon, snatched the waistband of George's trousers, and dragged him up the ladder. He pushed her away and, in doing so, lost his balance, falling in. She plopped on the wooden chest containing their dwindling food supplies and waited, her heart pounding in her ears. A bead of sweat formed on her upper lip, despite the coolness of the night air.

In the wagon's aisle, where Mary kept the floor unobstructed, George flailed his arms and mouthed incomprehensible words. He bowed his head, taking a deep breath, as if trying to resurrect his own thoughts. When he raised his head, he said, "Need supplies. Save half for supplies. Gotta go." Then he slumped over, succumbing to a deep snore, filling the wagon with the smell of beer.

Mary bowed her head, weariness tugging at her soul. Relieved that her magick stuck for George to remember they needed supplies, she was ready to depart for Butte, a day and a half trip. She clambered out of the back of the wagon and chuckled as she retracted the ladder, trying to avoid knocking George on the head. The oxen were ready to go, their patient loyalty clear as she moved from one to the next, whispering their names and stroking their necks.

With a jerk, the wagon set into motion; the oxen finding their rhythm along the empty streets of Bannack. Mary regretted not taking the time to tell her friends she had made in this raucous and vibrant town that she would be back soon. She had found a place for herself here, and the yearning to return already tugged at her heart. But for now, she needed to replenish supplies before she could come back.

The dark expanse stretched before her as they ventured north, heading toward Butte. Beyond the last building of the town, all she encountered was a black abyss. How would she navigate such obscurity to find their destination? She scanned the surroundings, straining to discern any semblance of a path. With only a few hours of sleep, she questioned how far she could travel without collapsing.

She focused on the simple act of putting one foot in front of the other, allowing it to become an instinctive rhythm.

In this inky shroud, she lost track of their progress, unable to discern if she veered off course or approached an unseen precipice. The moon, a mere sliver, hung low in the sky, casting no illumination upon the land. Above her, a vast ceiling of thousands upon thousands of stars twinkled, as they had on countless nights along the trail. Surrounded by emptiness, her own ragged breath and the oxen's hooves echoed in her ears.

One foot in front of the other, she pressed onward, her oxen displaying trepidation at their uncertain path. They communicated their doubts, but their unwavering loyalty kept them in line. Her life had taken an unforeseen turn, relying on the company of four majestic beasts in the dead of night, all because she had feared a conventional existence. Now, she possessed only those four oxen, an unborn child, and an unruly, petulant man-child. She sighed as she looked around.

In the distance, a faint flickering caught her attention, a distant fire she yearned to be Tony's, accompanied by his reassuring presence. She pushed that thought away. She approached on the lookout, aware that anyone could lurk in this wilderness. Outlaw road agents presented the grimmest possibility, as their encounter would be certain to end in robbery and death.

She had no choice but to press forward, praying that her direction remained true. Without discernible landmarks, she relied on the rhythm of her footsteps.

As she trudged onward, the sound of horse hooves echoed toward her. She hoped the darkness would shroud her from their view, but the jolting movement of the wagon might betray their presence. She urged Niall to slow their pace tapping his neck. Her body tensed. She held her breath. *Please pass by.*

Closer they came, the rising sun cast a faint light that turned the surrounding darkness to shades of gray and black. Still unable to distinguish their approaching figures, she knew their encounter was inevitable. To remain unseen seemed an implausible feat. Once again, she tapped Niall, further reducing their speed.

Mary halted for a moment, waiting for the back of the wagon to come to her. With a quick grasp of its edge, she hopped onto the step, relieved to find a secure foothold. She struggled to lift herself, her weary body burdened by the weight she carried within. She hoisted herself over the back, sliding into the wagon's interior. As she retrieved the rifle, she could feel the cold metal against her skin and her fingers closed around a handful of rounds, which she concealed in her pocket.

As she prepared to descend, the wagon halted. A man on horseback appeared at the wagon's rear, a pistol aimed in her direction.

"Get out!" the man yelled, his horse agitated as he struggled to rein it in.

In order to buy herself some time, she set the rifle on the edge of the wagon, extended the ladder and descended step by step, maintaining her composure. Her gaze scanned the surroundings. Three more men loomed, their forms somewhat discernible. There could be others lurking nearby—beyond a doubt, outlaws. The worst-case scenario had manifested before her eyes.

Desperate to divert their attention, she raised her hands, hoping her frail condition would be apparent. "I possess nothing of value. We lost it all in Bannack," she said, dropping to her knees, "Please, show mercy."

"Hey, we've got a pregnant one here. What do you think? She's got nothing." The man sneered, dismounted and advanced toward her. He seized her chin, forcing her to rise, tightening his grip when she resisted. "Feisty ones are the best. Nothing like a good fight."

Mary felt the heat rise within her, a primal force responding to her will. She focused her attention on the man's boots while commanding his horse to run. The horse unleashed its untamed spirit, reared, and galloped into the distance.

"Hey, get back here! Dammit!" The man released his hold on Mary, shoving her aside. "Ow! My feet! They're burning!" He sank to the ground, yanking off his burning boots and socks. In the pale light of the impending sunrise, his feet appeared red, and he blew on them for relief.

Another man approached, and Mary directed her power toward his rifle, intensifying its heat.

He dropped the weapon, his hand recoiling from the scorching metal. "What the hell!" He dismounted, attempted to retrieve the rifle, but its searing heat thwarted his efforts. Frustrated, he kicked it away.

Mary commanded his horse to flee, and it took off in a full gallop. She then focused on the man's boots, causing him to writhe in pain on the ground.

Two more men on horseback emerged. One of them said, "Quit playing around! Get up! Get your horses. We'll finish this. Useless fools."

Mary redirected her focus to the tops of their saddles, grinning as discomfort consumed them. Until it didn't. The lack of sleep sapped her strength, her magick dimmed. Panic set in, further clouding her concentration. Visions of potential calamities swirled in her mind, her grip on her magick gone. Her breathing quickened. They approached closer.

The crack of a gunshot shattered the air, and one man collapsed from his horse, thudding onto the ground. The other wheeled his mount around, only to meet the same fate. Both horses followed the path of the others. Two more shots rang out, ending the desperate crawl of the remaining men trying to escape. Their lifeless bodies would provide sustenance for Mary's cougar, who she sensed lurking a mile behind in the shadows.

Did George have the rifle? Mary risked a glance behind the wagon, her eyes discerning another man on horseback. Who was he? As daylight grew, his figure came into focus, and relief washed over her. Tony! She exhaled, the tension that gripped her dissipating. Grasping the corner of the wagon for support, she maneuvered hand over hand, traversing the perimeter. Fatigue overwhelmed her, and she crumpled to the ground before reaching her oxen.

Tony leaped off his horse, rushing to her side. "Mary, are you alright? Did they hurt you?"

A cascade of emotions flooded over her as she looked at his familiar face, reminiscent of the time he saved her from the river's clutches. Once again, he had rescued her, and tears of relief streamed on her cheeks. "I'm fine. You arrived just in time." She sobbed in heaves, releasing the pent-up fear and anguish.

He embraced her, cradling her, offering solace as she poured out her anguish. He stroked her head and whispered, "You are safe now. Shh."

When her sobs subsided, her body drained of energy, she said, "You have saved me once more."

"I'd left my campsite when I saw them heading for a wagon. Their horses took off. Strange. Where's George?" Tony asked.

Mary gestured toward the wagon.

Tony chuckled. "I had hoped you had left him behind. It might have been for the best."

Her shoulders slumped. While he spoke the truth, leaving George behind was out of the question. "I am doing my best. We're headed to Butte for supplies."

Tony carried her toward the back of the wagon. "I'll guide you to where I camped last night, then you can rest and recover before continuing to Butte. Get some sleep." Once Mary settled in the wagon, he hoisted the ladder, ensuring it wouldn't disturb George.

The wagon lurched forward, and Mary wrapped herself in a blanket, seeking comfort in its warmth. As her exhaustion overtook her, she found comfort that Tony, her unexpected savior again, would be a light in the darkness of the uncertain future that lay ahead.

Chapter Nineteen

THE GOLDEN GLOW OF the morning sun filtered through the canvas of the wagon, warming Mary's face as she emerged from her brief slumber. A vivid memory of the pistol pointed at her set her heart to racing, her breath quickening.

Mary crawled to the end of her narrow mattress, peering out the back of the wagon. The sight and sound of a babbling brook, its waters cascading in a soothing rhythm, brought a measure of solace. Her cougar rested in the dense brush on the other side of the stream, adding to her relief. For a fleeting moment, she closed her eyes, offering gratitude for surviving the attack.

Careful not to disturb George, Mary slid off the bed and stepped around his sleeping form. But as she made her way past his slumbering figure, George's foot jabbed at her ankle, his head raised. "Mary, why aren't you fixing my breakfast?" he yelled. "I need coffee!" A resentful groan escaped his lips before he let his head drop back to the floor. "Ow!"

Startled, Mary leaped away to avoid another unexpected strike. Irritation etched deep lines on her forehead as her head fell back in exasperation. "Why didn't you save us from those outlaws earlier this morning? Too drunk, as usual."

George leaned over on his elbow while trying to strike her again with his foot. "Well, you're not dead, are you? Where's my coffee?"

A familiar voice from outside the wagon interrupted them. "Get your own coffee, George!" Tony yelled.

George puffed out his chest, his anger simmering. His voice hissed like a deadly dose of venom, "What's *he* doing here?"

"*He* saved us from the outlaws." Mary's face dropped as she retorted, "*He's* the only reason you're able to have coffee this morning." She gave him a dismissive gesture as she put down the ladder and climbed out of the wagon, leaving George to fume.

Tony was a vision, sitting on a weathered log by the fire, drinking his coffee. His rugged countenance emanated an air of belonging to the outdoors. Despite his outward masculinity, his voice carried a softness. The intensity of his blue piercing eyes, deep pools brimming with mystery, drew her in like an irresistible current. Mary fought the tingling sensation below her growing belly, pushing such thoughts aside. Coffee was the only thing she should accept from him. *Stop!*

"I can't thank you enough for your help this morning," she said.

Tony reached into his pack and withdrew an extra mug. "It's nothing. I'm doing what any real man would do." He offered her a knowing wink, gesturing towards the wagon. "Care for some coffee, Mary?"

"I need strong coffee after this morning. Thank you again." When she took the mug from him, their fingers brushed, igniting an electric thrill that coursed through her. Mary took a steadying breath, redirecting her focus to the crystal-clear brook, its glistening waters mirroring the rosy hues of the sunrise. The crisp air, infused with the invigorating scent of pine, rejuvenated her weary spirit.

Mary rose and smiled. "I'll fix us some breakfast. I'm sure you must be hungry."

"A hot breakfast is something I can't refuse," Tony replied, his grin as warm as the morning sunlight. He raked his hand in a carefree motion through his tousled mane. "I was going to chew on some jerky, but your cooking is too good to pass up."

"After we eat, George and I will make our way to Butte," she said.

Tony shook his head. "I can escort you. The territory is dangerous. Well, you found that out yourself."

Mary sighed. "Oh no, aren't you heading to Peter and Anna's place?"

"I am, but they'd want me to lend you a hand."

George stomped around the wagon. "We don't need any help. I can get us to Butte."

"Then I'll follow you," Tony replied.

George puffed out his chest. "The hell you will!"

Tony winked at her, but said nothing more. Mary nodded her head, thankful he didn't provoke George further. It would only lead to trouble. She handed George his breakfast, and he snatched it from her. She threw up her hands.

George stormed off to eat by the nearby brook, plopping on a rock a bit too hard. "Dammit!"

Mary hoped the tranquil melody of the stream would soothe his volatile temperament for the journey to Butte.

Tony shook his head. "How do you do it? He's like that every day, but you remain calm with him. If I were in your shoes, I would have punched him."

"George's nothing more than a child trapped in a man's body." Mary whispered to prevent George from hearing her. "I treat him like one. It works better. Or it seems to. I'm too tired to get upset over his incessant complaints. They seem to flow one after another, as if life has been unfair to him."

Tony leaned closer, whispering, "Come with me once you've restocked your supplies."

Mary tilted her head, a resigned sigh eluding her lips. Tony never quit. "You think so, do you? And I suppose you, Peter, and Anna think I should leave George in Butte as well?"

Tony nodded, his smile unwavering. "Sounds like an excellent idea to me."

Mary handed him a plate of food. "I'll try to persuade George to make the journey to Bitterroot Valley instead of going back to Bannack."

Yet, whether Mary could sway George's stubbornness was no longer the primary question. The genuine question rested within her own heart. Bannack or Bitterroot Valley? What did she desire?

The journey to Butte was a taut, silent affair; unspoken tension charged the air. Tony trailed behind at a distance, far enough back to appease George, but Mary could still see his silhouette on the horizon.

Mary desired to retrieve the hidden money, secure supplies, and make their way back to Bannack. But her mind churned while calculating her best options.

The Bitterroot Valley was a venture of the unknown except for the three friends she had there who were people she could trust. Were there enough miners to sustain their livelihood? What would it take to stay well-supplied? The round trip to the valley would devour almost two weeks.

A swift journey to Bannack and back would need only three days. Of course, that was barring any outlaw encounters. On the negative side, Bannack had another mining outfitter, making them keep their prices low. The weight of the decision bore upon her, an unbearable burden that tormented her.

The snow-capped peaks of the Rockies provided an awe-inspiring backdrop to the thriving community of Butte. A wide and dusty main street bustled with horse-drawn carriages, wagons, and pedestrians. Conversations blended into a chaotic symphony, accompanied by the rhythmic clopping of hooves and the occasional clang of tools from nearby mines.

Tony hollered to a man carrying a bag over his shoulder, "Hey, where can I get mining supplies?"

The man nodded his head back. "Two blocks that way. They got everything."

Tony tipped his hat. "Thanks."

Navigating through the lively thoroughfare, they located the supply store, passing a saloon and a couple of boarding houses along the way. Mary climbed into the wagon, full of anticipation, as she reached for the hidden money. But her heart skipped a beat when her fingers found only emptiness. Panic surged. Had she misplaced it? She slid her hands under the mattress, searching the entire length and width. Her efforts yielded no results. She opened boxes and chests, tearing through the wagon in despair. Tears blurred her vision. It couldn't be. George must have found the money.

"George!" She scrambled out of the wagon. She scanned the street, her eyes darting from one figure to another. But he was nowhere to be seen. "George!"

Tony emerged from the supply store, concern etched across his face. "George went up the road. What's the matter?"

Stress spilled from Mary's voice like a river over its banks. "I can't find the money we made in Bannack! I don't know what to do!" She buried her head in Tony's chest, allowing herself a moment of vulnerability, releasing a flood of tears. Reason returned, and she pulled away. She raked her sleeves across her face. *This is wrong, so wrong.*

"We'll find George," Tony said. "If we start now, we might catch him before he squanders the money."

Mary nodded, wiping her eyes again. Tony's words brought a glimmer of hope. They had to locate George.

In the heart of Butte, Mary stood amidst the bustling streets, her eyes scanning for any sign of George. She clung to a fragile thread of optimism, hoping George would reappear, explaining his and the money's sudden disappearance. The weight of their dwindling funds and uncertain future pressed upon her shoulders, threatening to crush her resolve.

Tony darted into the nearest saloon. His quick return, accompanied by a despondent expression, announced the lack of favorable news. The pattern repeated itself at each establishment they visited until a bartender informed them that George had been there. But he had departed, seeking something unknown.

Mary's heart sank, her worst fears realized. The race against time to find George before he frittered away their earnings consumed her thoughts. The dream she held dear, the dream of building a better life, slipped away like sand through her fingers.

Mary and Tony scoured the boardwalk, their eyes scanning alleys, their footsteps quickening. But George remained elusive, leaving no other trace of his whereabouts. Night was falling.

After what felt like an eternity, Tony emerged from a saloon, eyebrows drawn together, his mouth pursed. Mary's heart sank as she recognized the somber tidings he carried. She braced herself for the blow she knew was coming.

"I found him at a poker table. He gambled it all away, Mary," Tony said, his tone soft but heavy. His gaze lowered. "I wasn't able to drag him away. Once he had no money left, he gambled the oxen and lost. The man who won the oxen intends to claim them in the morning. We must leave town. Now." He released a heavy sigh. "Don't wait for George."

Mary's breath caught in her throat, her mind struggling to process the full extent of George's actions. All this time, she had believed he had been drinking. The revelation that he would take their last hope and blow it away on the turn of a card dealt a devastating blow to her heart.

An emotional tornado swept through her—betrayal, wrath, and despondency. The realization that they now faced not only poverty but also the inability to continue their journey struck her hard.

Then, from the depths of the saloon, George stumbled out, reeking of liquor and wearing a foolish grin.

Mary rushed over to him, rage rising. "George, where's the money? What have you done with it?"

George shrugged, his grin fading. "Money? What money?"

"The money we earned in Bannack, you fool! I had it hidden in the wagon. Now it's gone. What did you do with it?"

"I didn't take no money," George slurred. "Ain't seen no money. You musta lost it yerself."

She knew George too well—when liquor flowed through his veins, lies dripped from his tongue. And now, amid the alcohol's embrace, deceit permeated his every word.

Mary clenched her fists while watching the wood of the boardwalk smoke. But she didn't care right now. It could all burn. She took a menacing step toward him, but Tony intervened, placing a restraining hand on her arm. "He's in no shape to talk sense now," Tony whispered. "Let's get him in the wagon."

Mary sighed, realizing the truth in Tony's words. They each grasped one of George's limp arms and dragged him down the street under the cloak of darkness. She paused as the thought of leaving him entered her mind. Tony stopped. Could she live with a broken promise? Head down, she yanked on her burden until they dumped him in the wagon.

Spiriting away before a gambler could claim her oxen, Mary's heart burned, as did her shattered hopes and dreams. A thought intruded. What would her mother do? Stella always cautioned her about their mother, making her dismissed that notion.

As the wagon wheels crunched on the dusty road due west from the town, Mary's mind swirled. The possibility of returning to Bannack now seemed remote, an unattainable mirage. The road to Peter and Anna's protected valley stretched before them, burdened by the weight of their meager provisions and no mining equipment to sell. Her predicament overwhelmed her, casting doubt on the judgment of her journey and the choices that had led her to this desolate crossroad.

CHAPTER TWENTY

THE SUN PLUNGED BEHIND the jagged horizon, painting the valley with fiery strokes of orange and crimson. As the first stars of the evening winked at Mary in the darkening sky, the high mountain air ran its fingers down her back and up her sleeves.

After a meager dinner, Mary scrambled into the wagon. She tossed her satchel on her bed and rummaged through it, searching for the two things she valued more than anything else: her mother's necklace and her grimoire. A simple spell that only she knew hid them from sight. Stella had warned her the necklace was too dangerous in anyone else's hands, even Mary's. *But I'm entitled to my mother's legacy, aren't I?*

Mary whispered a spell under her breath.

Visibility, I now bestow,
With this spell, let it show,
So mote it be!

There they were, a silver trinity knot pendant hanging on a fine silver chain, and her mother's grimoire, a leather-bound tome full of secrets and mysteries. She fastened the necklace around her neck, feeling its coolness against her skin.

She stared at the worn book, wondering what it held. The responsibilities of survival and travel gave her no time to read it earlier. But now she felt a surge of curiosity and hope. She thumbed through the yellowed pages, but the low light made it impossible to read the fading lettering. She would have to wait for better light during the day.

Her mother was a powerful witch. Maybe she could find something there that could help her with her current problems, something that might change her fate.

Before she left the wagon, she spoke the spell to hide the necklace from view.

Shroud this necklace in shadows deep,
Hidden from view, it's secrets to keep.
So mote it be!

Mary sat by the campfire, her eyes downcast, and lips pursed. Her slender fingers traced the delicate lines of her mother's charmed necklace, the bumps of the sapphire, ruby, and emerald. The cherished heirloom hung heavy on her neck, as if it carried the weight of her troubles. After uttering the incantation, it became invisible to anyone else. No questions to answer.

Tony sat beside Mary. "Mary, look at the surrounding beauty! The mountains stretch as far as the eye can see, endless possibilities. Imagine the gold and silver there. Our new destination will bring you a fresh start, you'll see."

Mary managed a weak smile, her thoughts consumed by the harsh reality of their circumstances. "Tony, I appreciate your optimism, but we barely have enough to get by."

George, his perpetual scowl present, sat across the fire, his eyes avoiding Mary's gaze. He shifted off a rock onto the ground. "Mary's always whining," George interjected. "She sold all the supplies and now we have none to sell."

Mary's eyes narrowed, a flicker of rage flashed within her. "George! You gambled away all the money *I* earned selling the supplies in Bannack. And you gambled away the oxen. Now we're thieves of our own oxen. Our future, our dreams, all gone because of your foolishness." Under her breath, she said, "Idiot."

Tony sighed and reached out to grasp Mary's hand. "I'm here for you."

Mary's heart ached at Tony's words, his steadfast support a glimmer of solace in her turbulent world. She squeezed his hand. "Thank you, Tony. Your presence gives me strength." For the rest of the evening, Mary forced a tight-lipped smile, but remained silent. She wrapped her shawl tight around her shoulders while her thoughts focused on the dwindling food supplies. She didn't aspire to be a charity case for her friends, Peter, and Anna, when she reached their place.

The next morning, Tony led on horseback with Mary and George walking beside their prairie schooner. By midmorning, Mary took time to ride in the wagon. She retrieved her mother's grimoire from the satchel. She was sure the book held the key to unlocking her potential, the spells, and knowledge within, offering a glimmer of hope.

Mary's fingers traced the well-worn yellowed pages. Her lips mouthed the incantations she read. She sought guidance, a solution improving their fragile existence without exposing her gifts. Many of her mother's spells were out of reach for her since she didn't have all the elemental magick powers like her mother did.

Her mother encased items in large drops of water and wondered if it was possible to drown someone this way. Oh, her mother had an evil heart. But Mary would think the same if she had the water gift.

What she got as she read page after page was a deeper understanding of her mother and herself. Mother and daughter were one in mind and manner.

She chuckled when her mother talked about her familiar, a magpie named Ean. If only she could have a relationship with Danu like that.

As the day of travel ended, the sun sank below the mountain, casting a cascade of colors across the prairie valley. Determined, Mary would face the trials ahead, both inner and outer, with the strength of her hidden powers. Her mother's grimoire gave her the confidence she needed in these dark times.

When they entered the Bitterroot Valley, the tension in Mary's neck and along her shoulders loosened. What would she have done without Tony? She knew she couldn't have navigated the treacherous roads alone, and George was useless.

After a while, they arrived at Tin Creek, a pitiful excuse for a town. It comprised nothing more than bunches of scattered tents along the muddy banks of the Bitterroot River. So many! Had none of them yet staked a claim? If they had, they would be at their plots, guarding them against intruders.

Mary didn't spot a single permanent building in sight. How would they make a living here? Hope slipped away.

Beyond the tents, lush green grasses, and wildflowers adorned the wide expanse of the valley, forming a vibrant tapestry of colors. Majestic cottonwood and ponderosa pine trees lined the meandering

Bitterroot River, offering shade and enhancing the scenic beauty of the surroundings. The strong flowing river was a relentless symphony, an orchestra of liquid power, as it surged and roared, conducting its own magnificent performance.

To the west, the mountain range stood tall and rugged, cloaked in dense forests and dotted with deep canyons and granite peaks. On the eastern side, gentler rolling hills and arid mountains unfolded, revealing open meadows and rocky outcrops. Above them, an eagle soared high in the sky, its wings slicing through the air.

Mary selected what she believed to be a favorable spot. She unhitched the oxen and allowed them to graze along the riverbank. A nearby water source would be a relief.

Tony had informed them about Hamilton, a larger town to the north, and Missoula, a day's journey beyond that. With a farewell, he departed for Peter and Anna's ranch, where his job waited. Their homestead lay nearby, where their cattle roamed the lush grasslands.

As Mary prepared dinner over the crackling fire, she turned to George and asked, "When do you think you should go to Hamilton to purchase some supplies?"

George scoffed, tossing his head back and rolling his eyes. "You never stop, do you?"

Mary clenched her teeth, suppressing the urge to slap him. If she weren't pregnant, she would have left him behind to rot and ventured to Hamilton on her own. But since that wasn't an option, she had to prod him into doing something useful. "It'll take you a day, maybe less, once we buy a horse. Without supplies, we'll starve."

George shot her a venomous glare as he rose and paced around the wagon. "As if I'm not aware of that!"

Mary tried to hold back a laugh, but it slipped out. If anyone would starve, it would be him if she abandoned him to his own devices. The thought tempted her to leave him behind and seek refuge at Peter and Anna's place. But she had made a vow, and she wasn't one to break it, even if it meant being bound to a lazy, self-centered man-child for the rest of her life. Mary sat to eat a plate of beans and biscuits in silence, assuming George would join her if he was hungry. But it wouldn't hurt her feelings if he didn't.

When he circled back around from the other side of the wagon, he said, "Why didn't you tell me the food was ready? Taking care of yourself and not your husband?"

"You walked away," Mary said as she continued eating.

George snatched his plate and moved several feet away. He sat on the ground, facing away from Mary. "You were the one who insisted on getting married. Therefore, it's your responsibility to take care of me."

Mary chuckled to herself, glancing over at the grown man she had pledged to care for. Children grew and stood on their own two feet, but this one never quite took flight. George would stay a spoiled one until the end, she was certain of it. Sometimes, in the darkest corners of her mind, she entertained the idea of hastening his demise. But she buried those thoughts as soon as they came.

Even at a young age, she had harbored such notions, but she knew better than to act on them. When her mother perished at the stake, she understood the dire consequences of embracing those dark desires. Stella's reminders of their mother's horrific fate struck fear in Mary's heart. The thoughts found their way into her mind during the day and invaded her dreams at night.

George tossed his plate near the fire. "Fine," he snapped. "Just fine. I'll go tomorrow. At least then I won't have to listen to you. Hand me the money I didn't find. I know you have more."

Mary rolled her eyes and handed him the money she had borrowed from Tony. She wouldn't tell him she borrowed it, since she knew that would set him off. The fear he would drink or gamble it away made her sweat. But going with him wouldn't help keep it safe as she learned in Butte. "There isn't much left, thanks to you."

George snatched the money. "Good luck staying safe without my protection."

Mary snickered. "That's funny!"

A man approached, hesitating for a moment before addressing George, "Do you have a claim yet?"

The mustached man sported a dirty white shirt, a red plaid vest, and gray trousers, supported by black leather suspenders. His black frock coat appeared dusty but not worn. He didn't seem like a miner, but a man of means. Mary had a favorable impression that he was an honest man, much like Tony. George needed that kind of influence.

George made a face. "No."

"Well," the man said, "I thought that if you needed to file a claim, we could travel to Hamilton together. It's safer on the road when we travel as a group." He turned, as if preparing to leave.

Mary said, "Wait, we don't have a claim, but we have some business in Hamilton."

The man halted and turned back. "So you might want some company, then?"

Mary nodded. "Yes."

George interjected, "No."

Mary shot George a disdainful look and smiled at the man. "Yes, we do. I'll see you when you return." She rose to her feet and walked toward the man. "Might as well get acquainted with a future customer."

She extended her hand. "I'm Mary, and this is George, my husband."

The man shook her hand. "My name is Jack. Jack Logan. Nice to meet you folks." He glanced at George. "I'm trying my hand at mining." He gestured to his attire. "Used to run a bar in Missoula." He shrugged. "You know, when you see your customers making more money than you, you do what they're doing."

At the mention of a bar, George's eyes gleamed and a wide grin spread across his face. "Well, Jack," he said, "let's get going then." He turned to Mary, looking smug. "I'm taking this one to carry the supplies." He grabbed Niall's reins and attempted to pull him along, but the stubborn ox refused to budge.

Mary sighed and whispered into Niall's ear while stroking his neck. The ox ceased its resistance against George. She observed them walking north toward Hamilton until she could see them no more. Tony had said it was reachable in a day by horse, but she didn't expect to see them for a few days. It would give her time to rearrange the wagon for a more permanent living arrangement and continue her study of her mother's grimoire.

Tin Creek, devoid of a bar, seemed like a better place for George. With fewer opportunities to get into trouble, perhaps he would become more focused on the business side of life. But Mary doubted it. George had a knack for attracting trouble. And she sent him off alone with a stranger. What was she thinking?

Chapter Twenty-One

THE MORNING SUN CAST a golden glow over the landscape as Mary stepped outside her wagon. She rested her hands on her hips and gazed out at the endless wilderness
before her. The meandering Bitterroot River sparkled in the dawn light. Birdsong and the whisper of wind in the trees were the only sounds breaking the stillness.

A gruff voice shattered the peace. "Hey lady! You want a tent and stove?"

Mary whirled around. A scruffy, bearded man stood, pushing a shrub over to show a faded canvas tent pitched nearby. His face was leathered from the elements, his voice rough as the bark on an old tree.

Mary's eyes grew large at the sight of the tent and stove. "Yes, I do! Can you help me move it?" she asked, taking a few steps closer to examine the tent's condition. The vegetation hid it well. She didn't even know he was there.

The man shook his head, his gaze fixed on the ground as if weighed by his own misfortunes. "Nah. I'm outta here. Dead broke and hungry." His shoulders slumped in defeat.

Mary's nostrils flared. She hurried after the retreating man, her boots leaving deep prints in the soft, wet bank. "Wait! What if I feed you? We can use my oxen to move it."

The man hesitated, hunger and hesitation warring on his face. His stomach rumbled. "You got a deal," he grunted. "What do ya got to eat?"

Mary prepared a hearty meal. The scent of warm food filled the air. The man dug in, the corners of his mouth raising. Between mouthfuls, he mumbled his name was Sam, and the tent was his mining partners until he did him dirty and put the claim in his name only. Left him the tent. Conversation didn't seem to be his strong suit.

After the last bite, Sam rose and dusted off his hands. "I'll be on my way now. Good luck with that tent." He shambled off without looking back, hollering, "Stove's heavy."

Mary's jaw dropped. "You promised to help me if I fed you!"

Sam kept walking.

Anger flared in Mary's chest. "Cess to you!" she yelled after him. "I hope you find the bees, but not the honey!" She stomped her foot, fists clenched. So much for relying on his word. She got a whiff of smoke and looked down. The dry grass. She double timed to the bank of the river until her temper dissipated enough she wouldn't start a fire. She didn't have the extra food to allow someone to betray her. Maybe she shouldn't have offered.

She sighed as she turned back to her wagon and the tasks that still awaited her. The fleeting encounter with the gruff stranger had left her feeling a mix of emotions—disappointment at broken promises, yet also a sense of compassion for a man struggling to survive in this rugged land.

Mary approached the tent, its proximity to the river bank unsettling her. It couldn't stay there. Since she had done everything else on this journey, there was no reason she couldn't move the tent and stove.

Mary disassembled the tent by yanking the stakes loose on one side. As she entered the tent, the poles smacked her on her head and legs, and the weighty canvas tangled around her. Grunting with effort, she extracted herself, though not without a few bumps and bruises.

Attaching the tent to an ox, Mary dragged it to her wagon. The stove she inched along herself with help from the same magick she used to handle the ox yokes. Not knowing anything about stoves except to use them, she thought it had to stay upright. The heavy iron sank into the soft earth, resisting her pulls. Her muscles burned with exertion.

Once in place, Mary faced her next challenge—rebuilding the tent. She spread the canvas over the stove, then crawled underneath, dragging several poles. Bracing a pole with her shoulder in the back center, she drove it into the ground. A slip of her hand along the wood to send magick energy kept the support upright. The pole shuddered but held firm. One by one, she erected the other poles the same way.

Outside again, Mary pounded in the stakes, securing the tent against the wind. Inside, she wrestled with the stovepipe and positioned the stove. Her new cozy home was coming together, albeit with the sweat of her brow alone. Far better than the wagon. And it was all hers.

Mary shuttled her belongings from the wagon to the tent. She placed her mattress by the stove, anticipating the chill of nights to come. Spent, she collapsed onto it and fell asleep.

When she awoke, she found Danu, her cougar familiar, curled beside her, warm with low rustling breaths of relaxed sleep. Memories of childhood washed over Mary - playing with a kitten in the garden while her mother and sister pulled weeds. She stroked Danu's fur, taking comfort in her presence.

Rested now, Mary gathered firewood, stoking the stove to life. The tent filled with dancing shadows and welcoming warmth. She and Danu explored the riverbank as the sun dipped below the horizon, ending her first day in the new home she'd carved out through grit and magick.

The road to Hamilton was rough and uneven, and their pace slow to navigate around rocks and gnarled tree roots. George winced as a protruding rock stabbed his foot through his worn boot. He wished he could ride the ox whose name started with an 'N' but for the life of him, he couldn't remember. Who names their oxen anyway?

It was fortunate that they decided against taking the wagon. No road made it challenging to find a decent route.

Beside him, Jack chattered away, oblivious to George's sour mood. "That's Trapper Peak over there. And that's Sugarloaf..."

George grunted, eyes forward. He didn't care what the cursed mountains were called.

"Your wife seems like a gracious lady," Jack said.

George whirled on him. "She has you fooled. She tricked me. I don't know how, but she did. Now I'm stuck with her nagging and blaming me for everything."

Jack chuckled. "You won't believe how many times I heard a man lament he got too drunk one night and found himself married in the morning. At least you have someone to cook for you."

George scowled. As if a full belly compensated for lost freedom.

"What brought you west, anyway?"

George tipped his head back, the sun's glare almost blinding him. "Wanted to do things on my own terms, not kowtow to my family's expectations." His voice turned bitter. "Thought I could strike it rich selling mining supplies."

"Well, still sounds like a fine dream," Jack said. "You might be able. One miner is following a silver vein on his claim. If word gets out, you'll need a storefront of supplies."

The mention of silver ignited a glow of hope in George's chest. By thunder, he needed a storefront! But he was flat broke except for the money Mary gave him to buy supplies which wasn't enough for the lumber. And they had to eat and make more money.

Then it hit him—he had a trust fund. He hadn't wanted to touch it, to admit defeat. But if it would secure his success now...

"I'm going to stop at the telegraph office. Gonna ask my brother to send me some of my money. I'll build the best store in the Montana territory. Why don't you build a saloon?"

Lost in his building fantasies, George didn't notice Jack's noncommittal murmurs. The store filled his mind's eye - living quarters upstairs, a stockroom bursting with mining gear. A proud storefront, gleaming white, 'Tin Creek Hardware' emblazoned in bold black lettering. It would be spectacular.

"You might be right," Jack said. "I'm no miner. But running a saloon...I know how to pour a drink and lend a friendly ear."

"And offer some gambling," George added. Every saloon needed poker and dice.

But Jack shook his head. "No gambling. Causes too many problems. I'm not a gambling man, myself."

George rubbed his chin. He'd work on Jack later about that.

"In fact," Jack continued, "if you help me build the saloon, I'll help build your store. And I'll buy food for all three of us. Your Mary can cook." He extended his hand. "Deal?"

George stared at Jack's open palm. A fair bargain? No one had ever offered him that before. His competitive instincts said to negotiate further, but something in Jack's genuine smile stopped him.

"Deal," George said at last, shaking Jack's hand. The camaraderie warmed him more than the prairie sun beating down on them. He fell quiet, unsure what to make of the unfamiliar feeling.

When they entered the lively streets of Hamilton, George's determined footsteps led him straight to the telegraph office. He pushed the creaking door open, revealing a small room charged by the clicking and clacking of telegraph keys. The telegraph operator, a wiry and bespectacled man, glanced over from his work, acknowledging George with a nod.

George wasted no time. "I need to send a telegram. It's urgent."

"Of course. Who are you sending it to, son?"

"Henry Perkins at Perkins Textiles in Chicago." As he said his brother's name out loud, it spurred George's pulse into a gallop. Henry would come through for him.

"What's the message, young man?" The operator slid a paper and pencil across the counter toward George. "Twenty words for forty cents."

George scribbled out what he had composed in his mind. The fewer the better. George wrote a concise message: Success. Need building. Send Trust.

The man glanced at the slip and bobbed his head. "Efficient. I like it."

George slid over the coins, which the man plunked into his cash box.

Cracking his knuckles, the operator began typing George's urgent plea in bursts of staccato code. The telegraph keys chattered like a woodpecker drilling a tree.

As the telegraph line carried the message across miles of wire, George stood there, a mixture of excitement and anxiety welling within him. The success of his dream store hinged on this very telegram, and he hoped that his brother would respond right away.

The operator gave George a reassuring pat on the shoulder. "Now comes the waiting, son. Good luck."

George hurried to the bank where he'd told Jack to meet him. There Jack stood, whistling and rocking on his heels. A grin spread throughout his face as he glimpsed George.

"There you are! Let's get to that lumberyard." Jack threw an arm across George's shoulders, guiding him along the busy street.

George laughed and joked with Jack as they walked, a curious sensation bubbling inside him. It was... enjoyment. Who would've thought he would like someone's company? The novelty left him speechless for a time.

When they reached the lumberyard, George proclaimed, using an exaggerated flourish, "Welcome, dear Jack, to the finest timber emporium in Montana!"

Jack chuckled. "Well, butter my backside! Look at all this!" He spread his arms wide, taking in the stacks of boards and beams.

A burly man ambled over to them, wiping his sweaty brow. "Help you gents?"

"I need to order lumber to build a saloon in Tin Creek," Jack explained. The man looked puzzled.

"About a day's walk south," George offered. "Gonna be a boom town once word gets out about the silver."

The yard man's face brightened. "Haven't done an order there. Well, c'mon back to the office and we'll get you sorted."

They entered the office where the yard man stepped around a desk, pulling out paper and sitting. Jack and George pulled a couple of chairs. Jack explained what he wanted, and the man sketched it out. He made calculations on the side of his sketch and tallied the order. Jack paid the lumberman, and they all shook hands.

George said, "I'll be back later for an order for my store."

Spirits high, they headed for the general store to buy equipment and provisions. George still had the money to get the mining supplies he needed, and he was proud he had spent none of it. That will show Mary. He was going to be successful on his own terms without his family or Mary nagging him. George bought pans, picks, and shovels, while Jack purchased food supplies for the three of them.

On the long walk back, the ox laden, George discovered he rather enjoyed listening to Jack's colorful stories instead of dwelling on his own troubles. And Jack's easy laughter proved contagious.

By the time Tin Creek's tents came into view, George felt lighter than he had in years, maybe ever. When he built his store, he'd show everyone he could succeed on his own terms. With Jack's infectious optimism beside him, he believed it for once.

Chapter Twenty-Two

A LOUD BIRD CALL pulled a far distant memory. Mary waddled out of the tent, a hand resting on the crest of her belly, full and taut as a sail catching the wind. She saw the cocky strut of a magpie, the flashes of iridescent green and blue shining in the afternoon sun. She saluted the bird as a smile spread across her face, remembering her mother's familiar, Ean. He protected her, watching over her as if she was his own. She whispered the old rhyme about magpies, "One for sorrow, two for mirth, three for a wedding, and four for a birth." *If only Stella were here to see this. She too would salute the bird to prevent the sorrow that comes from seeing a solitary magpie.* Tin Creek was becoming home more and more.

Raucous laughter echoed through the stillness of the valley. Mary's brows furrowed. She knew that laugh. It sounded like Henry.

George and Jack came into view over the hill. She watched George throw his head back, his usual sullen face creased with happiness. He clutched his side as another bout of laughter overtook him.

Mary blinked in astonishment. She had never heard George laugh like that. He looked... happy. Her gaze shifted to the pile of supplies strapped to Aengus. Mining pans glinted in the sun, and cloth sacks sagged, carrying unknown contents.

"You two did all this?" She hurried towards them, cradling her belly, unable to keep the grin from her face.

Jack flashed her a proud smile. "Yep, we got everything we need for the next few weeks. No need to worry about running out of food now." He patted one of the bulging sacks. "Mining supplies to sell, lumber coming for my new saloon. We're all set."

Mary glanced at George. So that explained his cheerful mood. She should have known it would take more than a successful supply run to crack through that dour exterior. "I thought you were going to Hamilton to place a claim?"

Jack shrugged. "I'm not a gambling man. Probably better I stick to what I know—running a saloon."

George arched an eyebrow at her. "Who'd you trick to get that tent, Mary?"

She pressed her lips together, stifling a sharp retort. Of course, he would assume she scammed someone. "It wasn't a trick, George. Sam left and offered it to me before he took off."

"It's true," Jack added. "Sam told me before we headed to Hamilton, he was eager to get out of here. His mining partner screwed him out of their claim and he ran out of supplies."

Mary shot him a grateful look. Jack knew when to intervene with George. She doubted either man would have lasted long in the mining camp without the tempering influence of the other's company. Jack's niceness would get him swindled or killed.

Over the next few days, life in the camp took on a new energy. The lumber Jack had ordered arrived, accompanied by grumbling from the freighter over the lack of road. Jack clapped the man on the shoulder. "Don't you worry, we'll have the worst parts fixed in no time."

George's eyes bulged in disbelief while he helped unload the wood. "How do you plan on doing that?"

"I'll gather some of the other miners to lend a hand. Fixing the road helps everyone, after all."

George shook his head, snorting. "Think anyone here is just going to volunteer their time?"

Jack shrugged, unperturbed by George's cynicism. "You'd be surprised what people will do for a common cause, especially if it benefits them, too."

Mary watched the exchange, marveling at how effortlessly Jack drew George out of his usual surliness. With Jack's easygoing good nature to counter his moods, George resembled a normal person.

The sounds of sawing and hammering rang out as Jack's saloon began taking shape. Mary wandered over to check on the progress. Jack's directions were met with George's skepticism, but they worked together to hoist walls and fit rafters into place.

During her breaks in selling supplies, Mary's thoughts turned to the mother's grimoire. She sat in the shade of her tent between customers and leafed through the crackling pages filled with spells and enchantments. Her mother had dabbled in all the magical arts. If only her mother had been around to teach her. Then perhaps she would have progressed beyond the random flames that sprang unbidden with her emotions.

She traced her fingers over the elaborate script and illustrations of plants murmuring the spells. The herbal remedies were indeed helpful, but the darker magick within the book intrigued and frightened her. Why would her mother resort to such spells? Bats in a house. The experiments in drowning living things in huge water droplets, wondering if she could kill someone that way. Terrible, dark magick.

Blowing fire. Mary had enough trouble not burning anything down when angry. Why would she do it on purpose? Her mother used wind spells to ruin crops. Absurd.

Spells for bewitching people. Mary's nose crinkled in distaste. She had learned her lesson in manipulating free will, no matter how useful she thought it would be. It went against 'do as you will, but harm none.' Karma came back threefold. She willed men to buy her mining supplies, only to have the money disappear from George's hand by his gambling.

Still, the prospect of brewing a storm cloud to hover over George on his grumpier days tempted her. She chuckled. Though perhaps he needed no magical intervention for that anymore. Jack's amiable presence already had a lightening effect on George's moods.

Mary closed the book, gazing at the new saloon taking shape nearby. Despite their differences, the two men balanced each other in a way she didn't expect. Jack's optimism and George's perseverance made them a formidable team.

While the magick she'd discovered in her mother's book unsettled her, a different magick was at work here. As Mary watched George bark orders while Jack smoothed ruffled feathers with his affable grin, she couldn't suppress her own smile. Perhaps she had under-estimated the transformative power of friendship. Jack's influence showed the promise of clearing George's own clouds at last.

After completing the shell of the saloon, George and Jack needed to make another trip to Hamilton for more supplies. At daybreak, they yoked the oxen and prepared the wagon. Their breaths came out in frosty puffs in the chill morning air as they worked.

George focused on his hope for a reply from Henry and money for his lumber order. Mary had given him the money made on the latest mining supplies, giving him an added stop in Hamilton to resupply. The wagon would make that easier.

George led the oxen-pulled wagon down the new road that led out of the mining camp. George regretted not paying for a wagon seat and thought he could seek that in Hamilton if he was going to do supply runs. He already walked to Montana because of his ill decision. Time to correct that. The wagon builder should have pushed him on the seat. Stupid man. The new road reduced their travel time and made the trip smoother.

As soon as they arrived in Hamilton the next morning, George rushed to the telegraph office. George, palms sweating, heart pounding, asked the telegraph operator, "Do you have a telegram for me, George Perkins?"

The man wrinkled his forehead and rolled his eyes to the ceiling. "You know, I believe I did. Let me get it." He pulled a slip of paper from a box on the wall labeled 'No Address' and handed it to George.

George glanced at it and then at the man. "You realize anyone can reach over and read people's telegrams?" He shook his head and stepped aside as Jack approached the counter. The telegram read: Bank of Montana. Congratulations. Hope all is well. Henry.

Now he was in a hurry to get to the bank. Not knowing the amount Henry had sent was a blessing, considering how vulnerable the telegrams were to being intercepted. But he wanted to wait for Jack.

Jack said, "Marisol at Brenda's Boarding House."

George watched him write out his message and give it to the operator. It left him curious about the woman's identity. Jack hadn't mentioned a wife or girlfriend. He didn't want to share his new friend. Maybe he wouldn't have time for him anymore.

When Jack turned around, George asked, "Who's Marisol?"

"She used to work for me. I wished it was more, but she feels like I'm family, a brother, something like that." Jack shrugged. "I asked her to come work for me again. That way, I'll have time to help you build your store. Did your brother come through for you?"

"I hope he did. I have to go to the bank to find out. Ready?"

The Bank of Montana, a small, drab wooden building, sat next to a vacant lot where men hammered away at the frame of a towering structure. George entered to find an old man ahead of him. Unfortunately, he would have to wait to discover the amount in his account. Just his luck.

George tapped his foot, causing the customer, the teller, and Jack to turn their attention to him. He kept on tapping. No sign said 'No tapping', which, of course, wouldn't stop him. Since their glares didn't work on him, the old man and the teller turned back to what they were doing.

Jack asked, "What in the world is wrong?"

"What are they doing? Printing money?" George turned on his heel and stormed out. Jack followed. He would go to the lumberyard to find out how much the lumber would cost.

Jack jogged to George's side. "You have no patience, do you?"

"No. None." George realized he was almost running and slowed.

"Your store will not materialize at this very moment. One step at a time." Jack shook his head.

At least, people moved faster at Hamilton Lumber. George approached the desk, pulling his sketch out of his pocket. "How much will this cost? It's a store, a storage room, and living quarters upstairs. I have the dimensions written on there." He slid over the sketch.

The man tilted his head as he examined George's drawing. "I'm going to need a few minutes to figure an estimate for you. And where to?"

"Tin Creek."

The lumber man pulled his head back. "Well, I hope there is a road this time. My freighter complained, but said someone was going to work on one."

George pushed his chest out. "We got it sorted out using help from miners and a rancher's crew." The reminder of Tony helping on the road made his muscles tense. He needed to focus on his lumber order, not some man trying to get Mary to leave. He didn't know why that bothered him. It's not like he had any feelings for her.

Jack nodded. "You'll have no problems this time. We are going to add a bridge over that one stream. It's not deep, but if there's some heavy rain, it might be a problem."

"Good. I like to see progress. I heard someone found a substantial vein of silver."

"Yeah, I'm selling a lot of mining supplies." George turned, eager to get back to the bank. "I'll be back later, then."

George's heart was pounding in his chest as he hurried back to the bank, hoping that the customer had left. The anticipation built and built until he felt like he was going to explode. When he opened the door, he found that the old man was no longer there, and in his place stood a woman. His face and shoulders dropped. She better be quick. His time was important. He tapped his foot. The teller glared at him again. Jack bumped his shoulder with his. George rolled his eyes and stopped tapping.

The thought of tripping the woman on her way out crossed his mind, but he was sure Jack wouldn't approve. Instead, he scanned the room. *Jack's saloon is better built and nicer than this bank.*

When he approached the crude counter, he said to the banker, "How is it that a bank is this pitiful looking?"

The banker twisted his mouth and pointed to a sketch of a big two story building on the wall. "We are waiting on the stone from back east to build on that large lot next door. *This* is only a temporary building."

"Oh. Hmm. My brother opened an account for me. I need the balance. George Perkins."

A smile crossed the man's face. "Yes, I received a telegram and then a wire from the main office to open your account."

"Well, what's the balance?"

"One thousand dollars."

A big smile spread across his face. What an odd sensation. George was sure his use of 'success' in his telegram sweetened the pot. "Good. Now I can build the first store in Tin Creek." He turned to Jack. "He built the first building, a saloon for the miners."

"Is there anything else I can help you with?"

"I'll be back to withdraw funds to pay the lumber yard once I receive my estimate. Everything is a wait in this town."

The man furrowed his brows and frowned. "It's first come, first serve as are most businesses."

George said on his way to the door, "I bet you don't treat Mr. I Built This Town Hamilton that way."

Twenty minutes later, George was back at the bank while Jack went to order a wood stove and alcohol for the saloon. The banker sat at his desk in front of a large ledger. As George stood at the counter, the man continued making entries. "Hey, I need to make a withdrawal."

The man kept his eyes on the book in front of him. "I'm working on Mr. Hamilton's account. You'll have to wait."

Wham! George slammed his hand on the counter. "I'm here to make a withdrawal," he said, enunciating each word. *How dare he speak to me like that?*

The banker jumped. A scowl formed, and he wrote a few more entries before taking his time rising from his chair. "Hmm. How much?" He yawned and looked at the clock on the wall.

George thrust his elbows out from his body and his chest out. He blew his breath out through his nostrils. He pounded his index finger on the counter. "One hundred ninety."

"One moment." The banker walked the short distance to a small safe on the floor. He kneeled and spun the dial.

George pretended not to watch as the banker turned the dial left and right. It didn't matter if he watched or not. The safe faced away from the counter.

The banker approached, bills in hand. He placed them on the counter in front of George and headed back to the small desk.

"Wait. Are you going to count it out?"

"I assumed you would count it yourself, anyway. I still have Mr. Hamilton's books to finish." The banker sat and returned to the ledger.

George stomped his foot. "That's no way to treat a valued customer. I'll be bringing a lot of money into this bank."

"They all say that. Good day, Mr. Perkins."

CHAPTER TWENTY-THREE

MARY HUMMED TO HERSELF as she arranged tin pans and pick-axes in neat rows along the tailgate of the prairie schooner. The air carried a hint of winter chill, and she pulled her coat tighter around her, frosty breath eluding from her lips. The sun glinted off the metal, making her squint against the brightness. Behind her, the sounds of hammers striking nails and men shouting echoed through the air—the beginnings of their general store.

A sudden flurry of hooves interrupted her and a rugged miner buying a pickax. Turning her gaze toward the approaching horse, Mary's eyes widened. It appeared to be a lone woman.

The woman drew her horse to a halt and surveyed the situation with dark eyes. "This Tin Creek then?" she hollered.

Mary froze in surprise—the striking lady wore men's trousers tucked into tall boots. A pair of ornate pistols hung on her hips. A colorful woven shawl draped over her shoulders, and pheasant feathers fluttered from her black wind-wild locks.

George straightened from his hammering, scowling at the interruption. "It is," he said. "And who might you be?"

The woman swung off her horse like one of her feathers floating in the air. "Name's Marisol. I'm looking for Jack."

Jack dropped his hammer, ran over, and embraced Marisol, spinning her off her feet. "I knew you would figure a way to get here!"

"You think a hundred miles of wilderness would stop me?" Her eyes glinted as she took in the ramshackle collection of tents and unfinished buildings. "And look at that brand new saloon. Let me decorate this time."

Jack shook his head. "I'm keeping it rustic, like my customers."

Marisol pouted and laughed. "Someday." A wink. "Who are your friends? Aren't you going to introduce me?" She spread her arms out and her infectious smile put Mary at ease.

Mary watched the exchange while she finished with the miner. This was the woman Jack had told them about, coming to help run the new saloon. She wore a bold independence and was not like any woman Mary had ever met.

George spat on the ground. "Women have no reason to wear men's trousers," he growled. "It's not proper."

Marisol raised one brow. "You'll find I'm not overly concerned with what's proper, mister. I dress for riding when that's what I'm doing and high fashion when I'm working."

Mary extended her hand, trying to hide her awe. "I'm Mary. Welcome to Tin Creek. Would you like some tea? We can get to know each other."

Marisol's eyes displayed a genuine warmth, shaking Mary's hand. "That sounds wonderful. I could use a nice cup of tea. Thanks for the offer."

They headed towards the tent while George grumbled under his breath and went back to work. Mary sneaked glances at the striking woman as she stoked the fire to heat water for tea. She envied Marisol's confidence and courage to travel alone and do as she pleased. Where would she go if she were the same as Marisol? Paris would be her first choice, but it required travel on a boat, which she would never do. Water. So much water.

"You'll have to excuse George," Mary said. "He comes from a traditional family, unused to independent women like yourself."

Marisol accepted the steaming cup. "Men seldom appreciate women taking charge and dressing practical. But I won't apologize for who I am."

"Nor should you," Mary agreed. She hesitated, afraid she would offend since she had never seen a woman wearing men's clothing. "If you don't mind my asking...how did you come to wear men's pants and use pistols?"

Settling on a empty crate, Marisol sipped her tea before answering. "I've been on my own since I was a young gal. I learned early that being female in this world makes you a target. That's when I decided not to play the part expected of me."

She tapped the pistols at her hips. "These keep those wolves at bay. The pants allow me to ride as competently as any man. Just had to prove it to 'em." Marisol smiled. "Most warm up to me after a while. The feathers help win 'em over."

Mary laughed aloud. She admired this woman's fierce independence and courage. "The feathers make quite the impression," she admitted. "You and I will be fast friends. I can already tell."

They chatted more about Marisol's travels and experiences in Jack's saloon in Missoula. The woman had led a life that was beyond Mary's imagination. She wished she could be fearless and free like that. But keeping her magick secret made her cautious and restrained.

"You're an inspiration, Marisol," Mary said. "It's difficult being a woman in these times, but you show that it's possible to be spirited and being guided by one's own heart."

Marisol chuckled. "I've had my fair share of challenges, believe me. But life's too short to be anything but who you are. It's not about being fearless; it's about being brave enough to face your fears and embrace your true self."

When the sun dipped below the horizon, George and Jack had made significant progress on the store's foundation. Mary started dinner on the wood stove while she shared her adventures on the Oregon and Montana trails.

"Why don't we eat in the saloon?" Marisol said. Mary grinned as she watched the feathers in Marisol's hair flow through the air as Marisol spoke.

Mary shrugged. "Sure. Why not? There's no table and chairs, but as long as someone helps me off the floor and you don't mind my appearance." Mary gave a rueful pat of her belly and glanced at her stained dress and swollen ankles.

Marisol tutted. "Nonsense. You look beautiful. I'll volunteer to help you anytime."

Spirit lifted, Mary nodded. It would do her soul good to get out of this tent and share a meal with this captivating new friend. Maybe Marisol was the medicine her lonely heart needed in this harsh place.

As they carried dinner to the saloon, Mary felt a newfound sense of hope and camaraderie. George and Jack ate on the front steps while the women sat on the floor, backs leaning against the bar.

Marisol said, "Men like George seek to control what they fear. Don't cede your power."

Mary bit her lip. Marisol was perceptive—had she seen the truth lurking beneath the surface?

Mary's witchery on George weighed on her conscience while George's subtle cruelties needled her raw. But she was bound to this life now.

As if sensing her mood, Marisol said, "Whatever shadows haunt you, know that you have a friend." She squeezed Mary's hand.

Mary managed a small smile. Marisol's friendship might bring a bright light to her dimmed spirit. Profound gratitude flooded Mary for the strong and remarkable women who had come into her life. Anna's kindness and support, and now Marisol's audacity and courage, ignited in Mary a sense of belonging and liberation.

The unexpected warm late afternoon sun on Mary's face was a welcome reprieve from the bitter cold that had gripped Tin Creek in late December. She leaned back against the rough canvas of her tent, soaking in the rare warmth. The snow had melted away, leaving the ground muddy and damp. It would freeze again overnight, but for now, the warm sun and cool breeze made it more like April than almost January.

Mary rested a hand on her swollen belly, the firm roundness beneath her dress. She hoped her baby would wait until the store was built, though at the rate the work was going, it seemed unlikely. She gazed at the half-finished frame of what would be the general store. George and Jack had run into delays getting supplies and their helpers not wanting to work in the bitter icy wind. It seemed her child would be born in a tent after all.

When a sharp cramp gripped her, she bent forward, gasping. But it passed—another false alarm. With effort, she reeled herself upright. Danu lifted his head from where he lay under the brush nearby, ready to aid her if needed.

"I'm alright," she assured him, and he laid her head back down with a soft chuff, mollified for now.

Mary sighed, then headed towards the river. The Bitterroot River flowed heavier than usual from the snowmelt, its waters swift and powerful. But she found drier areas along the bank where she gathered kindling under the tall cottonwoods growing nearby. The sun warmed her back while she hummed, and a gentle breeze rustled through the remaining dry leaves, carrying the smell of damp earth.

The lapping of the swollen river filled her ears, accompanied by the melodic calls of chickadees flitting through the bare cottonwood branches. As she stood, her lower back twinged in protest of the added weight she carried. She shifted the kindling bundle, trying to find a comfortable position. Out of the corner of her eye, she noticed a quick, furtive movement on the sandbar in the middle of the river.

A marten, sleek and agile, paced along the water's edge, its dainty paws sinking into the wet sand. It walked to the far end of the sandbar, gazed across at the far shore, then turned and paced back, its movements growing more frantic. In normal circumstances, the small creature would have been able to cross, but today, with the water rushing, it found itself trapped and distressed.

Poor thing. Mary bit her lip, considering options. She could freeze the water to make a narrow bridge, giving the marten an escape. But using her magick in the open made her nervous; she guarded her abilities. Though isolated, if anyone saw, there could be consequences. And the exertion of her magick while in late pregnancy was challenging.

The marten's distressed cries decided for her. Glancing around, she saw no one else. Mary sank to her knees on the soft sand, setting her kindling aside. The baby's weight made it difficult to find a comfortable position. She feared she might deliver her child at any moment. She leaned back on one hand, the other outstretched towards the sandbar.

Closing her eyes, Mary reached for her inner flame, channeling it along her arm. She embraced the licking fire flowing from her fingertips, not with heat to burn but with power to freeze. Her eyes snapped open, and she watched in satisfaction as ice crystals formed, stretching out in a narrow bridge from the shore to the sandbar.

As her icy bridge reached its intended destination, the river responded in anger. A wall of cold water surged forward, catching Mary off guard, almost pushing her into the river's treacherous embrace. She gasped, her heart pounding. Fear overcame her, transfixing her in place.

Danu sprang into action, pulling Mary by her dress further from the river's edge. Mary clung to the sand, trying to steady herself as she realized the unintended consequences of her magick. To her horror, the swelling current had shoved against her icy bridge, which was stronger and deeper than she intended. The river swirled around, seeking an alternative path. Frigid water surged towards Mary's wagon, the unfinished storefront, and several miners' tents yards away.

Mary despaired as the icy water swirled close to her possessions. If anything happened to her supplies or the building materials, it would be a major setback. Panic clawed at her chest until she struggled to breathe.

Feeling the weight of her actions, Mary's mind raced for a solution. The safety of her friends and prospectors depended on her quick thinking. Staggering upright, she thrust both hands towards the ice bridge, summoning her fire magick. Flames shot from her palms, melting the bridge in seconds. Shocked at the intensity of the flames from her hands, she looked at them, palms up.

As the minutes ticked by, the river corrected itself, leaving a dug-out swale on the shore. The water diverted away from the store and wagon, finding its natural path once more. Relief washed over her as she saw the potential disaster averted.

Mary's attention shifted to Danu, who had disappeared. The loyal cougar returned, his sleek fur damp, and he held the marten in his mouth. The small creature was freed from its dire predicament.

"Good boy, Danu," Mary murmured, a soft smile gracing her lips. Her familiar dropped the marten, allowing it to scamper away, back to safety. Danu's intelligent blue-green eyes gazed at her, radiating calm and comfort. Mary sank her hands into Danu's thick fur, forcing herself to take slow, deep breaths. Mary placed a hand on her heart while her eyes teared for her loyal companion, whose instincts and actions were always in tune to her needs.

As she took a moment to catch her breath, Mary reflected on the power of her magick and the responsibility that accompanied it. The marten's panicked cries still echoed in her mind. She had only wanted to help the poor creature but caused a disaster. Each spell, each action, carried consequences, and she knew she must stay vigilant and wise in her decisions. Her unborn child, and her newfound friends in Tin Creek, depended on her restraint and mastery over her magick.

Mary stroked Danu's back. "Remind me to think things through next time," she murmured. The cougar chuffed in agreement. She turned towards her tent as the first stars peeked out in the pale indigo sky. All she wanted now was to rest her aching back and swollen feet. Danu padded alongside, ready to keep watch through the night. The river roared on, no trace remaining of the day's events except the lessons engraved on Mary's heart.

Chapter Twenty-Four

They had moved the canvas tent to the floor of the unfinished store in time for a howling blizzard. The winds shrieked outside but did not pierce the heavy silence inside. Mary sat motionless in her chair, positioned beside the flap of the tent, peeking out as she watched the deep drifts blow in through the door frame. Then the snow danced in circles before settling into piles.

The cold seeped through the cracks and chilled Mary to her bones. Her breath formed frosty plumes as she moved her chair closer to the stove. Rubbing her arms for warmth, she glanced at the wood stove, its fire still burning. There was no worry about gathering more wood. Her secret magick sustained the flames burning no wood.

Across the cramped tent, George hunched in his chair, jaw clenched and brow furrowed. His brooding mood matched the gloomy weather.

The chair creaked as Mary shifted, the hard seat aggravating her aching back. Any day now she would deliver. She grimaced as she tried to find a more comfortable position.

George's head jerked at the movement, his scowl deepening. "Can't you sit still?"

Biting her tongue, Mary lowered her eyes and went motionless again. The silence stretched once more. She thought of her friends, far away in Chicago. What she wouldn't give for one of Stella's warm hugs or Henry's gentle smiles. Her heart twisted in loneliness and regret.

A painful tightness seized her belly. Mary bent forward, gasping, arms cradling her contracted womb. George shot her an irritated look, but said nothing.

The tension released, and Mary sat back, heart racing. These false alarms tormented her, making her yearn for her baby to arrive. At least she'd have someone to fill the dreary days trapped in this tent.

Her stomach growled in the silence. She pushed herself out of the chair and shuffled to the cast-iron stove. The beans from last night congealed in the pot, their appealing aroma now rancid to her. She scrunched her nose in distaste, but ladled some onto two tin plates.

On swollen feet, she lumbered part way over to George, holding out the meal as a peace offering.

"Bring it to me," he snapped.

Mary clenched her jaw, shuffled closer, and dropped the plate onto his lap. "Here."

"You're my wife. It's your job," he grumbled. But he shoveled the beans into his mouth without further protest.

Back in her seat, Mary forced herself to swallow the slimy lumps. She needed to keep her strength. The baby depended on her.

As she set the plate aside, another powerful contraction seized her, this time accompanied by a gush of warm liquid soaking her skirts. Mary doubled over, unable to contain a low moan.

The pain subsided, leaving her trembling and lightheaded. This was it. The baby was coming. Now. Here in this tent, her and George. Fear spiked her heart rate.

She stripped her sodden garments, exchanging them for a dry nightdress between more frequent contractions. George scowled as he tracked her efforts, but made no move to help.

At last she collapsed onto the bed, panting and clutching her swollen belly. She bit on a leather strap that had broken off her satchel on the trail as each wrenching pain crested. She appreciated Danu's concerned presence outside, along the back of the tent.

Mary rode the pain cycle of the contractions through the long night while George snored. Despite the coolness in the tent, Mary sweated profusely, making her clothes and bedding stick to her skin.

The morning light filtered into the tent, rousing Mary from her fitful dozing between agonizing contractions.

George snorted awake on his cot, oblivious to her ordeal. "Coffee," he grunted. "And where's my breakfast?"

Mary clenched her jaw as another vice-like contraction seized her swollen womb. She breathed through the piercing pain. "Get it yourself," she gasped. "I'm... indisposed."

Scowling, George shoved his feet into his boots and stomped outside, letting the tent flap fall closed behind him.

Mary sagged back, exhausted and drenched in sweat. She wasn't sure how much more she could endure. But another intense contraction crested, wringing a hoarse cry from her throat

The tent flap flew open. Marisol rushed to Mary's side, cloak dusted with snow.

"Oh Mary, why didn't you send for me? George said you wouldn't fix him breakfast, so I figured there was a problem," she murmured, grasping Mary's hand through the next agonizing peak. "Hush now, breathe. I'm here."

Time blurred into a haze of pain made more bearable by Marisol's soothing voice and Danu's comforting presence. Hours passed.

Mary let out a primal cry as she bore down on the next contraction. The urge to push was instinctive and irresistible. But the pain was endless, far worse than she'd expected.

Marisol coached her through the effort. "Breathe, just breathe." She touched Mary's knee. "I see the head! You're almost there. Push!"

Mary propped herself on her elbows. Keen to be done, she put everything into this push.

A thin, lusty cry pierced the air. Marisol placed the squirming purple newborn on Mary's chest. "It's a girl! Well done, Mama."

Boneless with relief, Mary laughed, cradling her daughter. "Hello, Isobel," she whispered. Waves of fierce love washed over her exhausted body. This tiny girl was hers, and she'd do everything for her.

After she dried Isobel and wrapped her in a soft blanket, Mary held her close, still trembling from the ordeal. Elation flooded her heart as she traced the wisps of hair peeking out. She memorized the tiny features through joyful tears.

Traces of Henry in her newborn created a deep pang in her heart. The long lashes and the cupid shape of her lips. He wasn't there to share the birth of his child and wouldn't be part of her life.

But all her mistakes and regrets seemed to fade for a moment as she stared into Isobel's emerald green eyes. Here was new hope. A clean slate. She would give this child the best life she could.

Marisol tidied up the soiled linens, stoking the stove's fading embers and adding a new log. Mary's magick had faded.

Mary gazed at Marisol. "Thank you. You are a genuine friend."

"Rest now. I'll look after you both." With an affectionate pat, Marisol gathered the bundles and slipped outside.

Alone with Isobel, Mary whispered fervent promises and pressed tender kisses to her downy crown. The winter wind howled outside, but Mary had never felt such joy and warmth as holding this precious child in her arms.

In the following days, falling into the rhythms of caring for a newborn brought Mary more joy and purpose than she'd ever known. Isobel's soft breaths and occasional gurgles were the only sounds breaking the icy silence within the tent.

When Isobel fussed for milk, Mary nestled beneath the blankets, ignoring George's remarks about 'Henry's spawn.' She endured his callous words for Isobel's sake, funneling love into the tiny girl snuggled against her breast.

As she soothed Isobel to sleep one evening, stroking her velvety cheek, she made a silent vow. No matter what the future held, she would protect this child with her whole heart and see her wants and needs provided for. She pressed a fierce kiss to Isobel's downy head.

"It's you and me, little one," she whispered into the stillness. "You and me against the world."

In the early morning, two weeks later, Mary heard the snort of a horse and the crunch of boots on the store floor. She stopped rocking Isobel in her arms and quit humming an Irish lullaby.

"Mary, are you here? It's Peter."

Mary's heart lifted at the sound of her dear friend. "Oh, Peter! Come in, come in," she urged, eager to see him, and hoping Anna was with him.

Peter ducked through the tent entrance, holding the heavy canvas open long enough to slip inside before it fell closed, locking out the chill air. "Ah, it's toasty warm in here. Good." He rubbed his hands together before removing his gloves. His kind eyes crinkled as he caught sight of the bundle cradled in Mary's arms.

"And what do you have there?" Peter stepped closer, peering down at the tiny face peeking out from under the blankets.

Mary beamed. "A girl. Isobel."

"She has your looks, thank heavens. Hopefully, she has your temperament and not George's."

Mary tensed at the mention of her surly husband, whose true knowledge about her child remained concealed. She prayed Peter's words did not tempt fate in the future if George overheard his name mentioned about Isobel. Eager to change the subject, she asked, "How is Anna? I've been worried about her."

"Well, I have news, too." Peter pulled a rickety chair next to Mary's. "We had a boy, John. Anna's doing good. Had an easy delivery." He tilted his head, brow furrowed. "And you? How was...?" His voice trailed off.

Mary sighed, hugging her delicate newborn closer. How would she know if it was easy? It didn't feel like it, and she was thankful Marisol was there for her. "She's here and healthy. That's all that matters."

Peter nodded, though his eyes remained troubled. "Did George help you through it?"

A startled laugh burst from Mary's lips. The image of George tending to her needs was nothing short of absurd. "That's a good one. He worried about getting fed. Slept through the rest. Marisol helped."

Peter shook his head, looking none too surprised. "I figured as much. I'm glad someone was here to help you. You'll have to tell me about Marisol. Why don't you come out to the house for a few days? Anna would love to spend time with you both. You can warm yourself by the fireplace." A grin spread across his weathered face. "I'm trying my hand at cooking and need some victims."

Mary wrinkled her nose in mock suspicion. "I was ready to say yes until you mentioned that last part. Now I'm scared." She smiled, a lump forming in her throat. "Truthfully, though, I would love nothing more than to visit you both. I've missed you."

Peter's eyes crinkled. "Well, that's settled then."

Mary transferred baby Isobel into Peter's waiting arms before grabbing her satchel to pack clothes for the visit. She hummed as she folded dresses and blankets. The thought of Anna's comforting presence and raucous laughter made her breathless and her heart pound.

George would grumble at having to fend solo, but Mary left a quick note — "Visiting friends. Back in a few days" — to curb any tantrums at her extended absence. She was sure George's friend, Jack, would feed him.

Mary allowed Peter to help her into the saddle, his firm hands steadying her still-sore body. She tucked Isobel snug against her chest under her coat before Peter hoisted himself behind them.

As the horse carried them off toward the ranch, Mary turned her face toward the mid-morning sun, letting its radiance soak into her numbed cheeks. A pang of remorse tempered her joy. If not for her selfish choices, she could have had a loving partner like Peter beside her long before now. But dwelling on past mistakes would not move her forward. For now, she focused only on the deep comfort of genuine friendship awaiting her.

Chapter Twenty-Five

As the horse picked its way along the snowy trail, a cozy homestead came into view, nestled in the valley below. The modest ranch, framed by a tall stand of Douglas fir and Ponderosa pine, made it look like the home sprouted from the forest. A barn stood sentinel over a corral.

"Incredible that just the three of you built all this in a few months," Mary remarked over her shoulder to Peter.

"It was backbreaking work," he replied, shaking his head. "Chopping down endless trees, hewing and stacking each log. My hands were covered in blisters and sap from sunup to sundown."

Mary glanced again at the snug cabin, smoke curling from its chimney. "But you did it - carved out a home using your own two hands. There's a lot of satisfaction in that."

"Without a doubt. This place may be humble, but we made it ours," Peter said. "Seeing Anna beam brighter than the sun when I come in each night makes it all worthwhile."

Mary smiled. She couldn't imagine a man laboring out of devotion for her that way. Peter had built this haven through tenacity and love. As the horse plodded the last stretch, Mary thought about how challenges had bonded Anna and Peter tighter than bricks and mortar ever could. She yearned for that sense of union they shared.

Mary stepped through the door of the two-room ranch house, and Anna enveloped her in a welcoming embrace.

"Oh, it's good to see you!" Anna exclaimed as she squeezed Mary's shoulders before pulling back.

Mary returned her smile. "I've missed you too!"

The two women turned their attention to the bundled infants nestled in their arms. "Oh, she's beautiful!" Anna cooed over baby Isobel. Meanwhile, Mary admired Anna's son, John, born a week before Isobel. His little fingers grasped at the air.

"Come sit by the fire. You must be cold and weary from the ride," Anna said, guiding Mary to a wooden chair near the crackling hearth. She added another log before taking a seat herself. Soon, the women chatted and giggled together like schoolgirls while their babies babbled and cooed. The harshness of frontier life melted away in their easy companionship.

Later, the front door creaked open and Peter entered. "We're having venison stew for dinner tonight," he announced, leaning over to kiss Anna's cheek in greeting.

Peter prepared dinner while the women got caught up on life since they last saw each other months ago. When the hearty stew was ready, the savory smell filled the cabin. The three friends gathered around the rough-hewn table with the two infants on their laps.

Peter leaned back in his chair and grinned. "Had quite the adventure checking the herd right before the big blizzard," he began. "I'm out there trying to round up the cattle, right? Now, these cows have minds of their own, especially Bessie, who thinks she's the queen of the pasture.

I'm on Duke, who's not too fond of the cold himself. He's shivering and looking at me like I owe him a seaside vacation. We're trudging through snow up to our knees, and I see Bessie leading the herd towards the only pond on the ranch.

I'm thinking, 'No, no, no, Bessie, not today!' But do you think Bessie listens? Of course not. She heads straight for the pond, and the rest of the herd follows like she's the Pied Piper of cows.

Now, here's where it gets interesting. I urge Duke to move faster to head them off, but what I didn't see was this patch of ice. Next thing I know, Duke slips, and we're both skidding across the ice. We must've looked like a winter rodeo act, slipping and sliding, trying to regain our balance.

Meanwhile, Bessie and the herd are having a field day, watching us with what I swear was amusement in their eyes. I get Duke back on solid ground, but by then, my toes are so cold I'm sure they've turned blue.

I round up the herd—finally—and get them back to the barn. But the kicker? When I get back to the house, Anna looks at me, tries not to laugh, and says, 'You know you have a snowball stuck in your beard, right?' And that's when I realized I had become a literal ice sculpture."

By now, Anna and Mary were laughing. Peter smiled and shook his head. "Never a dull day out there with those cattle."

As they ate, Tony came through the door. "I finished..." His face brightened when he spied Mary at the table. "Good to see you." He walked behind her, squeezing her shoulder. Though they had agreed any deeper relationship was impossible now, Tony's caring manner toward her had not diminished. He joined them at the table.

The sound of laughter and conversation continued to fill the room, even after the meal had ended. Mary cherished these carefree moments together, thankful for Peter's gift of finding humor, even in the day's mishaps.

Mary wiped her mouth and set her napkin on her empty dinner plate. "Excellent dinner, Peter. I had nothing to fear, after all. Before I forget." She left the table to retrieve her bag and rummage inside. She came back grasping an envelope that she held it out to Tony. "I know it's not much, yet."

"What's this?" he asked.

"The loan. In Butte. You really saved us."

Tony closed his large, calloused hand over hers. "You take care of your young one first." His eyes radiated sincerity. Mary nodded, warmed by his generosity.

Over the next few days, the two women savored every moment together, their babies beside them. During the day, they tended to chores, cooked hearty meals, and shared their dreams and frustrations about life on the frontier. At night, they retired to Anna's rope bed, whispering long into the darkness. Peter slept in the tack room with Tony.

Mary woke each morning to the aroma of coffee and sizzling venison sausage, feeling more rested than she had in months. Anna's presence brought a sense of radiant calm. They passed many hours sitting in silence, Isobel and John nestled between them as they knitted or mended clothes.

Mary gazed at the two sleeping infants nestled side-by-side in the willow bassinet. "To think our children will grow up together, forging a bond much like you and I."

Anna smiled, reaching over to adjust the blanket covering them. "They'll be as close as siblings. We'll make sure of it."

"Tell me how you picture them years from now," Mary said. Anna leaned back in her chair, contemplating.

"I see them roaming these hills, searching for adventure. They'll know every meadow, stream and cottonwood grove for miles..."

Mary smiled at the idyllic image. "Do you imagine they'll stay near after they're grown? Put down roots here?"

Anna sighed. "I hope so. But out here, it's hard to predict. They may strike out for the cities, or farther west. All we can do is give them a happy, wholesome childhood."

Mary nodded, a lump in her throat. She tried to etch this moment in her memory - the infants' tiny faces, Anna's company, the quiet cabin. A perfect capsule she could revisit years from now, whatever uncertainties the future held. As her past showed, nothing was guaranteed.

Anna gave her a knowing look and squeezed her hand. "But for now, we will raise them with an abundance of love."

Comforted, Mary returned her gaze to their sleeping babies. For now, this valley was their entire world. And they had each other's friendship. That was enough, though she missed Stella and Henry and wondered what her life would be like in Chicago.

But the idyllic days couldn't last forever. One crisp morning, snow still covering the meadow grasses, Mary gathered it was time to return home. After heartfelt goodbyes and promises to reunite soon, Peter took her back to town and to her canvas tent.

Though she would miss Anna and Peter's snug homestead, Mary's soul felt nourished by the gift of their unconditional love, comfort, and safety. Even in the isolated frontier, there were still hearths burning to gather 'round and kindred hearts ready to love.

When the winter weather took a turn for the better, the warm winds melted the snow. Marisol visited Mary every morning before she opened the saloon. George and Jack returned to finishing the store.

Isobel cried non-stop, unable to sleep because of the incessant banging of construction. Mary consulted her mother's grimoire and found a sound dampening spell.

Elements of silence weave your hush,
Cut off noise that causes a rush.
Wrap this tent in a muted fold,
Stop intrusions of noises too bold.
So mote it be!

As the last words of Mary's muffling spell faded, the canvas walls shimmered and wavered. A heavy silence descended within the tent, blocking out the racket of hammering and sawing from the store's construction.

Mary blew out her breath as a slow smile crossed her face. She closed the grimoire and tucked it under her pillow. She picked up Isobel from her cot and wrapped her arms around her kissing her forehead and whispering soothing words in her ear. Isobel's sobs subsided and her breathing slowed. Mary smiled and stroked her hair, humming a lullaby her mother used to sing.

Marisol ducked through the tent flaps, startling Mary. "Well, ain't that strange? I can't hear any of that ruckus in here."

Mary didn't remember how to undo the muffling spell and couldn't bring out the grimoire now. She forced a chuckle. "Funny how sturdy canvas can muffle noise." She held her breath, hoping that was the end of the noise discussion.

Marisol sank into the rickety wooden chair. It groaned under her weight. "I think this chair is trying to tell me something and it ain't nice."

"That chair is about to fall apart."

Marisol laughed and launched into describing more plans for her dream saloon.

Mary let her breath out. Why can't she use her magick as she pleased without worries of discovery? Life would be simpler.

As Marisol spoke, Mary drifted into her own thoughts. She'd craved wild freedom coming west, yet now found herself tethered by motherhood. The irony stabbed at her - she'd fled marriage and children, only to find herself married with a child on the frontier.

She shook her head, gazing at Isobel's rosebud lips. Yet her daughter was no burden, but a wellspring of joy. The warm weight nestled in her arms anchored Mary. For the first time, she understood true purpose.

She loved Isobel like nothing else in the world. Children were the dirty creatures she always thought they were, but it was nothing that couldn't be washed away. Her fears had been for naught.

Mary stood. "I hope you get the chance to have your own saloon. It sounds like a place I would like to visit." She had listened to Marisol's plans before. She envied the sense of direction her friend had. What could she do to ensure Isobel's future? "I feel like a walk. What do you say we walk over to the river?"

Marisol tilted her head. "Good idea. Been pent up like bears hibernating. Some fresh air would be good. Let's go."

Mary wrapped the blanket around Isobel tighter and pulled the tent flap aside. She walked through the doorframe of the store to find white puffy clouds covered the sky enough for the sun to play peek-a-boo between them. Mary blew out to see her frosty breath in front of her. She pulled Isobel tight against her chest and set out for the Bitterroot River bank.

Mary and Marisol strolled along the riverbank, their boots crunching on a mix of leftover snow and exposed earth. As Mary held her baby close, her heart swelled seeing Isobel's tiny pink face peek out from under the blanket.

The rushing river captivated Mary as they ambled along its banks. Sunlight danced across the rippling water, casting flickering reflections onto the shore. Ahead, a delicate willow sapling no taller than their knees swayed in the gentle breeze, its slender leafless branches beckoning.

Grasping Marisol's arm, Mary exclaimed, "Oh, look there! Isn't that little willow exquisite?" She turned to her friend, eyes alight. "Would you mind holding Isobel a moment? I simply must dig out this fellow and transplant him behind the store."

"I'd never miss a chance to hold this precious one." Marisol swept the cooing infant into her eager arms. Isobel gazed wide-eyed at the cottonwood branches swaying above, entranced by their hypnotic dance.

Kneeling on the muddy bank, Mary loosened the soil around the sapling's fragile roots, taking pains not to tear the tiny feeders. The earth crumbled under her hands as she freed the tree from its spot.

"There you are, little one," she murmured. Supporting the up-rooted willow like a newborn babe, she carried it to the creek's edge to wash its roots clean. Willow trees held a sacred place in her witchcraft, representing magick, intuition, and femininity.

Mary's eyes shone with excitement. "I'll plant this little willow behind the store, where its roots can spread and its branches reach for the open sky."

She pictured the slender tree in her mind's eye, grown tall and graceful beside the shop's rustic walls. Its trailing tendrils would sway in the breeze, welcoming all who passed beneath its canopy.

"It'll be beautiful," Marisol said, linking her arm through Mary's as they turned back. "We'll watch it grow together, season by season."

Mary gave her friend's arm an affectionate squeeze, heart brimming with gratitude. She had found the sisterhood lost when she'd fled Stella's stifling disapproval. In Marisol's steadfast loyalty, she'd found fertile soil for damaged roots to mend and grow strong again.

Mary knew that long after they were gone, this willow would stand as a living testament to the power of genuine friendship to uplift broken spirits and offer shelter from life's tempests.

CHAPTER TWENTY-SIX

GEORGE STOOD IN THE center of the finished store, hands on hips, chest puffed out. After months of backbreaking work, he had provided the little mining camp with its first mercantile. He let his gaze travel over the painted sign propped on the counter that read "Perkins General Store" in crisp black letters. Shelves lining the walls stretched from floor to ceiling, most empty and waiting to be stocked.

Barrels, crates, and sacks holding their current inventory surrounded the tent sitting in the middle of the floor. But soon enough, those shelves would overflow with tools, clothes, cast iron cookware, and dry goods.

Afternoon light flooded the space through the brand new glass windows. George nodded in satisfaction at the fine wooden counter they'd built, where he'd tally sales and collect payments.

The door opened and Jack strode in, giving a low whistle as he looked around. "Not too shabby, George." He clapped George on the back. "You should be open for business in no time."

George allowed himself a rare smile. He never expected to call the optimist a friend, but Jack proved his worth time and again. "Looks like all our hard work is paying off."

"What do you say we celebrate tomorrow night once we get the place presentable? We can invite our friends. Break open a case of whiskey too. I'd say we've earned it."

"All right, but I want *everyone*, including the miners." This new general store represented not only his own security, but that of the entire mining camp. A celebration was in order.

The next evening, George didn't recognize the place. They spent the morning moving the tent's contents, including the stove, up-stairs. Mary gave the tent away to a woman from Hamilton who planned to build a boarding house. They placed the inventory they had on shelves.

By the time Peter and Anna arrived, the smell of venison stew simmering over the wood stove permeated the air. The table from the saloon gracing the center of the room creaked under the weight of all the breads, beans, biscuits, and pies prepared by Mary, Marisol, and Anne. George's stomach rumbled.

The miners of the camp trickled through the door in their dusty clothes, clutching jugs of home brew. "Ain't seen a place so fine in a while," a grizzled old prospector, looking out of place with his tangled beard and tattered canvas pants, spun around as he marveled at the finished store.

The rowdy bunch echoed the sentiment as they found seats at the crowded table.

Ben, a miner who had helped frame, gave George a large sign carved with his name to hang outside. George had no words but managed a stuttered 'Thank you', eyes to the floor. No one had ever gone to such an effort to give him a gift. He wondered how long it took Ben to carve it, but he feared if he spoke a word more, he would blubber and make a fool of himself.

"Ya done good." The miner from South Carolina nodded his head. Murmurs of agreement rose among the scruffy lot.

For a man more accustomed to complaints and criticism, the praise made George shift in his chair. Mary's ladle clinked against the metal pot as she scooped steaming stew into bowls, causing a change in the conversations. Trust her to take the attention away from him. He wasn't sure if he was relieved or angry about it.

The merriment built as the whiskey flowed. George sensed a pleasant tingle on his lips as the powerful spirits slid along his throat. The sounds of people chatting and laughing in the background created a lively atmosphere. He watched as Jack climbed onto a wooden crate, his voice rising above the chatter as he called for attention. He admired the energy and enthusiasm of the crowd.

"Let's all raise a glass to George!" Jack hollered, lifting his cup high. "None of this would've been possible without his hard work and dedication!"

George waved off the boisterous cheers, but acceptance swelled in his heart. Here, among those who had toiled beside him to build this place from nothing, was applause worth savoring. This was all he ever wanted in his life but never received from anyone before, certainly not his father or mother. He was overcome and dumbstruck. At any moment, he feared he would cry. No way was he going to break down in front of anyone. He did like he always did—stuff his emotions away.

Several volunteers moved the table to one side to transform the room for music and dancing. A fiddler began a lively reel and Jack, Marisol, Peter, and Anna whirled about the floor. Laughter and off-key singing filled the air.

George watched Mary swaying with Henry's spawn in her arms across the room, the firelight dancing across her cheeks. He endured Tony's quiet presence beside him. Neither could dim his spirit tonight.

"You've made something worthwhile here," Tony said, handing George a fresh drink. "Should be proud."

George accepted the whiskey, nodding. As much as Tony irked him, the man had a knack for knowing when a kind word would mean something.

The night wore on in drinking, dancing and good-natured revelry. A little after midnight, the merrymakers trickled away in twos and threes. As the door closed behind the last guest, George sank into a chair by the wood stove, every limb leaden with exhaustion in a satisfying way. He watched Mary remove the remaining dishes from the table and head upstairs.

Jack dropped onto a crate nearby. His hair stood at odd angles and his eyes were bleary, but his grin still blazed. "Quite a celebration, eh?"

An answering smile crossed George's face. They marked his crowning achievement with a fine party. He had created something of value with Jack's help, of course.

For the first time in longer than he could recall, George realized he'd found a place where he belonged. It took a long journey to get here, but the payoff was right in front of him.

Early the next morning, George and Jack readied the wagon outside the now quiet store. They needed to make the haul to Hamilton to prepare the store for opening day.

As George struggled to yoke the oxen to the wagon, he glanced back at the dark shape of the store, a surge of satisfaction rushing through him. Maybe he'd hang that carved sign—George Perkins, Proprietor—to give himself a proper title. That would show his father. George had his own business and was going to be successful in his own way.

Jack tossed empty sacks and crates into the back of the creaking wagon with a series of thumps and thuds. "We've got a long road ahead today. But just think - when we come back to town, your store and my saloon will be stocked and open for business for both of us!"

As they set off on the dusty trail, George turned for another glimpse of the store that represented the first real fruits of his labors. For once, the future looked promising instead of uncertain.

With his new enterprise underway at last, George felt like a man standing atop a sturdy foundation. One he'd built with his own two hands through hard toil and determination. Out here on the frontier, he'd carved his own small pocket of civilization while making himself indispensable to the miners.

For the first time, people depended on him. The thought straightened his spine as he walked with the oxen and wagon, jostling along the rutted track toward Hamilton. He had built something permanent in this fleeting mining camp, a foothold in the wilderness. And that was reason enough to lift his chin high and walk tall.

The front door of the store flew open, banging against the wall, setting displays rattling as a brawny, bearded miner stormed in. George's headache redoubled. He'd already dealt with a messed up order and customers insisting on bartering. Now this ox, face purple with rage, was the last straw. Was he trying to break every pane in the door's window?

The miner slammed meaty fists on the counter. "This pickax broke first swing!" He brandished the tool, the tip chipped and mushroomed. "I want my money back, and I want it now!"

George crossed his arms, incensed by the bald-faced lie. That steel could fracture rock, not fail on a digger's carelessness. He knew quality, but this brute assumed him as a fool.

"You damaged it yourself," George retorted through clenched teeth. "I don't refund for incompetence."

"Why you cheating crook!" the miner bellowed. "I'll get my money's worth from your hide!"

Insults and threats ricocheted off the walls. Blood pounded in George's ears as his own shouts rang out. He leaned over the counter, veins bulging in his beet-red neck. No two-bit con would rip him off - he'd built this business from nothing!

Mary inserted herself between the purple-faced miner and himself, palms raised. "Gentlemen! I'm sure we can resolve this." Turning to the miner, she said, "Sir, I apologize profusely for the faulty pickax. Please accept a full refund today for the inconvenience."

George clenched his fists. That pickax wasn't faulty! Mary undercut his authority, and they'd lose money replacing goods broken by customers!

The miner paused his tirade, surprised. He looked wary, as if suspecting a trick.

Mary remained calm. "I insist. You've been wronged here." She placed a handful of banknotes on the counter. George watched as she counted out far too many bills, practically begging the scoundrel to take them. "This should more than cover what you paid."

The miner glanced down, his flush receding. He seemed torn, not knowing whether to stay angry or accept the apology.

"Please take it," Mary urged, pushing the bills closer. She lowered her voice. "Between you and me, we got a defective batch recently. But we'll make it right. Now, let's get you a new pickax that's to standard." She led him to the display and selected the finest one. "No charge at all. It's the least we can do."

George's face burned, watching Mary grovel at this brute. That ax was sound when sold! Mary would cost them a small fortune with her naïve mercy. No way would he let her usurp control again.

With the gleaming new tool in hand and anger soothed, the miner gave her a nod of grudging approval and headed out.

Mary turned to George, a self-righteous glint in her eye. Thought she knew better than him, did she? Just like when she tricked him into marriage with her charms. He wouldn't be sweet-talked again!

Before she opened her mouth, he roared, "Don't you ever go against me! Your doe-eyed act doesn't fool me."

Mary fell back, eyes widened. For an instant, she looked stricken. But her spine stiffened. "I won't let you bully me or customers. I saved you from a beating and the money is still on the counter."

George grew more livid at her stubbornness. "I would have won!" But maybe not. It didn't matter now. "See, you tricked him, too." Mary wheedled and manipulated people, yet thought herself so clever! He wouldn't tolerate her misguided decisions again - she'd shown her instincts couldn't be trusted. He'd be the sole authority in his store. "I see you give away your remedies, too. From now on, you sell them. No more giving away anything."

Using the claw of his hammer, he sent wood flying while opening a crate. No way would he let her ruin his success. George didn't come this far for a woman to destroy everything. Mary already had a noose around his neck, choking the living life out of him, which he would remove when he had the chance.

CHAPTER TWENTY-SEVEN

STELLA SANK INTO THE plush settee, gazing around at the lavish furnishings of her new home. Crystalline light from the chandelier glinted off the polished mahogany surfaces and papered walls. She didn't fathom this was her own parlor now, and that she belonged amid such finery.

It was a far cry from the cramped rooms she and her sister, Mary, had shared in the tenement above a tavern. Stella shuddered, remembering the leering drunks stumbling up the narrow stairs at all hours. They had been so young when their Uncle James died in a mining accident and her nanny job in Chicago fell through. It left them adrift in a big city where they knew no one.

Now, respectability and comfort were hers, thanks to new husband, Albert. He had lifted her from the shadows of her past into this sunlit life. They would fill these rooms with a family of their own soon. The thought wrapped Stella in contentment. She had all she dreamed of finding.

All except her sister, who she longed to be by her side. Worry for Mary, living in a tent with an infant, speared through her tranquility. The letter she'd penned sat atop the writing desk, awaiting the post. How irresponsible of Mary to be alone with an infant in the wilderness? That impetuous girl never considered consequences.

Stella fingered the gilded stationary. She had poured her heart into the page, beseeching Mary to return with her child, where she would offer them refuge. But she knew her independent sister, wild as an unbroken filly. Mary would resist any plea based on practicality.

Dearest Sister,

I'm happy to hear your news about baby Isobel and that you both are healthy. And it's special that you named her after our great-great-grandmother.

But I'm afraid for you and my niece to be living in those conditions. It's too much like when we first came to Chicago, living at the end of an alley without a roof over our heads. Those were scary and dreadful times.

Please come home. If not for yourself, then for your daughter.

Albert and I are married now. My home is beautiful and has plenty of room for you. I can and will help you. You just have to let me. Please, I'm begging you.

Love, Stella

Perhaps she should have appealed to Mary's sentimental side, reminding her of the closeness they once shared as children. She should have conveyed how their separation left a void in her heart, how Mary's presence would make her new home complete. Stella wrung her hands, wondering if she should rewrite the letter.

Stella sealed the letter, leaving it on her desk. She approached the wide bay window, watching a nanny push an ornate pram down the bricked street. Stella's arms ached to cradle her own baby. But she would surround her little niece with love and balm the hurts of Mary's rash choices if given the chance.

Turning from the window, Stella froze. Boots, her familiar, perched on the settee's rolled arm, regarding her with inscrutable yellow eyes.

Kneeling, Stella stroked Boots' sleek fur, tears welling. "Oh Boots, do you think she'll heed my plea? Will I ever see Mary again?"

The cat nudged his head into her hand, rumbling a consoling purr. Swiping at her eyes, Stella scooped Boots onto her lap as she settled by the hearth.

Stella let her mind drift back to their shared girlhood in Ireland - climbing trees and gathering wildflowers, spinning tales of fairies while their mother cooked over the peat fire. A pang of nostalgia pierced her. She longed to rekindle that glowing sisterly bond.

A log collapsed in the fireplace, scattering embers. Stella clung to hope that the same stubborn spark still smoldered inside Mary, beneath the layers of hurt and resentment accumulated over the years. They had allowed it to dim, but perhaps it was not too late to fan those embers back to life.

Boots nudged at her hand, reminding Stella she was not alone. She had a husband who adored her, a prosperous new life, and an independent spirit of her own now. She would carry the light of those memories within, even if Mary refused reconciliation.

With a deep breath, Stella set Boots down and rose to lift the letter from the desk. She held it to the fire's warmth, allowing love to flow from her heart through the inked lines. Though powerless to control her sister's choices, she could keep her own hopes kindled. She pressed a fervent kiss to the folded parchment.

"Find your way safely home," she whispered. Then, squaring her shoulders, Stella stepped out onto the sunlit streets. At the post, she consigned the missive to fate's hands. It was beyond her control now.

She could only trust that the bonds of blood would prevail, lighting Mary's road however she walked it. Until then, Stella would make her own joy, leaving the window open in hope.

Mary stretched to her full height, straining on tiptoes to shove a heavy box onto the top shelf. She didn't want it to drop and wake Isobel. As it seesawed on the edge, the mercantile door swung open, letting in a blast of crisp fall air.

Before she could turn to greet the customer, a large hand appeared in her periphery, nudging the box into place. Mary clasped her hands, stepping back in relief as she spun around. "Tony! Thank you. That was quite the balancing act."

Tony gave her a crooked smile beneath his unruly locks. "My pleasure, Mary. I'm always glad to lend a hand." His voice held a warm familiarity that caught her off guard.

Mary busied herself tidying the lower shelves, hoping to hide her flushed cheeks. She hadn't seen Tony since he came to their party when the store was completed. His affectionate manner around her had always been... confusing.

"Just stopping in while I'm in town. We've missed your lively company at the homestead," Tony remarked, leaning on the counter's end.

Mary kept her eyes averted, concentrating on aligning condensed milk cans with label edges lined up. "Yes, well, the store keeps me busy these days. And my daughter. I see Peter and Anna every Sunday when they come to the new church."

Mary stayed away, unnerved by Tony's obvious admiration. If only he directed it elsewhere instead of kindling complications. She peeked up to find him watching her, hat in hand.

Clearing her throat, Mary adopted a business-like tone. "Will you be needing any supplies today? We got a new shipment of tools in."

"No, no supplies. I came to ask something I can't get off my mind." Tony ambled closer and her pulse quickened. Mary needed an escape from this conversation's trajectory.

"You know, we expanded our dry goods selection," she redirected, edging toward the bolts of fabric. "Let me show you. I ordered the loveliest calico pattern…" What was she doing? Mary walked over to the hardware section.

Tony pursued, a determined look on his face, his jaw clenched in resolve. "Mary, leave George. He doesn't deserve you. Come away with me, and I'll show you a life full of love and devotion."

Despite the sincerity shining in his eyes, laughter bubbled in her chest. The sheer audacity was absurd. Yet a small part of her warmed at the idea of being treasured. Mary tamped it down.

"While I appreciate your concern, I gave my word to George's brother to stand by him and keep him safe. And I shan't break it." Mary lifted her chin, brooking no argument.

Tony wore a frown on his face, but he nodded anyway, conceding defeat. Donning his hat, he strode to the door and turned to face her. "The offer stands whenever you wish. I know your worth, Mary. Don't forget to value yourself." He walked out and closed the door behind him.

Mary sagged against the shelves, drained, as she watched him walk across the rutted road to the livery under construction. She had no intentions toward Tony, but the temptation to be cared for…it haunted the lonely corners of her spirit. But only Henry took space in her heart and soul. She resumed unpacking boxes, sorting through her jumbled feelings along with the contents.

Tony didn't comprehend the complications that bound her here. But his visit had awakened yearnings suppressed since leaving her former life behind—to be indulged and protected; to feel beautiful, admired, adored. Mary cherished his friendship, yet it stirred a longing for something more.

Henry would have offered what Tony did. But her rash actions destroyed that future. Her choices had painted her into a corner of her own making. Now she must live within the confines, taking solace in purpose over passion. Mary peered behind the counter at her nine-month-old daughter sleeping in a basket she bought from a local Salish woman.

With a deep breath, Mary straightened her shoulders and kept working. This was the life she had, the only one left available. It would have to suffice. Her dreams belonged only to herself now.

CHAPTER TWENTY-EIGHT

IN THE BACK ROOM of the store, Mary's fingers worked deftly, shaping a lump of rendered tallow. Her palms radiated an intense heat, not from any flame but from an inner fire, a gift she seldom revealed. She pressed a fresh wick into the center, molding the tallow into a perfect, creamy candle. The church bells tolled in the distance, marking the quiet Sunday morning, but here, Mary was enveloped in her own world of craft and concentration.

She repeated the process over and over, the soft whispers of wicks and tallow under her touch providing a comforting rhythm. Each candle she formed became a testament to her unique gift, a secret flame that danced at her fingertips, unseen but potent.

Her stock of candles, depleted from a surge in sales, replenished under her careful attention. This magick, subtle yet powerful, provided her and young Isobel with a modest but crucial income.

While Mary helped two-year-old Isobel count the candles, she heard the door rattle and the bell over the door tinkle. A woman's voice, ragged with coughing, called out, "Is anyone there? I see a light."

Mary unlocked the door, crossing her index and middle finger and spreading them with a flick. "Come in." It was a rare pleasure to have another woman's company, a respite from the usual male clientele seeking supplies. Marisol hadn't stopped by on Saturday or Sunday, as she slept in after a long night at work. And Anna, still in church, would stop by later.

The visitor, a blonde around thirty, appeared perplexed, her gaze lingering on the doorknob. "I need something for this damn cough," she said, her voice raspy. Mary recognized her from the local boarding house, a place Mary would rather sleep in the cold than frequent.

"I have a tea but not much. It's been in demand and I can't grow any of the herbs until spring."

"What do you want for it?"

Mary reached into a box behind the counter and retrieved a small paper wrapper containing sweetgrass, sage, and St. John's Wort. "It's fifty cents. It has to be steeped in hot water. Your cough will clear."

The woman dug into a pocket hidden in the waistband of her skirt and pulled out a few coins. "A card reader told me I would work as I am and get sick in the winter. I believe those cards."

Mary reached into her bag of supplies and pulled out her tarot cards, the darkest blue without being black, a gold triple crescent in the center. "You mean these?"

The woman's face beamed like a summer's day. "Yes! You read?"

"Aye, I read. If you tell others about your reading, you can have a free reading right now." Mary cleared the top of a box near the wood stove. She motioned for the woman to sit on a stool. "Isobel, play with your dolly for a while. John will be here soon."

"Okay, Mama." Isobel ran behind the counter and returned, dragging a rag doll. She sat on the floor and played tea party with an invisible teapot and cups. Mary wished she could afford to buy her an actual set.

The woman sat. "I will tell everyone. I'm not the only one who believes in the cards. Even the religious ones will sit for a reading as long as no one sees."

As Mary shuffled the deck, she focused on the cards. "Cut the deck for me," she instructed.

"First, what is your name? I'm Dawn." Dawn had a kind smile.

"I'm Mary." She chuckled and shook her head. "Sorry, I'm tired. I've lost my manners."

Dawn adjusted herself on the stool and cut the deck.

Mary grasped the deck and flipped the first card, setting it on the box. "Hmm. Lady Justice. You've faced injustice, but the universe seeks balance. Good begets good." *If you do bad, it comes back three-fold.*

Dawn's expression clouded, worry lines cut deep across her forehead. "Ya. That sums it up alright." She coughed a few times.

Mary's chair scuffed the floor when she rose and headed towards the wood stove, the floorboards creaking beneath her. She placed the kettle of water on with a loud clank. "Let's fix that tea now to get you some relief."

"That's kind of you. Thank you. I knew coming in here was going to change my life. I just knew it." Dawn sat straighter and let out a sigh that triggered more coughing. "This is annoying."

Mary returned to her seat. "You'll be better soon. I'll draw another card while we wait for the water to heat." For herself, she would heat the water with her hands, but she had to hide that ability, which was a shame. Witches had so much to offer, but people missed out. Such a pity she couldn't package it like her herbs and make a profit. If she were a wealthy woman, she could use her influence to change society's perception of witchcraft.

Mary turned over the next card. "The Nine of Swords. Your worries consume you, but they also show your desire for change."

Dawn nodded. "If I only knew what to do."

"Let's draw the next card. Maybe it will give you guidance. Or a warning."

"Yes. I need something, anything." Dawn rubbed her hands together.

Mary heard bubbles breaking the surface of the water and rose to approach the stove. She sprinkled the herbs into a cup and poured water over them. She carried the cup and placed it in front of Dawn. "Let it set to pull the herbs into the water." She returned to her seat. Stella, the master at reading cards, taught Mary. But the readings she did on the trail had helped improve her abilities. She enjoyed giving people the insights to change their lives. She should have read her own cards before she left Chicago.

The faded, smooth surfaces of the cards slid over one another like the rustle of dry leaves, full of character and a certain timeless grace. Mary placed the next card on top of the box. "The Three of Wands. A bold decision awaits you. A leap of faith."

"I have to do something different. I can't continue at the boarding house. It works for some, but I hate it. I want to do something I like, you know?" Dawn lifted the cup to her lips. "Hmm. Smells good." She took a cautious sip and another. "Tastes good, too."

Mary was doing something she liked right now, but that was only minutes out of her day. What would she do if she could do what she liked whenever she liked? Most likely making potions and doing spells. Doing magick made her happy. She had been told her whole life that she was mistaken to want things to always go her way by using magick. But if something made you happy, shouldn't you do that? That was what Dawn faced. What all women faced.

Dawn's face relaxed. "I don't feel the urge to cough now. That's a pleasant change."

The tea always worked. And that made Mary content for a moment. "Good. Ready for the next card?"

"Yes. A big decision and what's next?"

Once the card laid upright on the box, Mary said, "Knight of Swords."

"Oh. That looks good, right?"

Mary tilted her head. "Channel your frustration into positive change."

Dawn twisted her mouth and sighed. "I grumble too much. I need to take that and make something better out of it. Yeah, I can do that."

"Okay. Next card." Mary slid the card out of her hand and laid it on the box. "The Fool."

Shoulders pushed back and eyes wide open, Dawn exclaimed, "Oh no!"

Mary smiled. Everyone had that reaction. "It's fine. Fresh starts. New beginnings. Believe in yourself. What do you like to do?"

Dawn's face brightened. "I like to bake and I'm damn good, too. The boarding house has an oven, and I've been baking bread."

There it was. A new opportunity that Dawn was blind to. "Do you give it away or sell it?"

"Well, I give it to whoever wants it."

Mary noticed a glimmer of excitement in Dawn's eyes. "Oh, I could sell it. Which is fair because I have to buy the ingredients and I should get paid for my time. Oh, this is great. I never thought about making money with my baking. The cards are talking to me! Oh, Mary. This is wonderful." Dawn stood, knocking the empty cup off the box, but she caught it and handed it to Mary. "Thank you."

"Dawn, if you'd like, you can sell your bread here. I can put them on the front counter."

Dawn put her hands together at her chin. "That would be splendid. You are incredibly kind. I'm going to tell everyone about your card reading. It's a life changer."

As Dawn left, Mary reflected on the power of her readings, the joy of helping others find their way. She longed for more moments like this, where her magick and intuition could bring light to others' lives. The extra income would be helpful. But what she wanted to do was more magick.

The mercantile door flew open, letting in a biting gust of winter air that whipped the curtains into a frenzy. Mary's gaze jerked up from weighing nails for a customer, her transaction interrupted. A broad-shouldered man with a reddish beard stood waiting. His intense blue eyes sparked a sense of familiarity in Mary.

With an apologetic smile to her customer, Mary finished the sale. As the patron bundled their purchase and slipped outside, Mary's mind raced. Those piercing eyes—where had she seen them before?

The man removed his hat, releasing a mane of unruly curls the color of fox fur. "Afternoon, ma'am," he said. "You likely don't remember me, but—"

"The false nugget," Mary blurted out as realization struck. Heat rose in her cheeks. This was the swindler from Bannack who had tried to cheat her. She straightened her shoulders, on guard. "You're a long way from home. What brings you here?"

The man winced at her blunt recollection. "I admit I acted a fool in Bannack. A thieving partner gave me that false nugget. You saved me from further loss with your... special talent."

Mary tensed. How much did he know of her gift? She changed the subject. "If you've come seeking mining equipment, I'm well stocked."

The man shook his head. "It's you I seek. The name's Bill." He extended a hand in introduction. "I want to hire your services, if you're willing."

Mary balked, outrage flaming through her veins. How dare this scoundrel insult her dignity with his crude implications? "I suggest the boarding house for your sort of propositions, not my store," she seethed, fists clenched. From the corner of her eye, she noticed little Isobel watching the exchange. A pang of sadness pierced Mary's anger. Her child deserved better than this rough life they led.

Bill's eyes widened. He pulled his hand back and shook his hands, palms facing Mary. "Pardon my boldness, ma'am. I meant only to hire your unique talent for finding gold." He leaned in, dropping his voice. "You have a gift for sensing it. I saw it plain as day in Bannack."

Mary froze. Could her long-held secret ability be known? Unease trickled along her spine. She changed the subject again, feigning ignorance. "Unless you're buying, I must ask you to move along. I'm very busy."

Bill took a deep breath. "Alright." He paused. "You can detect gold." He paced in front of the counter and talked with his hands.

"Without even touching it. You can tell when it's there and not there. When I saw you do it in Bannack, I couldn't keep it out of my mind. People think I'm crazy, but I know what I saw. And here you are."

Now Mary realized what he wanted. It would've been nicer if he would've spit it out right away. "Yes, here I am. Working. I'm still in the dark about why you want to hire me, and I'm not sure I'm available."

Bill cocked his head. "Can we start with a name? I like to know the name of the person I'm talking to."

"Mary."

Bill bowed and continued. "Pleased to make your acquaintance, Mary. Now my idea is if you walk around, you can tell if there's gold in the ground."

Mary came around the counter and stood where she faced him and laughed. "You think I can take a stroll and find gold? If that were true, I'd be rich." Bill had a few screws loose. She marched to the back wall, two-year-old Isobel racing behind her, grabbed the broom, and began sweeping. The youngster swung around an imaginary broom, mimicking her mother.

Bill ambled closer and leaned over, his face close to hers. "It's possible. I propose a test. A quick one."

Mary sucked in a deep breath and released it. Bill was on her last nerve and stood in the way of her sweeping. "What's this test?" She took a step around him to continue.

"I want you to go to the Trails End Mine and..." Bill shrugged "...see if you sense anything. That's all." He backed away. "If you do, I want to commission you to find me a successful claim. Plain and simple. I have money, real money—no fake nuggets."

Mary leaned on her broom and considered what Bill said. It's true no one could pass fake gold on her. But could she tell if it was underground? Shouldn't she seek her own claim then? Her lack of trust in men made her uneasy about hiring them to work a claim. The only way for her to avoid the hassle of working on a claim was to earn a substantial amount of money by discovering one. This might be a way to gain enough money to take care of her and Isobel for a long time.

"Aye. I will go with you to the mine. On Saturday when I close early. I expect a gold eagle coin to find you gold and a twenty percent cut thereafter. Where do I find you?"

Bill smiled and put his arms out like he was going to hug her. When Mary retreated, he dropped his arms and shrugged. "Sounds fair. Meet me at the saloon. Thank you, Mary, for considering my idea. I'll leave you to your work. Thank you." He backed to the door and left, singing.

While Mary swept the floor, her mind raced with possibilities about Bill's proposition. Mary had always known that she had the fire gift, but she had never considered it would help her find gold. It made sense. When certain metals were nearby, a hum permeated her body. Her fingers would itch to touch it as if she were a magnet drawn to them.

Mary leaned her broom against a barrel of beans. She buried a silver coin deeper and deeper in the beans, testing the limits of her ability. Holding her hand over the beans, she could still sense the coin, no matter how deep she buried it. Her body acted like a compass, drawn to the metal like a magnet.

Excitement quickened Mary's pulse. Could she master this ability, transforming her circumstances? She envisioned returning to Chicago, buying a fine brick home, and Isobel attending school.

Isobel reached out her tiny hand. "Beans."

Mary scooped a few beans and handed them to her daughter. "Don't eat them. Just play with them."

Isobel plopped on the floor, placing the beans one by one in a row. Then she picked them up, counting, "One, two, four, fine."

Mary had a gift, a unique ability that might make her rich beyond her wildest dreams. She would meet Bill come Saturday, and see where this thread led. But she vowed to remain grounded and protect Isobel above all else. This gift was hers to use, not to be used by. With a deep breath, Mary returned to her sweeping, renewed purpose, steadying her steps.

CHAPTER TWENTY-NINE

THE DIN OF THE rowdy saloon assaulted Mary's ears as she pushed through the swinging doors. Little Isobel perched on her hip. The hazy air reeked of stale beer and tobacco, the din of off-key singing and raucous laughter mingling over the tinny notes plucked from a piano in the corner. Sawdust sprinkled over the scarred wooden floor muffled her footsteps as she scanned the crowded room.

Above the sea of battered hats and sweat-stained shirts, Mary spied her contact, Bill, sitting alone at the bar nursing a whiskey. She wove her way toward him, pulse quickening. This arrangement could be the windfall she needed to provide a stable life for her daughter. A dozen pairs of eyes sized her up as she passed by, but she kept her focus straight ahead, refusing to acknowledge their leers.

"There's my girl!" Mary turned to see her dear friend Marisol behind the bar, arms outstretched. Isobel lunged into Marisol's eager embrace, fingers fascinated by the colorful feathers decorating her hat.

Mary sighed in relief, the tension easing from her shoulders. "You'll watch her a spell? I've business across the way." At Marisol's nod, she planted a swift kiss atop Isobel's downy blond head. "Be good for Aunt Mari now, love."

The dancing plumes enthralled Isobel too much to notice her mother's departure. Mary joined Bill at the far end of the bar, taking a deep breath to gather her courage. His eyes held a speculative glint as he inclined his head toward the door, showing their transaction was best conducted outside. Mary's knees trembled as she preceded him into the dusty street. This was it—her chance to prove her rumored skills at divining gold. An opportunity that could change everything.

Outside, Bill guided her toward a rickety buckboard hitched to a sturdy roan gelding. He gave her rumpled split riding skirt a bemused once-over. "Reckon you can manage in that getup?"

Mary lifted her chin. "I've managed far more, in far less out on the trail." She hoisted herself onto the bench seat beside him, hands trembling. So much depended on what the next few hours would reveal. She focused on slowing her rapid breaths, willing her nerves to settle. Failure was not an option; Isobel's future happiness hinged on her success today.

Bill snapped the reins and eased the rig away from town toward the craggy foothills ringing the valley. As they bounced along the rutted track, Mary lifted her face to the sun, eyes drifting closed. The raw openness of the Big Sky country still called to her pioneer spirit, a siren song awakened on her westward journey. Yet she was no longer a lone adventurer but a mother with a child dependent on her wits and grit. The taste of unfettered freedom belonged to her alone no more.

The fading afternoon sunlight washed the rugged landscape in hues of burnished gold. Ahead, the ramshackle collection of tents and slapdash lean-tos marking the Trail's End mine came into view, tucked against the base of a craggy ridgeline. Mary inhaled the loamy scent of churned earth, wood smoke, and the acrid tang of dynamite fumes. The makeshift mining camp carried a charge of frenzied energy; the pulse of rough-hewn men feverishly working their claims.

When Bill reined his horses to a halt, Mary hopped down from the rig and stroked the dust off her skirt. She felt the weight of curious stares from nearby miners, eyeing this woman striding into camp. Her modest sage blouse and dark hair pinned beneath a woven hat marked her as no saloon girl. She kept her gaze fixed straight ahead.

Bill wove them along the steep ravine, pockmarked with tunnel entrances and piles of rocky debris. The screech and clank of a steam winch broke the stillness as they passed the deepest shaft. Mary paused, allowing the subtle thrum of the gold veins below to resonate through the soles of her boots. Yes, a rich load ran beneath this claim. Untold riches awaiting extraction from the earth's grasp.

At the edge of the existing claims, they stepped into an undisturbed valley. Mary tilted her face skyward, eyes tracing the wheeling path of a lone hawk. She ran a hand along the scraggly lodgepole pines they passed, relishing the sun-warmed roughness of the bark beneath her palms. How long had it been since she escaped the confines of the store to roam these open wilds that had sung their siren song and drawn her west? The landscape's stark grandeur stirred her soul.

Kneeling, Mary pressed both hands flat to the spongy earth, reaching out using more than ordinary touch. The ground seemed to thrum and vibrate beneath her skin, a magickal dance. She traced the subtle vibrations westward to a gentle rise blanketed in wildflowers. Here the enticing song deep below crescendoed, shivering through her palms like a beacon.

"The earth lies heavy here," she called out to Bill, pointing along
the hidden seam she had traced. He hurried over, tilting his head
as he inspected her coordinates, skepticism fading from his craggy
features. He tugged at his grizzled beard, nodding.

"Can't argue, missy." He dug in his pocket until he retrieved a
twenty-dollar gold eagle coin and placed it in her palm, winking.
"Earned yourself a finder's fee."

Mary closed her fingers around the solid heft of the coin, its edges
pressing into her flesh. A fierce surge of satisfaction kindled in her
core, setting her blood into a hum. The endless chores of the store
seemed petty now; she was meant for more than stocking pots and
weighing nails. Her uncommon gifts could earn a living here amidst
the savage beauty of this untamed land.

As the angle of the sun stretched the shadows long, they made
their way back toward the wagon in satisfied silence. Back on the
creaking buckboard bench, Bill glanced over his shoulder. "Much
obliged for your help today. I'll stop in the next trip I make to the
assayer and I'll have your cut ready."

Mary granted him a single brisk nod. She would wring all the
opportunity she could from this harsh but bountiful country. Isobel would not endure the pinching poverty of her own childhood.
Together they would claim a measure of comfort and security on
the frontier, come what may. She had talents beyond the ordinary
to rely on now.

The jostling wagon ride back toward town settled her restless-
ness, calm purpose replacing nervous anticipation within her. How
she had missed these wide open horizons and rugged lands, much
different from the crowded streets of Chicago where she'd lived.
Their wild, untrammeled spirit had called to her then, luring her

westward. She realized the siren song wasn't only for her—she now chased it for the sake of her daughter.

Mary traced the hard outline of the coin through the pocket of her skirt, finding comfort in its solidity. She harbored no regrets, for the freedom surrendered; Isobel's sweet face and dimpled laughter erased all doubts. The child had awakened instincts more powerful than the longing for adventure. Yet this raw, unpredictable country still held the opportunity for those bold enough to seek their destiny.

In the distance, the scattered buildings of Tin Creek emerged—the church, the assayer's office, the livery stable, the saloon, and her own mercantile. Isobel waited there, unaware of the future her mother now shaped for them both through will, grit, and uncommon gifts. But Mary envisioned the life ahead. They would manage, somehow, mother and child together. She squared her shoulders, weariness replaced by the fiery determination churning within her.

Isobel would not endure the biting poverty and uncertainty that haunted Mary's own childhood memories. She would wring every advantage she could from this harsh but bountiful land. They might bend beneath the heavy winds that gusted through this frontier existence, but they would not break. Using the aid of her uncommon skills, she would secure their place, carving out a free and prosperous future for them both. This wild country held possibilities untapped for those brave enough to seek them.

The saloon's raucous din once again buffeted Mary as she pushed into its smoky confines, eyes scanning for her daughter. There at a corner table sat Marisol, entertaining Isobel by swirling a feather under the child's nose. Her piping giggles warmed Mary's heart.

"Look who's back, my wee one," Marisol exclaimed. Isobel's rose-bud mouth opened wide in recognition, her chubby arms reaching out for her mother. Mary enfolded her in a fierce embrace, her child's downy head nestled in the crook of her neck, breathing in her comforting scent. No matter what destiny called, this child was her true home. Tomorrow's challenges could wait. Tonight, she held everything that mattered in her arms.

Mary hummed to herself as she arranged the jars of candy on the shelf behind the counter. She had to stretch her arm high to push the jars back against the wall. The merry tinkling of the bell over the door announced another customer. Mary turned, smiling, while brushing a loose strand of hair behind her ear.

"Morning Bill." He visited monthly to get supplies and deliver her cut from his latest mining haul. At first, the payments were small, just a few shiny nuggets or a small sack of gold dust. But over the months, they had grown larger as Bill struck it big on his claim. He entertained Mary with stories of his progress—starting construction, digging holes, discovering the valuable deposits that Mary had suspected. His enthusiastic stories always left her feeling both exhilarated and uneasy.

The money itself made Mary nervous. The small fortune Bill had paid her over the months remained upstairs, tucked away in the loose floorboard under her bed. Her eyes widened every time she glimpsed at the stack of cash, more money than she had ever seen in her life. She knew she couldn't keep it there forever. She planned on asking Peter to open a bank account for her at the new bank that opened next to the assayer's office. As a woman, she couldn't open an account on her own, so she would have him open the account in Henry's name.

This morning, however, Bill was not his usual jovial self. His smile was absent and worry lines creased his face. He waited until the other customers had left the store, then approached the counter, twisting his hat in his hands.

"Mary, I need to warn you about someone," he said in a low voice. "There's a man who has a claim above mine. I didn't even realize he was there until a week ago. But he saw you there, that day you came looking for gold."

Mary's breath caught in her throat. She steadied herself with one hand on the counter as Bill continued.

"He's been yelling threats at me for days, accusing me of cheating and claiming you have something to do with it."

Mary took a small step back, her heart pounding. All these months, she thought, no one had witnessed her secret ability to sense precious metals deep underground. Now this stranger knew her secret and made dangerous accusations.

"But I wasn't doing anything suspicious!" Mary protested. "I could have been picking wildflowers for all anyone knows."

Bill shook his head. "This one's not thinking straight. He's lost his marbles and could be dangerous. You need to watch your back."

Mary's mind raced, scenarios flashing through her mind. She needed more information about this angry stranger. "What does he look like?" she asked. "I need to know who to be on guard against."

Using her index finger, Mary traced a quick pentagram on the counter, hidden from Bill's view. She had cast protection spells around the store before, but she would have to reinforce them now.

Bill leaned back and stared at the ceiling for a moment. "You'll know him when you see him. He has long blond curly hair tied back, and wears a big floppy hat, probably to keep the sun off his skin since he's pale."

Bill moved toward the door, casting a worried glance back at Mary. "I gotta get back to my claim before he damages anything. You be safe now, Mary."

As soon as Bill left, Mary rushed to lock the front door and flip the sign to 'closed'. Fear and anger churned inside her as she tried to process this new threat. She had to protect herself and her child.

"Isobel!" she called out. "Come to Mama!"

Mary swept up her young daughter in her arms and carried her upstairs. The pounding of her own heart in her ears drowned out the sound of her new shoes pounding on the wooden stairs.

Isobel giggled and raised her arms. "Whee! Faster, Mama!"

Despite everything, her daughter's sweet face still made her smile. Mary would move heaven and earth to keep her safe. In her bedroom, she set Isobel on the floor. Then she moved to the bed and kneeled, feeling around under the frame for the loose floorboard. She pried it up and removed her most precious treasures - her mother's grimoire and enchanted necklace

The old leather-bound book contained many protection spells. Mary would need to weave the strongest magick she could summon to protect them from this new threat. She went into the kitchen carrying the book and necklace.

Once she set them on the rough wooden table, Mary opened the grimoire, running her fingers over the worn pages. The book seemed to open on its own to a candle spell for protection. Mary chuckled. Of course. She'd been making candles for weeks from rendered tallow. But the spell called for black candles, and she had none. She would need to improvise.

Mary moved towards the wood stove, opening the door. She stirred the ashes, creating a cloud of smoky dust. She rubbed the blackened residue over the surface of two pale candles, transforming them into darkened objects. The ash stained her hands, but she remained engrossed in her task.

After putting on her mother's enchanted necklace, she returned to the table. Mary would never remove it again; the power emanating from it spoke to her. Her fingers traced the trinity knot, finding the ruby, the emerald, and the sapphire.

Mary arranged the two black candles and one white candle in a triangle, white at the top, then seated herself before them. She wrote the angry man's name that Bill had mentioned - Sid - on a slip of paper and visualized his face and threats, anger simmering. She saw herself and Isobel surrounded by a glowing shield of protection, safe from harm.

As she lit the white candle, she envisioned it radiating a pure, bright light that represented protection. Mary spoke the spell while staring into the flame.

By the light of this flame, I call on the goddess Brigit,
Protect myself and my daughter, keep us safe and free.
Shield us from harm, banish Sid away,
May his threats and ill intentions never see the light of day.
With this binding spell, our safety I fortify,

So mote it be!

Then she lit the two black candles. Mary held the piece of paper with Sid's name on it over the white candle until it caught. She let it fall into the pot. As it burned, she visualized his negative energy being consumed by the flames, rendering him powerless.

The candles flickered as if responding to her urgent plea. Their light filled her with hope and courage. Regardless of the outcome of her spell, she took solace because she had stood up against this threat to her secret and her child. Mary would not let Sid intimidate or silence her. She was ready to stand her ground.

CHAPTER THIRTY

MARY HUMMED AS SHE wiped the worn wooden counter of her small general store. The morning had dragged by, only a handful of customers stopping in for supplies. She glanced over at Isobel, playing with dolls in the corner behind the counter.

Seeing her daughter safe and happy brought a soft smile to Mary's face, before her thoughts wandered back to the small fortune she had stashed in a brand new bank account.

George still believed them to be living hand-to-mouth from the store's profits while he spent his trust money at the saloon. If she explained where her money came from, it would mean revealing her supernatural ability to sense precious metals deep underground. Mary trusted Bill to keep her secret, but not George.

The jangling bell over the door shook her from her musings. Mary looked up to see a disheveled, wild-eyed man entering the store. Her heart sank as she recognized him as Sid, the angry miner who had been threatening Bill. His filthy clothes and unkempt beard matched Bill's description.

As Sid shuffled closer, muttering under his breath, Mary's muscles tensed and her pulse quickened. She wore her mother's enchanted necklace under her dress, the one she had used to cast a protection spell. But seeing Sid in person still made her anxious. Would her amateur spell work if confronted?

"I saw what I saw... I know what I know..." Sid repeated to himself as he wandered the store. He had never come in before, despite being in town for some time. Mary wondered if he was avoiding her, or preferred to travel the long distance to Hamilton for supplies.

"Can I help you find anything?" Mary asked, hoping he would make his purchase and leave.

Instead, Sid turned and barreled over to the counter, fixing her with an intense, unsettling stare. Mary recoiled from his wild eyes and pungent odor. George's imposing presence kept troublesome customers in line, but he was likely off drinking already at the saloon across the street.

"I know your secret," Sid declared in a gravelly voice, planting his grubby hands on the counter and leaning toward her.

Unsure how to respond, Mary feigned ignorance, buying time to assess the situation. "I'm not sure what you mean. What secret?"

Sid leaned further over the counter, his face inches from hers. "You've got some trick to show Bill where the gold is. Ain't no way he'd get that lucky on his first claim without help."

Mary forced a small laugh, hoping to show little concern for his accusations. "Oh, Bill likes to chat while he works. We've been friends for years."

Sid tilted his head, scrutinizing her face for any betrayal of dishonesty. He reached for a loaf of bread Dawn had dropped off that morning and slammed it on the counter, crushing it.

Mary seethed at the blatant disrespect for her friend's wares, but kept her expression neutral. "You think I'm helping Bill cheat somehow?" she asked. "I'm too busy running this store and caring for my daughter to get involved in claims."

"Maybe it ain't about claims," Sid leered. "George complains about you plenty at the saloon. Says you're frigid. Though I wouldn't blame you not giving yourself to that husband of yours. Reckon you and Bill got something going on the side?"

Anger flared in Mary at the offensive insinuation, but she tamped it, willing herself to remain calm. "I can assure you I'm faithful to my husband," she replied. "Now, you'll need to pay for that damaged bread."

Sid leaned further, pressing his advantage of size and gender. "I seen you in them hills more times than makes sense. Bill's striking it richer than anyone, and it's cause you're pointing him right to it!" He gestured at the dented loaf. "Ain't paying for nothing!"

Mary met his stare, refusing to be intimidated. "The vein on Bill's claim likely continues onto yours. If you keep digging, you'll profit too." She hoped appealing to his greed might distract him.

Sid paused, then leaned in closer, a nasty gleam in his eye. "Sometimes folks get chased off if others think they're cheating." He glanced at Isobel. "Might want to avoid the hills for a while, for you and the girl's sake."

The scalawag turned and stalked out, slamming the door behind him. Isobel scurried over with frightened eyes, and Mary hugged her shaking daughter close, stroking her hair. But her mind was spinning with ways to handle Sid. She would not let him bully or threaten them further.

Absently, she grasped the engraved pendant she wore, drawing strength from its subtle warmth. Mary would stop Sid for good. If she could prevent him from profiting off Bill's vein, it might curb his dangerous obsession. Bill didn't deserve to be chased off his claim, either. He was a nice man who discovered she had a skill she wasn't even aware of. And he paid her well.

What was the worst thing she could do? Mary didn't care anymore if it caused harm. She was past that point. Her mother had a spell that prevented someone from touching certain items and used it to protect her grimoire.

When a miner cannot touch the precious nuggets they dig for, they're no longer a miner. By incorporating a gold nugget into the spell, she could ensure the troublemaker would face a painful burn each time he laid his hands on gold. Mary needed to gather her materials. Fortunately, she had a nugget, and she was going to make Sid pay.

But it would have to wait until she closed the store for the day. That would try her patience.

Mary hastened up the stairs, her heart thumping with a mix of excitement and trepidation. Her day's business had ended, but her true work was just beginning. The floorboards groaned under her hurried steps as she entered her room; the door swinging open with a creak. Without shutting it, she dove into her task.

Dropping to her knees, her skirt billowing around her, Mary crawled under the bed. Her fingers, nimble and determined, sought the hidden compartment. Dust motes danced in the slanted light as she pried open the loose floorboard, revealing her most treasured secret—her mother's grimoire.

Standing, Mary dusted her hands and skirt, then opened the ancient tome. Its pages, yellowed with age, exhaled a scent of history and mystery. Her eyes found the spell she sought, its words a beacon calling to her.

Mary needed three things: an object to repel, in this case, gold, a magnet, and fire. The gold was easy. She had a small piece in her pocket that Bill had given her the last time he came. The magnet was a little harder, but she remembered a miner had given Isobel a lodestone once, a curious rock that stuck to anything metal. And fire, well, she had that in abundance.

Isobel came running to her, a cloth doll clutched in her hand. "Momma, what's that?" she asked, pointing to the book.

Mary smiled, trying to hide her excitement. "It's a book written by your Irish grandmother," she said.

"Oh. Pictures?" Isobel asked, trying to see over the counter.

"Not a storybook, dear," Mary said, stroking her daughter's red hair. "It's a book of recipes, things your grandmother and her mother before her knew. One day, you'll use it too."

Isobel's face fell, but then brightened again. "When, mama?"

Mary chuckled. "You'll know when. Now, go play. Mama has work to do."

Isobel ran off, her doll cradled in her arms.

Mary would have to wait to do the spell after her daughter was asleep. The desire was strong, almost overwhelming, to do it now, by the open window, where the moonlight streamed in. But she couldn't risk it. She had to keep her true self hidden, at least for now. A secret she kept, even from her own daughter.

Mary closed the grimoire. She had to get back to her mundane chores. But the knowledge of the spell, the power it gave her, was like a fire burning in her veins. She couldn't wait to unleash it. She was a fire witch, and she had the power to do great things.

But she had to be careful. She couldn't let anyone know about her powers, not even Isobel. It was a dangerous world for people like her, people who were different. Mary had heard stories of witches, like her mother, being burned at the stake, of people being persecuted for their beliefs. She had to keep her secret hidden, at least for now.

When it was time to put Isobel to bed, she read her a story, sang a soft lullaby while a sense of peace wash over her. When Isobel fell asleep, Mary headed back to the grimoire, calling to her.

She lit a candle; the flame flickered in the dim light. She opened the book, her fingers trembling. When it was time to do the spell, to test her powers, Mary's heart raced as she arranged the items on the table before her. The gold nugget, lodestone, and grimoire were all in place, ready for the spell she was about to cast. She rubbed her hands together, eager for the results of her magick and craved the exhilaration of revenge's power.

Sid thought he could intimidate her, threaten her, but he only fueled her determination. She was a fire witch who would not be silenced.

She drew a pentagram on the metal mining pan using chalk, placing the gold nugget and lodestone within its borders. They had to be touching as much as possible. Then, palms up, she summoned a small flame in her hands. The fire danced and flickered, casting shadows across the room.

Mary closed her eyes, focusing all her energy on Sid and his threats. As she chanted the words of the spell, the familiar surge of magickal energy coursed through her veins, exhilarating, empowering.

By nugget's gleam and lodestone's might,
In fire's dance, take flight this night.
Touched by Sid, let gold repel,
Enforced by this enchanted spell.
In golden hold, no hand shall dwell,
Lest they face the magick's knell.
So mote it be!

The fire in her hands leaped onto the objects, igniting them in a brilliant flare. Mary stumbled back, awed by the intensity of the magick she wielded.

The flames subsided, and Mary leaned forward, eager to see the results. Soot darkened the gold nugget and lodestone. She rubbed the soot away to find them unchanged.

Mary pushed her twinge of disappointment away. She needed to test the spell's effectiveness, to see if it worked. But how? Since Sid was the last person she wanted around her, she would have to get the nugget to him through someone else. But who?

Chapter Thirty-One

The bell on the shop's door tinkled, alerting Mary while she stocked shelves. She turned to find Marisol in a vibrant purple dress and hat adorned with her signature feathers. The day didn't start right without a visit from her friend.

"Good morning, Marisol."

Isobel ran to hug her Aunty Mari. Marisol lifted her into her arms. "Hello, my little chickadee. And good morning to your mama."

"Your dressmaking friend's shop is almost done." Mary walked around the counter and admired Marisol's dress. "She certainly does a beautiful job on your dresses. What about drab shop women's clothes?"

Marisol shook her head, feathers flowing back and forth, inciting giggles from Isobel. "Add some color to your dresses, dear. Perhaps something to match that gorgeous necklace you've been wearing. Who gave you that? A secret boyfriend?"

Mary rolled her eyes. "Who has time for that? It's my mother's necklace and my grandmother's before that. It's old."

"I figured a boyfriend since you've been tense since wearing it. You need one of your relaxing teas." Marisol set Isobel on the floor. "Or you can tell me what the problem is. We're friends." She walked over and took Mary's hand. "I worry about you."

Mary tilted her head. She didn't feel any different, though she worried her spell didn't work and Sid might follow through on his threat. But it wasn't something she would share with anyone. "A miner come in and threaten me because I'm friends with Bill. His name is Sid. Do you know him?"

Marisol's face dropped. "Oh, Sid. Yeah. He's a weird one. Comes in and sits by himself. Nurses a pint while mumbling to himself. Then leaves. A real sourpuss." She paused. "Come to think about it. I haven't seen him in the past two days."

Mary let out a breath through pursed lips. Her hand traveled to the pendant without her thinking about it. "I hope he leaves and never comes back."

"Well, I have to head back and open the saloon. It's been busier as the town grows. Gonna have to hire some more girls." Marisol headed to the door. "Have a good day. Bye, Isobel. Be good for mama."

Mary lifted her hand to wave. "You, too."

Isobel jumped and waved. "Bye-bye Aunt Mari."

Later, Bill came in dressed in the new dungarees he bought from her the last time she saw him, a huge smile on his face. Remembering she still needed to test if her spell worked, she would ask Bill to give the gold nugget to Sid. If he couldn't hold it, success, but if he could, she failed and lost the nugget.

Bill ambled to the counter, grinning ear to ear. "You'll never believe what happened. Want to guess?"

Mary tilted her head, grimacing. She hated guessing games, so she played her own game with him. "You're getting married? Having a child?" Those were unlikely.

"No."

"You've taken a job at the rodeo in Missoula."

Bill's smile vanished, replaced by a pinched expression. He shook his head. "No, Mary! I was all eager to tell you, and now you just took the wind out of my sails. Sid offered to sell his claim to me for dirt cheap and I bought it." Bill scratched his chin through his thick beard. "Funny thing was, we had to go to the bank to settle up because he wouldn't take any gold."

Mary grabbed the sides of her head, letting her hands slide down her cheeks. "Really? That's great news, Bill. Glad to see him go. Quite a bit of trouble, that one." Mary held her arms out. "Now you have that whole vein of gold to yourself." Mary hugged Bill in celebration, but had to pull back when he tried to hold it too long. She suspected he liked her a bit more than friends. Why can't a man be content with a friendship?

Bill stroked his beard. "Sid had his hands all bandaged. I asked him what happened, and he shrugged, never telling me. It was a strange ride to the bank with him. Odd chap."

My spell worked! Mary shrugged and sighed. "Sid came in here about a week ago and threatened me and my little girl. He ordered me not to assist you nor visit your claim. Why the complete turn-around? Strange." Mary couldn't wait for Bill to leave, breathless and eager to celebrate her own success.

"Hell if I know. Gotta go. I'm thinking of hiring a few chaps to help me. If you hear of anyone trustworthy and hardworking, let me know." Bill left the store and Mary watched him until he was out of sight.

Mary jumped, punching the air with her fists, relishing a successful spell. This opened the door to more magick beyond potions and herbal remedies. She was sure Stella kept the magick lessons to the mundane because she wanted to keep her safe. Spells like the one she did on Sid might backfire if you weren't careful.

Mary planned to study the grimoire every night after she put Isobel to bed. No reason she couldn't become a powerful witch like her mother. She was untouchable. She wanted to live and breathe power. Her hand again flew to the trinity necklace, where she relished the power that flowed through to her fingers.

Rain lashed against the windows, its rhythm a harbinger of the tumultuous thoughts churning in Mary's mind. The day, cloaked in a shroud of gloom, mirrored her unsettled spirit. She kindled the wood stove, its crackle and pop a soothing counterpoint to the storm outside. The ritual of preparing tea for Anna's post-church visit was a brief respite from the whirlwind of emotions that gripped her.

Isobel pressed her nose to the mercantile's window, her breath fogging the glass. "When will John get here, Mama?"

Mary smiled at her daughter's impatience. "Any minute now, little one."

With time to spare, Mary drew her tarot cards, seeking guidance. Her fingers trembled as she shuffled the deck, the cards whispering secrets as they slid against one another. The first card revealed itself - The Devil. Its sinister image evoked thoughts of George and Sid, emblems of toxic ties that shackled her. Next, The Fool leaped forth, its carefree visage mocking her inner turmoil. Mary's brow furrowed. The cards seemed to dance with her darkest thoughts, echoing her defiance against societal norms. But The Devil's presence was a sinister omen, hinting at perilous paths.

The last card, the Ten of Swords, emerged as a grim portent, its imagery of betrayal and ruin sending a shiver along her spine. Doubt clouded her mind; perhaps inner conflicts marred her focus. Hastily, she stowed the cards away, their message lingering like an unwelcome guest.

John, a whirlwind of youthful exuberance, burst into the shop, Anna trailing behind, breaking Mary's reverie. Isobel's squeal of delight filled the room as she collided with John in a tangle of laughter and limbs.

"Easy now, let's not destroy the place!" Mary playfully chided with a mischievous smile.

Mary had longed for the children's strong bond and their everlasting joy, but now she saw happiness as pointless. She found something better, giving rise to her smug smile.

As for the miner, who had a history of inappropriate behavior, came in for supplies yesterday, she confronted him using the full force of her newfound power. When she counted out his change, he had fondled her hand. Now he possesses an uncontrollable twitch in that hand. Served him right.

Anna gave Mary a concerned look. "Are you alright? The last time I saw you, you seemed like you were walking around with a dark cloud over you. I don't know how to describe it, really. But it's still there." She cocked her head, deep lines on her forehead.

Mary brushed it off, projecting an air of well-being, yet her thoughts were far from tranquil. "Me? I'm great. No clouds here."

"Hmm. If you're sure. I hope you would confide in me if you were out of sorts. We're friends after all. John and I look forward to coming here after church. I wish I could come to visit more often, but the ranch keeps Peter busy, and it's calving season now. It never stops."

Mary nodded. "The store has been more busy. I visit Marisol and Dawn when I can. Isobel is delightful every day and keeps me running." She thought about all the studying and experimenting she did using her mother's grimoire. It kept her all consumed that she had visited no one unless they came to the shop. And they all commented about a change in her without knowing what was different. If they could identify what they have a problem with, it wouldn't be so annoying. She felt better than she ever had, empowered even. Sorry if it bothered anyone. She was going to be who she was.

To change the subject, she brought Anna a cup of tea. "How about a nice cup of tea? Anything else new at the ranch?"

Anna's eyes grew large. "Oh, yes. Tony got up and left two weeks ago. Didn't come back, either. No note or any explanation. I forgot to tell you last week since the weather was so bad. I never considered he would be the type to do that." Head down, she shook her head.

Mary opened her mouth. What could she say? *I know why he left.* No. Best to keep that to herself. "I'm sorry. He's a good person. What happened?"

"It's put Peter in a bad spot. He went to Hamilton to find someone to replace him. They're meeting at the livery while we visit. I hope it works out. Peter is working himself to death."

"I hope it does." This visit was making Mary's head pound. First, her tarot reading was depressing. Anna thinks she's changed and now Tony disappears after asking her to leave with him. She drank the rest of her tea. Time for a much stronger blend to change her day.

"What's new in town?"

That's a better conversation. Mary tilted her head, her smile twisted. "A miner who threatened me and Isobel left town, thank goodness. The dressmaker's shop opened. Dawn's bakery is doing great. It helps bring more people to my shop early in the morning, though she's considering her own building now. That's it. Oh. Ah. My sister wrote asking that I return to Chicago to live with her and her new husband."

"Oh, my. That's a lot going on. Why would a miner threaten you? And would you go back to Chicago?"

Mary snorted. "This miner thought I was helping another miner strike it rich. He had some screws loose. And no, I will never go back to living with my sister." She didn't need someone to control her life. She had George. Why trade one for the other? Most times, George stayed away. Her sister would be on her night and day. Mary stretched her neck to check on Isobel and John.

"I would miss you terribly if you did. That's a beautiful necklace. Did George give you that?" Anna laughed.

A howl released from Mary and the two women both laughed hard and long. "I can't believe you asked that! Goodness, that was a good one." Mary touched the pendant. "It's my mother's. Before that, it extends through my grandmother and beyond, tracing back through generations." Now it was hers. Every day, she contemplated how it would best serve her.

"Very sentimental. That's nice." Anna set her cup down and turned to watch their children play.

Sentimental wasn't the word Mary would use. It was her birthright to have the privilege of power and ability to wield this type of magick. But sweet Anna would struggle to comprehend the reality of her ability. Anyone would. She slipped the necklace under her shirt to avoid further questions from anyone else.

Chapter Thirty-Two

George walked into the saloon, his eyes scanning the room for a glimpse of the beautiful new woman who came to work there. He had been searching for her all day, ever since he had laid eyes on her outside the dressmaker's shop early that morning. She had come out the door, her golden hair cascading along her back like a river of sunshine, her bright blue eyes sparkling like diamonds in the sunlight.

George had been smitten, but too shy to approach her. Unfortunately, he was heading out of town to Hamilton for his weekly supply run. Meeting that angel would have to wait.

It was the fastest supply run he ever did. George didn't take time to get a drink at his usual bar in Hamilton, even. Instead, he headed right back home. This new beauty was the only thing he thought of. He couldn't get her face out of his mind. No woman ever had this effect on him.

George pulled behind the store to the back door that led to the back room they used for storage. Grabbing bags of beans, rice, flour, and sugar, he dropped them on either side of the door inside. Next, he piled the boxes around, not putting them away. Mary could do it. He didn't have time. He drove the wagon over to the livery.

"Bernard! Take care of the horse. I'll pay you extra. I gotta to go."
He ran next door to Jack's saloon.

Once inside, he scanned the room, his eyes landing on a group
of girls gathered around the end of the bar. One of them caught
his eye, the same blond with a mischievous grin and a twinkle in
her eye. She was laughing at something one of the other girls had
said, and George's heart did a flip.

When he approached the group, the beauty was gone. "Hey,
girls," he said. "I want to meet the new one, blond, blue-eyed."

The girls looked at each other, then back at George. "You
must be looking for Pearl," a brunette said with a sly smile. "She
stepped out back, taking a break."

George's heart skipped a beat. "Out back?" he repeated.

The brunette nodded, her eyes sparkling. "Yeah, out back. But
be warned, she's a bit of a wild one. She's not for the faint of
heart."

George's excitement bubbled inside him, fueled by the
prospect of coming face to face with this enigmatic woman. He
thanked the girls and made his way outside, forcing himself to
walk slow though he wanted to run.

As he walked out the back door, he saw a figure standing
against the wall, a cigarette dangling from her pouty lips. It was
Pearl, and she was even more beautiful close-up.

George's mouth went dry. "Pearl?" he asked, trying to sound
confident, but stammered instead.

Pearl looked at him, a hint of surprise in her eyes. "Yeah?" she
replied, her voice husky and seductive.

George swallowed hard, trying to gather his thoughts. "I came
to meet you," he said. "I've heard a lot about you."

Pearl raised an eyebrow, a mischievous grin spreading across her face. "Oh, yeah?" she repeated with sarcasm. "Like what?"

George's face flushed, but he refused to back down. "I've heard you're a wild one," he said, his voice firm. "You're not for the faint of heart."

Pearl laughed, a deep, throaty sound that sent shivers along George's spine. "That's right," she said, her eyes sparkling. "I'm not for the faint of heart. But if you're up for a challenge, I might give you a chance."

The hairs on his arms and the nape of his neck rose, and he was breathless. This was an uncharted territory of emotions for him, and he wouldn't resist the urge to dive in headfirst. "I'm all for a challenge," he said, his voice firm.

Pearl grinned. "Good," she said. "I like a man who's not afraid to take risks. Let's see if you are."

Pearl took a step closer to him, her eyes never leaving his. "Kiss me," she said, her voice husky and seductive. "Show me what you're made of."

George noticed his heart pounding, his mouth moist. He leaned in, his lips meeting hers in a passionate kiss. It was an indescribable sensation, as if a current of electricity flowed through his body the moment their lips touched.

George deepened the kiss, his tongue exploring her mouth as she melted into his embrace.

Pearl pulled away from the kiss, her breathing heavy. "Wow," she whispered. "You're definitely not like any man I've ever met."

"I'm glad," George said, his voice husky. "I want to be the only man you'll ever need."

"We'll see about that," Pearl said, her voice playful. "But for now, let's enjoy the moment."

George nodded, his knees trembling and feeling like jelly. He had to make this moment count, to show Pearl that he was the man for her. He leaned in again, his lips meeting hers in another passionate kiss.

As they kissed, George's hands roamed over Pearl's body, exploring every curve and contour. He couldn't get enough of her. His desire for her was overwhelming. He longed to possess her, to make her his and his alone.

Pearl seemed to sense his desire, her body responding to his touch. She pressed against him, her lips never leaving his as they kissed. George sensed her heart racing, her breathing quickening. If she was as turned on as he was, he had to take things to the next level.

George broke off the kiss, his breathing heavy. "Pearl," he said, "I want you. I need you. Will you be mine?"

Pearl looked at him with desire. "Buy me a drink first."

Her words filled him with an overwhelming rush of excitement, causing his heart to race with joy. George had found the woman of his dreams, the one who would be by his side forever. He leaned in, his lips meeting hers in a passionate kiss as they sealed their love forever.

As they headed back into the saloon, George had found his happily ever after, the one that he had been searching for all his life. He would do anything to protect Pearl, to make her happy. He would love her until the end of time, and beyond.

The morning sun cast a warm glow over Mary's cozy kitchen as she placed a steaming plate of eggs and ham in front of George. The sizzling hot food illuminated his satisfied smile, his hunger clear in his eager eyes. She served Isobel and herself before finally settling down, the rich, warm aroma of the food enveloping the room.

As Mary took her first bite, relishing the delicious flavors, she noticed the far-off look in George's eyes. He seemed lost in thought, a hint of happiness lingering on his face. Curiosity tugged at her, and she asked, "What makes you so happy this morning?"

George snapped out of his reverie. His expression shifted into his usual scowl. "I think I've met my woman. I may be in love."

Mary raised an eyebrow. "Is that right?" she replied in disbelief. George could love?

George's face soured, his eyes narrowed. "Too bad I can't marry her since you tricked me. You ruined my life. You know that, don't you?"

A heavy sigh escaped Mary's lips as she rolled her eyes. He reminded her of his grievances every single day. "How could I not?"

George stared at Mary, his voice thick with malice. "Pearl is nicer than you. Prettier, too. She doesn't think she's better than everyone else like you have lately." He shot a glance at Isobel. "And she doesn't have a snot-nosed kid, either."

The anger within Mary surged, her jaw clenched tight. It struck a nerve when he brought Isobel into his tirades. "Leave her out of it. You got a problem with me, fine. But my child is off limits."

George's face twisted in a sneer. "Not as long as she is here, and I have to see or hear her."

Mary heated more when she saw the sad visage on her three-year-old Isobel's angelic face. The young girl was now old enough to understand George's lack of love towards her. Determined to change the subject, she said, "Thanks for taking the time to dump the supplies off. I'm surprised you bothered bringing them in. What do you plan to do today? We need some more wood for cooking."

George, putting on haughty airs as if he was still in his family's mansion back in Chicago, stood. "I'll be at Jack's getting to know Pearl better. Cut it yourself."

Mary jumped from the table, the scrape of her chair against the floor echoing through the kitchen. Storming into the bedroom, she slammed the door behind her, needing a moment to collect herself.

Mary returned to the table, holding a pair of dungarees. Her voice cut through the air. "See these?" she asked, her eyes fixed on him.

George looked at her with a mixture of confusion and irritation. "Those are mine. What of it, woman?"

Mary said, cold and sharp, "No, they are not. They are mine. I'm going to wear pants so everyone can see that I wear the pants around here. Not you. You're too delicate to do any sort of work at all. A pansy."

George's face flushed crimson, his eyes bulging. "I'm not a pansy and I'm not staying here to listen to this," he spat out, his voice seething. "I get supplies from Hamilton every week. That's work."

Mary tilted her head, her mouth twisting into a sardonic smirk. "The only reason you do that is because it is too dangerous for me to be on the road by myself. Otherwise, you would leave that to me, too."

George raised his voice. "You wanted adventure, didn't you? There's your adventure. Get to it, girl," he barked, storming towards the door, yanking it open and slamming it shut behind him, the force reverberating through the room.

Mary's heart raced, her hands trembling. She sank back into her chair, the weight of the argument lingering in the air. The words they exchanged hung heavy on her mind, echoing in the silence. She glanced at the dungarees in her lap, a symbol of her newfound determination to assert herself in the face of George's constant belittlement.

Now Mary would have to cut wood today after she closed the shop. Was there a spell for that?

The next morning, Mary woke to an empty bed. If George was up earlier than her, it was because he had to visit the outhouse. He was not one to keep early hours, as he stayed out all hours of the night. But she always woke up to his snoring lump next to her. He complained about sleeping with her, but he never got another bed, so Mary didn't worry about it. Only blustery George talk.

As the morning sun bathed the kitchen in a golden glow, Mary prepared a hearty breakfast, her hands moving with purpose and determination. Yet, as the minutes ticked by, George's absence became increasingly conspicuous.

Downstairs, Mary peeked out the windows. George, disheveled and disoriented, emerged from a boarding house down the street, his eyes clouded with the remnants of a night spent elsewhere. A surge of anger erupted within Mary, a tempest brewing deep within her core. Without a moment's hesitation, she charged out into the street, her night shift billowing around her like a battle flag. "What are you doing staying gone all night?" Ever since Pearl, the saloon's new bewitching siren, arrived, George spent more time and money there. As if that was possible.

George slurred his words. "It's none of your business what I do. You tricked me."

Same thing she heard all the time that she tricked him. Mary wanted to smack it out of him. "You flirted with me. Don't make it out like you didn't want me."

George tried to walk around Mary and nearly lost his balance. "I did that to make Henry mad, and you know it. I would never take the time to even talk to you." He made it to the door and turned around to Mary, who stood on the dirt road in front of the boardwalk. "I can fix it so you are on the street and Pearl moves in with me."

Weeds that lined the front of the boardwalk and surrounded the steps shriveled from the heat coming from Mary. She could not follow him without risking the entire building and Isobel was inside, standing at the window, looking out at her. The only thing she could do was try to extinguish her heat.

Mary took several long, deep breaths. She envisioned her favorite flower, a red rose, its heavenly scent, and big thorns. Slowly, she felt her temperature drop to a safe range to enter the store. And she stomped in. Then stopped. She had to stay calm for Isobel's sake.

But George tested her limits and now threatened her. What a fool. Her fingers stroked the silver of the trinity pendant, a symbol of her strength and resilience guiding her. And with each step she took, she carried an unwavering determination to overcome any obstacle that stood in her way by any means possible.

CHAPTER THIRTY-THREE

MARY WATCHED MARISOL SASHAYED across the dusty street, a vibrant new dress from the new dress shop swirling around her feet. Mary had little more than drab homespun dresses and worn boots. Even though George received a trust fund check every month, he would still take money from the till. Whenever she helped Bill with his claims, she stashed that money for later in an account she had Peter open in Henry's name for Isobel. The vision of her own brownstone in Chicago kept her from touching it.

Tapping the window pane, Mary caught Marisol's attention. Her friend waved a gloved hand and altered course toward the store, holding her purple dress clear of the ground.

"Oh Marisol, it's stunning!" Mary exclaimed as the door tinkled open and Marisol held the dress in front of her. Mary admired the off-shoulder neckline and flowing bustled skirt.

"Don't you just love it?" Marisol preened, angling to see her reflection in the glass jars. "I had it made special by Sybil in my favorite color. Worth every cent, if I do say so." Marisol picked up the bottom of the dress. "Sybil. You haven't met her yet, have you?"

Mary busied herself straightening the already orderly shelves, hiding her envy. She hadn't visited a dress shop in ages, but Sybil's work looked exquisite. "Only when she comes in the store. I don't have any money to spend on dresses."

"With as much as George fritters away over at Jack's place, seems you should have enough for a new dress."

Mary's fist clenched around a tin of coffee. George's frequent 'business meetings' with Pearl at Jack's saloon were common knowledge by now, fueling town gossip. Yet if she dared ask about the accounts, George accused her of overstepping her station.

The reminder that George had all the money and left her without bringing out her fire-y temper. "A married woman doesn't handle the purse strings. I make do." Her work finding gold on Bill's claims was a secret, therefore the money had to be as well.

"You mean you don't pocket some for yourself? You do it. I doubt he would notice."

Mary could slip the money made from her candles and herbal remedies into her apron. But that wasn't what was at the base of the anger rising. "Let's get some air, shall we?" The last thing she wanted was to burn the place down because her temper got out of hand.

Upon stepping outside, the warmth of a spring day greeted the ladies. As Mary turned towards the sun, its warmth comforted, but her stress lingered, seeking an outlet. "I had to chop wood after I closed the store yesterday so I could cook. George is too busy with Pearl. Pearl this and Pearl that."

Marisol chuckled. "Don't worry about Pearl. When George isn't in the saloon, she's with other men and doesn't think nothing about George. She follows the money, and that's it."

The ground sizzled under Mary's feet. She trembled with the effort of keeping her rage contained. The insults and derision were stinging, but George uttering his callous threat this morning made it intolerable. Mary stomped her foot. "He says he's going to divorce me and bring Pearl here, kicking me and Isobel out on the street."

"But Pearl doesn't like him that way. It'll never happen." Marisol let the skirt of her new dress fall and pulled Mary in for a hug. "You're very warm. Are you alright?"

Mary leaned into the hug, as it was the thing she needed most. Comfort. Someone who cared about her. She only saw Anna on Sunday, which was a shame since Isobel and John adored each other. But most days, she felt alone. Lonely. It's like she's stranded on a deserted island. George's verbal abuse didn't help. "I'm much better now. Thank you. I really needed to say it. I'm keeping things in and it's firing me up."

Marisol scanned the wide main street. "You know what we need is some benches in front of your place and Jack's. Then people can sit outside and socialize. I'll mention it to Jack."

That brought a smile to Mary's face. Marisol searched for answers to problems she saw under the surface of what people said. She had a knack for it. "That would be nice. Especially as the weather gets nicer."

"Well, dear. I have to get this dress on so I can make some money. Keep an eye out your window. I'll come out to show you." She gave Mary a wink and hurried into the saloon.

Mary turned around to face the store. After a big sigh, she went back inside to check on Isobel and get back to work. Marisol had the right inclination to find solutions, and Mary thought about her mother's grimoire as she fingered her necklace. There might be solutions for her there. For too long, she had resigned herself to womanly submission while seething over George's conduct. No more. She was a witch, with magick coursing through her. Why plead when you can command? It was up to her to improve her life because there was no one else to do it for her.

Mary stoked the fire in the wood stove to get it ready to bake her bread. When she slid the pan in, she dropped it with a loud thud on the floor. "Feck!" She picked it up and slid it in, closing the oven door.

George screamed from the bedroom, "God dammit, woman! What's all that racket? I'm trying to sleep. You did that on purpose."

Isobel ran to Mary and clung to her skirts.

"Well, it's not like I did it on purpose. Go back to sleep." Mary pulled Isobel into her to give her some comfort.

George stood in the doorway, glaring at her. "I talked to a lawyer yesterday in Hamilton about divorcing you. Then I can marry Pearl. She would live here and you would be out on that dirt road with your bastard brat."

Mary's hands rolled into fists. She whispered to Isobel. "Go downstairs and play nicely." When the child made her way downstairs, Mary perched her fists high on her hips. "You do it and see what happens. I know Pearl doesn't want to take care of a man-child."

George stomped over to the kitchen table. "You don't know that. She loves me. I love her. When I marry her, it will be my choice, not trickery. I can't wait to have you on the streets, no money and nowhere to go." George laughed. "What a sight that will be."

The fire in the wood stove grew strong. Her temper. Mary took a few deep breaths, but George standing there laughing continued to fuel her anger. She had no choice but to retreat as much as she detested that choice. She rushed downstairs to see Isobel playing with her rag doll. The sight of her sweet daughter tamped down her temper and hopefully the flames upstairs. The bread was ruined, but that was the least of her worries.

Dressed, George came downstairs, a smug look on his face. "I'll be gone all day, so I don't have to look at you. I suggest you pack." Out the door he went, making a beeline to the saloon.

Mary left out a sigh and blew a stray hair from her face. Pearl was a problem. The saloon was a problem. George was a problem. It would be perfect if she could get rid of all three. That would require some thought, but she better check on the bread that she ruined. Then breakfast. She had all day to come up with a plan.

Evening came and Mary still didn't know what to do with George, Pearl and that damn saloon. She stood at her bedroom window, pulling the curtain aside to peer down the street. In the front window of the saloon, she saw George pulling Pearl on his lap. Rage coiled around and through her. There was no way she was going to allow that woman to move into her home and take over the business she built with no help from George. She raced downstairs, through the store, and out the door. Afraid she would set her store and home aflame, she stood alone in the middle of the dirt road, with shops and businesses on each side. The only movement in Tin Creek was in the saloon.

George had needled her every day with his attitude and words since Independence, Missouri. He got them kicked out of the wagon train. His shortcut through a desert almost cut their lives short, and not crossing where they were told to cross the river nearly drowned her. Henry had asked too much of her when he asked her to keep him safe. Every single day, she wanted to slap George because of his attitude and behavior towards Isobel. But the last straw was the threat to kick her out onto the street.

Mary couldn't douse her temper with deep breaths this time. It burned through her, consuming every fiber of her body. Fiery power pulsed along her arms. The pendant at her neck pulsated and burned into her skin.

The power of the necklace encircled her, removing any doubt about what she should do. Mary would use her gifts to protect the most valuable person in her life—her daughter. *No one gets away with threatening me.*

Mary curled her hands into fists in front of her. When she opened them, she had a red ball of fire in each. As she focused on the pulsing orbs, thinking of all the ways George wronged her, they grew. Angry, warm tears rolled down her cheeks.

A tug on her skirt and the chuffs from Danu made her pause and turn around. The large cougar continued to pull on her skirt. Danu's fur furrowed between red eyes. She shook her head. "No, Danu. I must." She kicked her leg out to yank her skirt away from the cat and turned back to the saloon. The cougar ran fast and hard; he was leaving her, his spirit vanished. If George hadn't threatened her, this wouldn't be happening. It was his fault. She became more enraged.

Mary pulled back her right hand and lunged the fireball at the front window, where Pearl sat laughing. The glass shattered and the flames hungrily consuming the frame and walls. The crackling and popping of the fire satisfied her desire for revenge.

Mary slammed the left hand's fire ball into the saloon door. That one was for George. If he wanted to be at the saloon all the time, he would stay there. The fire overtook the door and frame, spreading quickly through the timber building.

Maniacal laughter replaced the rage in Mary's core. Turning, she ran behind the store to wait for her temperature to return to normal, breath ragged in her throat. She tuned out the screams from the saloon. All she wanted was the removal of her problems. George should have never challenged her.

Mary called out, "Danu!" She walked to the willow tree and hugged the tree while shouting Danu's name. Tears flowed as she realized she couldn't sense her familiar anymore. Why? When she needed her cougar spirit the most, he left her. A darkness enveloped her, hugged her, and her necklace burned yet again. She tried to lift it off her chest, but it was embedded. Who was she now? What had she done? Marisol and Jack were in the saloon, too!

Chapter Thirty-Four

George's heart fluttered as Pearl sat on his lap, her intoxicating presence overwhelming his senses. But beneath the surface, a mounting pressure threatened to burst through, demanding his attention. There was no ignoring it. With a deep breath, he mustered the courage to speak. "Pearl, I have to make a trip out back. And then I have something to ask you, something important."

Pearl rose from his lap, her movement deliberate and seductive. She leaned over, exposing her ample cleavage, and planted a lingering kiss on George's face. Her perfume filled his nostrils, clouding his judgment. "Don't be gone too long," she purred, her voice as smooth as the silken petal of a rose. "I need another drink."

"Yup, be right back. You know I can't bear to be away long."

He made his way to the bar, raising his hand to catch the bartender's attention. "Hey, Matt. I need a whiskey and make it the good stuff. Pearl needs one too. Be right back."

As he walked toward the back door, a wicked smile crept across George's face. He imagined Mary's belongings scattered on the street, a liberating symbol of their suffocating relationship ending. He couldn't wait to rid himself of her burdensome presence and her snot-nosed kid. To him, she was nothing more than an anchor, dragging him down while he longed for fun and freedom.

His monthly trust fund money provided him with the means to party in perpetual revelry in Montana. He didn't need to work; the money Mary made at the store was a bonus, affording him more time with Pearl. George chuckled at the irony of Mary toiling away while he indulged his desires.

A piercing scream shattered the air, jolting George from his thoughts. "Fire! Fire!" someone cried out, pointing toward the front door.

Horror washed over him as he turned to look, only to be met with a terrifying sight. Flames leaped and danced, devouring the saloon with relentless fury. Panic surged through George's veins, urging him to break through the frames to rescue Pearl, but Matt's firm grip halted his desperate escape.

"It's too late. You can't get to her." Matt's voice resonated with a mix of sadness and urgency. "See the flames? It's too much."

George moaned in despair, his hands clawing at Matt's restraining hold. "No! I have to try."

But Matt's grip tightened, pulling George toward the closest window on the side of the building. The glass shattered by Jack earlier. George fought against the invisible bonds, his eyes fixated on the front of the saloon, where a grotesque tableau of flames, smoke, and despair unfolded before him. Disoriented, he stumbled forward, propelled from behind by Matt.

How are the flames engulfing everything so swiftly, showing no mercy?

Matt nudged him. "Pull your shirt over your mouth and nose. The smoke is thick." George complied, the acrid smoke stinging his eyes, forcing tears to stream down his cheeks.

It was his turn to escape through the broken window. He cast one final, desperate glance toward the inferno, only to witness a massive timber crashing through the dense smoke. Pearl was gone, swallowed by the merciless flames. In that moment, George felt as if a part of him had died alongside her.

A strong shove sent him tumbling to the ground, and a pair of hands reached out, pulling him along. George looked up, his vision blurred by tears, to see Jack standing before him. George gasped, his voice choked with grief, "Pearl!"

Jack's solemn nod spoke volumes. "I know."

George clutched Jack's shoulders, his hands trembling. "My Pearl! She's gone." His knees buckled beneath him, and he crumbled to the ground, a torrent of tears consuming him.

Once again, Jack ferried him to the safety of the boardwalk in front of his store. Jack left to return to the chaos. Through blurred, tear-filled eyes, George surveyed the charred remains of the saloon, smoldering and lifeless. Before they embarked on their journey together, fate snatched away the love of his life. All he had ever wanted was to experience the warmth of love and to be embraced in return. Didn't he deserve that? How would he go on without Pearl?

An agonizing ache gripped his chest, and he curled into a fetal position, rocking back and forth in a futile attempt to soothe his shattered soul. He rolled over onto the boardwalk and stayed there until morning. No will to get up.

Sunlight struggled to pierce the morning fog, casting a pallid light into Mary's room. She stirred, her limbs heavy, an eerie tingling sensation lingering in her arms. Her gaze drifted to the window, where tendrils of smoke still rose from the remnants of the saloon, a haunting reminder of the night's calamity. The other side of the bed lay cold and deserted, a stark contrast to the warmth of the body that should have been there. Panic seized her as a chilling realization dawned: *I killed him. Who else?*

Guilt gnawed at her heart, the weight of her broken promise - to safeguard Henry's brother - crushing her. Marisol, Jack, and many others were inside the saloon when she released her vengeance. Mary had veered from the path of harmlessness into the shadowy realm of her mother's legacy. The thought clawed at her soul: *I am evil.*

Desperation drove her hand to the pendant, seared into her flesh. Mary tried to peel it out. But she hesitated, torn between the agony of its presence and the dread of confronting her actions without its influence.

Frantically, Mary descended the stairs, her heart racing. Outside, George's crumpled form lay on the boardwalk, a pitiable sight that offered a sliver of hope - maybe, just maybe, no one had perished.

The saloon's ruins stood as a grim monument to destruction, a stark reminder of the joy it once held. Memories of Jack and George, their excitement tangible as they built it, now lay in ashes.

Unlocking the door, Mary approached George, relieved. His mutterings of loss, "Pearl. My Pearl is gone," echoed the hollow ache in her own heart. She guided him inside, away from the prying eyes and the charred skeleton of her evil deed. She dreaded to know who else perished.

Upstairs, George's silent form lay curled in bed, a mere shell of the man he once was. His uncharacteristic quietude unnerved her. Mary covered him, expecting an outburst that never came, her own heart heavy with the burden of her deeds.

Mary closed the door. *I killed her.* This is what she had become. A destroyer. She had taken the two most important things in George's life, the saloon, and Pearl.

Mary set on pulling the necklace off her neck. She wanted it back under the floorboards, where it would not call to her. Was it the necklace that transformed her, or was she solely accountable for her actions? She wouldn't know until she got it out of her skin and off her neck.

Closing her eyes, she grasped the top of the trinity symbol and yanked. Mary clenched her lips together to not utter any noise, though she wanted to scream. It felt like she ripped her soul, a damaged soul, out of her, not only burned flesh.

Mary was to do no harm with her gifts, but now she killed someone. Holding the necklace with bits of her skin still encrusted in the design, she wiped the tears from the corner of her eyes. She placed the jewelry piece in a kitchen towel and wrapped it up. *I'm never wearing this again.*

Isobel came out of her room, making Mary jump. She tucked the package onto a shelf where she stored candles and put on a cheerful face. "Good morning, angel. Are you ready for breakfast?"

As Isobel rubbed the sleep from her eyes, she said, "Yes, mama. Did you burn the bread?"

Mary sighed. "No. Not this time. The saloon burned. It's what happens when you are not careful with fire." How could she be a good mother if she couldn't set a good example? How would she train her to use her gifts responsibly? The tarot's warning now seemed a prophetic mirror of her own descent. Her sister Stella's judgment loomed in her mind, a bitter acknowledgment of her likeness to her mother.

After Mary fixed breakfast, she entered the bedroom. "George, are you hungry? I can bring it in here." She waited for an answer, but none came. She strolled over to the bed and leaned over. His vacant gaze was a silent scream of anguish. "I'll fix you some tea to help."

While Isobel ate, Mary ran downstairs to retrieve the herbs she needed from the back room. This tea was not one she sold, as it was only for grief and regret. She would drink it, but she didn't want to stop feeling regretful. She deserved every bit of the pain plus more. As much as George was not a nice person, he didn't deserve to lose love, even if it wasn't reciprocated. How long before he would have discovered the real Pearl?

Mary realized she had acted in haste. Even Danu tried to warn her. She did not feel his presence anymore, leaving her heart and soul in shreds.

One half part wood betony and one part skullcap made a simple tea to deliver feelings of safety and composure to help George's traumatized mind. If he would take it. Mary also grabbed some salve for the burn on her chest. Fortunately, her shirt covered it so there would be no questions there.

Mary occupied Isobel with her chalkboard and chalk once the tea was ready. She took the cup and a spoon to the bedroom. "George, I made some tea for you. You need to drink some. You have been through so much." He was going to make this difficult, like everything else. She smirked, but would not be put off from her duty to help him. How else would she make amends?

Mary sat on the other side of the bed. "Do you want me to feed it to you?"

George blinked, and when he did, a tear slid to the bedsheet.

Mary's nursing attempts were met with passive acceptance, his tears a silent testament to his shattered world. "I'll bring you more later. Try to sleep." She peered out the window towards the charred skeleton of the saloon. Jack and Marisol were standing in front holding on to one another. Tears rolled down Mary's cheeks. *How could I do this to them?*

Mary wrestled with the haunting allure of the necklace. She steeled herself against its siren call, determined to bury its malevolent influence. Yet, the responsibility of her actions loomed over her, a specter of remorse and a reminder of the path she must now tread - one of atonement and redemption. She would wear it no more.

Chapter Thirty-Five

THE RELENTLESS HAMMERING ACROSS the street drilled into Mary's skull, echoing the turmoil in her heart. She clutched her mug of lavender tea like a lifeline, inhaling the earthy aroma. Anything to hold the darkness at bay that raged within since that fateful night. Never again would she dabble in vengeance. From now on, she needed only her child and this simple mercantile.

Isobel played behind the counter, murmuring to her doll in their secret language. Mary drank in the sight like a soothing balm. However, she strayed, Isobel was the one pure light left to her.

As she returned to tallying the ledger, a violent retch snapped her attention back. Isobel doubled over, vomit pooling down her dress as she cried. Mary rushed to her side, panic rising as she felt the raging fever on her daughter's skin. She grabbed a packet of herbs of willow bark, wild strawberry leaf, blackberry leaf, raspberry leaf, rosehip from a shelf. Scooping Isobel's limp body into her arms, she realized how rapidly her little girl deteriorated. "Oh, you are burning up." What cruel twist of fate was this?

She locked the front door and hurried upstairs, gagging at the stench of sickness permeating Isobel's hair. *My poor child.* There was nothing she cared about more than the little girl in her arms.

After stripping the soiled clothing, she swaddled Isobel in blankets. In the kitchen over the wood stove, she mixed a batch of the herbal tonic her own mother had used to treat childhood fevers and diarrhea. She only prayed it worked now.

Isobel soon soiled the bed linens too, but Mary rinsed and changed her, keeping the ill child as comfortable as possible. With a heavy heart, she fed Isobel the salty broth she prepared to ward off dehydration. It pained her to see her little one lethargic and frail.

Mary soaked a rag in some cool water and returned to the child's room. She sat by Isobel with the bowl of salty water, spoon in hand. Holding Isobel's head, she whispered, "Sip this." When it seemed she wasn't able, Mary poured it into her mouth and rubbed her throat to encourage swallowing. With every other sip, Mary stopped to dab the cool, wet cloth on the child's forehead.

At last, the herbal mixture was condensed enough. Mary administered it to Isobel drop by drop throughout the day while singing a lullaby her grandmother in Ireland sang to her.

Over in Killarney
Many years ago,
Me Mother sang a song to me
In tones so sweet and low.
Just a simple little ditty,
In her good old Irish way,
And I'd give the world if she could sing
That song to me this day.
Too-ra-loo-ra-loo-ral, Too-ra-loo-ra-li,
Too-ra-loo-ra-loo-ral, hush now, don't you cry!
Too-ra-loo-ra-loo-ral, Too-ra-loo-ra-li,

Too-ra-loo-ra-loo-ral, that's an Irish lullaby.

Oft in dreams I wander

To that cot again,

I feel her arms a-huggin' me

As when she held me then.

And I hear her voice a-hummin'

To me as in days of yore,

When she used to rock me fast asleep,

Outside the cabin door.

Too-ra-loo-ra-loo-ral, Too-ra-loo-ra-li,

Too-ra-loo-ra-loo-ral, hush now, don't you cry!

Too-ra-loo-ra-loo-ral, Too-ra-loo-ra-li,

Too-ra-loo-ra-loo-ral, that's an Irish lullaby.

In the anxious hours between administering sips of water, herbal tonic, and bathing Isobel's fevered brow, Mary berated herself. She was certain her daughter's dire illness was cosmic retribution for the harm Mary had inflicted in her selfish quest for vengeance.

As Isobel moaned and trembled, each cry lanced Mary's heart. She should suffer this torment, not her innocent child! Anguish and guilt churned inside her till she thought she might retch herself. She had been so blinded by rage that she failed to foresee the consequences which now manifested as her daughter's glistening, cholera-stricken body.

Mary implored any powers that would listen - let her take this punishment instead! But only a hollow silence replied, broken by Isobel's labored breathing. Useless! Her great powers had never given life, only leveraged suffering. And now cruelty's bitter harvest had come.

Rocking Isobel's fevered form, Mary unleashed her grief in a broken whisper. "Please forgive me, my sweet child. You know not what darkness poisons your mother's soul." She kissed Isobel's inflamed cheeks, tasting the salty heat of infection. This suffering should be hers alone to bear.

Downstairs, an insistent knock broke her despair. But whoever called now, she would not face them. Not with her failure visible in the child fading in her arms. She had neglected her most sacred duty - to protect this innocent life entrusted to her care. No penance would ever redeem this betrayal.

Mary closed her ears to the futile summons below. Eyes puffy with remorse, she clung to the ailing Isobel. All else faded to fog around her solitary vigil. Even if she could not turn back time's pitiless arrow, she would drain her very lifeblood if it might restore her child.

The mercantile's door creaked open as George shoved his way inside, face already locked in its habitual scowl.

"Mary!" he bellowed. Only stillness replied. With a huff, he hauled himself up the narrow stairs. Some blasted miner interrupted his work, clearing the saloon's charred remnants to beg him to open shop. As if it wasn't enough, he had to manage his own profound grief.

At the top, he hollered again. Mary's weary voice floated from Isobel's room. "In here. Isobel is gravely ill."

George leaned on the door frame, lip curling. The damned child was always underfoot, and now she had the audacity to fall ill? He had no time for such trifles.

"Get downstairs and mind the shop," he ordered. "I've work to do for Jack."

Mary's eyes flashed as she tended to the moaning girl. "It's your store too. Won't kill you to run it for once."

George clenched his fists, rage simmering. How dare this woman countermand him here in his own home! He advanced on her, teeth bared.

"I gave you an order! Now get downstairs before I put you there myself!" His shout rang through the little room. Behind Mary, the child flinched and whimpered.

He expected Mary to scurry away as she always did before. But she held her ground, regarding him. "Tomorrow," was all she said.

George rocked back, unbalanced. Where was this defiance coming from? The fiery temper he loved to provoke was nowhere in sight. For an instant, he glimpsed a formidable stranger staring back at him.

Unsure how to respond, he just nodded. "Fine. Tomorrow." He turned on his heel and clattered back downstairs, throwing the door bolt behind him. Less than a minute alone and the girl had unsettled him completely.

As he stood there, two women approached, carrying infants. George groaned. The whole blasted town wanted his wife's herb remedies today, apparently.

When he tried to shoo them off, they pleaded for Mary's help. The one woman, the wife of a carpenter he knew, said, "I came to get some herbs from Mary. My youngest is sick with vomiting, soiling, fever. I need Mary's help."

The carpenter built his store and the saloon and will rebuild the saloon. So George took some deep breaths while he twisted his mouth. "Fine." He turned to unlock the door. "Go upstairs and find Mary. She can let you out when you're done." He had enough burdens without playing nursemaid.

Both women said, "Thank you, thank you," as they entered the store. George locked the door behind them.

Crossing the rutted street back toward the saloon's ruins, George brooded. He should have put that woman in her place, showed her who commanded her. But the steel in Mary's eyes had given him pause. Truth be told, her new defiance impressed him, though he'd never admit it aloud.

Hands braced on a charred timber, George heaved it aside, muscles straining. He lost himself in the punishing work, trying to exhaust his simmering anger. But the image of Mary's cool authority lingered. Wherever she found this hidden well of strength, he sensed an unsettling shift coming that he was ill-prepared for.

Mary rested her head on her folded arms atop the mercantile counter, the wood grain's whorls swimming before her bleary eyes. Behind her, Isobel slept, curled beneath her favorite patchwork quilt. Though still wan, she was on the mend at last.

Mary reached a hand back to smooth Isobel's hair, relieved to find that the warmth was a sign of healing rather than the dangerous fever her child had endured. The memory of those harrowing days still haunted her.

The bells over the door roused Mary from her dozing. She sat up, combing her fingers through the greasy tangles of her hair. It needed washing, but hygiene had fallen low on the priority list during Isobel's illness and the rush of customers since.

"Good day, ma'am. I've come to check on young Isobel," said the young, bespectacled man who entered. Doc, as he called himself, had arrived from Hamilton when he heard cholera hit the small mining town. He helped Mary nurse Isobel from the brink. His steady guidance was the only thing that kept Mary from crumbling those dark nights when her child's life hung by a gossamer thread.

While Doc conducted his examination, Mary prepared a basket of the herbal tonic that had combated the outbreak. Though still weary in body and soul, she needn't worry over Isobel today. Her little girl continued improving.

"Your remedies and diligent care saved many lives, including this precious one's," Doc said as he joined Mary. "You've a true healing gift, Mrs. Perkins."

Mary's eyes welled with stinging tears as she looked at Doc's kind face. If only he was aware of her other gifts - the uncanny ability to burn one's hands when they touch gold or her murderous inferno at the saloon.

"Thank you, truly," she muttered, unable to meet Doc's compassionate gaze, keeping the shameful secrets hidden behind her watery smile. She desired to confess everything and relieve her soul, but feared his judgment upon learning the truth.

Doc reassured Mary with a pat on the shoulder before packing his bag. While it wouldn't alter what she had done, she made a resolute choice to dedicate her life to the selfless service of the townspeople, employing her gifts for healing and support. She would be generous, kind, and caring.

Perhaps in time, through humble service, she could make amends for the blackness in her own soul. But nothing ever restored a life. That weight would linger forever. For now, she would only move forward, step by step, down a righteous path. She would begin again today.

As she dispensed bottles of the curative tonic and offered hugs and encouragement, the parade of hopeful faces revived Mary's flattened spirit. The Hornsby boys gave her a handful of wildflowers, making her smile. Even Mr. Campbell, usually dour, grasped her hand and choked out gruff words of appreciation. Each small connection reassured her that though she was far from absolved, she was at least pointed the proper way again.

Anna and Peter arrived with John, who was also on the mend. Hugs and tears abound as they gave their thanks that both children made it. "I'm in your debt, always," Anna whispered in Mary's ear before leaving. "Anything you ever need, I'll do."

Near closing, Mary sent gratitude to the goddesses for this second chance. Glancing over at her sleeping child, she marveled anew that something so perfect came from her imperfect self. Isobel embodied the goodness Mary needed to nurture in herself.

Mary smoothed the quilt and planted a kiss on Isobel's cool forehead. Despite defeating the cholera outbreak, Mary knew the scars on her own soul would linger. Yet each minor act of service salved them bit by bit. One day, she might again feel deserving of this innocent, unconditional love.

CHAPTER THIRTY-SIX

THE FIRST PALE LIGHT of dawn crept across the worn wooden floorboards as Mary laid out her tarot cards on her scruffy kitchen table. With the house still silent, she relished this rare moment of solitude before the bustle of the day. Mary took a deep, steadying breath and focused her thoughts. It had been weeks since she last consulted the cards, not since before the fire and her decision to embrace a simpler path without magick. But now, with her life in turmoil after the fire and Isobel's recovery, she hoped the cards might offer insight.

With centered energy, Mary drew three cards for a standard past, present, future spread. Turning over the first representing her past, she was unsurprised to see The Tower, depicting a building struck by lightning, crumbling and aflame. An obvious reflection of her former reckless behavior that endangered her family.

The present card gave her pause - the Knight of Swords, depicting a mounted warrior charging into battle, wielding a sword. Its meaning might suggest conflict, aggression, even danger approaching and without warning. Mary's stomach knotted anxiously. She needed no more strife or violence.

Finally, she revealed the card symbolizing her future - Death. The skeletal rider on his pale horse was an ominous sign, signaling profound transformation, but perhaps a literal death. Mary shivered, pushing the card away. She refused to court more darkness.

Mary shuffled the cards again, drawing a second spread. Once more, The Tower and Death appeared, now joined by the 10 of Swords - a man lying prone, 10 blades piercing his back. A clear signal of impending betrayal, ruin. She swept the cards together, unsettled. Perhaps she read too much into arbitrary drawings.

"Morning, Mama!" Mary jumped at her daughter's sudden entrance, thoughts scattered. She pulled out a bright smile for Isobel, tucking the cards away in her apron pocket. "Let's get some breakfast, shall we?"

But throughout the morning, Mary's disquiet lingered. The cards' warnings echoed in her mind, impossible to disregard. After tidying up the kitchen, she fetched the deck again while Isobel practiced writing her name on her chalkboard. One more reading, for clarity. Again, the same ominous cards emerged, confirming her fears of approaching calamity.

Heavy footsteps announced George's entrance before his gruff voice. "Where's my breakfast then? You've time for playing with those damned cards?" Once his grief turned to rage after the fire, George had become a storm barely contained.

Mary prepared his plate, knowing any reply would see his tempest unleashed. As she set it in front of him, he tore the fork from her hand. "We'll be rebuilding soon," he declared. "And if I ever find who killed my Pearl..." His knuckles whitened around the fork. "I'll kill them."

Mary met Isobel's frightened eyes across the room. "Best we go downstairs and open up." They hurried out, but Mary's hands still trembled at George's threat. The cards had indeed warned of violence. She must protect Isobel from it.

Mary wondered if atonement would ever wash her conscience clean. But those who still showed her kindness even now, like Doc, gave her hope.

That evening, Mary lit a candle at the kitchen table and retrieved quill, ink, and parchment to right some wrongs to bring her closer to absolution. She sat at the table, her quill posed, struggling to find the right words. The letter to Henry was one she should have written long ago, but shame had stayed her hand. Now, with danger looming, she could wait no longer.

Mary wrote while biting her lip, her hand trembling.

My Dearest Henry,

I hope this letter finds you well. I think of you often and miss you. You deserved far better from me than I gave. I regret vanishing from your life. The weight of the secret I've kept from you has become unbearable.

I had a daughter, Isobel, after I left. She is your daughter. I was afraid to tell you back then, worried I would cause you strife with your family and social circle. I convinced myself it was better that you never knew. But that was selfish and cowardly. You had a right to know your own child.

I do not expect your forgiveness for keeping this truth from you. But I hope you might find it in your heart to connect with Isobel. She is a sweet, bright girl of four now who has never known a father's love. You would be proud of her, as I am every day.

If anything should happen to me, I hope you will help Stella care for her as your own. She is old enough now to understand her true parentage. Please give her the family she deserves, if I cannot.

I am sorry to lay this burden upon you now in a letter. You did not choose this, but Isobel is as much your flesh and blood as mine. I hope one day you might come to love her.

If you can find it in your heart to forgive me, please write me back. I wish only to make amends, and for Isobel to know her father.

With all my love,

Mary

Mary sat back, sighing as emotions swirled within her - sadness, regret, hope. She had revealed her deepest secret other than her magick, yet there was no relief. Would Henry ever be able to forgive her? And could she bear it if he refused, or worse, rejected Isobel?

Mary shook her head as she set the letter aside. She would have to gather the courage to post it soon. But first, she had another tough message to write.

With her quill once more, she started the second letter.

Dearest Stella,

I hope you are keeping well. It has been too long since I last wrote. I think of you often, and the happy childhood we shared.

How I wish I could turn back time and do so much differently. You tried to guide me on a righteous path, but I refused to listen. I'm vain and reckless with magick. And now, those actions may come back to haunt us all.

I must confess to wearing mother's necklace and performing the dark magick in her grimoire. Like our mother, I used my gifts in vengeance. I bound a miner to gold, so he suffered burns while working his claim. Then George threatened to kick me and Isobel out and move in 'the love of his life' saloon girl. In a rage, I burned the saloon to the ground, killing Pearl and two others.

Karma came. I almost lost Isobel to cholera, and many were sick in town. I made the tonic you taught me and distributed it in town to any who needed it, to save as many as possible.

For now, I have hidden the necklace and grimoire. I have vowed to only use my gifts to heal others.

But now, far worse karma may come. George speaks of vengeance against whoever burned down the saloon and killed Pearl. When he learns the truth, I fear what he may do.

I must beg one last favor that I have no right to ask. If the worst should happen, please take Isobel in as your own. She is an innocent in all this. Let her have the loving family I deprived you both for too long. She deserves that chance, away from this darkness that I poisoned my life with.

Forgive me for failing you as a sister, and for only reaching out now in my hour of need. I pray we might reconcile before it is too late. Please write back, so I know you received this.

All my love,
Mary

Mary brushed away tears that had fallen onto the letter, leaving tiny blotches like raindrops. In her heart, she yearned for her sister to show her generous nature by taking in Isobel, even though she felt she didn't deserve it.

Mary folded Stella's letter, making sure each crease was precise and neat before she sealed it with hot wax. Then she slipped it in her apron pocket. Henry's letter contained too painful of truths to send yet. Instead, she entered the bedroom and crawled under the bed to hide it under the loose floorboard. One day soon, she would find the courage.

Mary's hands trembled as she retrieved the wooden cigar box from its hiding spot on the bottom shelf of the kitchen hutch. Usually she'd resent George frittering away their scarce money on such frivolous luxuries. But today, she was thankful for the small sturdy box as she set it on the kitchen table. It would serve a vital purpose. She ran her fingers over the worn covers of her mother's grimoire before nestling them into the cigar box.

Mary poured a circle of salt around the closed box and placed her heavy cast-iron pot on top. Inside the pot, she lit a candle, letting its wax drip in the bottom. She held the candle in the small puddle of wax until it stood upright on its own. She repeated it with a second one. Her hands shook as she placed the necklace in the space between the candles. Instantly, the necklace's energy thrummed through her fingers. Its gemstones glinted brightly, beckoning her to put it on, to feel its intoxicating rush of power.

With immense effort, Mary, sweat on her brow, withdrew her hand, balling it into a fist. She chanted the sealing incantation she had prepared, a whisper at first but growing louder, more insistent.

Powers of illusion, deception, and sight,
Cloak this book from unwanted eyes.
Conceal its truth in darkness and night,
Until the key of the necklace lies.

By ruby, emerald, sapphire might,
I seal these pages out of sight.

Necklace near the book takes form,
Else, only shadows shall adorn.
So mote it be!

As her voice rose, the flames of the candles flickered and danced as if responding to her call. A sudden breeze whipped through the kitchen, blowing Mary's hair across her face. She watched as a phantom wind snuffed out the candles.

The moment she retrieved the necklace from the pot, she felt its energy pulsating in her hand. Mary hastily wrapped it in a kitchen towel and raced to the bedroom, dropping to the floor to release herself from its captivating hold. She laid there once she shoved it in its prison, relieved of its torture to her spirit. The missing piece of her soul was once more locked away.

On steadier legs, Mary returned to the kitchen and lifted the box's lid. When she looked inside, she found nothing but an empty void. The cigar box sealed shut with a soft snap, and she tiptoed through the night, making her way to Isobel's room under the pale light of the waning moon from her window.

Mary slid the box into the top drawer of Isobel's dresser. The book would remain hidden, only accessible to those who possessed the necklace. Its secrets would tempt Mary no more.

The morning sun streamed in through the kitchen window as Mary busied herself preparing tea. The familiar clatter of an approaching wagon and Isobel's squeal downstairs told her Anna and John had arrived for their weekly visit. Moments later, the two children broke into a whirlwind of laughter of excitement when John came through the door.

Mary smiled as they scampered off to play, then continued steeping the tea leaves, lost in thought. She had lain awake all night, turning over how to broach the subject weighing on her mind.

When Anna entered, Mary gestured for her to sit at the table. She carried over two steaming mugs and slid into the chair across from her friend. Her eyes fell on the small drawstring pouch resting on the tabletop, inside which lay the necklace she had sworn to never wear again.

After a deep breath, Mary said, "Anna, I... I have a confession to make, and a favor to ask."

Anna nodded, her gentle features full of warmth and concern.

Mary forced herself to continue. "You must have noticed how coldly George treats Isobel."

"I have," Anna replied. "It's quite sad."

Mary cast her eyes downward, her voice dropping to a hushed tone. "He has good reason for his resentment. Isobel... she isn't his daughter. Her father was George's brother."

Mary tensed, awaiting Anna's shock or disgust over such an admission. But her friend nodded for her to go on, no judgment in her eyes.

Encouraged, Mary continued, "I loved George's brother but feared I would never be happy living in his social circle. I was even sure I never wanted children. George's plans sounded so exciting. My heart aches every time I think about leaving Henry - it's my greatest regret."

The sting of tears overwhelmed Mary as she struggled to hold them back. "George's anger has become dangerous since the fire. I fear what he may do next." She slid the pouch forward. "So I need you to keep my necklace safe, and if anything happens to me... please see that Isobel goes to my sister, or Henry, where they will care for her."

Anna leaned forward, eyes widened, grasping Mary's hand. "Has George threatened you? You mustn't stay if you are unsafe!"

Mary managed a sad smile. "I cannot abandon him. I brought this darkness upon us, and must see it through." She squeezed Anna's hand. "Just promise me you will look after Isobel if the worst should happen."

"You have my word," Anna vowed.

An immense relief washed over Mary, knowing Anna's kindness would shelter her dear Isobel. She longed to confess the rest - her abilities, the harm she had wrought with them. But she had entrusted Anna enough for today.

Forcing a lighter tone, Mary said, "Enough gloom for now. Let's finish this tea, then I'll show how my garden looks."

The two women moved outside into the morning sunshine, watching John and Isobel play beneath the willow tree. Mary wished she could freeze this moment forever - the golden light, the children's laughter, the company of a genuine friend.

Whatever darkness loomed ahead, she knew Anna would be a beacon of light and hope for her daughter when she herself was gone. Mary could ask for no greater gift than that. For the first time in many years, a gentle calm washed over her.

Chapter Thirty-Seven

GEORGE SQUINTED AT THE dawn light streaming into his bedroom window. He felt Mary rise, but he could not fall back asleep. Every muscle in his body ached from the work on the new saloon. He got up and gazed out the window at Jack's new saloon framework across the street. Jack wanted a bigger one and the spot where his now burned building was too small with the livery and assayer on each side. Closer for George to get home.

George didn't find Mary in the kitchen, so he opened the door to the stairs and found she was by the wood stove downstairs. He watched her open the door, bend over and blow inside. The reflection on her face showed a roaring fire started. Not one from kindling, but a lit and burning log.

George sat motionless, his thoughts swirling in a tempest of confusion and disbelief. He replayed their past, each memory now cast in a sinister new light. How was he so oblivious? He had always perceived Mary as an enigma - her idiosyncrasies intriguing yet unsettling. But now, the truth loomed over him like a dark cloud: she was a witch. This revelation sent a shiver along his spine, reframing every moment they had shared.

George remembered resisting the idea of marrying her at first, yet somehow, he had been powerless to prevent it. Was it her magick that had bent his will?

Even out on the trail, she always seemed a step ahead. The first to kindle a fire, as if she commanded the flames themselves. He had admired her resourcefulness, but now he saw it as an unhuman capacity to manipulate the elements.

Her healing abilities were another piece of the puzzle that now fit into this alarming picture. People came to her with ailments and left, singing her praises. Her remedies, often simple, worked miracles that defied explanation. George had secretly marveled at her skill, attributing it to a natural talent. But now, he saw it as something far more sinister - an otherworldly power that she wielded with unsettling ease.

And then there was the way people gravitated towards her. Mary, odd and irksome, was beloved by all. He had seen it as a testament to her charm, but now he realized it was a calculated enchantment, a way to garner favor and influence.

It had all been trickery, a trap ensnaring him in a web of magick. George felt a sense of betrayal. It was as if he had been living in a constructed illusion, a trap of Mary's making. The woman was an enigma wrapped in a riddle, her true nature shrouded in mystery and now, in his eyes, darkness.

George's mind raced with a torrent of troubling thoughts, each more unsettling than the last. The image of the saloon engulfed in flames haunted him, a vivid reminder of the catastrophe that had unfolded. He wrestled with the possibility that Mary could have been the architect of such destruction. The thought that she might have set the saloon ablaze using a mere breath of her witchcraft sent chills down his spine. This wasn't just an accident; it was an act of inexplicable power, a dark, and uncontrollable manifestation.

The realization hit him like a tidal wave. He had been living alongside a witch without even knowing it. The enormity of this revelation left him reeling, struggling to reconcile this newfound truth. His life, as he had understood it, was crumbling around him, leaving him to grapple with a reality too bizarre and frightening to comprehend.

In the midst of chaos and bewilderment, one painfully clear thought emerged: Mary was responsible for Pearl's death, extinguishing his hope for true love and happiness. That Mary's witchcraft had robbed him of this possibility ignited a raging inferno of anger within him. His heart pounded with a mix of grief and fury, losing Pearl a wound that cut deep into his very soul.

Overwhelmed by his emotions, George's body mirrored his inner turmoil. He spun around, his movements fueled by a surge of anger and despair. The door slammed shut with a resounding thud, echoing the chaos in his mind. His head pounded in sync with the tumultuous rhythm of his thoughts, each beat a reminder of his loss and betrayal.

As he shook his head, trying in vain to dispel the onslaught of emotions, his fists clenched tightly. The physical manifestation of his inner conflict, his knuckles whitened with the intensity of his grip. He was a man driven to the edge, his world turned upside down by a revelation too surreal to process.

At that moment, a resolve crystallized within him. Revenge. The word echoed through his mind, a singular focus emerging from the chaos. He wouldn't let this betrayal go unanswered. The pain of losing Pearl, combined with the shock of Mary's true nature, left him with a burning desire to act. George knew nothing would bring back what he had lost, but he was determined to confront this betrayal head-on. The path forward was uncertain, fraught with danger and moral ambiguity, but George would seek retribution, whatever the cost.

With a determined stride, George stormed into the bedroom. His movements were brisk, filled with a singular purpose. He donned his clothes, each piece thrown on with a mix of urgency and resolve. He set his mind to grab breakfast at Jack and Marisol's makeshift tent behind the half-constructed saloon, then dive into a day's labor. But beneath this routine lay a darker intent. Today, he would craft a scheme to extricate Mary from his life, a plan shrouded in deceit and cunning, ensuring his hands remained clean.

As George ate breakfast amidst the hum of early morning activities, his mind was elsewhere, plotting, calculating. He needed to engineer a scenario where suspicion would never fall upon him. An alibi, solid and unquestionable, was crucial.

Later, perched on a ladder, he hoisted a rafter into place, his physical exertions a backdrop to his scheming thoughts. His mind wandered to a conversation he'd overheard - a miner boasting about the allure of French girls in Missoula. The thought tantalized him; a few days of carefree indulgence in a raucous town seemed like the perfect diversion. But duty called - Jack needed him here, to finish the saloon. His revenge could wait, simmering in the back of his mind, its sweetness undiminished by time.

George hammered crosspieces between the rafters, each strike a rhythmic release for his pent-up frustrations. He paused, his gaze drifting northward to the majestic mountain ranges that stood as silent witnesses to his plotting. His plan crystalized. Before departing for Missoula, he would stage a break-in. The ax, conveniently left by the woodpile, would serve as a tool of feigned violence, smashing the back door to simulate a forced entry. Inside, he would create chaos, overturning items and pilfering cash. As each detail slotted into place in his mind, a sense of exhilaration washed over him.

Eager to share a moment of levity amidst his dark contemplations, George called out to Jack below, "Why is a man who never lays a wager as bad as a regular gambler?"

Jack paused, his brows knitting in confusion. He tilted his head, pondering the riddle before shrugging in defeat. "I dunno know."

"Because he's no better," George chuckled, a brief respite from his sinister thoughts. But Jack's response was a mere shake of the head, a silent return to his work, cutting lumber with a steady hand. George's laughter faded into the morning air, his amusement fleeting as the gravity of his intentions reclaimed him. The joviality of the moment was but a brief interlude in the orchestration of his dark plan.

The sun was setting, casting long shadows across the room as Mary gathered the laundry from the line outside. Her movements were methodical, a dance of domesticity she had mastered over the years. She brought the clothes in, the fabric still warm from the sun's embrace, and set them on the kitchen table. "Isobel, do you want to help me?" she called out, her voice a gentle invitation.

Isobel, innocence of youth shining in her eyes, eagerly agreed. "Yes, mama." She approached the table, her small stature just allow-

ing her to peer over its edge. Carefully, she placed her beloved doll -
a handcrafted token of her mother's love - beside the pile of clothes.
"Mama, dolly help?" she asked.

Mary's smile was a soft curve of affection. "Yes, Dolly can help."
She handed Isobel some kitchen towels to fold, a task well within her
little hands' capabilities. Then Mary's fingers lingered on George's
shirt, her mind drifting to his recent moodiness that cast a shadow
over their home. She was grateful for his absence. Deep down, she
suspected he knew about her role in the recent events, and it worried
her. Yet, she was prepared, having made contingency plans should
the situation escalate.

The door swung open abruptly, breaking the tranquility of the
moment. George strode in, his presence like a storm cloud entering
the room. "I'm going to Missoula to get some supplies. Be gone a
few days," he announced, his tone clipped and cold. He approached
Mary, too close for comfort, his face inches from hers. His eyes
burned, an intensity that sent a wave of fear through Mary. She
instinctively stepped back, but George's grip was iron, his fingers
clamping onto her shoulders before forcefully pushing her to the
ground.

"Isobel, get help. Go!" Mary's voice was a desperate cry amidst the
chaos. "Stop, George. I'll leave if that's what you want. I'll go back to
Chicago. Don't hurt me, please," she pleaded, her voice trembling.

But George's rage was unyielding, his eyes wide with fury. "You
set that fire. I know you did. You're a witch," he accused. "I've seen
you light fires without a match. You are evil, and I will set things
right. You killed all those people. You killed the only woman I have
ever loved." His hands encircled her neck, squeezing with relentless
force.

Mary, struggling for air, uttered a curse in her native tongue, "Briseadh agus brú ort." The words were a last-ditch effort, a spell to curse him to his final breath.

Isobel, witnessing the horror unfolding before her, rushed to her mother's aid. "No, Papa! No! Don't hurt Mama!" Her tiny hands pulled at George's arm, but he was unmovable. With one hand, he flung Isobel aside, his roar echoing through the room. "I'm not your Papa. Never call me that again." His words were a dagger to Isobel's heart, sending her retreating to the wall, tears streaming down her face.

Mary gasped for air as she futilely tried to pry George's hands from her neck. Her legs kicked, seeking leverage, seeking escape. Realizing her impending fate, she turned her gaze to Isobel, her eyes conveying a mother's love in her last moments. "I..love...you," she whispered. With the last of her strength, she cast a spell, ensuring Isobel would not remember this day until she found the grimoires.

Until the necklace and grimoires reunite,
Keep her mind from the darkest night.
Let her laughter ring true and free,
Unburdened by past agony.

With this spell, I weave protection,
Guiding her in a safe direction.
When mother's legacy she does see,
Restore her memories, so mote it be!

Mary's gaze tore away from Isobel, the sight of her daughter's tear-streaked face an unbearable torment. Her heart ached with a mother's profound sorrow, the realization that she would never again witness Isobel's smile, hear her laughter, or feel her small arms wrapped in an embrace. She couldn't bear the finality of their parting, the cruel severance of their bond.

Her eyes, heavy with pain and defiance, found the willow tree outside the window. Its branches swayed gently in the breeze, a stark contrast to the violence unfolding within. Using the last vestiges of her strength, Mary summoned a deep, guttural curse. The words, born of anguish and wrath, rolled off her tongue, each syllable a potent mix of magick and emotion.

Twist and turn, oh willow's frame,
Let it bear the mark of the witch's bane.
From roots to crown, in moon's eerie light,
Cloak its bark in shades of night.

Leaves once green, now turn anew,
Paint them red, a bloodied hue.
A symbol of loss, a reminder so dire,
A testament to a witch's pyre.

Let this tree stand tall in memory,
Of the witch who met her destiny.
By my power, this change I decree,
A solemn sentinel, so mote it be!

The curse was more than a spell; it was a manifestation of her spirit, a last stand against the injustice she suffered. The curse was aimed at the willow, a silent sentinel to her ordeal. She intended it to be a perpetual reminder to George, a haunting echo of her presence that he could never escape. The tree would stand as a testament to her life, her struggles, and the depth of her love for Isobel.

A wave of exhaustion swept over Mary. Her body, wracked with pain and depleted by the effort of casting the spells, surrendered. She felt herself slipping away, her physical form succumbing to the inevitable. But even as her body went limp, her spirit blazed with a fierce intensity. In her last moments, Mary held onto the hope that her actions would protect Isobel, and that George would forever be haunted by the memory of the woman he had wronged. Her last thoughts were a blend of sorrow for leaving Isobel and a fierce satisfaction that her curse would endure, a lingering shadow in George's life.

George stood, his breaths ragged. A cold, merciless look etched on his face, he spat out the words, "Good riddance, you wretched witch." His voice was a venomous hiss. Each syllable reverberated in the room, marking the end of his tumultuous struggle. With calculated strides, he crossed the room, his remorseless eyes piercing. His destination was the wood stove, where he reached to grasp a poker, its metal cold and unyielding - a fitting extension of his hardened heart.

Meanwhile, Isobel crawled over to Mary's lifeless form. Her tiny hands, trembling, reached out to her mother. "Mama. Mama. Wake up," she pleaded. She shook Mary but her mother remained still, her body devoid of the warmth and vitality that had once defined her. Isobel laid herself across Mary's chest, her sobs filling the room. Her tears soaked into Mary's clothes, a silent testament to the bond between mother and daughter, now severed.

In that moment, the room was a stark contrast of emotions - George's cold wrath against the innocent grief of a child. The events that had transpired would leave an indelible mark on both their lives, setting them on divergent paths forever altered by the day's tragic events.

George returned with the poker. He lifted Mary's skirt, pushing the child away again. He took the poker and jabbed it into Mary. Blood spilled and pooled on the floor.

Isobel darted towards George. Her slight frame trembled. She unleashed a fury upon him. Her tiny feet kicked fiercely, each strike a testament to her anguish and desperation. Her hands, so small and delicate, transformed into instruments of defiance as she pummeled him with all the strength her young body could muster.

Surprised by her sudden onslaught, George dropped the poker. His reaction was swift and brutal. One large hand clamped around her tiny throat, cutting off her breath, silencing her cries. His grip was iron, unyielding, as he held her aloft. He peered into her face, wet with tears, and in it, he saw a haunting reminder of his brother Henry - the brother who had always been the golden child, the one who cast George into the shadows.

In a fit of rage and bitter memories, George hurled Isobel across the room with a terrifying force. Her small body arced through the air before crumpling into a soft, forlorn heap, her cries and resistance silenced.

Cold and emotionless, George turned away from the havoc he had wrought. Each deliberate step he took towards the door echoed the finality of his actions. The door slammed shut behind him with a resounding finality, its sound reverberating through the room like a death knell. The violence and turmoil he had unleashed lingered in the air, a palpable force that contrasted with his silent departure.

CHAPTER THIRTY-EIGHT

ISOBEL STIRRED FROM THE pain along her back, her throat burning, a harsh cough tearing through her. Her eyes fluttered open to a scene that struck her with a bone-chilling terror. The sight of her mother, lifeless in a crimson pool that had seeped across the floor, overwhelmed her young mind. Her father was nowhere to be seen, a haunting absence in the nightmare's aftermath. Tears streamed down Isobel's cheeks, a river of grief and confusion, until exhaustion rendered her tear ducts dry.

Trembling, she crawled towards the table, her every movement hesitant, as if the very air around her was tainted with the horror of the scene. She couldn't bear to glance at her mother again, that image too harrowing for her fragile heart. Grasping her doll - a symbol of safer, happier times - she sought refuge under her bed. In that cramped, shadowy space, she curled into a tight ball, clutching her doll like a lifeline, her small body wracked in silent sobs.

As the evening crept in, a gnawing hunger and thirst set in. Yet, the thought of facing the grim reality outside her makeshift sanctuary petrified her. With great effort, she crawled to the door, her movements slow and deliberate. She closed it, a barrier between her and the unbearable sight of her mother. Retreating under her bed, she held her doll close, her heart pounding with the fear that her father might return. The threat of more harm from him loomed large in her mind, a shadow that haunted her fitful sleep.

The morning light brought no relief to Isobel. Sunbeams streamed through her window, casting patterns on the floor that would have fascinated her any other day. But today, they were mere flickers in her world of darkness. She realized her mother hadn't woken her as usual, but the reason eluded her, lost in a fog of trauma and confusion. She cried noiselessly, her face buried in her doll. Thirst clawed at her throat, hunger gnawed at her belly, but fear anchored her in place. The fear of seeing her mother motionless, the fear of her father's potential return - these fears bound her to her hiding spot.

Isobel lay there, lost in the play of sunlight, trying to make sense of the silence, the absence of her mother's voice. The sound of knocks on the door stirred her. Was it be Sunday? She knew Sunday meant visits from John and his mother, a routine that had always brought joy. But today, even the prospect of friendly faces wouldn't coax her from her sanctuary. She remained hidden, holding on to the fragile hope that somehow, when she woke next, the world would be right again. But as she drifted back to sleep, the harsh reality remained - her mother was gone, her father was a source of fear, and she was alone, save for the doll in her arms.

The sun was high in the sky, casting a harsh light on the dusty street as townsfolk congregated outside the general store. They appeared concerned as they peered through the dusty windows, trying to discern why the bustling store remained shuttered.

Jack emerged from his new saloon, his brow furrowed. "What's wrong?" he inquired.

A woman from the crowd responded, "I've been trying to get supplies for two days now, but they haven't opened. Mary opens the store every day, except Sundays and holidays. What do you think's wrong? Last time this happened, their child was deathly ill. I just hope everything's alright."

Jack's gaze shifted to the store's window, his eyes searching for any sign of life within. Finding none, he rapped on the door, his knocks echoing in the tense silence. After several minutes with no response, he circled to the back door, knocking and calling out, "George! Mary! Can you come down? Are you okay?"

Receiving no answer, a sense of unease settled over him. He returned to the store's front, his expression growing grimmer. "No one's seen them? I haven't seen George in a few days, and I see him every day. Something ain't right," he murmured, a knot of apprehension forming in his stomach.

Pointing at Bernard, he asked for help. "You wanna give me a hand? Maybe we can get in through the back door. I'm sure George has an axe or something in the shed." Together, they retrieved two axes from the shed, and with a few powerful swings, they broke open the back door.

Stepping inside, Jack called out again, "George! Mary!" The silence that greeted him was ominous. He ascended the stairs, turning to Bernard. "Wait here. I don't want to startle anyone when I open their door."

Fumbling with the doorknob, he found it unlocked and entered. The sight that met his eyes made him stagger back, a hand flying to his head in shock. Mary laid on the floor, motionless. "Oh, no! Mary!" He rushed to her side, kneeling in the growing pool of blood. Her lips were a chilling shade of blue, and the amount of blood was staggering. "George, are you here?" he called out as he searched the rooms.

Then, a chilling thought struck him - Isobel. "Isobel? It's Jack." He entered her room, but it appeared empty. Bending down, he spotted her cowering under the bed. "Isobel, come out, sweetie. Let's get you out of here, okay?"

Isobel, her eyes wide, backed further into her hiding place, shaking her head and crying.

Jack's heart ached at the sight. "Will you come out for Marisol?" he asked, but Isobel only turned her face away, refusing to budge. Jack's mind raced, trying to piece together the events that had led to this tragedy.

He opened the window and shouted for help, "Get Marisol and then Doc. And hurry!" His voice was urgent and panicked.

A man responded with a quick "Gotcha ya!" and dashed off, kicking up dust as he went.

Returning his focus to Isobel, Jack reassured her. "Marisol will be here soon. Then we can get you fed. I bet you're thirsty, huh? Where is your daddy?"

At the mention of her father, Isobel turned away, her actions speaking volumes. Jack's stomach turned. He glanced over at Mary's lifeless body, a growing suspicion gnawing at him. "What did George do?"

Soon, Marisol arrived, breathless. Jack instructed her, "Wait. Don't look at anything except Isobel's room. Do you understand? Go into her room and close the door. She's under the bed. I need you to coax her out."

Marisol nodded. "Is Isobel alright? Where is Mary?" Her eyes brimmed with tears, but she held them back, focusing on Isobel.

Jack returned to Mary and George's bedroom and removed the sheet from their bed. He covered Mary, sparing Marisol and Isobel the horrific sight.

As Marisol emerged with Isobel wrapped in a quilt and clutching some clothes, Jack led them outside. A crowd had gathered, and Doc approached. "Mary is dead upstairs," Jack whispered. "Isobel's been under her bed for days. Marisol will take care of her."

Doc, concern etching his features, asked, "Where's George?"

Jack shook his head. "I don't know. I haven't seen him for a few days and he said nothing out of the ordinary. His usual moaning and bellyaching." Jack said. "Do you want to see Mary first or Isobel?"

"Mary."

They returned to Mary, where Doc examined her body, noting the bruising and the lack of defensive wounds. "She was murdered," he concluded.

Jack stood there, his mind a whirlwind of emotions and questions. The suspicion that George could commit such an act was a bitter pill to swallow. He had known George was unhappy, but murder? The reality of the situation was a heavy burden, and Jack felt the weight of it pressing on him as he tried to make sense of the unimaginable tragedy.

Doc, having finished his grim assessment of Mary's body, followed Jack across the street where Marisol had taken Isobel. Isobel, wrapped in a quilt, appeared small and fragile in Marisol's arms. Her eyes were distant, lost in a world of her own, a stark contrast to the bustling activity around her.

As they entered Marisol's room, Doc set his bag down and kneeled in front of Isobel. Gently, he coaxed, "Let me look at you, sweetheart." His voice was soft, trying to pierce the veil of trauma that enveloped the little girl. Isobel, however, remained silent, her gaze fixed on some unseen point in the distance.

Doc examined her neck, where distinct bruises marred her delicate skin. The marks were a telltale sign of the ordeal she had endured. He touched them lightly, causing Isobel to flinch, but she remained otherwise unresponsive, her silence a heavy shroud around her.

Jack and Marisol exchanged worried glances as they watched. Doc's expression grew concerned. "She's in shock," he murmured, more to himself than to the others. "The physical wounds will heal, but the emotional trauma... that will take time."

Turning to Jack and Marisol, he instructed, "Keep her warm, make sure she drinks water, and try to get her to eat something, even if it's just a little. She needs rest and a safe environment. She needs your support and patience."

After Doc left, Marisol led Isobel to a cozy corner of the room, laying her on a cushioned seat. She offered her a cup of water, which Isobel accepted, sipping without a word.

Jack watched them, a profound sadness filling him. The once lively and chattering Isobel was now silent, a stark reminder of the tragedy that had befallen their small community. The questions of what had happened and why loomed large, but for now, the priority was Isobel's well-being.

Chapter Thirty-Nine

In his office in his grand home on Prairie Avenue in Chicago, Henry worked on his company's books. It was a warm, bustling afternoon, with the sun casting a golden hue through the large, paneled windows. Outside, the sounds of horse-drawn carriages and the distant hum of the bustling city filtered through the windows, mingling with the quiet scratching of his pen.

His office was a testament to the opulence of the era and his success. Rich, dark mahogany wood lined the room, from the bookshelves brimming with leather-bound volumes to the large, imposing desk dominating the center. The desk was a clutter of activity: piles of papers, a few opened letters, an inkwell with a feathered quill perched at its edge, and a brass stand holding several more pens.

Henry sat behind the desk, his posture upright and commanding. Dressed in a tailored suit, his waistcoat buttoned up, he exuded an air of authority and wealth. His hair, neatly combed, had a few strands rebelliously falling over his forehead. His brows furrowed as he concentrated on a ledger making notes or ticking off items.

The sharp rap at the door jolted Henry from his deep concentration.

"Come in," he called out, his voice echoing in the spacious, book-lined study.

The door creaked open, and Estelle, his housekeeper, stepped in. Her nose was scrunched in apparent distaste, her lips pressed into a thin line. Henry caught a fleeting glimpse of anger flickering in her eyes as she shut the door behind her.

"There's a woman here demanding to see you," Estelle announced, her arms folded across her chest. "She claims it's urgent business from George and insists on consequences if we turn her away."

Henry's brows furrowed in perplexity. George, his estranged brother, hadn't made contact in several months. What prompted this unexpected intrusion now?

"Did she mention what it's regarding?" Henry inquired.

Estelle's expression remained impassive, her gray hair pinned, betraying no hint of movement. "She was quite secretive, refusing to divulge any details, insisting only that she must speak with you immediately." As she leaned forward, her voice dropped to a near-whisper. "She's not a woman of means, if you take my meaning. I would not feel comfortable allowing her into your office, but she did mention George."

Nodding in understanding, Henry rose from his chair, smoothing the fabric of his vest. "Very well, Estelle. Have her wait in the foyer. I shall see to this matter momentarily."

Estelle departed with a brisk nod, her heels echoing along the hallway. Henry exhaled, a sense of foreboding settling over him as he prepared to confront the mysterious visitor.

Stepping into the foyer, Henry paused. The woman waiting for him was a stark contrast to the opulent surroundings of his Prairie Avenue home. Her dress, once perhaps of decent quality, was now faded and frayed, hanging on her slender frame. Stray strands of hair peeked out from under a hat that had seen better days. As she turned to face him, the overpowering combination of stale rose perfume and sweat hit him, causing him to recoil.

"How may I assist you?" Henry asked, maintaining a polite but guarded demeanor.

The woman's lips curled into a sly grin, revealing a chipped front tooth. "George sent me," she declared smugly. "I have something—or rather, someone—you care about. But my help comes at a price."

Henry's heart raced, his mind swirling with possibilities. Blackmail? Abduction? His fingers clenched into fists at the thought of this stranger wielding power over him or his family. "And who might you be referring to?" he asked, struggling to keep his composure.

She tilted her head. "The girl's name is Isobel."

The mention of Isobel, his niece, tightened a knot in Henry's stomach. His thoughts whirled. "I'm at a loss. What has happened to Mary? Why do you have Isobel?"

The woman's eyes narrowed. "Mary's dead. George doesn't want the child."

Henry felt the room spin, his knees weakening. He turned away, struggling to maintain his facade. Mary, the woman he had once held dear, was gone. And now Isobel was thrust into this chaos. George's indifference was no surprise, but the reality of it stung.

Composing himself, he faced the woman again. "You've come a long way, and for that, you deserve fair compensation. Let's discuss a reasonable agreement to ensure Isobel's well-being."

The woman hesitated before seating herself on an ornate chair, her worn attire contrasted the luxurious surroundings.

"What do you consider a fair price for your... services?" Henry inquired, his voice steady despite the turmoil within.

Fingering her tattered shawl, she avoided his gaze. "Considering the travel and care for the girl, I reckon $2,000 should suffice."

Henry stood, his chair scraping against the floor. "$2,000!" he exclaimed, pacing the room in frustration. This was extortion. Yet, he was cornered. Isobel's safety was paramount.

He faced the woman, his resolve firm. "I offer $1,000, payable upon Isobel's safe arrival tomorrow. That is my final offer."

The woman agreed, and Henry drafted a contract, which she signed with a shaky 'X'. He escorted her out, his mind reeling.

Back in his study, Henry sank into his chair, overwhelmed by grief and responsibility. Mary, his long-lost love, was gone, leaving behind a myriad of unspoken words and unfulfilled dreams. And now, Isobel, an innocent caught in this tragic web, would be his to care for.

He steeled himself for the challenges ahead. Isobel would need a home, love, and stability—everything her father had failed to provide. Despite the unexpected turn his life had taken, Henry was determined to give Isobel a future worthy of her mother's memory.

The faint knock at the door pierced the quiet atmosphere of the house, startling Henry from his thoughts. He leaped to his feet, propelled by a mix of anticipation and anxiety, and hurried to the front door, reaching it before Estelle could.

He swung the door open and was met with a sight that tugged at his heartstrings. Standing before him was a small, forlorn figure: a child, dirty and disheveled. Her torn and tattered dress hung on her tiny frame, her bare feet caked with grime. Her bowed head revealed a mop of chestnut brown hair, matted and unkempt.

Henry's hand flew to his mouth in shock, and he kneeled in front of the child, taking her tiny, dirt-smudged hand in his. As he looked into her sad green eyes, reminiscent of Mary's, a wave of emotion washed over him. His voice trembled as he spoke. "Isobel, I am so relieved you are here, safe and sound. You're with family now, and I promise you, I will keep you safe." Gently, he scooped her into his arms, her slight weight a stark reminder of her vulnerability.

Henry turned around to find Estelle closing the door for him. "Isobel, this is Estelle," Henry introduced, though the child remained silent and distant. "She must be starving and in need of a bath. Could you perhaps start with that? I need to make some arrangements for her—clothes and whatever else girls need."

Estelle offered Isobel a warm, reassuring smile. "You're home, dear. Henry, you'll find a children's clothing store next to the bakery. Stella should know the place. You'll need a few essentials to start with. I'll reheat some stew for her in the meantime."

Henry gently set Isobel down, watching as she cautiously explored her new surroundings, her toes curling into the plush fabric of the Turkish rug. "Do you like the rug, Isobel?" he asked, though she remained silent, her gaze wandering curiously around the room.

He patted her head. "She's been through a lot. It'll take time for her to adjust. I'll leave you to it, Estelle, and head out for those errands." With a deep sense of responsibility weighing on him, he made his way out to prepare his carriage.

Alone with Estelle, Isobel appeared small and fragile, yet her curiosity was clear as she ran her fingers along the smooth wainscoting. Estelle thought aloud about the child's past living conditions. "I can't imagine what life was like for you in Montana. But you're safe here now."

In the kitchen, Estelle busied herself preparing the stew, her movements efficient and nurturing. She lit the wood stove, the gentle crackle of the fire providing a comforting background noise. "Are you cold, Isobel? You can stand by the stove to warm up," she suggested.

Isobel, drawn to the warmth, stood close to Estelle, seeking comfort. Estelle kneeled and enveloped the child in a gentle embrace. "You're home now, sweetheart. We'll take good care of you."

When the stew was ready, Estelle served Isobel a bowlful, along with a biscuit. The child ate with a voracity that spoke of days without proper nourishment. "You must have been starving," Estelle observed.

Isobel nodded, her actions speaking louder than words.

"Ready to get clean? I hate to think about when you last had a bath. I'm sure your mother kept you clean, but I'm guessing not since she died."

Isobel looked downcast at the mention of her mother, a shadow of grief passing over her face.

Estelle regretted her thoughtless words. "I'm sorry, Isobel. I shouldn't have said that. You've been through a lot."

Isobel's slow nod was a silent acceptance of Estelle's apology.

Estelle led Isobel upstairs for a bath, starting a small fire in the bathroom stove to warm the water. She grabbed her hairbrush. "I guess we might as well see if we get these mats out while the water warms up. I hope so or I will have to cut your hair short. A pixie cut might be okay, and it will grow out, anyway. Pretty bows and everything will be fine."

After several minutes on one of the child's dreadlocks, Estelle opened a drawer to retrieve a pair of scissors. She sighed. "I keep telling myself it grows back, but I hate to cut your hair. But here goes nothing." Estelle cut each of the matted clumps and they fell to the bathroom floor. Isobel didn't respond and stood still. After the clumps laid on the floor, she thought of what she could do to salvage Isobel's chestnut hair. She clipped it into a short bob with bangs that swept to one side.

Holding up a mirror, Estelle asked, "What do you think?"

Isobel's smile was a rare glimpse of the child within, breaking through her shell of silence.

"Let's get rid of the clothes." She pulled the tattered dress over Isobel's head and took a whiff. "Oh my. Phew. Stray dogs smell better."

Estelle helped Isobel into the bath, the water darkening as the dirt washed away. "So much dirt for a little girl." After drying her off and dressing her in a clean shirt, Estelle brushed Isobel's newly cut hair, noticing its resemblance to Henry's. She eyed the little girl and found no semblance to George but more of Henry and Mary. Was she Henry's child and not George's? Lucky for her.

As she settled Isobel into bed for a nap, Estelle pondered the child's future in this new home. She left the door ajar, a silent promise of safety and care always within reach.

Returning to the kitchen, Estelle set about cleaning up, her mind abuzz with thoughts and concerns for Isobel. The house, once filled with quiet routine, was now the start of a new chapter, one that held promise and hope for a child who had experienced too much sorrow at her tender age.

Chapter Forty

Henry's carriage rolled to a halt in front of Albert and Stella's elegant brownstone. He leaped from the carriage and bounded up the steps, his heart pounding. When he reached the door, he rapped, his foot tapping a restless rhythm as he paced the landing.

Albert answered the door, his face lighting up at the sight of his friend. "Henry, what a pleasant surprise! Do come in. I'll fetch Stella," he said.

Henry, unable to contain his eagerness, blurted out, "I have good news and bad news." His heart and soul struggled with the conflicting news he carried.

Henry sat in the ornate living room of Stella and Albert's brownstone, his hands clasped in his lap. The room, usually a place of warmth and laughter, felt oppressively silent. Stella and Albert sat opposite him, looks of concern and curiosity on their faces, unaware of the devastating news he was about to deliver.

Stella leaned forward, her eyes searching Henry's face. "Henry, you seem troubled. What brings you here today?"

Taking a deep breath, Henry met her gaze, his eyes brimming with unshed tears. "Stella, Albert... I have some very difficult news to share." His voice trembled as he struggled to find the words. "It's about Mary."

Stella's hand flew to her mouth, her eyes widening in alarm. "Mary? What about her? Is she alright?" The fear in her voice was palpable.

Henry shook his head, a lone tear escaping down his cheek. "No, she's not alright. I'm so sorry to have to tell you this, but... Mary is gone. She passed away."

A gasp escaped Stella's lips, her hand clutching at her heart. Albert reached out, wrapping an arm around her shoulders, his own face etched with shock. "Gone? But how? What happened?" Albert's voice was barely a whisper.

Henry swallowed hard, the pain of his loss raw and all-consuming. "I don't know all the details yet. But Mary's daughter, Isobel, is here now. She arrived on my doorstep this morning."

Stella's tears flowed, her body shaking with sobs. "Poor Mary... and little Isobel. Oh, Henry, this is dreadful." She leaned into Albert, seeking comfort in his embrace.

Henry nodded, his own grief now overshadowed by a sense of duty and responsibility. "Yes, it's a terrible tragedy. But right now, we need to focus on Isobel. She's only four years old and has been through so much. She needs us, Stella, Albert. We're her family now."

Albert, his face somber, nodded in agreement. "Of course, Henry. We'll do whatever we can for Isobel. She's family."

Stella, wiping her tears, looked up with a newfound resolve. "You're right, Henry. We must be strong for Isobel. She needs our love and support now more than ever. What can we do to help?"

Henry offered a weak smile, grateful for their support. "I thought we could start by getting her some clothes and things she'll need. She arrived with nothing but the clothes on her back. Marshall Field's would be the ideal place to shop for her needs. They have everything we could want for her."

Stella rose, determination in her eyes. "Let's do it. We'll make sure Isobel has everything she needs. And we'll help her through this, together." Stella, now bustling with activity, echoed his suggestion. "Absolutely, Marshall Field's is perfect. They have such lovely children's wear. Let me grab my reticle, and I'll be ready to go."

Henry laughed. "You should have seen her when she arrived. Such a sight. Though she seems healthy, she hasn't spoken a word yet. I hope it's the exhaustion from her journey."

"The poor child. But we'll do everything we can for her. Let's not waste any more time. I can't wait to see her."

Together, they stepped out of the brownstone and into the carriage, ready to embark on their mission. Henry's heart swelled. Isobel's arrival had brought a seismic shift in his life, but with their support, they would provide Isobel a loving home and help her heal from the unimaginable loss of her mother. Mary's death would leave a void in their lives, but in Isobel, they had a part of Mary to cherish and protect. The journey of healing was just beginning, not only for Isobel, but for all of them.

Henry, Albert, and Estelle bustled into Henry's foyer with an assortment of shopping bags. Preparing for Isobel's arrival had been a whirlwind of activity, a bittersweet blend of joy and sorrow. Stella's heart ached for her lost sister, but the prospect of caring for Isobel brought a new sense of purpose.

Estelle descended the stairs. "She's just woken from her nap," she announced. "I had to cut her hair. The mats were beyond saving. But it'll grow back."

Stella dug through the bags, her hands finding a beautiful dress along with socks, underwear, and shoes. Handing them to Estelle, she expressed her enthusiasm. "How are you, Estelle? I can't believe she's here and I can't wait to see her in this dress. What do you think?"

Estelle accepted the clothes with a smile. "I'm doing well, thanks. Isobel will look absolutely charming in this. I'll bring her shortly, then get some refreshments ready." She then disappeared upstairs.

Henry said, "Come into the parlor. I have to excuse myself to take care of the horse and carriage. I will be back soon."

As Stella and Albert made themselves comfortable on a settee, her emotions surged. "I miss Mary so much. And now, having Isobel here... it feels like a part of her is still with us. I can't believe Henry agreed to let us care for her. I've always wanted a little girl, and now Mary has given me that."

Albert's voice was low. "Are you planning to teach her the craft?"

Stella nodded, her voice a whisper. "Yes, but we must keep it from Henry. Mary never revealed her true nature to him. She was afraid he wouldn't understand. Mary always had a wild streak, much like our mother. Unfortunately, it led her to some poor choices."

As Stella reflected on her sister's life, Estelle reappeared with Isobel in tow. The child hid behind Estelle, her eyes downcast.

Stella kneeled, tears brimming in her eyes. "Oh, my dear Isobel. I'm your Aunt Stella, your mama's sister. You're going to live with us now." She cradled Isobel's hands, her heart swelling with love.

Henry reentered the parlor, settling himself on the couch. "So, you've met Isobel. What do you think?"

Isobel walked over to Henry and took his hand. Henry's expression softened, and he gestured for her to sit beside him. She complied, still clutching his hand.

Stella observed a curious phenomenon—the parlor palm near Isobel appeared to flourish, its leaves perking up as if energized by her presence. Stella masked her surprise; the child's abilities were manifesting already. She needed to train Isobel soon to help her harness her powers.

"She's delightful. I can see Mary in her," Stella remarked, then hesitated, a realization dawning on her. "Henry, she looks like you. Could it be...?"

Henry's gaze drifted to a painting over the fireplace. "The past is behind us. I'm focused on the present. Isobel's staying a few more days would be wonderful. I need time to get to know her better."

Stella's mind raced with plans and preparations. "Then it's settled. She'll stay with you for a few days while we get everything ready. There's much to do, and much to teach her. She's going to bring joy to all our lives."

Stella felt a sense of destiny unfolding. Isobel, carrying the legacy of her mother and hinting at hidden depths, was about to embark on a journey that would span generations. Stella knew that in the years to come, Isobel's story would unfold in ways they couldn't yet imagine, leading to adventures and challenges that would test and reveal the true extent of her inherited powers. With the seeds of the future planted, Stella was resolute in her mission to prevent the past mistakes made by her mother and sister to repeat.

THE END

If you enjoyed Fire Witch, please leave a review where you purchased this book and on Goodreads. Subscribe to my newsletter at annettegrantham.com/fire-witch-newsletter.com for updates on new releases, exclusive stories, and sneak peeks. You'll want to be the first to know when Earth Witch is published to follow Isobel's journey.

Acknowledgements

"Fire Witch" is not just a story; it's a journey—a tapestry of early mornings and unwavering dedication. It's the second tale I've spun in The Frontier Witch Series, a testament to my penchant for crafting tales in a whimsical order. The seeds for this series were sown with "Earth Witch" during NaNoWriMo 2018, followed by "Fire Witch" as my 2021 NaNo project, and "Dark Witch" blossomed from NaNoWriMo's April 2023 camp. The silent pre-dawn hours have witnessed the relentless reworking of these narratives, my favorite time to weave the magick of words.

The camaraderie and critiques from the Lewis County Writers Guild has been the whetstone for my skills, sharpening my ability to present you with a story worthy of your time. The collective wisdom of Amy Flugel, Margie Keck Smith, Wayne Wallace, Beverley Gowan, Johanna Flynn, and Kristen Franklin has been a blessing to my writer's journey. Their generosity of spirit is a debt of gratitude I carry, hoping to pay it forward with each word I write

The vibrant community of 20Booksto50K has been a beacon, illuminating the path from manuscript to marketplace. The collective knowledge shared through Facebook interactions and annual congregations has armed me with the tools to bring this book to you, coupled with a dose of inspiration and an atlas of authorship.

Margie Keck Smith deserves a special mention for her role as a beta reader par excellence, whose insights have been crucial in refining the pages you hold.

To my children and stalwart cheerleaders, Rick Garza and Jennifer Swafford: their unwavering support and boundless enthusiasm have been my guiding lights. Their beliefs in my dreams fuels my courage to chase them.

At the heart of it all is Dale Grantham, my partner and kindred spirit, who embraces my dawn-bound rituals with love and understanding. And to Twilight, my faithful canine companion, who insists on daily doses of nature's inspiration and unwittingly becomes the star of many a Zoom call.

Last, to you, dear reader—your journey through the pages to the end fills this endeavor with meaning. Thank you for your time, your thoughts, and, if you're so inclined, your reviews. They are the lifeblood of a writer's evolution. The tale continues, and Isobel's story awaits—her path as unforeseen as the magick it's woven from.

About the Author

Annette Grantham's life reads like one of her richly imagined fantasy novels—filled with journeys, discovery, and the pursuit of passions. Hailing from the bustling streets of New York, Annette's early years were a nomadic odyssey from the historic Northeast to the expansive heart of Texas. Her adventurous spirit found a home in the military, where she served with dedication and honor, before she embarked on a tech odyssey as a software engineer. However, beneath the code and uniform, a storyteller's heart beat with fervent imagination.

Annette's pen has always been mightier than a sword, and her lifelong dream to weave tales has come to fruition in her writing. She now crafts enthralling fantasy novels that stitch together her fascination with bygone eras and the mystical. Her four-book series, "The Frontier Witches," is where the grit of "Deadwood" meets the enchanting allure of "Practical Magic." Here, readers find themselves alongside bold and spirited heroines—witches who don't just navigate but flourish in the untamed frontiers of the Old West. The prequel to the series, "Dark Witch", sets you on the journey on how Mary and Stella end up in America after their mother, Lillian, is arrested for witchcraft.

Nestled in a snug cabin in Washington, where the wild whispers of nature are but a window away, Annette lives with her high school sweetheart, a lovably eccentric dog, and under the watchful eyes of a lively squirrel congregation. Her home is not just a retreat but a wellspring of inspiration where she conjures her next spellbinding adventure.

Website: https://www.annettegrantham.com
Facebook: AnnetteGranthamAuthor
Instagram: annettegranthamauthor

Other books by Annette Grantham:

https://www.
books2read.co
m/u/4NgYxY

Coming soon in 2024: Earth Witch—the continuing saga of Isobel.

Made in United States
Troutdale, OR
02/06/2024